the OBSIDIAN EYES of KLIEF

WAR OF THE TWELVE
BOOK FOUR

· ALEX ROBINS ·

Copyright © 2022 by Alex Robins

Cover and Interior Design by Damonza
Maps by Alex Robins

ISBN 978-2-9576580-8-4 (paperback)
ISBN 978-2-9576580-7-7 (ebook)

Published by Bradypus Publishing
49380 Bellevigne en Layon
Dépôt Légal : juin 2022

www.warofthetwelve.com

For Jon and Elleanor

Hoi-Hoi and Elfling

The greatest gift our parents gave us was each other

Thanks for the memories

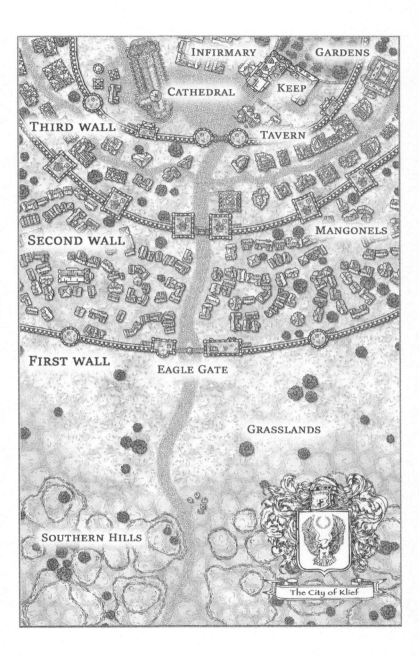

INFIRMARY · GARDENS

CATHEDRAL · KEEP

THIRD WALL

TAVERN

SECOND WALL

MANGONELS

FIRST WALL

EAGLE GATE

GRASSLANDS

SOUTHERN HILLS

The City of Klief

TABLE OF CONTENTS

LOSTTHORN

"It did not take long for the consequences of the wyrm's destruction of Morlak to ripple through the Barony. Refugees flooded the outlying villages, adding considerable strain to their already meagre winter stores. Trade shuddered to a halt as the quarries and mines closed. Even worse, the severely depleted Morlakian town guard no longer had the numbers to patrol the roads, leading to a significant rise in theft and banditry. It was a dark time."

FROM 'THE WAR OF THE TWELVE', 427 AT

∽

THE POURING RAIN fell relentlessly from the slate-grey storm clouds, swollen droplets rattling off the tiled roofs of Lostthorn and turning the dirt streets into sludge. Henke could feel it squelch under his leather boots as he walked. He had lost his hooded cloak a few weeks back, and his threadbare clothes were soaked through.

Pit-spawned weather, he thought. A particularly large pear-shaped drop trickled down from his bald scalp to the end of his hooked nose and hung there. They had never had rain this late in the year before. Something was off.

"How much further?" asked his companion, his voice muffled by the wide hood of his own cloak. *Probably nice and dry under there. The bastard.*

"Hundred yards or so. Keep close."

The two men trudged along, eventually arriving on the edge of a small square, deserted save for a crotchety old bar-keep, grumbling to himself as he moved his tables and chairs inside out of the rain.

Henke was yearning for a smoke, but his pipe would never light in this weather, so he took out a match instead and chewed on the wooden tip.

"Should be snowing, not raining," he said with a sniff. "Spent my whole life in Morlak, never had any rain during the winter months."

His companion only grunted.

"Not much of a talker, are you?" said Henke, squinting as he peered into the depths of the other man's hood. He could make out the vague shapes of two eyes and a nose but not much else. "Where did you say you came from, again?"

"Here and there."

"Not very helpful, are you?"

There was no reply. Henke had had a much better rapport with his last partner, Grundle, a big muscle-bound brute with biceps the size of boulders. Not the brightest pea in the pod but with more than enough brawn to make up for it. He had boasted that he had once lifted a full-size cow right off the ground, and Henke had had little reason to doubt him. Unfortunately, Grundle had gone missing three days ago, and after a fruitless search, there had been no other choice but to find a suitable replacement.

He stopped short, realising that his feet had mechanically taken them to their destination. A grimy locked door at one end of a dingy alleyway, far from prying eyes.

"This the place?" his companion asked.

"Aye. Be careful. They're a bit of a handful." He fished around inside his sodden tunic until he found a hefty key. The door creaked open, revealing a set of stone steps leading down into the darkness. Henke stepped hurriedly inside, eager to get dry.

The stairs led to another door, one that opened with the same key. The room beyond was cramped and poorly lit. Two single beds and a bucket were enough to fill most of the floorspace. It was unoccupied, although someone had spread a blanket on the ground. Upon it lay three scraggly toy figures made of straw; a miniature family, maybe, a father, mother, and daughter.

"Where are they?" muttered Henke, his eyes narrowing suspiciously. The room was windowless, the only way in or out was through the door, and Henke had the sole key. His employers had assured him that the lock was unpickable.

He took a tentative step. There was nowhere to hide. Nowhere except ... behind the door! He whirled just as a shadow leapt out of its hiding place, a high-pitched scream bursting from its mouth. Nails raked across Henke's face, hard enough to draw blood. He pushed his attacker away, and it fell onto the blanket.

"Stupid whore, you nearly blinded me! I ought to—" he began but was interrupted by another, smaller figure who charged out of the darkness and bit down onto his ankle.

"PIT!" he yelled, shaking his foot to dislodge the struggling form. One last twist of his leg made it lose its grip and sent it tumbling down next to its fellow prisoner. The dim light of the cell revealed the dirt-smudged faces of a mother and her daughter.

Henke put a hand to his cheek. It came away smeared with blood. "Damn you both," he said angrily. "I don't know why you can't just behave." The woman glared at him defiantly. She was strikingly beautiful, the long strands of her ivory hair giving her face an almost ethereal glow. A purplish bruise discoloured one cheek. She put a protective arm around her child.

"*You don't know why?*" she snapped. "You come to my home! You kidnap us and lock us up in this ... *pigsty* without any explanation! Feed us scraps! Make us both use that Pit-spawned bucket over there! And you don't know why?" She made to move towards him again but stopped when Henke raised his fist menacingly.

"Stay where you are. As I've already told you, I don't know why you're here, my employers didn't disclose that information. This can only work if you both respect me, and you *will* respect me." He began to unbuckle his belt. "Five strokes for you and two for the child, does that sound fair?"

"Cerra," came a choked voice from behind him. He turned to see his usually stoic companion visibly shaking, one hand pressed against the wall for support. "I didn't want to believe it ... I couldn't bring myself to believe it, but it's true, it's all true ..."

"Everything all right, there, friend?" asked Henke anxiously. "This isn't the best time to let the bats loose in the belfry, eh? I'm gonna need your help holding them down while I dish out the punishment."

In a flash, the man was inches from his face. Henke's belt was ripped from his hands and whipped across his knees with surprising force. "What ... what are you doing?"

The reverse stroke caught him in the mouth. The tip of the belt buckle cracked two teeth. Henke cried out and staggered backwards. A third stroke further deepened the open wound in his cheek.

"I believe it was five strokes?" the man said calmly, lashing out twice more in quick succession. Henke stumbled. His elbow caught the slop bucket as he fell, and foul-smelling muck splattered all over his head and tunic.

"I should probably kill you now," the man continued. "And there was a time when I would have done so without hesitation ... but I am trying to change. It is the only way I can hope to win back the trust of my wife."

"Nissus?"

The man turned and removed the hood of his cloak revealing a plain, nondescript face with narrow eyebrows and balding hair. His eyes were glistening with tears. "There was once a man who answered to that name," he said softly. "He was a selfish man; a proud man. Driven by ambition to the point that he forgot all else. He neglected his family, his friends. He put his own needs before those of others. That man lost everything ... and that man is gone."

The child peeked out from under her mother's arm and looked up at him. "Who are you, then?"

"My name is Jeffson." He smiled.

"Hello, Jeffson. My name is Daelle, and this is my mother, Cerra."

"It is a great pleasure to meet you both."

Cerra looked up at him, myriad emotions flickering across her features. "You ... you have spoken with Ner'alla, then?"

"I have. And I have also *spoken* with the people who ordered your imprisonment. They will not bother you again."

"Nissus ..."

"The woman who told me where to find you is still alive," he said gently. "I *have* changed. It's Jeffson now, not Nissus."

"My daddy was called Nissus," Daelle said, picking up one of the straw figures and holding it up for him to see. "Although you don't look like him at all. He was as thin as a twig but strong — really strong — with lots and lots of hair. You don't have any hair at all." She gave the toy a kiss. "He's gone now."

Jeffson bit his bottom lip and kept silent. Henke let out a quiet moan from the far corner of the room.

Cerra stood up and made a half-hearted attempt to rearrange her dirty hair. "Well, it was nice to meet you, Jeffson. Thank you for freeing us. I think we should be on our way. It's a long road to Morlak. Say goodbye, Daelle."

"Bye-bye, nice man."

"Morlak?" Jeffson asked. "You do not wish to stay here in Lostthorn?"

"No. They wrecked my house and vandalised my workshop. I have nothing left. Ner'alla always said there would be a place for me at *The Crimson Wing* if I needed it."

"*The Crimson Wing* is gone."

"What?"

"Not just that, the whole of Morlak is gone. All that you will find there now are despair and desolation."

"Oh, Pit! We don't have anywhere else to go. Ner'alla was my last hope!"

"Morlak is gone, but Ner'alla is still alive. If … if it is agreeable to you, I can take you to him."

Cerra glanced at her daughter. "Where is he?"

"I'm not exactly sure."

"Jeffson …"

"I did not say that I knew where he was, only that I can take you to him. There's a refugee camp about a mile outside Morlak, a place for the survivors to regroup. That was where I last saw him. Either he is still there, or we will find someone who can tell us where he went."

Cerra thought for a moment. "Very well. It will be safer for us to travel together. And you can explain to me what in the Pit has been going on since we've been locked up in this slum hole. But, Jeffson …"

"Yes?"

"Once we meet up with Ner'alla, we will go our separate ways. Agreed?"

"Of course."

"Right. Daelle, gather your things. We're leaving. Oh, one more thing." She marched over to the prone form of Henke and kicked him hard in the stomach.

"*That* was for calling me a whore."

CHAPTER 1

COMRADES IN ARMS

"There will come a time, in each of your lives, when your faith will be tested. Sceptics will seek to cloud your mind with petty half-truths and unproved theories, brought on by jealousy or fear. It is during these moments that you must pray to the Twelve, so that they may add their strength to yours. Makara's wisdom. Brachyura's ingenuity. Simha's strength. Mithuna's guile. All are freely given. The Twelve are our shepherds, and the Twelve are with us all."

HIGH PRIEST OF THE TWELVE, 361 AT

∽

THE FLAT STONE bounced twice off the mirror-like surface of the lake and disappeared with a disappointing plop. "Pit!" shouted Aldarin, clapping his hands together in frustration. The noise spooked a flock of wild geese nesting further down the shore, and they took flight, squawking angrily.

"I'm sure you'll get the hang of it, eventually," said Jelaïa, trying unsuccessfully to hide her smile.

"Don't think I can't tell when you are mocking me," fumed Aldarin. "I should be good at this. I have spent close to two decades honing my mind and body, pushing myself beyond what I thought was possible. I climbed the cliffs of Kessrin with my bare hands—"

"Very impressive."

"Don't interrupt. Climbed the cliffs of Kessrin, survived an ambush by the Knights of Mithuna, the battle of the Bay of Doves, the siege of Talth ..."

"Yes, Aldarin, I was there."

"So, why can't I make this Pit-spawned pebble ricochet across this Pit-spawned lake?" He reached up and scratched at his head where an ugly scar wormed its way through his cropped hair, from behind his ear to the dome of his forehead.

Jelaïa tilted her face towards the early morning sun, relishing the warmth on her skin. She looked around and found a suitable log near the shore for them both to sit on. "Come and sit next to me for a moment, would you?"

He sat, his considerable bulk making the wood crack.

"How are you doing, Aldarin?" Jelaïa asked.

"Fine."

She laid a hand on his arm. "If you're not going to be honest with me, I'll head back to camp and leave you to sulk in peace."

He sighed, deflating a little. "I ... I am troubled. My

head aches. Constantly. It feels like there is something pushing against the inside of my skull, struggling to get out."

He looked at her, and she could see the pain writhing in the depths of his ocean-blue eyes.

"Sleep is difficult. Both Kumbha and Belen, the healer, have given me concoctions that help somewhat, but it is always there. Sometimes as loud as a cavalry charge, other times as soft as raindrops on a window. But always there. At every waking moment."

"Aldarin! Why did you not say something?"

"I did not wish to trouble you."

She slapped him lightly on the arm. "That's not how it works."

"How what works?"

"This." Jelaïa gestured back and forth between the two of them. "Us. You need to be able to share this sort of thing with me. It's what couples do. They confront problems together."

"Hmmm." Aldarin reached up with his free hand and brushed back a lock of chestnut hair that had escaped Jelaïa's ponytail. "Since when did you become such an expert on the subject?"

"I …" She faltered, looking out over the lake. There was no wind, and the morning sky was almost perfectly reflected in the water, the sun a disc of liquid gold. "My parents had that sort of connection. That complicity. I don't think many people knew it, as they were careful to avoid being overly familiar in public …" She felt a lump in her throat. "I cannot even begin to imagine what my mother must have felt when she lost him. And I was not even there to help. I should have been there. And Father …" A quiet sob escaped her lips. "I miss him so much."

Jelaïa could almost see him in the clear surface of the lake, standing tall and proud in his golden armour, the hint of a smile playing across his lips. So real she could reach out and touch him.

She felt an arm wrap around her shoulders, and Aldarin drew her into his embrace. "He was a great man," he said gently. "We did not always see eye-to-eye, but he was a good leader, a good husband, and a good father. And he would be proud to see what you have become."

"Proud?" Jelaïa said, dabbing at her eyes with the sleeve of her dress. "I ran away from my duties as Baroness to become a priestess. Then, when I finally accepted my inheritance, the first thing I did was to lead his loyal subjects on a foolhardy trip north to take back a burnt-out husk of a city. I do not think he would be proud."

Aldarin was shaking his head. "Your lack of self-confidence makes you twist the truth. Your visions were crucial to us foiling the attack on Kessrin. You helped reforge and strengthen alliances among the western Baronies. Your intervention on the field of Talth was instrumental in turning the tide of battle. And, of course, you saved my life." He kissed her on the cheek. "You need to start seeing yourself as others do. As I do."

Jelaïa gazed up into his honest face, feeding off his words, drawing on his courage to make it hers and smother her feelings of grief. She let out a slow breath and began to feel a little better.

A pair of geese alighted on the surface of the lake with a fluttering of wings and a spate of bickering squawks. The sudden noise made Aldarin jolt up in surprise, his hand reaching automatically over his shoulder to draw an axe that wasn't there. Jelaïa caught sight of his expression and burst out laughing.

"Oh no, geese!" she shouted in mock distress. "Whatever shall I do? Save me, my brave knight, from these devious birds of death!" She batted her eyelashes.

Aldarin scowled, then the corner of his mouth twitched, and he let out a deep laugh of his own.

"You are insufferable, Baroness!" He picked up a flat stone and sent it spinning out over the water. It ricocheted a half-dozen times before sinking. "Hah! There! See! I improve! Soon the student will surpass the master ... or mistress!"

"It's not a competition, Aldarin."

"Sorry."

"Besides, you have some way to go yet." The geese had stopped their discordant prattling and were probing the shallows, looking for food.

It's so peaceful, Jelaïa thought. *I could stay here forever. But there is no time. Never enough time.*

"We should be heading back," she said reluctantly. "They'll be breaking camp, soon."

"Just a moment longer."

"But they will be waiting for us ..."

Aldarin pulled her close. "Then, let them wait."

"Where have you been?" scolded Loré del Conte, frowning down at Jelaïa from his stallion. "Derello and Brachyura were tired of twiddling their thumbs and set off half an hour ago with the wagon train. Need I remind you we are close to the Kliefien border? They are adamant we reach the capital before nightfall."

"I very much doubt that Lord Brachyura, Fourth of the Twelve, 'twiddled his thumbs'," interceded Aldarin, his huge frame even more imposing now it was enclosed in his burnished plate armour. "The Baroness was with me. Taking a very short break from her ever-increasing workload. I hope that isn't a problem?"

Loré was about to offer an angry retort, but something in Aldarin's expression made him catch himself. "No ... no, Sir Knight. No problem. I will inform the honour guard you are ready to depart." He jerked hard on the reins and sent his horse trotting over to a large group of riders waiting by the edge of the deserted campsite. Further out, the Arelian rank and file were formed up in units of ten or twelve, huddled around their sergeants to receive last-minute instructions. A clarion sounded from somewhere up near the head of the line, and the men began to move.

"Insufferable man," muttered Aldarin, looking around for his own horse. "He still speaks to you like you were a child."

Or like he was my father, Jelaïa thought, but that was one secret she had yet to share.

She skirted the remains of a rapidly cooling fire pit and spied her snow-white palfrey munching on a nosebag of grain, its saddlebags bulging with food and winter clothes.

"I think Loré is finding it difficult to adjust," she said, unhooking the bag and climbing into the saddle. "I am a very different person from the scared young woman he knew back in Arelium."

"Very different? More assertive, certainly, but your core values have not changed." Aldarin smiled up at her. "And that is a good thing." He gave her horse a playful tap on the rump and turned away to search for his lost mount, locking his pronged helm in place as he did so.

Jelaïa moved slowly up the column of Arelian foot soldiers, waving or nodding to those she knew, which was, as it turned out, a good many. She recognised men from the infirmary of Arelium, either recovered from their wounds or healed by Kumbha's miraculous gift. Men from the Battle of the Bay of Doves, including those who had protected her with their spearwall so that she could unleash the fires of Brachyura on one of Mina's krakens. And lastly, men from the siege tower of Talth; brave, hardy volunteers who had assaulted the ancient walls under Orkam's watchful eye and helped the knights unbar the gates.

This is what my father must have felt, she thought, as one man doffed his morion helmet and bowed respectfully. *They are more than just faces to me now, they are … comrades in arms.*

"My thanks to you, M'Lady," one of the soldiers mumbled as she passed him. She slowed her horse to match his pace. The soldier's face was covered in pink streaks and completely devoid of eyebrows and lashes. He grinned up at her.

"Thanks for what?" she asked, confused.

"Ah, you don't remember me, M'Lady. I weren't sure you would, someone all-important like y'self."

"I …. No, I'm sorry, soldier, I do not."

"I was up on the wall of Talth, M'Lady. Greylin' son of a whore jumped me, tore off 'alf my face like it were skinnin' a rabbit."

All of a sudden, she remembered. Emerging from the top of the siege tower. Picking her way through the Arelian dead. A hand grasping her boot.

"You sent for 'elp, M'Lady, I 'eard you. Sent your man runnin' for the stretcher-bearers. I was one of the first ones they brought back. Lady Kumbha—" he said her name with a hint of zeal "—said that another five minutes and it would've been too late to save me."

Jelaïa was unprepared for the overwhelming surge of emotion triggered by the man's words. She tightened her grip on the reins, careful not to let anything show on her face.

"I am glad you are still with us, soldier," she said. "But you should have returned with the injured to Arelium. You deserve some rest."

The man shook his head stubbornly. "Go 'ome? Now? Beggin' M'Lady's pardon, but I'm not turnin' back until I see this 'ole thing through. Not gonna abandon my unit either. Besides, who knows what we'll face in Klief, you might need me to protect you."

"By the Twelve, let us hope not! The only things I want waiting for me in Klief are a warm bath and a nice, soft, feather bed. What's your name, soldier?"

"Anton, M'Lady."

"Arelium thanks you for your service, Anton." She inclined her head and nudged her palfrey onwards with a squeeze of her calves, moving up the line of men towards the vanguard.

She heard Loré before she saw him. The charismatic noble was roaring with laughter at some lewd joke that one of his sycophants had regaled him with, his loud voice drowning out the quieter chuckles of his fellows. Jelaïa was only slightly surprised to see Taile Bansworth among them. The disgraced Kessrin was still excluded from Derello's inner circle, with both men taking great pains to avoid each other as much as possible.

The laughter petered out into an embarrassed silence as Jelaïa drew level with them.

Right, she thought. *How do you tame a tiger?*

"My Lady," Loré said, trying to compose himself. "How good of you to join us. Apologies. We were just discussing—"

"A woman announces to her friend that she is getting married for the fourth time," Jelaïa interrupted.

"What? Who?"

"Ask me what happened to her previous husbands."

"Yes, um, what happened to the first husband?"

"He ate poisonous mushrooms and died."

"Ah, and the second?"

"He ate poisonous mushrooms, too ... and died."

"Ah?" Loré appeared flummoxed. "A most unfortunate coincidence. Please don't tell me the third suffered a similar fate." The nobles riding next to them were idling closer, inconspicuously trying to get within earshot.

"The third? No, he died of a broken neck."

"A broken neck?"

"Yes," replied Jelaïa, deadpan. "He wouldn't eat the mushrooms."

There was no reply. For a moment, she thought she'd made a terrible mistake, then Bansworth, his eyes twinkling, let out an explosive guffaw. His mirth was contagious, and soon the entire vanguard was chuckling amiably at Jelaïa's joke.

"She got you there, my Lord," the Kessrin said, his cheeks tomato-red.

Loré tapped a gauntleted finger against his teeth as if thinking something over. "Not bad, my Lady, not bad," he said finally. "But have you heard the one about the farmer, the pig, and the overripe pumpkin?"

The rest of the day passed by in a blur as Jelaïa and the high nobility of Arelium exchanged stories. They crossed over into Klief unimpeded. The only notable sign that they had entered the Barony was the road, which suddenly changed from a dusty dirt track into a well-maintained paved highway. After the group had paused for a light lunch and a few glasses of wine, the stories grew even more vulgar. Bansworth, in particular, had a seemingly unending number of tasteless tales, some of them so pornographic that even Loré had to ask him to stop.

The Barony of Klief reminded Jelaïa of Arelium. Acres of flat farmland divided the countryside into neat, rectangular shapes of green and brown. The autumn harvest had stripped the fields of their crops leaving behind hard, dry soil. The only signs of life were the occasional curious herds of cows, munching on what little grass remained and staring stupidly at the Arelian foot soldiers as they passed.

The capital city itself was visible from miles away, a triangular hill rising up out of the surrounding low-lying hills like a shark's fin. As they approached, Jelaïa realised just how massive a place it was, in all likelihood bigger than Kessrin and Arelium combined. The exterior curtain wall was a thing of beauty; gleaming white granite decorated with hundreds of golden banners and dotted with guard towers. Behind it, a second wall, just as ostentatious as the first, with twelve flat platforms upon which were positioned large catapults.

No, not catapults, mangonels, Jelaïa thought, correcting herself, thinking back to Sir Gaelin's lecture on siege warfare. *Less range and power but easier to crew and maintain.*

At the very top of the hill, a third protective ring of stone encircled what appeared to be some sort of religious building, the tip of its lone spire high enough to pierce the clouds. Late afternoon sunlight reflected off stained-glass windows.

"It is a temple to the Twelve," Aldarin said, following her gaze. "I believe the Kliefien call it a cathedral. The priests of the Twelve have a strong presence here, partly because the Baron is a devout follower himself."

Jelaïa couldn't take her eyes off the glittering spire. The view from the top must be extraordinary.

"The priests of the Twelve? You mean the black-robed travellers who wander from village to village preaching far-fetched fairy tales? My father tolerated them and allowed them passage through Arelium — he believed them to be relatively harmless. From what I gather, most of their sermons are met with benign indifference."

"'Tis the same in Kessrin, although I would not under-estimate their rhetoric. There were several priests present during the siege of Arelium, and those on the walls who believed in their creed did so in a most fervent manner."

"How can they deify a group of people who actually existed? Who do they think built our towns and cities? Helped us to defeat the greylings?"

"They do not refute any of that. Their faith is based on what happened after. They believe that the Twelve's disappearance was planned, that once their work here was done, they ascended to the heavens and abide there still, guiding us from among the stars."

"Hmm," huffed Jelaïa, not convinced. She turned her attention back to the distant city. Squinting, she saw that a multitude of red and blue tents had been set up at the base of the first wall, just out of arrow range. Derello, Brachyura, and the rest of the Kessrin forces.

"That's odd," she said. "Why are they camped outside? Waiting for us to arrive, perhaps?"

Aldarin shook his head. "I doubt it. I hold a deep respect for Lord Brachyura, but patience is not one of his strong suits." He pointed at a rapidly approaching cloud of dust on the road. "We will have our answer soon enough."

A messenger dressed in the blue livery of Kessrin clattered to a halt, pressed a sheaf of paper into Jelaïa's hands, then wheeled his horse around and set off at a gallop along the paved highway back towards the distant camp.

"What does it say?" asked Loré impatiently.

Jelaïa scanned the page. "It's from Derello," she said. "The High Priest of the Twelve is refusing to see us." She frowned. "He has named us blasphemers … and forbidden us entry into Klief."

CHAPTER 2

THE SANDS OF SHAKALLA

"I took the time to explore those arid southern lands, but there was nothing for me there. How could I ever attempt to build something with all that sand and in blistering heat? Water is scarce. There are no construction materials. No solid ground for the foundations. Even if I did manage to overcome the economic and technical problems, whatever I built would eventually be swallowed by the desert. Let us forget about that inhospitable place. It is highly unlikely that any of the human tribes will be strong enough to thrive there."

BRACHYURA, FOURTH OF THE TWELVE 21 AT

∽

K A'ARKA'S HORSE GAVE an exhausted snort and shuddered to a standstill, its dry tongue lolling from its mouth. "Pit," swore the ebony-skinned

Knight of Brachyura, wincing as the movement stretched his own cracked lips.

The boiling hot sun beat down on the tired horse and rider, relentless and persistent. The air offered no respite: it was so hot and stifling that Ka'arka felt like he was standing in front of a blazing fireplace. He was dressed in a simple sky-blue tunic, dry and chafing against his skin; the sweat from his body evaporating before he could sense its wetness. The lack of humidity did not lessen the smell, however, the rank stench of it permeating his entire body, from his knotted dreadlocks to his bare arms and legs.

He slid down from the saddle and reached for his water bottle, giving it a tentative shake. A gentle sloshing sound told him there was less than a third left. Not enough. Not nearly enough. He unscrewed the cap and took the tiniest of sips, just sufficient to wet his lips. It took a considerable effort of will not to tip it all down his throat. Instead, he screwed the top back on and took stock of his surroundings.

Sand. Endless rolling dunes of golden sand, shining so brightly it hurt his eyes. The same, never-ending landscape day after day, ever since he had left the relative comfort of Ak'Shah over a week ago. The tiny nomadic village was on the very edge of the Shakalla Desert, at the frontier between soil and sand where the last of the scrubby bushes leached what little life remained from the earth. It was also the place where Ka'arka had been born.

He did not remember any of his time spent there. His parents were traders and had left the sun-drenched south when Ka'arka was two years old to ply their wares in Arelium, finally settling in the town of Cogdon close to the border. It was the perfect location as the busy main trade route from

Da'arra to Arelium passed straight through Cogdon, and the introverted Da'arran merchants were much more amenable to trading with those of their own kind. Ka'arka's parents had their pick of the best and most valuable commodities before they even reached the capital.

Consequently, Ka'arka had had a rich, sheltered childhood, albeit a lonely one. He had been a short, skinny little boy. His dark skin and accentuated speech had made him an easy target for the town bullies, and those with him had often suffered the same fate, leaving him with few friends. He had instead spent the greater part of his early years helping his father run the trading post. Long hours of stacking shelves and unloading crates had soon filled out his slender frame, packing enough hard muscle onto his arms and legs that he no longer had anything to fear from his tormentors.

A plaintive whinny from his horse brought him back to the present. He poured a small amount of water into the cap of his flask and held it up to the beast's swollen tongue. The liquid was gone in an instant, flaring nostrils searching his hand and forearm for more.

"I'm sorry," he said, patting its neck consolingly. "We have to be sparing with our supplies. This is the last of our water, and I'm not sure how much further we have to go."

The horse pawed the ground, making the armour strapped to its back jingle. Ka'arka glanced at the heavy set of interlocking metal plates guiltily. As a Knight of Brachyura, his armour was like a second skin, forged and tempered by his own hand after years of training. He had refused to leave it behind when departing the temple, wearing it constantly on the long trip down through Arelium and over the treacherous mountains known as The Lion's Teeth, but half a day in the hot desert sun had been enough to make him capitulate. And now, his steed was paying for his own weakness.

Judging by the sun's position, he was still heading in the right direction, southeast towards the capital city of Da'arra itself and the cool waters of the Oasis that brought life to the desert. The thought of it made his parched throat itch. It was in Da'arra that he hoped to find answers to an enigmatic warning spoken by one of the priestesses of his Order.

Unless the interpretation of the Conclave was wrong, of course, in which case he had travelled all this way for nothing.

There was a flash of something on the edge of his vision, a shadow on the top of a nearby dune. He blinked his dry eyes and tried to focus. A gust of warm wind sprinkled him with sand and grit.

Nothing.

His parents had told him of the desert sickness: fatigue, undernourishment, and thirst leading to hallucinations. Visions of water, trees, grass, or even people. To fall prey to these apparitions was to risk death. He took a cautious step back and released the straps tying his double-headed axe to his saddle. He hefted the axe in both hands, feeling its comforting weight. The word 'Brachyura' was carved into the handle in his own eloquent script.

"You will not be needing that," came a muffled voice from atop the dune. The figure was willow-thin, garbed in tight-fitting black cloth, its head covered by a turban, its face masked. The top of a curved glaive protruded from behind its back.

There was a crunching of sand, and Ka'arka turned to see a similar figure appear behind him. Its mask was also drawn up over its nose. Only two dark brown eyes were visible, ringed with kohl to protect them from the intense glare of the sun.

"What brings you here, traveller?" the figure asked, its voice distorted by the mask. "So far from civilisation and with a horse that looks more dead than alive?"

Ka'arka shifted his grip on his axe. "I am bound for Da'arra, on urgent business," he said. "I do not wish to cause any offence. If you have any water to spare, I would be willing to trade you for it. Otherwise, I suggest we part ways peacefully."

There was a bark of laughter. "You *suggest*, do you, Knight of Brachyura?"

Pit! thought Ka'arka. *They know who I am.* "I am indeed a Knight of the Twelve," he said warily. "Brachyura himself charged me with a mission of the utmost importance. There is a possibility that Da'arra is in danger."

There was a slight change in the stance of the figure on the dune. "Brachyura? The Twelve no longer walk these lands, Knight. What do you gain by tempting us with these falsehoods?"

"I do not lie. He has returned to us. It could be that others have returned too."

The nomad behind Ka'arka shook its head. "This changes nothing, I'm afraid, Knight of Brachyura. We cannot let you continue. We have our own orders, given to us by Baron del Da'arra himself. Even if Brachyura was here in the flesh, our answer would be the same. The road forward is blocked."

"What? Why?"

"It ... It is not for me to say. The only road open to Da'arra now is the western route, past La'desh and Jira Lake."

"Ridiculous!" exclaimed Ka'arka. The heat was starting to make him feel dizzy. "That's a hundred miles in the wrong direction! I have been on the road for weeks. I am tired. My horse is tired. I cannot afford any more delays."

"Then, we have a problem," the figure said, drawing its glaive. The glaive was a fearsome weapon, a curved blade roughly eighteen inches long socketed onto the end of a long pole. The metal tip gleamed as it caught the sunlight. "Last chance."

"I am sorry," Ka'arka replied. "I do not wish to disappoint my Lord." He shifted his leather boots and brought up his axe into a defensive pose.

The figure nodded, then sprang forwards in a cloud of sand. It thrust its glaive at Ka'arka with alarming speed, slipping through his defences and nicking him on the shoulder. With a cry, the Knight of Brachyura knocked the glaive aside and charged at his opponent, who dodged easily out of range.

"You are not equipped for fighting on this terrain, Knight. Nor in this heat." The nomad tapped its cloth sandals with the butt of its glaive.

Ka'arka tried to catch his breath, each inhalation of hot air burning his lungs. "Perhaps," he said. "But failure is not an option." He attacked again, ducking under a horizontal sweep of the glaive and raising his axe. The nomad pivoted, the axe whistling harmlessly past its face.

"Pit, you're fast," Ka'arka complained as the nomad danced away. He could feel grains of sand in his mouth, rubbing against his gums, but his body was too dehydrated to make the saliva needed to spit them out.

His head was throbbing.

"Enough," the nomad said. "We have water, which I am happy to share. Let us eat together, and we will escort you part of the way back."

Ka'arka smiled and, with a twist of his hand, sent his axe spinning away into the sand. The nomad's mahogany eyes flickered as they followed the axe's trajectory. A simple distraction but an effective one. The Knight of Brachyura dealt his adversary a stinging blow to the head and tackled the surprised nomad to the ground. He sat down hard, pinning the struggling figure's arms under his knees.

"Now," Ka'arka said. "If you would tell your friend to join us, I think …" he trailed off, his eyes drawn to a glint of metal. A medallion dislodged during the skirmish. A silver dagger. "I have seen this sigil before," he said, trying to force his tired mind to remember. "During my training. It means something. Something important."

He heard the thrum of displaced air too late and failed to avoid the butt of the second figure's glaive. It thwacked into his forehead, toppling him off his fallen opponent and onto his back. His former captive now stood over him, blocking out the glare of the sun. He felt the tip of a glaive press gently against his throat.

"It is *more* than important," the nomad said, slowly unwrapping the turban with its free hand. "It defines who I am. It is the sign of the one I strive to imitate. It is the sign of my Order."

Ka'arka gazed up into a face of captivating beauty; a woman with short braided hair and smooth dusky skin the colour of ink. An ugly welt was forming on one cheek, an unfortunate consequence of their duel.

The woman set aside her glaive and offered him her

hand. He accepted gladly and was pulled to his feet, surprised by the strength in her supple arms.

"My name is Xer'ana," she said. "Xer'ana, Knight of
Luridae, Eighth of the Twelve. I think I may have been going
about this the wrong way. Come with us back to our camp,
and tell me all about this vital mission you are stubbornly
willing to risk your life for."

"I am ... most grateful for your hospitality," Ka'arka said, a
cup of water in one hand and a date in the other. He was
sitting cross-legged in the shade of a tent awning, covered in
sweat but mercifully out of the sun. The Knights of Luridae
had set up three tents in such a fashion that each one would
provide some shade throughout the day. The tents formed
a semi-circle around a six-foot hole in the ground: a hole
containing a small puddle of muddy water.

Xer'ana had explained that finding such underground
treasure was difficult but far from impossible with the right
training. Water in the desert acts similarly to how it would
in any other terrain: it collects at dividing lines in the landscape, such as at the base of the dunes or beneath the surface
of sandstone outcrops. Xer'ana and her fellow knights had
been out in the desert for weeks now, living off such underground caches, supplemented by the morning dew and a
carefully-rationed supply of dried fruits and meats.

The leader of the Knights of Luridae was sitting opposite
him, seemingly unbothered by the heat, sipping what smelt
like mint tea from a small porcelain cup. "You are welcome,

Knight of Brachyura," she said calmly. "I have asked one of my sisters to see to your horse. I hope we are not too late."

"Too late?"

"The animal is on the verge of death." She arched a disapproving eyebrow. "You have not been taking sufficient care of it."

"Oh ... That was not my intention."

"I am sure. In any case, either it will survive the night, and you may ride it back to La'desh, or it will not, and we will be able to replenish our food supplies."

He held her gaze, wondering if she was joking. She stared back at him, impassively.

"I have already told you, Xer'ana, I am not going back," he said, looking away and taking a sip of water. "One of the priestesses of our Order had a vision, and the Conclave believes it has something to do with Da'arra."

"Priestesses? Visions? Our Order does not have such things. What do you mean?"

"Ah. Well, there are no female Knights of Brachyura. The male initiates become knights, the female initiates priestesses."

"What a ludicrous notion. Our own Order has no such frivolous inequalities. Continue."

"The priestesses share a particular gift, supposedly bestowed upon them by the Twelve. They can receive disjointed images of current or future events. These visions were few and far between until roughly a year ago when the Twelve began to awaken and the dreams intensified."

"I see. What was the vision that brought you here, Knight of Brachyura?"

"My name is Ka'arka. If I remember correctly, it went

as follows: *Crater. Darkness. Scratching claws. Golden sands. Forgotten depths. Misery.*"

Xer'ana's stolid demeanour cracked a little at hearing this. "Im ... impossible," she stammered. "How could they know?"

"Know what?"

She set down her tea and studied his face, gauging his trust. The kohl around her eyes added a sternness to her gaze. Finally, she came to a decision. "We have been charged with turning travellers away from this area, Knight of Brachyura, because we are less than half a day's ride from the Da'arran Pit, and there has been some ... activity there."

Ka'arka felt his heart skip a beat. "Activity? Is it—"

"Greylings? Yes."

"Then, this is a most fortuitous encounter!" he said, smiling broadly. "I have stumbled across the very reason for my presence here. If we work together, we can contain them before they do any harm!"

"That is not our mission. There are only four Knights of Luridae here, myself included. Our orders are to scout out the Pit and surrounding area, assess the situation, and send word for reinforcements. Your help is not needed."

Ka'arka ground his teeth in frustration. "You would be foolish to exclude me from this. I was instructed by Brachyura himself to—"

"Do not try my patience," Xer'ana interrupted sharply. "If you want to talk of fairy tales and children's stories, I will leave you to do so by yourself."

"I am not lying," Ka'arka shot back hotly. "I swear it. I swear it on my honour. I swear it on the Great Lake. My patron guides us once more. I spoke with him, as did our

First Priestess. He told us of many things. How the Schism was a mistake. The Pact a lie. The greylings are returning to the surface. And the relative state of peace we have known for the last three hundred years is coming to an end."

Xer'ana leant forwards with renewed interest. "Tell me what you know," she said, her voice low and penetrating. "Tell me everything."

CHAPTER 3

ONE DAY AT A TIME

"There was certainly some resentment among the Morlakians when Baroness Syrella announced she would be joining the expedition north to Klief. A small but vociferous group accused her of shirking her duties and abandoning her people. I do not believe that to be true. I have not known the Baroness long, but she is no coward. If she chose to go to Klief, it was because she was convinced something or someone there would provide the means to strike back at the creature that had destroyed her Barony. A means for her to have her vengeance."

FROM 'THE WAR OF THE TWELVE', 427 AT

✧

R EED WAS GOING to die. He was sure of it. There was no other explanation for the mind-numbing pain slowly crushing his brain to a pulp. He squeezed his eyes tightly shut, hoping it would help soften the steel hammer thudding against his forehead, but it did nothing whatsoever.

What in the Pit had happened last night? He vaguely remembered some sort of argument between Vohanen and Ner'alla. Something to do with which was better, wine or ale. A stupid, stupid question. He should have left the campfire while he still had the chance. Left with his dignity. In fact, he probably would have, if Syrella had not intervened. The Baroness had not only assured them all that red wine was the far superior beverage but also insisted that the Morlakian variety outclassed the Arelian-grown vine in every respect.

Vohanen had bristled at hearing this, running to his tent to fetch his own 'personal' supply of ale. Ner'alla, not to be outdone, had asked his servant, Stick, to bring out a few choice bottles of Morlakian red. And they had started drinking. Then what?

He sorted through a blurry hodgepodge of memories.

Vohanen, badgering Kriari to give his opinion on two near-identical glasses of wine (and only getting a bemused 'Kriari' in reply).

Krelbe, taking an unopened bottle for himself and wandering off into the darkness to drink it alone.

Reed, his beard wet with white froth, bellowing out the lyrics to "*The Girl at the Country Fair*" and miming spear thrusts with an imaginary spear.

Caddox, fumbling his mug of ale with his broken hand and spilling the contents all down his front.

Reed, taking Syrella by the hand and spinning her around, marvelling at how her dress bloomed outwards as she danced, like the petals of a flower caressed by the wind.

Reed, bending close and kissing Syrella on the mouth.

Kissing the Baroness of Morlak, the White Rose, one of the most powerful women in the nine Baronies, on the *mouth*.

Pit.

He groaned, pulling the sheet cover over his head, willing himself to disappear into the darkness.

What had he done? What sort of idiotic, foolish, Pit-spawned thing had he done? For once in his life, he had found someone who seemed to be at least partially interested in him, and he had thrown it all away.

Idiot.

It was only early morning, and already he knew that the day was ruined. It could not get any worse. Definitely not.

There was the rustling sound of a parting tent flap.

"Good morning, my Lord, I trust you had an excellent evening?" The familiar bland voice filtered down through the sheets into the warm den Reed had made for himself. He groaned. He was wrong. It could *always* get worse.

"I believe it would be best for you to get up now, my Lord," the voice continued, a tad smugly. "We will be departing soon, and it would be a shame for his Lordship to be left behind, would it not?"

Reed lifted one corner of the sheet and cracked open his left eye as much as he dared. A nondescript middle-aged man stood in the centre of his tent, a pile of clean clothes balanced delicately on one arm and a jug of cold water held in the other.

"Jeffson," Reed croaked. "You're back! What are you doing bringing me clothes? We don't have to keep up this charade anymore. I saw you stab Mithuna in the face, remember? I know who you are now. I release you from my service."

"Nonsense, my Lord. A noble of your standing cannot arrive in Klief without an *entourage*. It would most assuredly be frowned upon."

Reed risked opening his other eye. "An entour-what?"

"A retinue or group of followers, my Lord. The rules of high society state that—"

"Fine. Fine. I'm too tired to argue, we can discuss this later. When did you arrive?"

"Late last night, my Lord. We made good time from Lostthorn to Morlak. One of the side-effects of the wyrm's onslaught seems to be a slight change in the weather. We encountered little snow, only a few hours of rain, and not enough to make the roads impracticable."

"How did you find us?"

"Some guards at the refugee camp told us you were heading to Klief. And the trail was still fairly fresh. Enough for someone with my ... particular talents to follow you without much trouble."

"Hmm." Reed sat up and immediately clutched his head as the movement sent more angry pulses thudding into his skull. "You said 'we'. You found them?"

Jeffson paused. "I did."

"That's excellent news! You must be overjoyed to see them alive again after all this time."

"It was ... I mean ... yes, I was pleased to find them."

Reed scratched at his beard. "Well, you'll have to introduce me, I have lots of embarrassing stories to tell."

"I ... you will have to ask Ner'alla. My wife and child are staying with him for the moment." Jeffson's unflappable facade slipped for a moment, and Reed caught a look of anguish in the manservant's eyes before the mask dropped back into place.

"Of course, Jeffson," he said softly. "Whenever the time is right."

"Thank you, my Lord. Now, do you require any *assistance* in dressing yourself?"

Reed let out a short laugh. "That may have managed to embarrass me a few months ago when I had just arrived in Arelium, Jeffson, but it will take more than that to fluster me now. Bring me a basin to go with that jug of water, help me get this nightshirt off, and we'll see just how much of last night's shame we can scrub off me in the next half-hour."

⁓

Reed emerged a short time later. It was a crisp, winter morning, and the trees at the edge of the campsite were covered in a thin sheen of frost. Armoured Knights of Kriari, their fur mantles ruffled by the breeze, were packing up their tents and securing their travel bags. Reed was pleased to see Taleck among them. The veteran had his arm in a sling but at least appeared sufficiently recovered from his poisoning to stand on his own two feet again.

At the far end of the clearing was a line of four wagons: Ner'alla's cart, a covered wagon for supplies, a makeshift prison currently housing Verona, and one that was used by Syrella and her handmaiden. Syrella … Reed cringed inwardly at the prospect of seeing her again after last night's debauchery.

The man known as 'Stick' was sitting on the back of

Ner'alla's cart, picking at his teeth with a sliver of wood. Reed gave him a hesitant wave, which was acknowledged by a brief nod.

"I would suggest some sustenance, my Lord," said Jeffson, appearing silently behind Reed's left shoulder.

He grunted in reply and traipsed across the hard earth to the cooking pot still simmering in the glowing ashes of the campfire. He ladled what appeared to be vegetable soup into a bowl, the steam making his eyes water.

"If you will excuse me, my Lord, I will start dismantling the tent."

Reed had a mouthful of stew. It was watery and far too salty. He swallowed with difficulty. "Pit, that's foul! Not one of Krelbe's better efforts."

"Wasn't Krelbe," said Stick from his perch. "That old grump spent the night with his bottle. I think Vohanen made that, and I wouldn't tell him you don't like it, he's in a terrible mood this morning."

"I wonder why?" said Reed sarcastically, massaging his aching forehead with his free hand. "He must have drunk twice as much as me. And why are you so chirpy?"

Stick shrugged. "Walked it off."

"Kriari," came a rumbling baritone from behind Reed, nearly making him drop his soup. The First of the Twelve was standing a few feet away, his smile stretching the burnt skin of his face. The burns were recent, acquired when the giant had rung the bell atop Morlak keep just before the entire building had been consumed by the wyrm's fiery breath. A selfless act that had surely saved many Morlakian lives and earned him Reed's respect.

"Good morning, Lord."

"Kriari," the colossus corrected gently.

"Good morning, Kriari. I hope you … slept well?"

The First of the Twelve turned his gaze on Reed, and he shivered. All of the Twelve had those same dark reflective orbits that sucked you in and pulled your psyche apart. No one, not even Vohanen or Jefferson, could stare into those eyes for more than a few seconds before being forced to look away.

"Come," Kriari said.

"Can I finish my meal, first?"

"Come."

Reed put down his soup. The palm of his right hand was starting to itch. There was a three-inch-long scab there, running from thumb to little finger. A gruesome souvenir of his time spent in Morlak. Sighing, he got up and followed Kriari to the supply wagon.

"Barrel," the colossus said, pointing inside.

"Yes, it is," Reed replied cautiously. "It's definitely a barrel … um, well done." Was the First of the Twelve still inebriated?

"Barrel," Kriari repeated and wandered away, still limping slightly from his wounded leg.

Reed frowned and clambered up into the back of the wagon, using one of the rimmed wheels as support. Six wooden bows arched overhead, covered with canvas. The interior was packed with burlap sacks, crates, and barrels. Strings of onions and garlic hung down from the arches, along with various other herbs and condiments that Reed did not recognise. A creaking sound came from one of the barrels at the very back of the wagon, almost indistinguishable in the gloom.

"Right," muttered Reed to himself. He clambered over sacks of grain and squeezed round a salted leg of pork, narrowly avoiding hitting his head on the wagon roof. The barrel creaked again.

"Um. Hello?" he asked, feeling stupid. There was no reply. He rapped his knuckles on the side of the barrel. The barrel knocked back.

"I ... I think you should come out now," Reed said tentatively.

"Am I in trouble?" came a high-pitched, quavering reply.

"For hiding in a barrel? I don't think so."

With a final creak, the top of the barrel slid open, and the grimy face of a young girl appeared, an apologetic look on her face.

"Mila?" said Reed incredulously, recognising the child he had carried out of Morlak while the town was collapsing under the wyrm's bombardment.

"And bunny," the girl said seriously, reaching into the depths of the barrel and producing a scruffy stuffed rabbit with one ear missing and an eye hanging by a thread.

"What are you doing here? I left you with a nice man who was going to help you find your parents; why are you not with them?"

"We couldn't find them," answered Mila with a sniffle. "We looked and looked everywhere, but we couldn't find them. Then the man told me that Daddy and Mummy were de ... de ... dead and that I had to go with a n ... new family, but I don't *want* to go with them, I want to go with you and the magic lady."

"The magic lady?"

"The one with the special eyes."

"Ah, Syrella. Well, I don't think that's a good idea. Syrella and I are both very busy and—"

Mila burst into tears.

"No, no, listen," said Reed hurriedly, the girl's cries further adding to the pain in his skull. "We can find a solution, I'm sure someone will—"

"I want the MAGIC LADY!" Mila bawled, tears streaming down her face.

There was movement outside.

"Reed, is everything all right?"

Pit! Syrella.

"Um, yes, my Lady!"

"Merad?"

"Yes, my Lady?"

"Come out here right now, and bring whoever's with you."

"That's the magic lady!" Mila exclaimed happily and pushed past Reed to climb out. He extricated himself from the labyrinth of food to find that Mila had wrapped her arms around Syrella's leg and was chatting with her animatedly, apparently forgetting to breathe in the process.

"So, then I got inside when the guard wasn't looking, and I saw that the barrel of apples was half-empty, and I knew that I shouldn't have gone inside, but I really wanted to see you again, and there was nothing else for me to do so I hid, and then I thought that maybe you *didn't* want to see me and that you'd be angry so I didn't want to come out, and then the kind man found me."

"He *is* a kind man, isn't he?" said Syrella, patting down Mila's hair that was sprouting out in all directions like it was trying to escape her head.

"Sorry, my Lady," Reed said, staring firmly at a point behind Syrella's shoulder. "I didn't mean to bother you with this."

The Baroness let out a peal of laughter. "You are so ... honourable, Merad, it's something I like about you. Mila? Would you like to ride with me in my wagon today? It's better than hiding in a barrel, and my handmaiden is an excellent seamstress, I'm sure she can fix bunny's eye in a trice!"

"Oh, yes please, magic lady, that would be wonderful!"

"Off we go then!"

Reed rubbed his head. *I should probably say something.*

"Um, my Lady?"

"Yes?"

"About last night ... I would just like to apologise for being a bit too ... I mean for my improper behaviour."

"Merad?"

"Yes?"

"There's no need to apologise. One must only apologise when one has done something wrong. Everything that happened last night did so because I wanted it to."

"I ... right. Um. It's just that all this is a bit new to me, and I'm not quite sure how to proceed with the, er, courtship ..." he floundered about as if he had just been thrown into the sea and didn't know how to swim.

"My father was not a great parent," said Syrella, coming to his rescue. "He berated me, kept important things from me, tried to manipulate me and emotionally break me. I do not have very many good memories of him. Although I do have one. I must have been seven or eight years old, and I was trying to learn to ride a particularly stubborn pony.

There was to be a parade at the end of the year, and I wanted to be part of it. The mean animal kept throwing me off. My father found me in tears. "I will never be ready," I remember telling him. "It's useless." He smiled and told me he would share his secret with me, a trick to help me tackle every challenge life puts in my way."

"What was that?" Reed asked softly, lulled by the sound of her voice.

"Take things one day at a time," Syrella replied simply, her eyes sparkling. She took a step closer and kissed him on the cheek.

"One day at a time," mused Reed, rolling the thought around in his head. It didn't sound so bad.

"Magic Lady!" came the impatient cry.

Syrella smiled warmly. "Coming!"

Reed watched her leave, his addled mind desperately trying to make sense of the conversation. *Everything that happened last night did so because I wanted it to. So that meant ...*

"Think she likes you." Stick had not moved from his spot on Ner'alla's cart. He smirked.

"I think so too," agreed Reed. "We've been spending a lot of time together since leaving Morlak. Although I'm not sure what to do about it."

"I could give ya a few pointers if ya like. Why, when I was last in Kessrin, we went to this 'orehouse and ... 'Old up, 'ere comes more bother."

Vohanen was storming across the campsite, his face a dark shade of crimson. "Was it one of you?" he yelled angrily. "Well? Was it?"

Why is everyone shouting today? thought Reed wearily as the knight's voice bounced around his skull.

"One of us what?" he asked innocently.

Vohanen scowled. "Verona's no longer in her cell," he said. "The door was unbarred from the *outside*. Someone let her out."

"What? When?"

"Probably last night while we were pissing drunk, Reed! Damn that Pit-spawned Da'arran and his Pit-spawned wine!"

"No, that doesn't sound right. There were dozens of us gathered around the campfire, and you can see the door from here. One of us would have seen something. It must have been after that. Which means she hasn't gone far." Reed turned and called loudly to his manservant. "Jeffson? Would you join us by the prison wagon, please? Oh, and bring my spear."

The prison wagon was just a flat-bedded cart with a wooden cabin bolted on top. They could immediately see that Vohanen was right; there were no exterior signs of effraction, the metal-banded door was ajar but otherwise untouched. Reed peered inside. A cot, a slop bucket, and a half-eaten plate of food. No Verona.

"Jeffson, you told me you arrived here late last night, did you see anything?"

"No. At least, nothing seemed to be amiss. But it was dark, and we were all tired ..." He knelt in the dirt next to the wagon, his hand tracing a faint footprint. "It appears she went north into the forest. Barefoot." Jeffson stood, walked a few paces, and found another print. "Walking on the balls of her feet."

He followed the tracks to the edge of the campsite

and disappeared into the trees. Vohanen looked at Reed, shrugged, and set off in pursuit.

They had gone about a hundred yards when Jeffson pointed at something spattered on one of the pine trunks; a dry, sap-like substance. He scratched at it with his fingernail and touched his finger to the tip of his tongue.

"Blood."

Vohanen drew his short sword. "Verona's? Did she cut herself escaping?"

Jeffson looked ahead. More dark patches dotted the ground.

"I think she did more than cut herself, Sir Knight."

They proceeded cautiously. Verona's tracks became clearer and more erratic. A broken twig, crushed leaves, muddy footprints. Then, at last, they found her.

The priestess of Zygos was slumped against the trunk of one of the larger pine trees. Her throat had been cut, the jagged red line already covered in frost. Frozen droplets of blood hung from the open wound like a ruby necklace. Below her bare feet, on a basket of leaves, sat her swollen tongue, a splash of dark purple against the green. Her dull, wide eyes stared at the three men accusingly.

Reed could feel the vegetable soup swirl around his stomach. He grimaced and looked away.

"This is bad," Vohanen said quietly.

"I know," Reed agreed. "No one deserves to die like that."

"What? No, I couldn't care less about that Pit-spawned woman. Her scheming got my son killed and more besides. It's bad because someone let her out. Someone from the campsite did this."

He sheathed his sword, his face grim.

"One of our travelling companions is a traitor."

CHAPTER 4

THE HIGH PRIEST OF KLIEF

"What is the point of even having a Council of Baronies if none of the Barons ever shows up? Del Quayjin pretexts he is too old to make the trip over the Redenfell Mountains, del Da'arra claims to be swamped by internal matters, and del Klief flat out refuses to come altogether! The Twelve did not reunite the tribes and create the Council for us to piss it all away! It's crass, disrespectful, and downright stupid."

BARON LISTUS DEL ARELIUM, 424 AT

J ELAÏA STARED UP at the twenty-foot-high walls of Klief, the golden banners fluttering overhead. Mocking her. "Did you explain to them who we were?" she asked Derello testily. The Kessrin Baron was dressed in his chainmail coat and pink sash, his black hair slicked back behind his ears with copious amounts of pomade.

"Of course."

"And?"

"The city gates must remain closed, on orders of the High Priest."

"You are telling me The Baron of Kessrin, the Baroness of Arelium, and two of the Twelve aren't important enough? Preposterous! We don't have time for this. The weaver said she would send the wyrm to decimate a Barony every month. *Every month*, Derello! And that was over two weeks ago."

"I agree, but what would you have us do?"

Jelaïa chewed on a rebellious strand of chestnut hair. "I'm going to remind them who we are." She walked closer, stepping into the shadow of the gatehouse. An enormous embossed eagle, its wings outstretched, covered almost the entirety of the closed double doors. The heraldry of Klief. There was no movement from the ramparts.

This is how the ancient tribes of men were nearly annihilated, she thought. *Mistrust and division.*

She cracked open her amulet and dabbed a smear of Aldarin's blood onto her lips.

"I am Baroness Jelaïa del Arelium, Lady of the White Wolf and a priestess of Brachyura." She snapped her fingers, and her hand caught fire with a *whoomph* of blue flame. "We come on urgent business. The Baronies of men are at war, and Klief is a part of it, whether you wish it to be or not."

Silence, save for the rustling of banners and the distant cawing of a murder of crows.

Right, thought Jelaïa. She stretched out her hand, fingers spread wide, and concentrated. A scorching cerulean stream streaked upwards from her palm, setting the nearest banner ablaze. It burned well, leaving a charred mark on the pristine white wall as it was consumed. A slight odour of burnt fabric permeated the air.

"This is what the enemy wants," Jelaïa continued, her face a mask of concentration as she fought to contain the fires of Brachyura. "They want us to fight among ourselves, squandering what little time we have. We have come a long way and sacrificed much to get here. So, this is what is going to happen. I will carry on burning your banners from your walls, and when they are all gone, I will burn down your gate. Perhaps once your eagle is a pile of molten sludge, you will listen to me." She swept her arm to the left, and another pennant caught fire.

There was a flurry of activity behind the gate and after a few moments, one of the doors opened a crack. A bandy-legged official appeared wearing bulging stuffed hose, a golden lace doublet, and a felt cap. He was carrying a rolled-up scroll under one arm and what looked like an elaborate spiral horn or trumpet. Catching sight of Jelaïa, he bowed slowly and pressed the horn to his lips. The instrument made a sound like two mallards fighting over a chunk of bread.

"Hear ye!" he crowed, spittle flying from his mouth. "His most illustrious eminence, Baron Azael del Klief, and his first counsellor, the High Priest of the Twelve, welcome you to our magnificent city." He set down the horn and unrolled the scroll. "I will now read to you a personal message written by the hand of his holiness. Ahem."

Jelaïa, caught off guard, dropped her arm and let the energy drain away. She had expected an armed guard, or the Baron himself, not … whatever this was. She risked a

sideways glance at Derello and saw that the Baron was studying the richly-dressed messenger with amusement.

"Ahem." The man cleared his throat again noisily. "The
message reads … My friends! It brings me such joy to see you
here before our gates. Long have I yearned for a time when
we would all meet. My melancholy days were filled with
hues of grey, but now your presence will illuminate my life
with a thousand vibrant colours. My only regret is that you
felt subterfuge was necessary to garner my attention. The
names of the Twelve should never be used in vain, even by
such prominent figures as yourselves. My congregation will
be concerned if you attempt to humanise those whom they
worship and terrified if you continue to assert that some of
the Twelve walk among you. Such twisted fantasies must be
put aside if you wish to enter our walls."

Subterfuge? Fantasies? Jelaïa bit back an angry retort, simmering with indignation. The messenger seemed completely
oblivious to the effect his words were having. He flipped the
scroll over and began to read the other side.

"I would ask but a simple boon. We have learnt that
others approach. More travellers seeking counsel. If you can
find the patience in your hearts to wait a scant few hours
longer, I will meet with you all face-to-face, here before the
Eagle Gate, to clear up any unfortunate misunderstandings."

The messenger rolled up the scroll then bowed so low
he nearly lost his felt cap. "If you would be so kind as to give
me your answer, Baron, Baroness, so that I might inform his
holiness of your decision?"

Jelaïa motioned Derello closer. "This High Priest sounds
like a pompous fool," she said in a hushed tone. "Have you
ever seen him before?"

Del Kessrin shook his head. "No. Nor the Baron. Klief always sends emissaries to the annual Council. They have done so for years. My father never met the Baron in person. And you?"

"Never. Listus used to complain about his constant absenteeism. Do you think they even have a clue as to what's going on outside their Barony? The High Priest obviously doesn't believe that the Twelve have returned. And behind all that flowery speech were a good many poorly veiled threats. I'm not sure we should let him make demands of us like this."

Derello gestured to the walls above them. "Perhaps, but look at the size of this place! There must be tens of thousands of men stationed here. Our own forces are hardly a match for them, even if you factor in the Knights of Brachyura. I'm not sure trying to strong-arm the Baron to let us in is going to be effective."

Jelaïa let out an exasperated breath. "So, what, we wait?"

"It's just a few hours."

"Fine. You tell him. I don't want to get covered in drool." She spun around and walked angrily away.

"Stop nibbling on your hair, Jeli," Praedora admonished. The two priestesses were sitting on fold-out chairs under the awning of Jelaïa's tent, a couple of hundred yards from the city wall. It was cool in the shade, and Jelaïa had pulled a long fur-trimmed coat over her traditional green dress. The coat was crimson-red, the colour of Arelium, and strangely enough, wearing it made her feel more like a Baroness.

"How can you tell?" she asked curiously, brushing the hair away from her face.

Praedora smiled. "I think with the loss of my sight, my hearing is slowly improving to compensate. You sound like a masticating cow."

"Aunt!"

"Well, you asked. Eating your own hair won't make the time pass any faster."

"He said a few hours. We've been here nearly all day," said Jelaïa petulantly. "Our one advantage is time. And that advantage is shrinking."

Xandris hurried past, pushing a wheelbarrow loaded with what appeared to be charcoal. He saw Jelaïa looking at him and raised one of his hands from the handle long enough to give her an enthusiastic wave.

"It's only wasted if you procrastinate," Praedora said. "I thought Loré brought you some missives to sign. Have you finished?"

Between the two women stood a table, bowed under the weight of unsigned documents. There was also a pair of well-worn reading glasses, an ink pot, and a quill. Jelaïa looked guiltily at the pile of parchments. She had signed nothing. The ink had been open so long it was beginning to harden.

"I've ... I'm nearly done," she said innocently.

"You'll have to learn to lie better than that if you wish to be a successful Baroness," teased Praedora, although Jelaïa could detect a slight melancholy in her words.

"Are you all right, Prae?"

The First Priestess of Brachyura fondled the axe-shaped medallion at her breast, empty since the death of Sir Manfeld.

"I'm fine. It's just that sometimes I miss things. I miss

my cousin. I miss being able to stand on my balcony and look out over the Sea of Sorrow. And I miss …"

"Yes?"

"I miss the fires, Jelaïa. That feeling when the azure lightning strikes, that inimitable sensation right on the threshold between pleasure and pain. When I called upon the fires of Brachyura, all my problems faded away, and the impossible became possible. You know what I am describing. Without my gift I am useless."

"Useless?"

"I don't need to have eyes to see what the others think of me," Praedora said. "The whispers. The … *pity*. As if my being here is an act of charity."

Jelaïa leant over and grasped her aunt's hand firmly. "Nonsense. I value your counsel and friendship. And in any case, since when does Praedora, First Priestess of Brachyura, care about what other people think? The priestess who chased after a Knight of the Twelve in her undergarments armed with a kitchen knife?"

The corners of Praedora's mouth twitched, and she groaned. "I told that story to Aldarin in confidence. I should have known he'd pass it on. He is utterly terrible at keeping secrets."

"He is. Although he is much better at so many other things."

"I'm sure he is."

"What? No? I didn't mean that. I— What's going on?"

The sound of raised voices was coming from the edge of the campsite, hidden by the rows of blue and red tents. Soldiers and Knights of the Twelve were being drawn to the noise, stopping what they were doing and heading towards it.

"What can you see, Jeli?" asked Praedora, cocking her ear.

Aldarin appeared at a jog, pushing his way through the Arelian bystanders to reach Jelaïa's tent. He looked exuberant.

"They've arrived!" he said ecstatically, his face split in a wide grin. "I didn't think it possible! By the Twelve, Jelaïa, this is the happiest of days." He picked her up easily and spun her round, knocking the pot of ink off the table. He kissed her hard on the lips before setting her back down.

"Come on!" he shouted, grabbing her hand. "Let's go!"

Jelaïa looked towards her aunt. "Praedora?"

"Off you go, dear, you can come and tell me all about it afterwards." Jelaïa gave her a peck on the cheek and allowed herself to be pulled along by an excited Aldarin.

"Make way," he ordered as they reached the crowd of onlookers. "Make way for the Baroness."

The crowd parted, revealing a small group of men and women. In front of them, his hand raised in greeting, was the tired, skinny shape of Merad Reed.

"Reed!" she cried happily, running forwards and throwing her arms around his neck. "We've missed you! Loré told me you had been sent to Morlak. I feared the worst! What happened?"

"I am also here, my Lady," came a monotone voice, and Jeffson appeared at Reed's side. He bowed expertly. "I am pleased to see that both your Ladyship and Sir Aldarin survived the siege of Arelium unharmed. You have changed."

"As have you, Jeffson," Jelaïa replied, sizing him up. "You seem to be a bit less ... morose."

"I imagine that is all thanks to Sir Reed's positive influence," Jeffson said dryly. "He is such a joy to be around."

"Do you know what I think, Jeffson?" said Jelaïa, watching as Aldarin, laughing, enveloped Reed in a crushing hug. "I think that you say things sarcastically in the hope that people won't realise you are telling the truth."

A spark twinkled deep in Jeffson's eyes. "I couldn't say, my Lady. Now, if you will excuse me, I will find a place to set up Sir Reed's tent."

"Oh, I wouldn't bother. The High Priest of Klief knew you were coming. He wanted to wait for you all to arrive before letting us inside."

A huge figure appeared, looming over them both. Ink-black eyes stared at them from a burn-scarred face.

"Kriari," the giant said, in a voice so deep it made Jelaïa's skin vibrate.

"Then again," she said, "maybe we should take a moment to share the events of the last few months. It looks like we have both made some interesting acquaintances."

∿

The impromptu meeting took place in Derello's command tent, the only place big enough to accommodate three members of the Twelve. Brachyura and Kumbha's joy at seeing Kriari again quickly turned to despair as they discovered his impaired mental state. Kumbha tried briefly to use her gift, but it proved just as useless at healing him as it had for other patients afflicted with a disease of the mind.

The First of the Twelve now sat in one of the corners of the tent. Derello had given him his bronze eyeglass, and the giant was captivated by the metal tube, turning it over and over in his hands and occasionally pressing it to one eye. The other participants were crowded around a detailed map of the nine Baronies. Jelaïa scanned the multitude of familiar and unfamiliar faces. Never in the last three hundred years had so many disparate factions banded together with a common purpose.

Brachyura and Kumbha stood side by side, so different in their physique, yet so alike in their mannerisms. Aldarin and Vohanen, each representing his Order. Derello del Kessrin and Syrella del Morlak. Captain Reed. Praedora. Loré. Outside the tent waited dozens more. Orkam, Krelbe, Taleck, Ner'alla, Caddox, Jeffson ... survivors of Arelium, of Kessrin, of Morlak, and of Talth.

All eyes were on Jelaïa. She took a deep breath and began. She told them of her father's murder and of the man responsible: Praxis, Knight of Zygos. She told them of the ambush on the banks of the River Stahl, of her awakening and subsequent training at the temple. How they had convinced Brachyura that the Pact was wrong. The battle of the Bay of Doves. The death of Mina. Kumbha's plan to use a brood mother to locate the weaver. Praxis's escape. The siege of Talth. And lastly, her fateful conversation with the weaver that had set in motion the destruction of Morlak.

Her throat was dry by the time she had finished, and she felt physically and emotionally drained. Aldarin moved wordlessly to her side, offering her his arm in support.

Reed was the first to break the silence. "You have walked a long road, my Lady," he said softly. "I was there for your first steps, and they were not easy. But when I look at you now, I can see the courage and charisma of your father intertwined with the empathy and compassion of your mother. They would both be proud."

"Thank you, Reed. Loré tells me my mother is not well since the death of my father. I know she misses me. I just hope she understands why I have to see this through."

"Of course she does," interjected Loré blithely with a pearly smile. "Listus was always galivanting off to save Arelium. This is no different." He turned to Reed. "And what about you, my fellow invalid? It seems you have lost your metal chair, as I have lost my metal brace!"

Reed gave a short chuckle. "Pit, my Lord, I feel like I have lived a lifetime since our last meeting by that crackling fire. I'll do my best to relate our own sorry tale, although I will need Syrella and Vohanen's help for part of it, as I was somewhat … indisposed."

He closed his eyes for a moment. Then he spoke. He spoke of the last days of Nidore del Conte. Loré showed no emotion at hearing his son's betrayal, nor when Reed described how he had slowly convinced the young noble to help him escape Morlak prison. The del Conte patriarch was quiet and still. Only his finger moved, running up and down his cheek as if remembering an old wound. When Reed described Nidore's final moments, the finger stopped abruptly.

"I … If you would excuse me," Loré said in a choked voice and pushed past Vohanen as he fled the tent.

"He had to know," Reed said sadly as the flap dropped back into place. "Nidore deserved that much." He took a moment to compose himself, then finished recounting the death of Mithuna and the wyrm's destruction of Morlak.

"Our worst fears are thus realised," said Brachyura

ominously when Reed had finished. "Despite all the progress humanity has made. Despite your new weapons of war and your reforged alliances. The wyrm is just as unstoppable now as it was three hundred years ago."

"All the more reason to find Makara," said Kumbha firmly. "He will be able to help us, I am sure of it. Let us go bang on the gates of Klief and make them let us in."

Vohanen coughed and took a timid step forward with a jangle of beads. "Lady, if I may, I would ask a favour of you before we leave."

"Of course, Sir Knight."

"I have a comrade in arms, Sir Caddox is his name, who fought bravely by my side to free Morlak and did so willingly in the name of honour. He has lost the use of one arm—"

"Caddox!" boomed Brachyura. He looked almost bashful. "I am afraid I am responsible for that poor man's dilemma. Please, send him in."

Vohanen nodded gratefully and left the tent, returning with the broad-shouldered Knight of the Twelve, his arm still bound to his side. Brachyura strode over to him and, to the surprise of all present, bent down on one knee and bowed his head.

"Sir Caddox," the giant said. "I fear I have not sufficiently apologised for the wrong I have caused you. Without your intervention, we would surely not all be standing here today. Please, forgive me."

"There is nothing to forgive, Lord," Caddox replied, his face level with that of Brachyura's. "We all do things we regret." He shared a glance with Aldarin, and Jelaïa saw something unspoken pass between the two.

Kumbha laid a delicate hand on his shoulder. "This will

hurt," she warned. Caddox started to reply, then screamed. There was a cracking of bone, horrendously loud in the cramped confines of the tent. Kriari dropped the eyeglass and looked up, concerned. Then, in an instant, it was over.

Caddox removed his arm from its makeshift sling and flexed his fingers. "It's not possible," he said, his voice filled with wonder. "What is this ... sorcery?"

"It is my gift," Kumbha replied simply. "For better or for worse." A droplet of blood trickled from her left nostril, and she wiped it away absently.

"I will repay you for this, Lady," Caddox said fervently. "Even if it takes me a hundred years."

"I applaud your optimism if you really think you are going to live that long," Derello said cheerily. "The day is not getting any longer. Shall we go meet with Baron del Klief and the High Priest? Just the ten of us here I think, at first? Diplomacy before military might? No need to overwhelm them."

There was a chorus of muttered agreements, and they left the stifling confines of Derello's command tent for the fresh afternoon air. Jelaïa felt herself tingling with anticipation. She was still leaning on Aldarin's arm, the cool metal of his gauntlets familiar and reassuring.

Brachyura furrowed his brow as they came closer to the gate. He reached out his hand and brushed his fingers across the smooth granite.

"My Lord?" Aldarin prompted.

"I recognise this stone," he said curiously. "It is my own handiwork. And this place. It is familiar, but ... wrong, somehow."

"Do we turn back?" asked Jelaïa.

Brachyura shook his head. "No. Too much is at stake." He rapped an armoured fist on the Eagle Gate.

"WE ARE READY!"

His voice resonated off the bright white walls. For an instant, nothing happened. Brachyura was just about to call again when the double doors were pulled open, revealing the lower city of Klief. A paved road, straight and wide, ran from the gatehouse to the second wall roughly three hundred yards away. Hundreds of soldiers lined its entirety, backs ramrod stiff, eyes fixed forwards, and bedecked in enough finery to buy a small Barony. Each man had a gold breastplate and helmet, both polished to a mirror-like sheen that reflected the winter sun. Steel-tipped spears were held unwaveringly, each weapon decorated with a golden tassel affixed to the base of the blade.

In the middle of the road, a curtained palanquin was waiting for them, carried on the shoulders of four burly, golden-clothed bearers. The official from earlier was standing close by, horn at the ready.

"Hear ye!" he proclaimed in his grating voice. "May I present to you his holiness the High Priest of the Twelve. Bathe yourselves in his radiance!" He drew back the curtain, revealing a figure so old and wizened that Jelaïa was not sure that he was even still alive.

Wrinkles wormed their way all over his liver-spotted bald head, disappearing down his neck. His priest's robes, another lavish mixture of white silk and gold thread, were not enough to conceal his misshapen back and emaciated form. He sat cross-legged on a bed of cushions, his shrivelled hands folded in his lap.

How can this man be the High Priest? wondered Jelaïa. *He*

barely looks able to use a chamber pot let alone preach a sermon.
Then she saw his eyes. They were untouched by age, crystal
clear, the colour of uncut amethyst. The irises shone with a
mysterious brilliance as if harbouring some unfathomable
secret.

"Impossible," the High Priest began in a wavering voice
they had to strain to hear. He raised a lorgnette and peered
at them through the lenses. "Is it you? Is it really you? The
resemblance is remarkable ... I could almost believe ...
almost ..."

"Brother."

It was Brachyura who had spoken. Jelaïa had never seen
him so distressed. His black eyes were opened wide, his
mouth agape. He shook his head as if trying to shake away
his disbelief.

"Brother! What happened to you? What have you
become?"

Makara, Tenth of the Twelve, one of the most powerful
beings ever to walk the nine Baronies, tilted his head to one
side, and a roaring voice louder than a hundred waterfalls
exploded into Jelaïa's mind.

**What have I become? You are asking the wrong ques-
tions. I have done nothing other than suffer the passage
of time. But you! Who are you? You wear the faces of my
brothers and sisters, but I saw you die! I saw you all die!
By all that is merciful! What has the weaver done to you?
What has she done to your eyes?**

CHAPTER 5

GOLDEN RIVERS

"I have made an extraordinary discovery, Brother! An enormous body of fresh water, larger even than Terris Lake, hidden deep in the shifting sands of Shakalla Desert. A haven of peace and tranquillity. An oasis! Trees grow along its shores. Fish swim in its clear waters. No longer will the southern tribes be forced to suffer the harsh conditions of Da'arra. I will build my temple on the banks of this oasis, and next to it, I will build them a city."

LURIDAE, EIGHTH OF THE TWELVE, 21 AT

⋙

I T WAS DARK by the time Ka'arka had finished, and the oppressing desert heat had waned with the setting sun. The silvery glow of a thousand shining stars reflected off Xer'ana's face as she set down her umpteenth cup of tea.

"Interesting."

"*Interesting?* That's all you've got to say?" Ka'arka replied incredulously. "The Twelve are returning! My fellow knights nearly died trying to convince our patron to break the Pact!"

"Yes, an interesting and compelling tale, Knight of Brachyura, but one that does not concern us. I find it rather ironic that you and the other Knightly Orders only remember our existence when it serves your purpose. What exactly did you expect to find, coming here with your shining armour and your barded steed? A frightened group of old women, cowering in the ruins of their temple, waiting for someone to come and save them?"

"What? No, I ..."

"Ever since the Schism, we have been down at the edge of the world, fighting our own battles, alone and unaided, and we will continue to do so until the ground splits asunder and the stars tumble from the sky. Why don't you return to your patron and tell him that?"

Ka'arka could hear the disdain in her voice, see the wrinkles around her tired eyes, and the bloated blood vessels that ringed her brown irises. It was the face of someone who was slowly being ground into the dirt but was too proud and too stubborn to admit it.

"How long have the greylings been here?" he said softly.

"Greylings? Those Pit-spawned sons of whores are the least of our worries." She uncurled her legs and stood, wriggling her sandalled feet to send some warmth to her toes. "Jira Lake has been reduced to a crater of cracked earth. Even the Oasis is shrinking. What was believed to be an everlasting supply of water is another lie. Without it, we cannot irrigate our crops, or drink, or bathe our children. Without it, the city of Da'arra will cease to exist, and we will be forced back into the sands."

She gave a low-pitched whistle, and the other Knights of Luridae approached, their dark garments making them one with the night.

"So, you see, Knight of Brachyura, greylings or not, our Barony will fall. It will fall to an enemy we cannot defeat, and it is inevitable."

"I am sorry, Xer'ana."

"Why? It's not your fault. Da'arra will live on. Our people are strong, they will adapt." She let out a long, tired breath. "Enough talk of things that cannot be changed. The Da'arran Pit is a problem we may be able to do something about. Shen'alla, come here please."

Ka'arka recognised the second woman who had ambushed him in the dunes earlier that day.

"The Pit is always watched," Xer'ana continued. "A task given by the Twelve themselves, shared between the Knights of Luridae and the desert nomads. It was Shen'alla who first saw the greylings appear."

The younger knight nodded. "'Twas near the end of summer," she said. Her voice was the opposite of Xer'ana's, husky and warm like the caress of the desert wind. "Only at night. Five of the grey-skinned ones. Then more. They spread out in all directions, canvassing the area like they were searching for something."

"And did they find it?" Ka'arka asked.

"I think so." She glanced at Xer'ana. "If my mistress allows it, I will show you."

Xer'ana was adjusting her turban and mask. "We will all go. Knight of Brachyura, I won't have you clanking around out there in your metal coffin. What else did you bring?"

"Um, just a spare tunic, leather boots, and my riding cloak."

"Well, that will have to do. You can bring your axe but wrap it up in something so it doesn't reveal our position. We will be there to observe, not to be observed."

"Understood. How will we travel there?"

Xer'ana looked up at the twinkling sky and smiled thinly. "It's a nice night. I think we will walk. Try to keep up."

It took them just under an hour to reach the Da'arran Pit. The journey would have been shorter if the Knights of Luridae had not been forced to adapt their pace to that of Ka'arka. He struggled along, his natural weight making him sink into the desert sand at every step while his light-footed companions slid across the surface unimpeded.

Before long, his calves began to ache with the continuous effort.

They are doing this on purpose, he thought to himself, dragging one foot after the other. *Intending to make me fail. Well, it won't work. And when all this is over, I'll invite them back to Kessrin. Take them for a swim out in the Sea of Sorrow.* He grinned silently, picturing Xer'ana thrashing around in the emerald waters.

"Stop mumbling," Xer'ana hissed at him. "We're here. The Pit is just over the top of this dune. On your belly, Knight of Brachyura. We crawl."

Ka'arka lay down on his stomach and wormed his way up the sandy incline. Dozens of stinging grains rubbed against his tunic and bare arms. He crested the rise, and suddenly the Pit was there before him, filling his vision; a deep, gaping hole far darker than the night sky. Aldarin had tried to describe the Arelian Pit to him, but Ka'arka now realised that it was impossible to put into words the enormity of what he was seeing and the suffocating feeling that came with it, sapping his will.

The Da'arran Pit was surrounded by high rocks, protruding from the desert sand like the massive bones of forgotten giants. There were enough of them to form a natural barrier against the flow of sand, although a handful of golden rivers had managed to serpentine through the cracks, cascading over the edge of the Pit and down into the darkness below like waterfalls. Ka'arka watched for a moment, transfixed by the millions of tumbling, sparkling grains of sand. *Beauty can be found in all things,* he thought, forgetting briefly the crushing oblivion of the Pit itself.

Shen'alla slithered up next to him. "They leave from a tunnel to the west," she whispered, pointing to an entrance close by.

"Leave to do what?"

"You'll see."

They didn't have to wait long before three huge creatures emerged from the darkness. Ka'arka shuffled closer, frowning. Aldarin had described the greylings as cavorting, childlike beasts, screeching and yelling among themselves. These were far larger, their bodies packed with muscle. His friend had told him of the other creatures that he had fought on the walls of Arelium. What was it he had called them?

"Threshers," Ka'arka growled. "Far more dangerous."

The threshers below moved calmly and silently up the

side of the Pit before disappearing over one of the western dunes.

"They usually leave for about an hour," Shen'alla said in a low voice.

Ka'arka looked up at the stars. "I ... I am afraid I cannot read the constellations," he admitted, embarrassed. "I will have to rely on your guidance."

He heard a sigh of exasperation to his right, and Xer'ana dropped a small glass object on the sand in front of him. "We do not read the constellations, either, Knight of Brachyura." The object turned out to be a sandglass: two glass bulbs connected by a narrow passage through which a fine stream of sand was now flowing.

"Each bulb is one hour," Xer'ana said. "Watch."

Pit, what an annoying woman! thought Ka'arka. He observed the trickling sand for a time before his mind began to wander back to Kessrin. It had been wonderful to see Aldarin again; the brawny knight was like a brother to Ka'arka, and he knew the feeling was mutual. Ever since they had wound up on adjacent beds in the temple infirmary, each covered in a colourful assortment of cuts and bruises. Two scriers against the world. In the years that followed, more and more bullied outsiders had joined their scrappy group of misfits, but Ka'arka and Aldarin would always be the first.

Siblings. And as with all siblings, there was rivalry between them. There was no denying that Aldarin had been the right choice to send to investigate Praedora's visions, but Ka'arka had felt a pang of jealousy when his friend had returned victorious, his blue eyes sparkling with the gleam of his success, his lips overflowing with countless tales from the siege of Arelium.

And now it was Ka'arka's turn. The Conclave had shown him the same trust they had shown Aldarin. A trust he did not take lightly. He would prove himself to them and return with his own stories of courage and glory.

How long had he been gone? A month? Two months? It was easy to lose track of time on the road. He wondered what Aldarin was doing now. Probably still relaxing in the temple of Brachyura, indulging in some fine cuisine and sharing a bottle of white wine with Praedora. Or maybe with that young woman, what was her name? Jelaïa? Lucky man.

"They're returning," said Shen'alla quietly, her voice pulling him brusquely back to the present.

The threshers were approaching the Pit, moving slowly, each pushing a large cream-coloured oval more than half their size.

Eggs.

"What in the Pit ...?" murmured Ka'arka in confusion. The eggs seemed heavy, leaving great furrows in the sand as they were moved closer and closer to the Pit, the threshers carefully manoeuvring the bulky objects around the rocks.

"They are taking them into the tunnels," Shen'alla said. "This is what they've been doing. Eggs are brought up to the surface, left here for a week or so, then carried back down again."

"A week? Where do they leave them?" asked Ka'arka as the first of the eggs reached the top of the Pit and began to roll down the slope, the thresher grunting as it controlled the speed of descent.

"We don't know for sure, but I think they bury them in the sand."

"What do you mean, you don't know for sure, have you not followed them?"

"No, we—"

"I forbade it," Xer'ana interrupted. "I told you, Knight of Brachyura, whatever they are doing does not concern us. Unless they become overtly hostile, we should not intervene."

"Understandable," Ka'arka replied. "But the status quo has changed. Greylings have attacked Arelium. Do not think Da'arra will be spared a similar fate. For all we know, whatever they are doing here is the prelude to a greater plan." The first two eggs and their bearers had been swallowed by the darkness. "We must act now or risk losing them!"

For the first time since they had met, Xer'ana looked unsure. "I don't know …"

"Misery, Xer'ana. The priestess's vision spoke of misery. They have never been wrong before. If the waters of the Oasis are diminishing, then you are right, Da'arra's decline is unavoidable. But your complacency here may cause pain to the *Da'arrans*. Not to your city but to your *people*. When you are called to the shores of the Great Lake, what will you tell them? That you stood by and watched? Or that you tried to intervene?" He sprang to his feet in a shower of sand. "I am going. You may join me or stay here, it matters not."

He crested the dune and powered down the other side, his momentum carrying him forwards. The last egg was at the mouth of the tunnel. The thresher pushing it spotted Ka'arka careening towards it and let out a guttural cry for help.

There goes the element of surprise, Ka'arka thought as the beast's roar echoed off the cavernous sides of the Pit. There was an answering growl from somewhere inside the tunnel. Another huge shape lumbered out of the darkness, gesturing impatiently for the egg carrier to hurry up. Two round, button-like eyes locked onto Ka'arka. The thing snarled and pointed.

A challenge.

Ka'arka reached over his shoulder and unsheathed his axe, tearing off the old tunic he had wrapped around the blades. He slowed, searching for a flat area of rock where he could plant his feet.

The thresher came to meet him, beating a massive fist against its naked chest. *What I wouldn't give to have my armour now,* Ka'arka thought. He shifted his stance, anchoring his right foot behind him, with his axe held high over his head to block his opponent's attacks. He deflected the first two punches with the flat of his blade and the third with the tip, slicing open the thresher's knuckles.

It grunted and came at him again, using both its fists to pummel him from either side. A low jab broke through his guard and thumped against his thigh. He stumbled, barely warding off an uppercut to the face.

"Uuu—" the thresher began, then the shining tip of a steel glaive burst forth from its ribcage in an explosion of bone and gore, spattering Ka'arka's head and body like rain. The beast looked down stupidly at the length of metal protruding from its chest. One hand brushed weakly against the sharp tip before the creature crumpled to the ground, revealing the sylphlike form of Xer'ana, her shoulders heaving.

"Your distraction proved most effective, Knight of Brachyura," she said, pulling her weapon clear and wiping the blade on the thresher's loin cloth. "Although perhaps next time we could plan our assault together, rather than us being forced to run after you and clean up all your mess."

Ka'arka sighed. "Of course, mistress. I will try to remember that."

"See that you do. I take it you are still set on following those creatures into the Pit?"

"I am."

"I thought as much. I have sent Shen'alla back to camp to fetch your armour and some oil lamps. It would be foolish to proceed unprepared. We will both accompany you when she returns."

"Really? Why?"

"Because ... and I am loath to admit it ... because I think you might be right. We have become complacent, wrapped in our own ideals of self-preservation. You need to understand something, Knight of Brachyura. When the Order of Zygos told us of the Pact, we refused to believe it. Our patron, Luridae, was one of the greatest of the Twelve, unparalleled in his martial prowess. He left us little, but the parchments in the temple archives paint the picture of a man filled with an irrepressible hatred for the greylings. He would never have bowed to them, never agreed to any Pact or Treaty, no matter the odds ..."

Ka'arka ripped a piece of tunic from his arm and set about cleaning the muck off his face. "I thought the same of Brachyura, but he swore to us the Pact was real."

"Bah! An engineer, cowering behind his walls! He would have signed it without a second thought! Luridae would not have given up so easily. We were sure the acolytes of Zygos were wrong. The Schism broke us. We were never the most numerous of the Knightly Orders, and we lost more than half our number trying to defend what we thought was right ..." She trailed off, at a loss for words.

"The shadow war was a difficult time for all of us," Ka'arka said softly.

"It was. And so were the years that followed. We were fighting on too many fronts. The fallen Knights of the Twelve, the increasingly harsh living conditions of the desert, the roaming bands of raiders, and now this ... We are few ... too few. It is hard to see the light of the sun when you are surrounded by so many shadows." Xer'ana pulled down her mask and breathed in a lungful of night air. "Hard, too, to see the faces of our true friends. I may have judged you somewhat hastily, Knight of Brachyura."

"Think nothing of it, mistress." Ka'arka dropped the ichor-stained scrap of fabric. "It is a failure to be shared. We should have come here sooner. I should have come here sooner. I am a knight, but I am also Da'arran. I apologise for waiting so long before seeking you out." He held out his hand. "Let us start anew. Ka'arka, Knight of Brachyura, at your service."

Xer'ana hesitated for a moment then grasped his wrist. Her fingertips were smooth and icy-cold. "Xer'ana, temple mistress of the Knights of Luridae," she said, fixing him with her dark eyes. "... and daughter of Baron del Da'arra."

CHAPTER 6

Ominous Revelations

"We cannot force the other Baronies to welcome the priests of the Twelve, no more than they can force us to renounce our faith. Nevertheless, I would suggest allowing our most fervent believers to travel beyond our borders, not to convert others to our cause but simply to perpetuate the memory of the Twelve and the values they represent. So much of who they were has been lost, and some things must never be forgotten."

High Priest of the Twelve, 289 AT

"So, Verona is dead?" Aldarin asked Reed as they followed the ungainly palanquin up the main road of Klief. Makara had refused to say anything more after seeing Brachyura's inhuman eyes, only closing the curtain and motioning to his bearers to take him back to the cathedral.

"Not just dead," Reed replied. "Her throat was cut and her tongue removed."

"Removed? Before or after she was killed?"

"After, thank the Twelve. It wasn't done to torture her but to send a message. Taleck thinks it symbolises that she was murdered for something she said or was going to say. I don't know." Reed scratched at his beard and glanced at the line of Kliefien town guard stretching up the road as far as the second wall. Behind them, he could see rows of shops and houses, their doors closed and their shutters shut. There was no sign of any of the town's inhabitants. "Whatever the case may be," he continued, "we are no closer to finding her killer. Vohanen has assured me that none of his knights would do such a thing, and I think we can rule out Syrella."

"Jeffson? He and his family arrived on the exact same night, a suspicious coincidence."

"Once, maybe, when he called himself Nissus. He has promised to leave that life behind, and I believe him. Besides, if he had wanted her dead, he could have killed her in the Great Hall of Morlak. Why spare her then only to kill her later?"

"What about that peg-legged fellow who hides in Ner'alla's shadow?"

"Who? Stick? Or whatever his real name is. He's a strange one, for sure. Good with a knife, too. Nearly got the better of Jeffson. But what would he gain from killing Verona? I don't think he even knew who she was before we brought her back to camp." He readjusted the clasp of his vermilion cloak.

"Still have your wolf's head clasp, I see," Aldarin said. "And that tattered old thing."

"Recently reunited. I lost them both when I was being dragged back to Morlak. Vohanen found them while following my captor's trail and kept them for me."

"I'm sure we can find you a new one."

Reed touched the vermilion fabric affectionately. "I'd prefer not. Remember, in Jaelem, when you refused to relinquish your axe? We all have objects that are not easily replaced, those that soak up memories as we go through life, like the parched earth swallows the rain. And in doing so, they become a part of us, a part of who we are."

Aldarin smiled in agreement.

They passed through the second gate. The wall here was significantly more fortified: mangonels graced the roof of every tower, their spoon-like arms turned towards the grasslands to the south. Reed was surprised to see that this part of the city was just as deserted as the first. Even the honour guard had vanished. The only sounds were an unattached shutter banging in the wind and the distant barking of stray dogs. Makara's palanquin plodded steadily onwards.

"Where is everyone?" Reed wondered.

"Maybe the Baron had the town evacuated?"

"Or maybe they all ran away when they heard Jeffson was coming. He has that effect on people."

Aldarin let out a bark of laughter. "I've missed your jokes, friend Reed."

"Have you?" Reed said slyly. "I'm surprised you've had time to miss anything, what with Lady Jelaïa keeping you so busy." He stole a look at Aldarin and saw that the tall knight was blushing furiously.

"I ... I mean, yes, the Baroness and I have entered a relationship, but I have not neglected my duties—"

Reed gave him a playful tap on the pauldron. "Relax, Aldarin, it's not an interrogation. I'm happy for you both. I think you make a good fit."

"You do? I am worried that … we are too different. We have both led very divergent lives. A Knight of Brachyura and a priestess … a butcher's son and a Baroness. And what about the contrast in age? I am nearly nine years her senior …" He looked over his shoulder. Jelaïa was far behind, chatting animatedly with Derello and Syrella. "Perhaps she needs someone more in line with her own sensibilities and social standing."

"Pit, Aldarin!" exclaimed Reed. "I'm the last person you should be coming to for relationship advice, I am far from an expert in the matter!"

The palanquin had reached the final wall, and this time the gates were barred. One of the bearers rapped a complicated series of knocks on the door and shortly afterwards, they swung open.

"What I *can* say," Reed continued, "is that I believe that for us to grow, we need to be challenged. I have changed more in the last three months than in the last ten years, all because I have met people who have broadened my horizons. This is how we better ourselves, by gaining new insights, opinions, and perspectives. Don't try and make Jelaïa's choices for her; if she wants to be with you, there must be a good reason."

Aldarin studied him with his piercing blue eyes. "Thank you, friend Reed."

"You don't need to thank me. Besides," Reed said smugly, "you are not the only one to have kissed a Baroness."

"What? What in the Pit are you talking abou—"

The discordant blare of the ceremonial horn cut him

off. "All bow before Baron del Klief," the golden-dressed messenger bawled. They had reached the cathedral, an over-indulgent architectural nightmare of buttresses, towers, and gables, topped by a single spire that ascended to vertiginous heights. A wide flight of steps led to a three-doored portal under an enormous rose window, dazzling in red and blue glass. The jambs dividing the portals were decorated with sculpted effigies of who were presumably the Twelve. Reed could make out the bald axe-wielder Brachyura, the square-jawed Mithuna, Kriari, Kumbha, and many more. On the lintel above the central portal stood a life-size statue of Makara in his robes, one hand raised in blessing.

Twenty or so Kliefien nobles milled around the cathedral's entrance like a flock of lost sheep waiting for their shepherd. Reed had never seen such a collection of hats, brocades, hose, doublets, pantaloons, skirts, and shoes. And the colours! It looked like someone had thrown a half-dozen pots of paint onto the ground and let the noble men and women of Klief roll around in the resulting mess. Bright-red feathered caps clashed with sky-blue capes and yellow leggings. Golden lace was everywhere.

"Which one's the Baron?" Reed asked Aldarin, out of the corner of his mouth.

"No idea," the knight murmured back.

Reed scratched at his beard again. Jelaïa and the others were still a long way behind. His eyes roamed the crowd and alighted on a little boy of about ten sitting apart from the others.

"Hey, you!" he whispered furtively. "Help us out. Which one of these Pit-spawned cockerels is the Baron?"

The boy shot to his feet, his eyes flashing. The nobles

behind him fell silent. "How DARE you!" he cried angrily. "How dare you talk to me this way! Blasphemy! I should have you whipped! Guards! Take this man away!"

Aldarin stepped forwards hurriedly before Reed could reply and sank swiftly to one knee. "My most sincere apologies, my Lord," he said, bowing his head. "Lord Reed, Captain of the Old Guard and Defender of Arelium, is recovering from a long and arduous imprisonment—"

"Yes, I am regularly briefed on Morlak's and Arelium's current affairs," the boy interjected. "I would not be a very good Baron if I wasn't."

"Of course, my Lord. It's just ..." He moved closer. "The poor man's mind is a bit addled from weeks of solitary confinement, my Lord. Captured while facing off against impossible odds. I am responsible for him. The transgression is mine. If you wish to have someone whipped, it should be me."

Baron Azael del Klief mellowed somewhat. "No, Sir Knight. That will not be necessary. War takes its toll on us all. You must be Sir Aldarin. I believe you played a prominent role in all three major conflicts in our ongoing battle with the greylings. You have my thanks." He held out a pale hand, its fingers covered with golden rings.

"My Lord," Aldarin replied respectfully, bending to kiss one of the rings briefly.

"What are you doing playing with children, Aldarin?" Jelaïa, Derello, and the other members of the delegation had arrived, with Brachyura, Kriari, and Kumbha close behind.

"I am greeting *Baron del Klief*, my Lady," said Aldarin pointedly.

Jelaïa's eyes flickered as her mind switched gears. "My

Lord Baron," she said, turning to the boy and performing an elaborate curtsy. "What a great pleasure to meet you at long last. My father Listus has told me great things about the Barony of Klief and its fabulous riches. I see his praise was far from exaggerated."

Azael clicked his heels together and bowed in return. "At last, some decorum! My Lady, allow me to welcome you to our humble city." He looked past her. "Although it galls me to extend the same courtesy to these charlatans. If not for our High Priest's counsel, we would have left you on the other side of the Eagle Gate, where you belong."

"Charlatans?" Brachyura repeated. He seemed more confused than angry.

"Naturally. Sent to test our faith. It is the only rational explanation for your presence here. Let us proceed into the cathedral of the Twelve where we will be able to talk undisturbed." Spinning around to face the crowd of nobles, he clapped his hands. "Vassals! You are dismissed. Return to your homes and wait there until first mass! The Twelve be praised!"

The visitors followed Azael through the rapidly dispersing multi-coloured adulators. Kriari paused at the top of the steps and tugged on Brachyura's arm. "Kriari!" the First of the Twelve exclaimed happily, pointing to the stone figure crafted in his image.

"Indeed," Brachyura replied with a sad smile. "Our brother has been quite busy deifying us while we spent three hundred years in hibernation."

"He must have his reasons," Kumbha commented. "You know Makara as well as I do, Brother. Has he ever struck you as egotistical or self-centred?"

"No," Brachyura admitted. "Quite the opposite."

"Then, let us trust him, for now." She gave her own statue a passing glance. "They've got my hair wrong."

The interior of the cathedral was just as flamboyant as its facade. Stained-glass windows bathed the floor with red and blue light. The nave was one long rectangle, lined with alternating white and gold columns. Each of the twelve side chapels, six on either side, was dedicated to a member of the Twelve. Far above, self-supporting arches formed a vaulted ceiling, the repeating lines of marble resembling the bleached ribs of an enormous whale.

Rows and rows of well-worn pews stretched from the narthex to the far end of the cathedral where a simple circular structure rose up out of the paved floor, looking strangely out of place among the surrounding finery. As Reed came closer, he could see that its surface wasn't quite flat but concave, and the circumference was decorated with miniature towers. Signal towers.

By the Twelve, he thought. *It looks like a model of the Southern Pit!*

The palanquin was set down in front of the bizarre maquette, and Makara emerged, leaning heavily on a steel-tipped ebony cane. Azael rushed to his side with a fold-out chair, and Makara slowly lowered himself into it.

"You may leave us," he wheezed to the bearers, who bowed and retreated silently.

"We have been patient," Brachyura began. "I think it is time for you to—"

"Wait." Makara turned to the young Baron del Klief. "Sleep," he ordered, and the boy's eyes snapped shut. He slid to the ground.

"Someone put him in the palanquin, please," the Tenth of the Twelve said wearily. "What I have to say is not for him to hear. Worse, it could destroy the delicate equilibrium I have spent years maintaining."

"... He does not know you are Makara," Jelaïa said hesitantly. "How is that possible? There is a life-size statue of you above the cathedral entrance!"

"No," Makara replied cynically. "There is the statue of the current High Priest of Klief above the cathedral entrance. The effigy of Makara is on the furthest jamb, next to that of Dhanusa. I doubt you even saw it. An image of me in my prime or, at the very least, much younger than I am now. I am very careful, Jelaïa del Arelium. I have had three hundred years to be careful. You won't find any representation of Makara that looks anything like I do now."

Jelaïa was shaking her head. "And no one is surprised that the High Priest has been the same man ever since this place was built?"

"My public appearances are rare. I no longer give sermons. Only a select few ever see me outside my palanquin. The Baron, his official messenger, the bearers ... all are easy enough to manipulate. The human mind is a fragile thing. One only needs to find the right thread and tug."

"You have explained how, but not why," Kumbha said, her lips pursed.

"Why what?"

"Why deify the Twelve? Why build this cathedral?"

Makara coughed, a harsh, wracking sound that made his whole body shake. It reverberated off the vaulted ceiling, magnified tenfold. Azael shifted on his bed of pillows but did not wake.

"This is not a cathedral," he said, wiping a drop of spittle from the corner of his mouth with a wrinkled thumb. "It is a *crypt*. I built it to honour their lives and their sacrifice, to have something to remember them by, and to help others remember. Did you know that Klief is the only Barony where all of its subjects know the names of each and every member of the Twelve? By perpetuating their legend, we cement their place in history."

"Crypt," Kriari grunted. "Dead?"

Makara gazed at the giant, his face filled with pity.

"Answer his question," Brachyura said softly, his obsidian eyes unreadable.

"Yes, I am the last surviving member of the Twelve. They are dead. They are all dead."

Makara's words cut into all those present like the blade of a carving knife, punching through bone and muscle, piercing the heart. Reed felt an icy chill run through his body and could see that all of his friends were similarly affected but none more so than Brachyura. The dark-skinned colossus was livid, angry veins pulsing on his forehead.

"FOOLISHNESS!" he shouted, slamming his gauntleted hand into one of the pews. The wooden seat exploded. Splinters clattered to the floor like hailstones.

Makara hadn't moved. "Look into my eyes," he said calmly. "I saw it happen. You say you know me. Look deep. You will see that I am telling the truth."

"All this time spent alone has loosened your already tenuous grip on reality, Brother," snarled Brachyura. "Or perhaps you are becoming senile in your old age. I—"

Quiet.

Brachyura's jaw slammed shut.

Makara leant forwards in his seat, his brow furrowed in concentration. "Calm yourself," he said through gritted teeth. "We must discuss this rationally. It is the only way."

The Fourth of the Twelve nodded, and his jaw was released. "Very well. I will listen to what you have to say. We will all listen. But if this turns out to be some sort of trick, Brother, I will throw you off the walls of Klief myself."

"That is acceptable."

"Then start by answering me this. I have the body of Brachyura. The memories of Brachyura. Yet, you still have doubts as to my identity. Why?"

"A good question. There are three glaring issues. Firstly, you *do* bear an uncanny resemblance to the Fourth of the Twelve ... but only as he would have appeared three hundred years ago. Why have you not aged?"

"We were in hibernation—" Kumbha began.

"Let me finish. Secondly, my gift has always allowed me to sense my brothers and sisters all over the nine Baronies and project myself into their thoughts. The four of you are ... *empty*. I cannot feel you. I cannot speak to you. When I enter your minds, I hear nothing. The silence of the abyss."

Kumbha shivered and crossed her arms.

"Thirdly, and most importantly, I *saw* my brother die. His body crushed. There was no way he could have survived what happened to him."

Brachyura looked unconvinced.

"Let us, for a moment, humour you and agree that the Twelve are dead," he said reluctantly. "Or, more realistically, that *we* were dead and have been revived in some way. Who killed us? We had no enemies once we all agreed to sign the Pact."

"The Pact?"

"Yes, you doddering old fool. The Pact, the Treaty of Peace with the greylings. It bought three hundred years of borrowed time for the nine Baronies. And, in exchange, we surrendered unconditionally to the weaver, agreeing to all of her demands."

There was a high-pitched rattling sound, and Reed realised that Makara was laughing. "*Agreed? Surrendered?* Those two words have never been part of our vocabulary. Listen to your instincts. Do you think Kriari would have bowed down and accepted defeat? That Luridae, who once faced four-score greylings alone, would have meekly surrendered? Simha, the most headstrong and reckless of us all?"

"I …" Brachyura clenched and unclenched his fists, at a loss for words.

"You feel it don't you? You *feel* that this is wrong."

"But … the Pact. Our years in exile. We were confined to statues. I don't understand."

"You have been manipulated. There was no Pact. What do you remember of that Midsummer's Day?"

"We … we descended into the Morlakian Pit. All twelve of us. We were met by a thresher who led us deep into the earth. We met their leader, a creature called the weaver, who appeared to us through a … portal of sorts. Discovered what she was hiding from us. Something we could never hope to defeat. A monstrous serpent, birthed when the world was still young. A wyrm. It was then that we abandoned all hope and capitulated."

"Oh, no," Makara replied sorrowfully. "That's not what happened. That's not what happened at all."

CHAPTER 7

THE FINAL SACRIFICE

*"Perfectionism or, at the very least, perceived perfectionism was
a major issue throughout our later years. The human tribes still
saw us as the invincible victors of the Battle of the Northern
Plains, despite our diminished reflexes and slowly ageing bodies.
I think maybe our decision to sue for peace was not entirely
altruistic. Many of my brothers and sisters feared that another
prolonged conflict with the greylings would reveal just how tired
and weak we had become."*

MAKARA, TENTH OF THE TWELVE, 427 AT

∽

MAKARA SQUEEZED THROUGH the fissure at the
end of the underground cavern. The insufferable
heat was burning his lungs, making it hard to
breathe. Sweat poured off him, soaking his robes. He had
removed his half-moon spectacles, and his eyes wept salty

tears that blurred his vision. He wiped them dry with his sleeve and took stock of his surroundings.

His siblings and the creature known to him as the weaver were standing on the shore of a vast underground lake of boiling magma. Its red-hot surface bubbled and swirled angrily, covering the entirety of the cave they were now in. Towering over them loomed something so astronomically huge that it defied all thought and reason. A scaled head, a hundred feet long, ancient and reptilian. Two of the largest eyes Makara had ever seen glared down at him, yellow flames dancing along their lidless edges.

"A wyrm," the weaver said. "We found it resting, deep within the earth. It killed so many of us. Thousands. Hundreds of thousands. Until we learnt how to stop it. How to control it." She closed her hand into a fist, and the wyrm opened its mouth and let out a roar. Makara dropped his cane and covered his ears as the acoustic vibrations rattled his bones.

Brachyura drew his double-bladed axe. "So, it was a trap," he said. "I should have listened. We were foolish to believe that you and your kind desired peace."

"You mistake me, warrior of the Twelve," the weaver replied in her strangely accented voice, the syllables of each word chained together in an ungainly fashion. "We *do* wish for peace. Peace between your race and mine."

Makara felt his heartbeat slow, and he breathed a sigh of relief. "That is all we have ever wanted … my Lady," he said. "If we are both willing to make compromises, there is no reason why humans and greylings cannot come to a mutually beneficial agreement."

The weaver cocked her head and blinked her

almond-shaped eyes. "You do not understand. This language of yours is twisting my words. You are not human. You are the Twelve. I am offering you peace between the Twelve and my children."

Makara looked at her in stunned disbelief. "And what of the human race?"

She shrugged. "There is no place for them in the future I envisage for my children. They must be purged."

Simha gave an incredulous snort. "You can't be serious."

"Why not? I do not wish to unleash the wyrm unless I must. The lands above must remain intact if my children are to settle there. The wyrm will render them uninhabitable. If you ally yourselves with me, our combined strength alone will be enough to destroy the nine Baronies. But you know this. I can see it in your minds."

Makara frowned at hearing the weaver's words. She could see it in their minds? He thought back to what he had felt earlier when the weaver had touched the brood mother. A faint pulse had travelled between the two. Did that mean she could communicate with other greylings, as he could with his brothers and sisters? Maybe this was how the greylings remained so organised. So efficient. So dangerous. What would happen if that advantage was taken away from them?

He tried to send out questing mental tendrils of his own, but nothing happened. Since entering the depths of the Pit, his gift of telepathy no longer worked, just as Shala had lost her ability to manipulate the elements, and Mithuna her talent for physical transmutation. Worse still, he feared that this meant his siblings no longer had the latent shared reflexes that made them so invincible when fighting together.

There must be a way out of this, he thought. His mind analysed a thousand different strategies, each leading to the same outcome. Failure. He dug deeper, racing through a hundred years of memories, searching for something, anything, that might turn the tide.

"I will have your answer, warriors of the Twelve," the weaver said. High above her, the wyrm twisted and turned.

The others were all looking expectantly at him now. He had never wanted to be their leader. He was an advisor. A diplomat. How could they rely on him to decide the fate of so many? It was hopeless.

Then, he felt it. An itch at the very back of his mind. A dark thought that he had purposefully buried in the depths of his psyche. In all his calculations, in all his simulations, one parameter had always stayed the same.

The survival of his siblings. That was the solution. The only way to win. Through sacrifice.

He turned slowly to his brothers and sisters, the only family he had ever known. To the casual eye, they seemed just as unconquerable as when they had first appeared among the human tribes over a hundred and twenty years ago, but Makara knew that not to be true. He could see the cracks in their facade; the way Mina leant too heavily on her sword, how Guanna hunched his shoulders, the bags that hung under Shala's eyes, the deep lines that creased Brachyura's forehead. Makara remembered the Fourth of the Twelve nearly collapsing after the Hellin Pass, overwhelmed with exhaustion. The near-invincible demigods from the Battle of the Northern Plains were a distant memory. They had walked these lands too long and stretched themselves too thinly. Time leaves none unscathed.

They had given everything to safeguard the realms of men. All their strength. And now he was going to ask them to give even more. And he hated himself for it.

"Well?" the weaver prompted impatiently.

Makara ignored her. "I have an idea," he said to his siblings. "But it will cost us. It will cost us everything we have. We are tired. We are weak. Our gifts have been taken from us. All we have left is our courage. Are you willing to go that far for them? Are you willing to give your lives to protect the humans?"

"What are you talking about?" said the weaver crossly. "That is not an answer."

"I am ready," Brachyura said firmly, a fierce glint in his eye. "I would rather die fighting than live as a coward."

"As would I," agreed Kriari, swiftly echoed by Guanna and Simha. Luridae and Shala nodded. Dhanusa grunted.

"Of course, Brother," murmured Kumbha. "If we do not make our stand here, all we have done since our arrival will amount to nothing."

"I have come to the same logical conclusion," Zygos agreed.

"It is I who instigated this, and it appears that I was wrong," Mithuna added sourly. "I have no great love for the humans, but I must, at the very least, attempt to atone for my lack of judgement."

Mina was the only one not to answer. She shook her head and looked away.

"Very well," Makara said, apprehension rising in his chest. He swivelled back to the weaver. "Then, you have our answer, my Lady. Our answer is no."

"FOOLS" shrieked the weaver. "YOU WILL DIE HERE!" She raised a stick-like arm to direct the wyrm.

"BRACHYURA, KILL HER!" shouted Makara. The Fourth of the Twelve grasped the butt of his axe with both hands, raised it over his head, and threw it at the weaver with all his strength. The weapon punched into the weaver's chest like a ballista bolt, smashing through her rib cage and knocking her off her feet. The wyrm let out an ear-splitting bellow that shook the very earth. Cracks appeared on the cavern ceiling.

"We need to leave! Now!" Makara ran for the fissure in the rock, the muscles in his legs on fire. He tripped on a loose rock and went sprawling, chipping a tooth as his head hit the hard floor. Kumbha was the first to reach him. She pulled him up. "Leave me!" he ordered hoarsely. "Help the others!" She shook her head. "No, Brother. You are wrong for once. The others don't need me, you do. I will carry you." She heaved him up onto her back and shimmied through the gap. On the other side, a thousand greylings waited for them, threshers driving them on.

"They are too many!" Kumbha screamed as the first of the greylings came within range. Mina pushed past her in a flash of golden plate, her immense double-handed sword already swinging. Six greylings were felled with a single stroke.

"Get Makara out!" the Last of the Twelve ordered, ichor dripping down her blade. "We will deal with this rabble." Kriari appeared at her side, grinning madly. "You should wait for me, Sister. It's much more fun fighting together than alone." He set down his tower shield with an audible clang and drew his short sword, dispatching two greylings with a rapid stabbing motion.

The other members of the Twelve had made it through the gap. Brachyura was the last one through, his axe covered with dark blood. He quickly assessed the situation. "Guanna, Shala, Luridae. With Kumbha. Make a path. Get Makara out of danger then return here to help. The rest of you, on me. Heptagon formation. If we can get to the threshers and eliminate them, our job here will be much easier."

Roughly two hundred yards away, Kumbha could see the narrow snaking path they had used earlier to descend from the tunnel to the cavern floor. She veered away from the mass of greylings crowding around the crevice and concentrated on the distant goal. Her escort soon caught up with her, Guanna positioning himself to the fore, Shala and Luridae to the rear.

They heard the strident cry of a brood mother followed by the pattering of clawed feet as greylings hurried to block their escape. Shala pirouetted, her bronze sickle decapitating a pursuing enemy and slicing the arm from another. Guanna cut down three more, braining a fourth with his buckler.

"Nearly there," muttered Makara. Luridae took a trio of daggers from his belt and threw them in quick succession, each blade finding its target with unerring accuracy. They had reached the bottom of the path now. Makara risked a glance back down into the cavern and saw that the seven members of the Twelve had formed a heptagon and were pushing slowly through the chittering greylings in an attempt to reach the threshers.

A movement near the fissure.

"Kumbha!" he called. "Something's wrong!"

"Not now!" The Eleventh of the Twelve was tiring, her breathing laboured.

He cursed his blurry eyes and craned his neck as far forward as he could. There was definitely a shape, razor-thin, with four spider-like appendages. His blood ran cold. It was the weaver, on all fours, scuttling along the wall of the chasm like an insect.

He had to warn them. He took a deep breath and concentrated, willing his thoughts out of his body, searching for the familiar glow of his siblings' presence that would allow him to speak directly into their minds. Nothing. His gift had still not returned.

The weaver pounced.

Kriari heard the rush of air and swung his shield around, but the weaver was fast. Faster than any greyling. Faster than any thresher. And faster than one of the Twelve. She landed on the giant's chest and tore out his throat.

"NO!" Makara wailed in anguish as Kriari fell, his life-blood spilling from his ruined neck. Mina leapt over her brother's fallen form and crashed into the weaver, sending them both tumbling into the mass of greylings.

How had the weaver survived Brachyura's axe? He had seen her fall! His entire strategy had hinged on her death, in the hope that it would set the wyrm free and disrupt the horde.

They had reached the vantage point. Kumbha lowered him down. "We have to go back," he said to her.

"What? No! They are giving their lives down there so we can escape!"

"If we don't stop the weaver, it won't matter whether we escape or not!" Makara shouted in frustration. "Listen!"

When I first saw her, she touched one of the brood mothers. I heard something pass between them. A projection of her thoughts. Just like me. I believe *this* is how the greylings still manage to resist us, how they can coordinate their attacks over great distances. And, worst of all, I think this is how the weaver can control the wyrm."

There was a scream from below. Mina was on her feet, her left arm a bloody lump of mangled flesh, her long hair matted with ichor. The defensive pentagon had collapsed, and the survivors were beset upon on all sides by greylings and threshers.

"I have to go," Kumbha said, her eyes filled with tears.

"Your gift won't work, Sister! You cannot heal them!"

"I know. I don't care. I have to go."

Dhanusa was wrestling with the weaver, yelling incoherently, stabbing at her again and again with his knife. She thrust her head forwards and bit off his ear in a spray of blood.

"Please, just hear me out!" implored Makara. "The weaver is the key! Kill her and the war ends. Kill her, or—" he looked at the archway filled with pulsating black liquid, "—get her away from here. Break her hold."

Kumbha nodded, then bent and kissed him gently on the forehead. "Goodbye, Brother," she said tenderly. "May we meet again."

Simha and Mithuna were down, the boisterous Fifth of the Twelve the victim of a lucky punch from one of the threshers that had crushed his nose and sent a shard of bone up into his brain. Zygos was trading blows with the weaver, his face and arms a web of red lines from her talons.

Brachyura had his back to his brother, dispatching any greylings or threshers that came near.

As Makara watched, Zygos ducked under a slash of the
weaver's nails and rammed his stiletto under her chin, up
into her skull.

Please, Makara thought. *Please let this be the end of it.*

The weaver, laughing, pulled the stiletto free and, before
Zygos could react, thrust it through his cheek and out the
back of his head.

*This is insane! We are the Twelve! Despite our weakened
state, we are still demi-gods! Yet, she has killed four of us!*

Kumbha, Guanna, Shala, and Luridae crunched into
the back of the greylings, shattering them. Kumbha was gesticulating wildly, calling out to Brachyura and pointing to
the open archway. The Fourth of the Twelve eviscerated a
thresher and nodded.

The weaver turned, her claws raised to meet this new
threat. Guanna and Luridae baited her, keeping her attention on them while Shala circled round to her blind spot and
jumped onto her back, wrapping two powerful arms around
her neck. The weaver twisted and turned, but couldn't shake
off her attacker.

Guanna saw an opening and grabbed the weaver's
left arm, pinning it tightly between his gauntleted hands.
Luridae took hold of the other, and together they began
dragging the creature towards the portal.

"Brachyura, clear the way!" Guanna bellowed, his face
lined with effort.

Five threshers barred the way forwards, and Brachyura
waded into them, carving a path with his axe. Black ichor

rained down on him with each powerful sweep of his weapon. They were getting steadily closer, thirty feet away now.

Twenty.

The weaver closed her almond eyes, concentrating. A deafening roar exploded into the cavern.

The wyrm, Makara thought through a haze of fear. *She is trying to summon the wyrm.*

Guanna and Luridae were hauling the weaver to the base of the arch. The brood mothers surrounding it slithered away, mewling.

The entire cavern was shaking. An enormous stalactite, three times the size of Brachyura, fell from the ceiling, impaling a squealing brood mother. Cracks appeared along the narrow fissure as the wyrm tried to break out.

"PUSH HER THROUGH!" Brachyura screamed desperately. More stalactites fell. Luridae was thrown aside as one pierced his shoulder. The weaver tore her hand free from his grasp and jabbed her talons into Guanna's side, slicing open his plate armour as if it were made of paper.

Shala, still on the creature's back, pulled with all her strength. The weaver staggered backwards, teetering on the edge of the portal. A clawed hand latched onto the side of the archway. Brachyura threw down his axe, lowered his shoulder and charged, slamming into her chest. With a frustrated scream, the weaver disappeared into the blackness, taking Shala with her.

Brachyura stood alone as the cavern collapsed around him, surrounded by the bodies of the fallen. He turned, and his wandering gaze found Makara. The tenth of the Twelve did not need his gift to know what his brother was thinking.

Goodbye.

Brachyura inclined his head and returned his attention to the portal. Squaring his shoulders, he pressed his hands against the archway and pushed.

For a moment, nothing happened. Then, with a crack loud enough to be heard over the falling rocks, the portal toppled over in a cascade of broken stone and black liquid. The way had been blocked. The weaver could no longer return.

The last thing Makara saw was his brother smile, then the cavern ceiling caved in, and he was buried under a mountain of rubble.

And Makara wept.

"And so, I left that place," Makara concluded in his croaky voice. "I fled, like a coward, running with my tail between my legs. My memory of our descent and Dhanusa's arrows guided me back to the tunnel entrance, where Mina's ropes were still in place. The few greylings I came across were near-catatonic; staring blankly at nothing. My theory proved true: without the weaver to guide them, they were far less dangerous."

He fell silent. Kumbha began to cry quietly. Brachyura put a comforting arm around her shoulders and pulled her close.

"The ... the Pact," Aldarin stammered. "It tore the Knightly Orders apart. Are you telling us there is no such thing?"

Makara nodded sadly. "When I returned to the surface, I had to decide what to reveal to the Barons. Understand that the Twelve were living legends. Demi-gods who had never been defeated. I could not bring myself to sully their reputation. Besides, if I had revealed that the Twelve had perished, it would have plunged the Baronies into chaos."

"So, you lied."

"No. I told them a simple truth: that thanks to the actions of the Twelve, the greyling threat had been ended. No more, no less."

"It was not you, then, who created this false 'Pact'?"

Makara looked taken aback. "Of course not! Why would I even consider such a thing? Where did the idea first come from?"

Praedora bit her lower lip. "The priestesses of Zygos. They called a meeting sixty years ago. My predecessor was there. In fact, all the Orders were supposed to have been there. Including the Order of Makara."

"I have no Order. Not anymore. I was already an old man when the Twelve reunited the tribes, too old for children. I had a few indiscretions over the years, but my bloodline soon petered out. What did the priestess claim?"

"That she had found documents hidden deep in their temple archives."

"And did you find any such documents in the temple of Brachyura?"

She shook her head.

"So, the Schism was based on the findings of a single Order. Did none of you ever stop to think you were being manipulated? The Pact was surely a trick of the weaver to sow discord among you, and it worked perfectly."

Brachyura massaged his head with the palms of his hands. "But I remember signing it," he moaned in frustration. "And now you tell me these memories aren't mine. Am I even Brachyura? And if not, who am I? What am I?"

"I don't know. The only person who holds the answer is the weaver herself." Makara's eyes flickered around the room. "I would suggest that until we know for sure exactly who you are, we do not divulge what we have discussed here. I will inform Azael that I have spoken with you and that you truly are the Twelve, sent from the heavens to aid us. It is the best way to be sure of his compliance."

"Agreed," Brachyura said. "So, what is our next move?"

"Everything leads to the weaver," Aldarin said. "She is the key to ending the greyling invasion, to stopping the wyrm, and to elucidating the return of the Twelve. We need to find her. Lord Makara, if we can locate a brood mother, would it be possible for you to use your gift to enter its mind and discern the weaver's whereabouts?"

"A brood mother? I have never tried, but if her gift functions in a similar fashion to mine, it should be possible."

"Then, hope is not lost," Brachyura said, standing a little straighter. "We will scour the nine Baronies for one of these creatures. It will lead us to the weaver. And we will make her reveal what she has done to us."

Baron Azael was stirring. Makara gave him a look of almost fatherly affection.

"There is no need for you to leave, Brother," he said softly to Brachyura. "I already know where to find one. Zygos is marching on Klief at the head of an army of one hundred thousand greylings. He will be here tomorrow."

CHAPTER 8

THE UNESCAPABLE PRISON

"As the Oasis desiccates and shrinks, so too does the will of our people. But we must not despair. We will survive this new hardship as we have all others. The desert has always been both harsh and forgiving, merciless and beautiful. When the infrequent rain sweeps over the dunes, withered stumps burst into flower, green shoots sprout from shrivelled husks. And so it is for the Da'arran people. We will endure this drought, and when the time is right, we will thrive once more."

BARON DEL DA'ARRA, 420 AT

⤲

K A'ARKA LIFTED HIS sputtering oil lantern and squinted down the tunnel. It looked exactly the same as the last three.

"We've lost them," he growled at Xer'ana.

She squeezed past him and knelt in the dirt, her hand brushing an imprint made by one of the large egg-shaped objects. "*You* have lost them, Knight of Brachyura. I have not."

Xer'ana, Daughter of the Baron of Da'arra. That new nugget of information certainly explained the permanent haughty expression she wore and why she spoke to everyone as if they were beneath her. He had tried to learn more while waiting for Shen'alla to return, but it had been like pulling teeth. From what little he could gather, the first Knights of Luridae had been trained to guard the Oasis by Luridae himself, and thus their temple was not built in a remote part of the desert but adjacent to the capital city of Da'arra.

Consequently, the initiates were closely intertwined with Da'arran high society; far more than any of the other Orders. It was only a matter of time before Luridae's bloodline mingled with that of the Da'arran Barons.

Ka'arka watched Xer'ana move confidently down the tunnel, her glaive thrust out in front of her like a divining rod. She had removed her turban, and the soft yellow light of the lanterns accentuated the supple curve of her neck.

"Careful," murmured Shen'alla, a few paces behind him. "Xer'ana is notoriously swift to anger, and does not like to be … admired."

"I was only—"

"I know what you were doing. I'm just trying to help you keep your head attached to your shoulders."

Another junction. The descending path to the left was covered in greyling tracks.

"By the Twelve, how deep do the Pits go?" Ka'arka asked.

"No one knows," Xer'ana replied. "Luridae supposedly

led expeditions down here before his untimely disappearance, but whatever records he may have made of his discoveries have been lost."

They walked past a series of side-tunnels; dark, gaping holes in the rock, like giant-size maws. Ka'arka imagined hundreds of greylings waiting in the darkness, just outside the circle of lantern light. Waiting and watching.

"We'll have to turn back soon," Xer'ana said as if reading his mind. "We've burned through more than half the oil, and we'll need the lanterns to see our way out again. Unless you want to make the return journey in the dark ..."

"Definitely not," said Ka'arka decisively. "This place is scary enough as it is." His breastplate felt too tight, the metal pushing uncomfortably against his chest. He had donned his armour too hastily and was starting to regret it.

"There seems to be some sort of underground cave up ahead," said Xer'ana, peering into the gloom. "That shall be our final destination. If we don't find them there, we'll have to turn around."

Ka'arka drew his axe with some difficulty, his arms scraping against the sides of the narrow tunnel. He stepped warily into the cave. It was empty and much smaller than he had expected; only forty feet or so in length, its walls dry and smooth. The light cast by the trio of lanterns was strong enough to illuminate the far wall. There was no other discernible way in or out. A dead end.

In the centre of the cave stood an archway, its crumbling slabs decorated with whorls and symbols he didn't understand. The interior was filled with a thick black liquid that pulsed and rippled like the waters of a windswept lake. Five wide, circular pools surrounded the archway, connected to it by channels cut into the floor of the cavern. The same dark substance flowed along these channels, from the base of the archway into the pools themselves.

"What is this new evil?" Ka'arka wondered, stepping closer. The stones bordering each pool were decorated with the same unreadable symbols found on the archway and one new, unique image he recognised. Animals. An eagle. A wolf. A bear. A stag. A fox.

"The tracks end here," Xer'ana said, her eyes scanning the walls for hidden exits. "They came into this cave and didn't come out again. Look." She pointed to the pool with the image of an eagle. There were unmistakable egg-shaped tracks, mixed with clawed footprints. Lots and lots of footprints.

"They went into the pool? Could it be the entrance to some sort of underground tunnel?"

"Perhaps, but that doesn't make any sense. Greylings can't swim. They abhor water."

"So, what now?"

Xer'ana held her lantern over the pool. Nothing could be seen beyond its slick, reflective surface.

"If it's a tunnel, I'll see where it goes," she said, donning her turban and extinguishing her light. "Wait for me as long as you can." She knelt and put one hand into the liquid, then withdrew it in shock. "Pit, it's cold!"

Ka'arka put a hand on her shoulder and gently drew her back. "I will go first," he said calmly.

"But—"

"How often do you swim, my Lady? I have not seen many rivers or lakes around here. My temple is on the coast. I have swum in the icy waters of the Sea of Sorrow nearly every day for the last fifteen years. Fighting against the undertow and the bitter cold. A good leader should know how to use the strengths of the men and women they command. Let me do this."

Xer'ana fixed him with her hard eyes. He stared back unflinchingly.

"I do not need lessons in leadership, Knight of Brachyura. Nor do I like being interrupted. But your argument is sound. We will keep watch. Shen'alla! Help him remove his armour."

Ka'arka stripped down to his tunic and dipped one bare foot into the pool. A glacial chill ran up his leg, making him shiver.

Pit! he thought. *That's colder than the seas of Kessrin. Much colder.*

The black liquid felt like oil against his skin but had a thicker quality; dripping slowly and sluggishly like tar. Ka'arka forced himself to breathe calmly, focusing on the rise and fall of his chest. He relaxed his tense muscles, rolling his shoulders and shaking his arms.

Then, with one final look at Xer'ana, he plunged into the darkness.

Fire. Fire everywhere.

Blue flame, the colour of sapphires.

He was blind, pulled left and right by hidden currents. The biting cold was agonising. More chaotic images flashed behind his eyelids.

The beating of wings.

Plumes of green smoke.

Suddenly, he was catapulted from the pool into a

pitch-black cavern, crashing into something. A creature. It squirmed under him, trying to rake his face with its claws.

Greyling!

He turned his head. A sharp talon cut a red line across his cheek. His groping hands found a scrawny neck and twisted it. There was a crack. The greyling fell limp. Ka'arka rolled off the corpse, his chest heaving. He coughed up a lungful of black liquid and sat up slowly. As his eyes adjusted to the gloom, he began to get a clearer idea of his surroundings.

The cavern he now found himself in was near-identical to the one he had left. The same ancient, mysterious arch-way, the same series of pools. He crawled over to the one he had been thrown out of. The image carved into the stone border was different. He couldn't quite make out what it was; a snake or a lizard maybe. He traced the carving. Legs. A lizard. His eyes widened in understanding.

Taking another deep breath, he dived back into the pool. He was ready for the cold and the disparate images this time, letting himself be carried by the current instead of trying to fight against it. With a splash, he was ejected from the pool again, narrowly avoiding Xer'ana.

"That was fast," she said as he rubbed some warmth back into his limbs. "You must have swum only a short distance. Where does it end?"

"It's … not … a … tunnel," he said, his teeth chattering. "Remind me … of your … heraldry."

She shot him a quizzical look. "You have been away from your birthplace too long, Knight of Brachyura. The coat of arms of Da'arra is an emerald lizard on a field of yellow. Every Da'arran should know this."

"Apologies," he said, grinning despite his clacketing

teeth. He pointed a trembling finger at the other pools. "The wolf ... Arelium. The bear of Morlak. The stag of Talth. The fox of Quayjin. The eagle ..."

"... of Klief," Xer'ana finished.

Ka'arka nodded. "It's not a tunnel. It's a portal. A portal to Klief."

⁓

Praxis had known the inside of many prisons during his life; from the hold of a carrack to a Baron's tent, from a Kessrin guesthouse to an underground cave. They all paled, however, in comparison to his current predicament. He was trapped inside the worst possible place imaginable: his own body. A prison from which he would never escape. And he had no one to blame but himself.

When did I become so arrogant? he thought, trying unsuccessfully for the hundredth time to move the little finger of his right hand. Arrogance. He had fallen prey to the very thing the teachings of his Order warned against. Ironic, really, considering the name of his captor.

For years, he had managed to follow his temple's creed to the letter. Logic unhampered by feeling. Logic and balance in all things. Emotions were fallible. Logic was not. His detachment from any form of sentiment had initially served him well, allowing him to win Listus del Arelium's trust then murder him without hesitation. Gaining Derello del Kessrin's support had been just as easy.

But then ... one of the emotions he had worked so hard to push away had managed to worm its way back in. The most despicable of them all. *Lust.* Lust for the power granted

to him by the Regency of Arelium. A power he had refused
to give up. He had kept telling himself it was only a means
to an end …

Stupid, self-delusional fool.

Quiet, came the echoing boom of Zygos's voice, cutting
through his thoughts like a knife. **I can hear you buzzing
around in there, initiate. Like an annoying wasp. Stop it.**
The last two words were accompanied by a stinging pain. A
lash of the whip. A reminder of who was in charge.

Fortunately, Praxis's psyche was not imprisoned in total
darkness. He could see the outside world, or rather a sim-
plified version of it. There was no colour in the Seventh of
the Twelve's sight, only varied hues of black and grey, most
assuredly the consequence of replacing Praxis's eyes with
those shadowy pools of viscous liquid.

It was night, with the moon hidden behind the clouds
making it even harder to see. The only light came from the
twenty-odd Knights of Zygos surrounding their patron.
They rode horses captured from the ill-fated Kessrin expedition that had been sent after Praxis. An expedition that had
been led by Hirkuin. Moments before his death, the Captain
of the Guard had unwittingly revealed Jelaïa and Derello's
final destination: Klief.

Zygos twisted in the saddle, allowing Praxis to see what
followed in their wake. Greylings. Tens of thousands, maybe
even hundreds of thousands. They covered the ground as far
as the distant horizon like a swarm of angry locusts, destroying everything in their path. Unstoppable. Unbeatable.

Klief would fall in a day.

A brood mother, its slug-like form transported on a rick-
ety litter by four burly threshers, detached itself from the

chittering tide and approached. The vanguard halted. One of the knights drew his stilettos and barred its way, scowling.

"Let it pass, Helios," Zygos said to the man. "We have nothing to fear from our allies."

"Yes, Lord," the initiate replied, sheathing his weapon and bobbing his head.

The brood mother gave a shudder. Drool dribbled from its ugly mouth. Another shudder. Then its putrid maw opened and a voice spoke. "Zygos. You are making excellent progress. Am I correct in thinking you have nearly arrived at the city?"

The weaver, using the bloated birther as a proxy. Praxis could feel his patron's disgust.

"We have," Zygos replied irritably. "As you would know yourself if you deigned to grace us with your presence rather than use this creature as your mouthpiece. It is most inefficient."

"I cannot," the weaver countered. "I am the keystone. If I fall, the entire greyling race falls with me. It is too dangerous."

Which is why she sent us, Praxis thought. *We're expendable.*

"We should have retaken Talth first," Zygos said. "They may not be much of a threat, but it is a poor strategy to have an enemy at our backs."

"Do not question my decisions. Obliterating Talth was my original intent. However, that was before learning of this new serendipitous opportunity. Four Barons and four traitorous members of the Twelve bottled up in one place. It is not a gift to be squandered."

"Then, why not use the portals to move from Talth to Klief?"

"Send one hundred thousand greylings through the pool? That would take days! Besides, the Kliefien Pit is not as ... accessible as it once was."

The brood mother made a pitiful keening sound. A small hole opened in its cheek with a wet squelch.

"I will be brief," the weaver continued. "This flesh will not suffer me long. By the time you reach Klief, night will be fading. My children have made great progress in resisting the sun's rays, but they will still be weakened by the light. The surrounding hills are riddled with tunnels. You must let my army rest underground or in the shade."

"As you wish. And what shall the Knights of Zygos do while the greylings recover?"

"Send out an emissary. Try to negotiate."

Zygos ran a finger along his scarred cheek, mimicking one of Praxis's old habits. "Negotiate?"

"A lie, of course, but it will allow us to gauge the strength of their defences and judge their readiness. This version of Klief did not exist when I last walked the lands of the nine Baronies. I hear they have erected a monument to the Twelve. A temple ... a cathedral. Despicable. They are not gods. They scream and die like everyone else. I will grind that aberration to dust."

"As you wish. And the eggs we were promised?"

There was a crack of distended bone. "Almost ready. The boiling sands of Da'arra were perfect for their final incubation. They are coming through the portal now. Although if the defence is as weak as your spy reports, we will not need them. Klief will have already fallen by the time they hatch."

Zygos frowned. "Perhaps. I am not sure how much I can trust him. He is one of our more recent recruits, still unskilled in the art of discarding his emotions. We lacked the time to mould him into a true Knight of the Order. Conversely, the information he fed us concerning Praxis's location was correct, as were his reports of the allied army's movements."

The brood mother squealed as its other cheek ripped nearly in two. Spittle leaked from the open wound. "Details," the weaver said, the syllables garbled. "I must leave, this mother is dying. Just answer me this. Is he loyal? Will he fulfil his mission? If, for some reason, the attack fails, will he let us into the city?"

"Yes," Zygos answered without hesitation.

"Yes, he will."

CHAPTER 9
THE WHITE FLAG

"I have strived throughout the pages of this book to record the recent conjuncture factually and objectively. A task far more complicated than I initially thought. History is built from the memories of those who have lived through past events, yet how can one efficiently merge historical accuracy with the unreliability of the human mind?"

FROM 'THE WAR OF THE TWELVE', 427 AT

∼

J ELAÏA AWOKE TO Aldarin's soft snores, his warm body pressed up against hers. She lay silently next to him for a while, relishing the intimacy. They had shared the same tent on the trip north to Klief, but this, at last, was a *bed*. A real bed, with fluffy pillows and a proper feather mattress. Far more agreeable. And speaking of agreeable …

She wriggled round and put a hand on his naked chest, feeling it move as he breathed.

He looked at peace. The resolute expression he so often wore during the day was nowhere to be seen. It was the scar on his scalp that worried her. She had managed to bring him back from the brink of death thanks to Praedora and the Unbroken Circle, but there was a cost. Always a cost. The constant headaches.

"What are you thinking about?" murmured Aldarin groggily without opening his eyes.

She kissed him on the neck. "How happy I am to be in this bed. And you?"

"Hmm … Breakfast."

Jelaïa gave a mock cry of anger and slapped him on the arm. "*Pit*, Aldarin!"

A smile tugged at the corner of his lips. "I jest, my Lady. I jest. In all honesty, I was reminiscing on exactly how we arrived in our current predicament." He turned his head towards the bedroom window. Their quarters were situated right next to the cathedral, the hazy shape of the spire visible through the thin curtains.

"Do you believe Makara?" Aldarin asked, gazing absently at the church of the Twelve. "If what he says is true, then hundreds of my brothers died for nothing. The Pact. The Return of the Twelve. Lies upon lies upon lies. Enough to fill an entire graveyard with rotten corpses. We have been deceived so many times, I am not sure I can ever trust again."

Jelaïa felt cold all of a sudden. She snuggled closer and sensed Aldarin's reassuring arms wrap around her. "I believe … that he is telling the truth," she said after a moment's pause. "As for the Pact, we are all to blame. The nine Baronies have evolved at a blistering pace. Culture. Science. Medicine. Warfare. But in chasing our dreams of the future, we have neglected our past. We are …" she shook her head in exasperation. "We are building the roof of our house before consolidating the foundations. We are writing the second chapter of a book without reading the first."

A bell tolled three times, summoning the faithful to morning prayer.

"It is only by understanding the mistakes of the past that we can avoid repeating them in the future," Jelaïa continued, brushing a strand of chestnut hair from her forehead. "How could our predecessors not think to keep detailed archives? So little was recorded, and what *does* exist is contradictory and poorly maintained. I do not agree with deifying the Twelve, but Makara was right when he said Klief was the only Barony that knows their names. None in Arelium has that knowledge, not even my father. And we had a statue of Kumbha in our *garden*!"

"Knowledge the Twelve had and did not share," Aldarin rumbled.

"True, but we did not ask for it either. Pit, we didn't even ask each other. The Council of the nine Baronies meets once a year and instead of trying to learn more about each other's culture, we waste that precious time bickering about trade routes and tithes."

"Both are important to Arelium."

"Agreed. However, money and good fortune will not stop the greylings from killing every last one of us."

"A fair point."

"What's so frustrating is that this has happened before. The human race almost failed due to mistrust and division.

And now it is happening again; the nine Baronies are drifting apart like shattered ice on a frozen lake."

Aldarin scratched at the scar on his scalp. "They *were* drifting, perhaps, before the greylings crawled out of the Pits. Their reappearance has achieved what the Council of Baronies could not. Kessrin stands with Arelium. Talth has joined us. Morlak is here. New bonds are being forged. Forged in the fires of battle. Tempered by blood, grief, and loss. The Baronies will emerge not only victorious but stronger and more united than ever before."

"That will amount to nought if all we do here is forgotten."

"Then, we will have to make sure that does not happen," said Aldarin encouragingly. His stomach gave a menacing growl. Jelaïa couldn't help but laugh.

"Breakfast?" she asked teasingly.

"Breakfast."

≼

The keep of Klief was more a manor house than a defensive bastion; a sprawling two-storey building filled with columned hallways and marble statues. The eagle heraldry was everywhere; carved into the decorated capitals of the columns, painted on the walls, chiselled into the doors. Aureate banners hung in every available free space. There was easily enough gold thread to clothe the entirety of the city's occupants.

In fact, that's another strange thing, thought Jelaïa, walking briskly down one of the corridors behind a starved

Aldarin. *We've only seen a score of nobles and a smattering of servants since we arrived. Where is everybody?*

Aldarin pushed open a set of double doors, and they were immediately assailed by the mouth-watering odour of freshly-baked bread. Kessrin, Arelians, and Morlakians were clustered around an impressively large rectangular table creaking under the weight of a tempting array of delicacies. Bread and pastries, of course, but also all manner of fruit — including lemons and limes from Da'arra — honey from the hives of Morlak, salted fish from Kessrin, and more besides. There was even a small pot of tea, partially hidden by Xandris and Belen, who were guarding it jealously.

Aldarin practically ran to the table, grabbing a plate from a passing servant with a word of thanks. Jelaïa paused by the door for a moment, wanting to take it all in. Praedora and Derello were deep in conversation, the young Baron as red as a beetroot. Vohanen was in the midst of explaining something to a grim-faced Taleck, gesticulating excitedly with both hands, the mug of ale he was holding dangerously close to overflowing. Syrella and Reed were a few tables away, talking quietly. The Baroness of Morlak had a little girl sitting on her knee who appeared to be stuffing her face with scones coated in honey.

Everywhere Jelaïa looked people from different places and divergent lives were mingling, learning more about each other, coming together like the links of a chain. Only Loré del Conte ate alone, picking listlessly at a crust of dry bread and staring vaguely at nothing in particular. Jelaïa selected a few choice pastries, accepted the cup of tea handed to her by Xandris, and pulled up a chair next to her biological father.

He looked terrible, his face drawn and gaunt,

charcoal-grey bags under his eyes. He was wearing the same clothes as the day before, smelling slightly of mud and old wine. He attempted a smile on seeing her, but it came out as a tired grimace.

"Daughter," he said.

"Loré," she cautioned. "No."

"Apologies." He withdrew a flask from the inside of his dirty jerkin and took a small sip. Jelaïa could smell the alcohol.

"How are you?" she asked tentatively.

Loré chuckled sadly in reply. "It is a strange thing, is it not, the randomness of life? Four months ago, I was lying on my back in the dirt, my leg broken, my eye torn from its socket. I was sure I was going to die. It was an indescribable feeling, being so close to death, a kind of elation that I would not have to live with the shame of my defeat. The pain didn't seem so bad, knowing release would come."

He unscrewed his flask and took another sip. There was a shout from the end of the hall as Krelbe lost another hand of cards to Ner'alla, Sir Bansworth, and the man who called himself Stick. Jeffson was watching them over a steaming cup of tea.

"It didn't, of course," Loré continued. "Instead, I reawakened to constant, numbing pain. I learnt that my wife had been dragged screaming to the barges of Kessrin. Soon after, my son disappeared on the field of battle. It was a dark time."

"And then you were healed," Jelaïa said quietly.

"Yes, Daugh— my Lady. Healed. And I thought the Twelve had smiled upon me once more, naive as I was. Praxis, curse his shrivelled heart, used to tell me that for every action there is a reaction. Something to balance the scales. Now, I understand what he was trying to say. My happiness could not last. My son is gone."

He began to bring the flask to his lips once more, but Jelaïa caught his hand.

"He is," she said. "You heard what Reed said. He made the choice to sacrifice himself to save his friends. He was like you, lying in the dirt after your disastrous cavalry charge. He had made mistakes, lots of mistakes. His actions caused the deaths of many including, if I recall, several brave men of the Old Guard. But he did not give in to despair. He tried to change. I, for one, am proud of my half-brother. I would rather die attempting to redeem myself than live out my life as a traitor and a murderer."

Loré stared at her for a moment, then closed the flask and put it away. "There is so much of Listus in you, child. Even though you are not of his blood, I look at you, and I see the same steel in your eyes. Pit, you even sound like him. I hated the bastard sometimes, but he always knew what to say … I miss him. I miss them both."

Jelaïa swallowed to try and clear the lump in her throat. "So do I, Loré." She scanned the room until she found the tall bearded form of Vohanen. "Sir Knight," she called loudly, beckoning him over.

"My Lady?" The Knight of Kriari put down his ale and came to stand by her shoulder, munching on a chicken leg.

"May I present to you one of my closest advisors, Sir Loré del Conte?"

Vohanen inclined his head respectfully. "My Lord."

"As you may know, Sir Knight, Loré learnt of the death of his son yesterday. I was aggrieved to discover that your son suffered the same fate. Perhaps you have some advice for his Lordship?"

"Aye," said Vohanen slowly, taking a seat. "I do. Something a good friend of mine told me when I was in a bad place."

"Excellent." Jelaïa stood up. "I'll leave you to it. Those muffins aren't going to eat themselves." She wandered towards the overladen table.

"Ah, my Lady!" said Xandris brightly, appearing by her side like an excited child. "I've been waiting for the chance to talk with you. I have been experimenting with—"

The doors to the dining hall banged open, and Azael del Klief made his entrance, flanked by two guardsmen with polished golden breastplates and tasselled spears. They towered over him like threshers over a greyling. His roaming eyes found Jelaïa, and he marched to meet her.

"My Lord Baron," she said with a curtsy.

Azael took her hand and pressed it to his lips. "My Lady," he said. "The room is suddenly more radiant now that you are here to illuminate it with your beauty."

She coughed to hide her smile.

"My thanks, Lord Baron. The High Priest does not accompany you?"

He waved the question away. "The High Priest is in communion with the Twelve, evidently. Three of them have descended from the heavens to guide us in our darkest hour! Three! Is it not miraculous?"

More like two and a half, thought Jelaïa to herself, remembering Kriari's bemused smile. *In communion ... clever. A way to keep them close.*

"It is," she said aloud. "We are so incredibly fortunate to see them walk these lands once more."

"It is as was foretold," Azael said seriously. "They return to end the greyling threat once and for all."

Jelaïa wondered just how much the child-Baron knew. He seemed oblivious to the fact that other members of the Twelve were under the control of the weaver, and that two of their number, Mithuna and Mina, had been killed by people calmly eating breakfast in the same room as him.

Before she could reply, the door crashed open once again, and Caddox marched into the room, his burnished silver armour polished to a fine sheen, his holstered axe gleaming.

"I come from the wall," he said ominously. "The enemy host approaches. It is ... substantial in size. One of their number wishes to parley. Dressed in black, with a scar on one cheek. He comes bearing the white flag."

"Praxis," murmured Jelaïa. She wasn't hungry anymore.

"An envoy?" scoffed Azael. "I can see why. The city of Klief has never been taken. They have seen our walls and realised their folly. Let us go and discuss the terms of their surrender."

∽

The four Barons and Baronesses rode to meet the enemy envoy, escorted by an honour guard of the Knights of the Twelve.

Jelaïa chewed moodily on a strand of hair. *Of course, it would be Praxis. It was always Praxis.*

Aldarin had told her what he had overheard after being

stabbed by the former Regent of Arelium. Once he had been set free, Praxis had fled to the temple of Zygos. The conniving weasel had obviously wasted no time in slinking back into his patron's good graces.

She spied him waiting, sitting on a pale grey mare, impeccably dressed in his leather armour. He held a spear in one hand, a white flag attached to the tip.

Then she saw his eyes.

Oh no.

"Lady Baroness," Praxis said calmly, his voice as emotionless as the void. "We meet at last. I have heard great things about you from … the one who occupied this flesh before me. Allow me to introduce myself. My name is Zygos, Seventh of the Twelve."

No!

Jelaïa tried to calm her beating heart. "Greetings, Lord Zygos," she replied, feeling the burning touch of those jet-black globes.

"I hope it does not cause you too much pain to gaze upon the face of the man who murdered your father," Zygos continued, studying her carefully.

Jelaïa's hand went instinctively to her axe medallion, her fingers clenching the metal so hard that the tiny blades bit into her flesh. *This is what he wants,* she thought. *To exploit my emotions, to make me angry enough to try something stupid.*

Twenty knights waited patiently ten yards behind their master. Zygos had come under a flag of truce. Attacking him now would be foolish. She marshalled her thoughts.

"It is not easy, no. My father was a great man, Lord. If not for him, we would not be talking now. He was instrumental in crushing the greyling horde at Arelium. He did not deserve to be callously murdered while weak and unable to defend himself. Nonetheless, it is not pain I feel when looking upon the face of his killer but pity. This punishment you inflict on him is far worse than death."

Zygos's lips twitched in a terrible parody of Praxis's half-smile. "Punishment? I have bestowed upon this man the greatest possible honour. He is host to a demi-god. We barely age, we are stronger, faster, and more intelligent than you humans. He will bear witness to incalculable wonders through my eyes. What greater gifts are there than time and knowledge?"

"Immortality ... at the cost of all freedom and sentiment," said Syrella coldly. "That does not sound like a gift to me."

"Ah, Baroness del Morlak. I see you survived the purge of your city. Are you still a Baroness when there is no one left for you to govern?"

Syrella said nothing for a moment then, to the astonishment of all present, she burst out laughing. "By the Twelve, Zygos, is that really the best you've got? Pitiful! I've been picked on by my father my entire life! I was a disappointment to him as soon as I left my mother's womb! If you think a poorly veiled insult like that is going to ruffle my feathers, you will be sorely disappointed."

"Enough," said Azael crossly. He was sitting astride a coal-black pony, its barding crafted from thousands of glittering golden scales. "We did not come here to engage in small talk. We came to discuss the terms of your surrender."

Zygos seemed to notice him for the first time. "Ah, little Baron. I failed to see you there, hidden by those so much greater than you. Tell me, is religion a good surrogate for two loving parents? Have the nightmares stopped now that you worship the Twelve? Do the peals of the cathedral's bells drown out the sobs of misery born from the grief only an orphan can know?"

Azael paled. "QUIET!" he raged, his face flushed. "Do not mock the Twelve; it is by their grace that we resist the darkness."

"Stupid child. *I am one of the Twelve*. How can I mock myself? Should you not be on your knees, pledging yourself to me?"

"I ... I don't know who you are," stammered the Baron. "But you are not Zygos. I have seen his effigy carved into the pillars of the great cathedral of Klief and in the chapel that carries his name. You are an imposter, and I will never bow to you."

Zygos shook his head in bemusement. "Belief. Love. Anger. Working together to distort reality. It is only when one can strip away all superfluous emotions that the mind becomes pure and clear."

"Stop speaking in riddles," Azael said. "What do you offer us in exchange for your lives?"

Zygos blinked and turned away from the boy, addressing Derello, Jelaïa, and Syrella. "You cannot win," he said assertively. "I have one hundred thousand greylings at my command."

"And we stand on the walls of the greatest fortress the nine Baronies have ever known," Derello replied, staring courageously into Zygos's eyes. "Your army will break on these walls like water on stone. You do not scare me, Seventh of the Twelve. Your late sister was infinitely more threatening than you."

"I do not threaten," said Zygos with a frown. "That is not efficient. I deal in simple facts. I am merely stating the obvious. I have a hundred thousand greylings. Even if Klief has ten thousand men, which I doubt, statistically you are outnumbered ten to one. No one will come to your aid. The Baronies to the south, Morlak and Talth, are too busy licking their own wounds to send help. And the northern mountains are buried under heavy snow. Quayjin and the other Baronies could not reach you even if they tried. You stand alone. It is illogical not to capitulate."

"We have faced worse odds," Derello replied.

"I do not think you have. And even if by some miracle you resist the greyling tide, the month of respite offered by the weaver is nearly at an end. She does not make idle threats; she will send the wyrm against Klief. She will melt the stained-glass windows of your cathedral and reduce your monument to slag."

"We do not—" Jelaïa began, then fireworks detonated in her brain, searing the inside of her skull. She tumbled from her horse, hitting the ground hard.

"No," she moaned, her entire body on fire. "Not now. Not here."

The visions ignored her, blinding her to all else, forcing her to see.

A wolf cub, white as snow, its paws covered in blood.

A vermilion cloak, torn to tattered shreds, the ripped fabric sinking into a lake of tar.

A ram's horn, split into two halves, one bright and clear as day, the other chipped and scarred.

And darkness, covering the land, darker than shadow,

darker than night. Darker than the Pit. Obscuring everything. Destroying everything. Nothing will be safe. All will be lost.

"Jelaïa?" Derello was kneeling at her side, his face lined with worry. "Are you all right? You're bleeding."

She put her hand to her nose and felt the blood trickling from her nostrils. "It's nothing. A vision."

She stood, unaided, and turned to Zygos who was looking at her with interest. She took a deep breath.

"Tell your mistress we have met with Makara, the last surviving member of the Twelve. We no longer believe her lies. We know that the Twelve fought to the very end to protect the nine Baronies. Even you, Zygos, before you became the puppet you are now. You all resisted. To the bitter end. And we will do the same. Arelium did not fall. Kessrin did not fall. Klief will not fall. A hundred thousand, two hundred thousand … it matters not. You will never take this city. Not while any one of us still draws breath. Go. Go and tell the weaver that we will not submit. Go tell the weaver you have failed."

Zygos nodded as if expecting this. He let go of his spear and wheeled his horse back towards his men, trampling the white flag into the mud.

"Well said," murmured Syrella. "What now?"

Jelaïa wiped the blood from her nose.

"Now, we rouse our allies to war. Now, we prepare."

CHAPTER 10

The Calm Before
the Storm

"We see some extremely violent weather along the western coasts.
Heavy rain pummels the cliffs of Kessrin, strong winds churn
the waters of the Sea of Sorrow. Lightning lights up the sky. And
there is always a moment just before these brutal demonstrations
of nature's ferocity. When the clouds begin to gather on the
horizon, the marine birds fall silent, and you can feel a tingling
in the air. A whispered hush of anticipation. I have grown to
love those moments. The calm before the storm."

PRAEDORA, FIRST PRIESTESS OF BRACHYURA, 426 AT

❧

"I ... SAW A girl at the country fair, prettiest I could see," Reed sang to himself, readjusting the wolf's head clasp of his vermilion cloak. He strolled out of the Klief cantonment and turned his face to the sun, feeling it warm his skin. It was amazing what a good night's sleep and a hearty meal could do for morale.

"Saw a girl at the country fair, her name was Marjorie." A troop of golden-armoured town guard jogged past him, breastplates clanking, heading for the first wall. He walked east, past the massive form of the cathedral, to the gates of Baron del Klief's manor. Two stern-faced guards barred the way with their spears. He dug around in his pocket and fished out a crumpled piece of paper stamped with Azael's seal. The guards gave the seal a cursory glance and waved him through.

"Saw a girl at the country fair, but she didn't want to dance with me." He bounced up the marble steps two at a time, passed through twin sets of doors, cut left down a corridor, then right, then left again.

"So, she took me up for a tumble in the lo o o o ft ..." he pushed open the last set of doors and entered the Great Hall of Klief. The Barons, Baronesses, and the High Priest were already there, engaged in a heated debate. Aldarin, Praedora, Vohanen, and the three members of the Twelve stood close by. A War Council. Reed took one look at the angry faces and decided it would be best to stop singing.

"What did you say? How many men?" Jelaïa was demanding hotly, her cheeks flushed.

"Two thousand, my Lady," Azael repeated apologetically, glancing at Makara, or rather the man he only knew as the High Priest.

"This must be some sort of joke," Derello said with an incredulous chuckle, running one hand through his pomaded hair. "There were at least that many guardsmen lining the roads when we arrived."

"Yes ... that was close to the entirety of our town guard. I wanted to put on a good display. It's not every day we receive a visit from three Barons. You deserved a magnanimous welcome."

"I don't understand," Syrella said. "Klief is twice the size of Morlak, maybe even three times. You can't properly defend somewhere like this with two thousand men. What in the Pit is going on?"

Azael shot another glance at Makara, his eyes pleading.

The High Priest let out a despondent sigh. "We are dying," he said. "An unfortunate consequence of our self-imposed isolationism. By refusing to open our Barony to outsiders, we have precipitated our own decline. There are not enough births to renew the population. Trade has slowed to a trickle. We have plenty of gold mines to the north, but gold cannot buy everything. The people are leaving. There are no more merchants. We have no livestock, so the tanneries, leatherworkers, and butchers have all closed down. We have no wheat and no bakeries."

"We have the cathedral," Azael said defiantly. "And we have the faithful."

"Yes, my Lord. Faith sustains our minds. But it cannot sustain our bodies. It cannot provide us with food and amenities."

"But ... all those houses," Syrella said. "The lower city alone must have close to a thousand structures. I did notice that many were empty, but I thought you had simply ordered an evacuation, as we did in Arelium."

Makara shook his head. "The exodus predates the return of the greylings. The buildings are not just abandoned, they are in ruins. Dilapidated and neglected. You were so fixed on the guards lining the road that you did not think to look too closely at what lay beyond. Those citizens who remain have relocated to the upper levels, between the second and third walls."

Reed cleared his throat. "Then, the first wall should be given up for lost. We pull back and deploy the bulk of our forces on the other two."

"Unacceptable," Azael snapped. "I will not merely hand over a third of my city without a fight. You're the man who insulted me yesterday, aren't you? Who are you, again?"

"Sir Merad Reed, Captain of the Old Guard."

"Old Guard? Oh yes, that bunch of deluded has-beens who believe they were appointed by the Twelve themselves to protect the nine Baronies from the Pits. Laughable. I hope you won't feel too insulted if I take everything you say with a particularly large grain of salt."

"Sir Reed is right," Aldarin said sternly, crossing his arms. "We should not spread ourselves too thinly."

Azael frowned, chewing his lower lip thoughtfully. He turned to the three members of the Twelve and sank to one knee. "Lord Brachyura, Lady Kumbha, Lord ... um, Kriari," he said reverently. "You have descended from the heavens to lead us to victory. Your counsel in this matter would be greatly appreciated."

Brachyura motioned for the Baron to rise. He looked tired as if he hadn't slept.

And he probably hasn't, Reed thought. *I mean, who can blame him? He has learnt that his memories are not his own. Not only that, the weaver is somehow responsible for his current predicament. How deep does she have her hooks in him? In all of them? What is left of a man when his memories and identity are stripped away?*

"I ... cannot help you," Brachyura said in his deep, cavernous voice. "None of us can. Our judgement cannot be trusted. In fact, we should not even be here. Our very presence could be detrimental. We would be best to recluse ourselves. Kriari, Kumbha. With me." He spun on his heel and strode quickly from the Great Hall, his siblings close behind.

"What ... what does he mean?" Azael asked. He looked baffled. His question lingered in the air, no one present daring to answer.

Derello broke the uncomfortable silence. "The Fourth of the Twelve gives sage advice. We have survived for three hundred years without their guidance, there is no reason why we should not continue to do so. Tell us, Azael, why do you believe we should not relinquish the first wall?"

Azael drew himself up proudly. "I know what you think of me," he said. "You see a rich little boy dressed in white and gold. You see a spoilt brat coddled by the High Priest. You are not wrong. I have led a sheltered life. But I have also been schooled in the economics, art, history, philosophy, and architecture of Klief. I know this city well, better than any of you. The first wall can be held with two thousand men. Do any among you know how to work a mangonel?"

"During the siege of Talth, a Knight of Guanna, Sir Gaelin, instructed me and many of my fellow initiates in their use," Aldarin replied.

"Very well. The distance between the two walls is not random but carefully calculated. The open space before the first wall is within the optimum firing range of the mangonels. Properly manned, they can turn that patch of land into a killing ground. If we abandon the first wall, that advantage will be lost."

"Your argument is sound," Derello agreed. "Sir Gaelin was constantly vaunting the merits of his war machines and with good reason. I vote we attempt to use them."

"Then, we shall," Jelaïa concurred. "But that leaves us with the difficult decision of who should man the wall? It will be hit the first. And the hardest. Not the most enviable of prospects."

"It is my city," Azael replied. "My men will hold the ramparts as they always have. Besides, the Knights of Brachyura will be needed on the second."

"Sir Bansworth and the Kessrin will support them," Derello said. "I only have two hundred men, but they have fought the greylings twice now; they will prove their worth, I am sure of it."

"Then, it falls to Arelium to take the final wall," Jelaïa declared. "Sir Vohanen, would you and your knights care to assist us?"

"Of course, my Lady. We are few, but we would be honoured to stand with you."

Jelaïa nodded. "In that case, it is decided. Orkam will take command. Loré del Conte has found somewhere he can convert into stables. We'll keep the horses there and use what cavalry we have to plug any gaps. Excellent. We have our defensive strategy. My Lord Baron, do you have a place for the injured? Medical supplies? Food?"

"Klief has a fully-stocked infirmary," Azael replied proudly. "Your healer was most impressed. Food, on the other hand, is a real concern. We have the winter stores, but five thousand voracious men will devour what little we have squirrelled away in a couple of weeks."

"It will take more than bandages and cots to treat the wounded," Syrella cautioned. "We will need stretcher-bearers, nurses, orderlies ..."

"You will have them. Hundreds of Kliefien faithful are still here. My subjects may not be fighters, but they are obedient and willing. Runners to carry messages to the walls, nurses for the infirmary, cooks for the kitchens ... no able-bodied man or woman will stand idle. Perhaps you would like to assist me in this matter, Lady Baroness?"

"With pleasure. I will be far more useful in the infirmary than on the battlements."

"Then, we are decided," Jelaïa said. "The greylings will most likely attack at dusk. Let us use the time we have to prepare as best we can. May ... May the Twelve guide our way."

There was a chorus of murmured acknowledgements. Vohanen and the three leaders filed out. Reed hung back, not quite sure where to go, but knowing he wanted to stick close to Aldarin.

Praedora, who had remained silent throughout the exchange, opened her mouth to speak. "I will stand with the Kliefien town guard on the ramparts of the first wall," she blurted out, her blind eyes unreadable.

"What? Why?" Jelaïa asked in surprise. "What use could you possibly be?"

"What use? Don't be impertinent. The fires of Brachyura have helped us even the odds many times before."

"What are you talking about, Aunt? You cannot use your gift. Sir Manfeld is ..."

Praedora smiled knowingly. "Once again, child, you hear but you do not listen. What did I tell you during our time together at the temple?"

"That Manfeld was the source of your gift. He is gone, Prae, and with him your powers."

"You have become too sure of yourself, Jeli. I sometimes miss that wide-eyed, innocent girl who Aldarin brought to my door. I told you that I have only reacted strongly to *two* Knights of the Twelve. Sir Manfeld ... and Aldarin."

Something akin to doubt flickered in the depths of Jelaïa's eyes. "You are grasping at straws, Aunt. Just because you reacted to Aldarin during the Scrying doesn't mean that your bond is potent enough to awaken the fires."

"Agreed. That's why I tested it. Aldarin filled my vial yesterday. It works. I can call upon my gift."

"But ... but ... your blindness, Prae, how can you fight?"

"I cannot. At least, not unaided. I will need a chaperone."

Jelaïa's eyes went from Praedora to Aldarin. "No. No way."

"I have already accepted," the big knight said softly. "I am sorry, Jelaïa. I owe Praedora so much. I would not have survived those early years at the temple without her guidance. This is my way of repaying her."

"Then, I will come with you," Jelaïa said stubbornly. Reed was surprised to see tears glistening in the corners of her eyes.

"No," Aldarin replied gently with a shake of his head. "You said yourself that the first wall will be hit the hardest. We cannot risk the Baroness of Arelium on the front line. Your place is behind the third wall, with the others."

"You ... you ... you tricked me!" Jelaïa shouted shrilly.

"You are the two people I trust the most, and you went behind my back, scheming and plotting. How could you?"

"Jeli …"

"Don't you dare! I will not hear it! Out of my sight! If you are so eager to throw your lives away, then hurry down to the first wall and find a good spot to die, before they are all taken!"

"Please …"

"OUT! Both of you, out!"

Aldarin reached out a hand, but she pushed it away. His face fell. He turned and offered his arm to Praedora instead, and the two of them shuffled out of the Hall, the tall knight guiding the older woman's steps.

Jelaïa waited until they were gone then collapsed, sobbing.

Reed took a deep breath and went to sit beside her.

"Merad," Jelaïa said, stifling her sobs and wiping her eyes with the sleeve of her dress. "Apologies. I thought I was alone. A moment of weakness. What can I do for you?"

"I hated living in Jaelem," Reed said conversationally. "There was nothing to do. No excitement, not a single thing to look forward to. Every day the same. I just wanted to accomplish *something*, you know? Make my mark on the world. Be proud of myself. That's why I joined the Old Guard. The recruiter, Captain Yusifel was his name, painted such a vivid picture. The shield against the unknown, he called us. You can imagine how my eyes lit up at hearing that."

Jelaïa gave a sad smile. "I gather it didn't turn out quite how you had hoped."

"That's one way of putting it," said Reed ruefully.

"Twenty years of monotonous, menial tasks. And nothing to show for it. And the Pit ... it leached the life from me, Jelaïa. From all of us."

"I know what it's like, to an extent. I spent most of my adolescence as a prisoner of my father's over-protective paternalism. A long, lonely tunnel with no end in sight."

"Right. It's just so frustrating to see others change and grow while we cannot do so ourselves."

"Exactly ... Oh, I see."

"Praedora is like us, Jelaïa. If I had to guess, I would say that she has felt frustrated and left out ever since she lost her sight. Her gift defined who she was. Imagine having that taken away. How helpless she must have felt. I wonder how long it took her to work up the courage to ask Aldarin for help, knowing what effect it would have on you."

"She ... she could have come to me."

"Maybe, but I think she is too proud for that."

"Pit, Reed, I sent them away. What shall I do?"

Reed helped her up. "I'm sure they'll be fine," he said kindly. "They are both far from defenceless."

"That's not what bothers me. It's Aldarin's recklessness. He gets all caught up in his oaths and his honour without stopping to think of the consequences. The night before the siege of Talth, he attacked a group of threshers single-handedly. If Brachyura had not been there, he would have died."

"That does sound like him, he did something similar on the walls of Arelium. Head-butted a thresher."

Jelaïa chewed nervously on a lock of chestnut hair. "And another thing. He would not want me telling you this, but he has been having headaches. Terrible headaches. I'm ... worried."

Reed felt his good humour drain away. *Pit*, he thought. *Why do I always let myself get roped into other people's problems?*

"How about I go and join them?" he said aloud, ignoring the fluttering of butterflies in his belly. "I'll be the voice of reason, sitting on his shoulder and whispering in his ear. If things get too troublesome, I'll get them both out before we are overrun."

"You would do this for me?"

"Of course, my Lady. You forget that you are the Baroness of Arelium and I your loyal subject. I am yours to command."

"I will never command you, Reed. I am asking you, as a friend, will you help me?"

Reed bowed and gave what he hoped was a reassuring smile. "I will, my Lady. I will. And with me at his side, what could possibly go wrong?"

∽

Aldarin and Praedora were easy to find. They had chosen a spot on the roof of the gatehouse, directly above the eagle-embossed double doors; two dark figures in a sea of gold. The Kliefien town guard lined the ramparts on either side. From afar, they looked like rows of wheat, ready for harvest.

Not a very apt comparison, thought Reed as he climbed the stairs to the battlements. *Especially as they will be facing threshers.* He skirted around a duo of tasselled spears and elbowed his way through the crowd towards the familiar pronged helm.

"Ah, Reed," said Aldarin, his ocean-blue eyes conveying no surprise at seeing him. "Jelaïa sent you, I imagine?"

"Yes," Reed replied tersely. "You've got some ruffled feathers to smooth, my friend."

"She will understand. And there is no turning back now. For some incomprehensible reason, Azael has deemed I should be in command of the wall. Something about courage and experience." He looked out over the crenels. Far below, a handful of black tents had been pitched just beyond arrow range. On the largest of them, a flag displaying a set of silver scales whipped back and forth. "I can't believe I didn't see it," he murmured.

"See what?"

"That Praxis was a Knight of Zygos! He wore a set of scales around his neck, for Pit's sake! I was so focused on my mission ... so trusting. Never again."

The sun was dipping below the horizon, and the last of the day's warmth was fading. Reed pulled his cloak closer to his body. "I wouldn't blame yourself, Aldarin," he said. "You weren't the only one he fooled. Jeffson always used to say that the perfect way to go unnoticed is to hide in plain sight."

Aldarin grunted noncommittally, his eyes still on the tents. "Why haven't they attacked yet? We know they no longer fear the sun."

Praedora gave a short laugh. "Your temple masters have taught you better than that, initiate. You know why."

He thought for a moment. "Because one must think of not only what is advantageous to the attacker but also what is disadvantageous to the defender."

"Precisely. They may have begun to adapt to our

sunlight, but they still have excellent night vision. We do not. Despite their recent evolution, the basic principle has not changed. They are stronger at night. We are weaker. And they have time on their side."

The town guard were pulling up the golden banners that hung from the ramparts, the same ones Jelaïa had threatened to burn two days ago. Aldarin contemplated them with a slight frown on his face. "I took a closer look at that flashy armour they wear," he said. "I thought at first it was iron or steel coated in gold paint. It isn't. It's solid gold. Two thousand suits of solid gold armour."

Reed's mouth dropped open. "That's got to be more gold than can be found in all the southern Baronies!"

"Assuredly. And it's a complete and utter waste. Gold is a strange metal, paradoxically both soft and heavy. See how they are sweating? That breastplate must weigh fifty pounds. And it won't stop a greyling claw any more than a piece of leather or a plank of wood."

"Well, you are in command. Maybe you should tell them?" said Reed sarcastically.

"You are right, friend Reed, maybe I should," Aldarin replied earnestly, missing the point entirely. "I—"

"MOVEMENT!" came the cry from further down the wall.

Twilight, Reed thought. *Just like during the siege of Arelium. A time for monsters.*

When he was a child, his father had often told him scary stories to dissuade him from going out at night. Naturally, they were all completely fictitious, but to a six-year-old Reed, they were very, very real. Twilight, his father used to say. When the shadows intertwine … and the monsters come out to play.

Now, more than thirty-five years later, Reed heard his long-dead father's words once more, except this time, they were true. Greylings covered every available inch of ground, from the tents of the Knights of Zygos to the very edge of the surrounding hills and beyond. Thousands upon thousands upon thousands, more than the human brain could comprehend. Like an immense swarm of buzzing flies. Immeasurable. Unstoppable.

Two thousand shining toy soldiers in their paper-thin armour against the horde. They were going to be ripped apart.

"TORCHES!" Aldarin yelled. "LIGHT THE FIRES! BOWMEN TO THE FORE! MAKE WAY!"

The darkness moved.

"STAND FAST! FOR KLIEF! FOR THE TWELVE! THE ENEMY ARE COMING!"

CHAPTER 11

SAFE HAVEN

"My siblings are all equally predictable when it comes to dealing with a particularly tenacious enemy. Makara will try to negotiate. Guanna will construct his engines of war. Simha will charge in recklessly. Mithuna will attempt to convert them to her cause. Using the same tactics time and again is a foolhardy strategy, one destined for failure. Each obstacle we face should be tackled differently. Logic and reason are not incompatible with experimentation."

ZYGOS, SEVENTH OF THE TWELVE, 109 AT

❧

THE PASSAGE THROUGH the portal was significantly less disorienting the second time, but Ka'arka still felt the numbing cold, despite the added protection of his plate armour. The same images danced through his brain as he was thrown through the void: sapphire flames, beating wings, and green smoke.

Why am I seeing this? he thought. It was eerily similar to what Niane and the other priestesses of Brachyura had experienced, although he felt no pain, just slight discomfort. Was there some link between wherever he was now and the visions? What was it Sir Manfeld had said? That they represented things that could happen or that were already happening?

Ka'arka's musings were cut short as he reached the end of his journey and was ejected forcibly from the oily pool into the pitch-black cavern. He was ready this time, tucking his armoured knees under him as best he could, transforming his clumsy fall into an equally clumsy roll. Rising to his feet, he heard an indignant shriek and turned just in time to be thwacked in the face by the butt of Xer'ana's glaive as she crashed into him. They both collapsed in a jumble of flailing limbs.

Her turban became caught on his pauldron. Her face was inches from his. He could still smell the faint spicy odour of herbal tea on her breath. Feel her body pressed against his.

"Knight of Brachyura. It's dark in here. We need light. Light from the lantern tied to my belt. A belt I cannot reach because your legs are wrapped around mine. What would you suggest? Are you thinking of moving sometime soon, or shall we stay here like this until the greylings find us?"

Ka'arka felt his cheeks burn and, for once, was glad of the shadows. "No, my Lady." He twisted his lower body and pulled at her turban with his free hand. Xer'ana disentangled herself, took the lantern and flint from her belt and set to work trying to light it. A moment later, Shen'alla shot forth from the pool, landing gracefully.

"What a strange substance," she said, looking at her gloved hands curiously. "We should be soaking but my clothes are barely damp." The lantern sputtered into life. Ka'arka examined his gauntlets and saw that the Knight of Luridae was right. They bore traces of the liquid but appeared greasy rather than wet as if he had plunged his arms into a barrel of oil.

"Let us hope it is not flammable," he said.

Xer'ana held up the flint and lantern. "A bit late for that, wouldn't you say? I didn't set myself on fire, so I think we are safe." She aimed the light at the pool from which they had all emerged. "Definitely a lizard. This could explain how the greylings can assemble such large numbers so quickly. If each of these portals really does lead to one of the six Pits, they have the means of travelling astronomical distances in a day. And this central archway, what could it be, I wonder?"

The stone portal looked identical to the one in Da'arra, covered in the same symbols and filled with the same tarry liquid that pulsed rhythmically like a heartbeat.

"I don't know," Ka'arka said. "And I don't want to try and find out. What if it leads us straight into a horde of greylings? Or worse, straight to the bottom of the ocean? Let's concentrate on finding out where those eggs went."

He scanned the dirt of the cavern floor, easily picking up the threshers' trail.

Xer'ana brushed past him. "I have the light," she said quietly. "I will lead. This lantern holds all our remaining fuel. If it dies before we reach the surface … well, we will have to try and feel our way out."

Ka'arka imagined the three of them trapped in the dark, groping their way blindly along the tunnels. He suppressed a shudder. "They must be taking the eggs topside," he said in what he hoped was a confident tone of voice. "Why go to all the trouble of bringing them to Klief just to roll them back down into the depths of the earth. The trail will lead upwards, you'll see."

"I admire your conviction, Knight of Brachyura, but I think that is enough talking. The constant squeaking of that metal coffin you're wearing is already eroding whatever chance we may have had at stealth. Let's not make it even worse."

They ventured once more into the tunnels. The fresh tracks made by the eggs and their handlers mingled with a multitude of older claw prints, hundreds upon hundreds on top of one another. The tunnel taken by Ka'arka and his two companions grew wider, wide enough for them to walk abreast without touching the walls.

A greyling highway, Ka'arka thought, straightening his back. The air smelt slightly less foul, the stench of faeces and sulphur offset by something more neutral.

"Light," whispered Xer'ana, pointing at a distant pin-prick shining like a star in the blackness. They picked up the pace, using the far-off glimmer as a beacon. Ka'arka gave a sigh of relief when it became apparent that they were heading for the mouth of an enormous cave. And beyond, a row of grassy hills, still and silent like sleeping giants under a moonlit sky.

It was night and, for the moment at least, they were alone.

"A way out!" Ka'arka cried as he stepped out of the stuffy

confines of the cave, grinning happily. "Out, at last! The Twelve be praised! I thought I was going to go mad down there."

"Madder, you mean," said Xer'ana. Her face was as inexpressive as always, but her eyes were shining.

"Why, my Lady, you have a sense of humour! Let me praise the Twelve a second time."

"Just because I choose not to use something doesn't mean it's non-existent, Ka'arka."

The Knight of Brachyura was still grinning at her. "You slipped up, my Lady. You called me by my name."

"I did, didn't I? Let's not make a habit of it. Shen'alla? Can you see anything to confirm we are in Klief?"

"Nothing definitive," the younger Knight of Luridae said, looking up at the stars. "I recognise some of the constellations, but they are not where they should be. And some are missing altogether. One thing is certain: we are a long way from Da'arra."

"Cold, too," Ka'arka added. A gust of wind shrieked past him, rushing down into the valley where the low hills were clustered around a large, flat basin filled with strange circular rocks. Hunched figures moved among them, shadows among shadows.

No, not rocks.

"I've found our eggs," he said, pointing. "Pit, there must be at least a hundred. What now?"

"We find a way to destroy them."

"What, just the three of us? Those are threshers guarding them. We'll get torn to pieces. Best wait until dawn, at least, when we—"

"Quiet!" Xer'ana snapped. "What was that?"

The wind wailed once more. Ka'arka realised it was not the noise of the wind itself he was hearing but a mix of discordant screeches and screams carried through the air.

"Greylings," he cursed. "It's coming from somewhere over the ridge, behind us."

They moved cautiously up the hillside, weapons drawn, eyes probing every rocky outcrop and skeletal bush. Ka'arka was first to the top. He let out a gasp. Half a mile away, rising out of the plain like a single white tooth, stood Klief, its trio of walls lit by signal fires, its cathedral spire reaching for the moon.

An army of greylings carpeted the land before the city with numerous smaller groups snaking out from the central mass like a kraken's tentacles, spreading out to assault the entire length of the first wall.

"I ... I have never seen so many," Shen'alla said breathlessly, her eyes wide.

"I do not think any of us has," Ka'arka replied. "Their numbers rival those recorded during the Battle of the Northern Plains four hundred years ago. How did they manage to regain their strength so quickly?"

"The defences appear to be holding," Xer'ana remarked. As she spoke, the twelve mangonels positioned on the second wall thrummed in unison, sending massive boulders raining down on the attackers. The scant few greylings that managed to make it through the deadly hail were mercilessly pummelled by golden-clothed archers.

"That is because the enemy are committing but a fraction of their strength." Ka'arka gestured with the butt of his axe to the main force waiting beyond the range of the mangonels. "The assault must be in its early stages; they are testing the defences for weaknesses. A sound tactic, and one I would not have expected from greylings."

"We need to tell the defenders about the eggs," said Xer'ana resolutely. "And the portal."

"And how do you propose we do that, mistress?" Shen'alla asked in consternation. "There is an army between us and Klief."

"Not so," countered Ka'arka. "Look. We are on their far-right flank. We can ignore the bulk of their troops completely. If we keep close to the hills, using them for cover, we will only have to contend with the vanguard assaulting the walls."

"That's … That's still hundreds of greylings, Ka'arka."

"Those mangonels will soon reduce that number to something more manageable if they continue firing."

"And what if they fire on us?"

"We'll just have to hope they can tell the difference between a Knight of the Twelve and a greyling, won't we?"

Xer'ana stepped in between the two. "Stop your prattling, both of you. The Knight of Brachyura is right. If we want to attempt to link up with the Kliefien defenders, it's now or never. I cannot ask you to follow me, Shen'alla. No one will think any less of you if you choose to remain behind."

"Remain behind? No, mistress. I have followed you across the sands of Shakalla, into the depths of the Pit, and through the nameless void. I do not intend to stop now."

Xer'ana looked pleased. "I expected nothing less. Knight of Brachyura. How fast can you run in that metal coffin of yours?"

"Not fast enough," grumbled Ka'arka, shrugging off his

gauntlets and pulling at the leather straps of his breastplate. Shen'alla moved to help him.

"We will have to move at speed," Xer'ana continued. "We should aim for the far right-hand side of the wall. We'll attempt to stick together, but if one of us falls, we do not stop. It only takes one of us to deliver the warning. Agreed?"

Ka'arka and Shen'alla nodded. The Knight of Brachyura was wrapping strips of fabric around his bare feet, his sky-blue tunic damp with sweat, his armour lying in pieces all around him.

They made their way quickly down the slope. The city of Klief grew larger, filling their vision. The infernal uproar of one hundred thousand greylings was deafening, easily masking the sound of their approach. The first wall was tantalisingly close, less than three hundred yards away, enough to make out each individual soldier manning the ramparts. But they were reaching the edge of the hills. Soon there would be no more cover. Nowhere to hide. It would be a race across several hundred yards of flat, hard earth.

A killing ground.

Ka'arka took a deep breath and began to accelerate, hearing his two companions do the same. A large group of greylings, straight ahead. A thresher was urging them towards the wall with vigorous cracks of its whip. Ka'arka raised his axe and swung with all his strength at the thresher's unprotected back. The twin blades bit deep, cutting through the thing's spinal cord. It collapsed, arms flapping uselessly, mouth opening and closing like a fish out of water.

Ka'arka barely slowed, leaping over his fallen opponent and ploughing into the rear of the greylings, lashing out left and right, carving a bloody path to the city of Klief. He broke through, his face smeared with filth, his axe slick with blood.

So close.

A boulder from one of the mangonels soared overhead, close enough for him to feel its passage. It landed among the greylings behind him, crushing nine and maiming five more. A hundred and fifty yards left. Within bow range. He lifted his axe high and started screaming "Knight of the Twelve! Knight of the Twelve seeking asylum!"

Smoke from the braziers atop the ramparts spiralled down, hampering his vision. He coughed, stumbled, and almost ran into a pair of threshers. They turned on him in surprise, weapons raised. He desperately parried a wicked-looking mace with the flat of his blade but could do nothing to stop the second thresher's cudgel hurtling towards his head.

Then Xer'ana was there, her glaive singing, cutting the thresher's hand off at the wrist. "GO!" she yelled as the creature bellowed in pain. "GET OUT OF HERE!" Shen'alla dived past his right, her own glaive whirling in a complicated figure-of-eight.

Ka'arka forced his aching legs to move. A hundred yards. They had been spotted now by a middle-aged man with greying hair and beard, dressed in a vermilion cloak. He was ordering a group of guards to lower a golden banner over the battlements.

A scream of terrible agony made Ka'arka turn, just in time to see a thresher crush Shen'alla's skull with its hand, her pulped brain running down the beast's gargantuan fingers like jelly. It threw the still-twitching body aside and advanced on Xer'ana, grunting to its fellow.

Two against one. She would be dead in seconds.

Ka'arka looked up at the wall. The grey-haired man was beckoning to him. A safe haven just a few yards away. The eggs. The portal. They needed to be warned.

A recent memory flashed before his eyes. Xer'ana sitting opposite him, her face illuminated by starlight, surrounded by the silent beauty of the desert. A Knight of the Twelve. A Da'arran. Like himself.

"PIT!" he screamed and turned away from Klief, sprinting back to help the Knight of Luridae. Xer'ana had lost her turban and was bleeding from a deep cut across her forehead.

"How dare you disobey me!" she shouted angrily, dodging a sweep of the thresher's mace.

"I'm afraid I'm one of the few people you can't order around!" he replied blithely. "Head to the wall. I'll hold them."

"No. Two against two is fair odds. We dispatch them together."

A score of arrows buzzed from the walls. Two or three found their mark but only appeared to enrage the threshers further. Luckily, it was just the sort of distraction Ka'arka needed. He sprang at the mace-wielding thresher, burying his axe in the thing's groin. It roared, blood and ichor pumping from the lethal wound. With an ultimate cry of fury, it brought its mace down hard on Ka'arka's shoulder. He heard the crack of his scapula breaking just before the intense wave of pain hit his brain, bringing him to his knees.

Xer'ana reached him, her tunic torn in several places. "More are coming. They won't hold the banner for us forever. We have to move."

Ka'arka sheathed his axe, tried to move, and almost

blacked out. "I ... can't," he said between gritted teeth. "Leave me."

"Aggggh! Foolish man! I told you not to come back for me!" Indistinct hulking figures lumbered through the smoke. Coming closer. "Lean on me, Knight of Brachyura!" She took his weight on her shoulder and put one arm halfway around his waist. They hobbled forwards like an elderly couple, clinging to one another.

The smoke parted, revealing four armoured threshers blocking their path. There was no way around them.

So close, Ka'arka thought, wanting to scream in frustration. *Pit! So close!*

"I am sorry," he grimaced. "Shen'alla has sacrificed herself for nothing."

Xer'ana looked at him, and for a brief instant the hard shell she had built around herself fell away, and he caught a glimpse of the tired, scared, lonely woman beneath. "I am sorry too, Ka'arka," she said softly.

He smiled, holding her gaze.

A blinding bolt of cerulean flame streaked down from the ramparts and set one of the threshers ablaze. It howled, its armour melting, metal and flesh liquifying.

"RUN!" A familiar female voice shouted, and a ball of blue fire exploded among two of the remaining threshers.

Xer'ana tugged at his arm, and they dragged themselves onwards, inch by laborious inch. There was a loud whoosh as a fiery curtain sprang up behind them, dissuading any further pursuit.

Sapphire flame, Ka'arka thought. *The image I saw when I traversed the portal.*

They arrived at the base of the wall, and Ka'arka grasped

a handful of golden fabric with his uninjured hand. "PULL" yelled the man in the vermilion cloak, and they were hoisted into the air, slowly but surely rising up the white stone until they reached the battlements.

Ka'arka let go of the banner and lay on his back, panting. The man stood over him, a strange mix of anger and admiration on his face.

"What sort of Pit-spawned foolishness was that, Knight of the Twelve?" he growled.

"I wouldn't bother, Reed, he never listens anyway." The crotchety female voice sent a tingle of joy down Ka'arka's spine, and he smiled despite the pain.

"Praedora. I thought it was you. We have you to thank for the fires of Brachyura, I take it?" He focused his weary eyes on her face. "By the Twelve, you ... you are blind. Then how did you—"

"I guided her," said Aldarin.

"A ... Aldarin?" Seeing his friend, his companion, his brother, was too much for Ka'arka who, lying on the cold stone slabs of the first wall ramparts, dissolved into an uncontrollable fit of incredulous laughter.

CHAPTER 12

THE SCENT OF HONEYSUCKLE

"It's incomparable, that feeling you get when you realise you have done something useful. I know your life at the temple was hard, Aldarin, but I also remember the look on your face all those years ago when I offered to take you away from your abusive father. That look of unbridled hope. I have known many hardships over these last few weeks, but as long as I can still feel useful, the rest of it doesn't seem so bad."

PRAEDORA, FIRST PRIESTESS OF BRACHYURA, 427 AT

"STRETCHERS!" REED CALLED out loudly. The dark-skinned Knight of Brachyura was fading in and out of consciousness, still chuckling quietly to himself. The woman who had accompanied him tugged at Reed's cloak. "You, whatever your name is. We have an urgent message for the Baron. You will take us to him immediately."

Pit, another woman ordering me around. Just what I need.

"My Lady," he said icily. "If you haven't noticed, we are under attack. I cannot leave the wall at this time. The War Council is coordinating our defences from the keep. Which, as luck would have it, is close to where the infirmary is located. If you follow the stretcher-bearers, they will lead you there."

"Very well." Her face softened. "I apologise for my bluntness; it has been a long day and an even longer night. May I know the name of the man who saved my life?"

Reed relaxed slightly. "Captain Merad Reed," he said. "Although I didn't do much. It is Praedora you must thank, the priestess of Brachyura; it was her handiwork that cleared a path to the wall. Ah, here they are."

The soldiers on the wall parted to let the stretcher-bearers through. Reed thought he recognised one of the two, but he couldn't quite put his finger on it.

"If you could both spare a moment to help me, my Lords," the man said in a strained nasal voice that jolted Reed's memory. Of course. The Baron's mouthpiece. That overdressed, frilly, lacy fool of a horn blower. Oh, the irony.

Reed was itching to say something sarcastic, but after taking in the man's dirt-streaked face and unkempt hair, he thought better of it. He bit his tongue and helped Aldarin manoeuvre Ka'arka onto the stretcher while Praedora stood by anxiously.

"Prae, do you wish to go with them?" Aldarin asked.

"No ... no. I will be more useful here."

"Back to the gatehouse, then," the Knight of Brachyura said, offering her his arm.

A group of soldiers pushed past them carrying bundles of golden-fletched arrows. The mangonels spoke once more, slinging their deadly payloads down onto the attackers. Reed watched them pass overhead with a frown.

"MESSENGER!" he yelled. A small pug-nosed adolescent appeared at his side as if by magic, his face losing its battle against the ravages of pubescent acne. He locked his thumbs together and spread his palms wide, making the sign of an eagle. The official salute of Klief.

"Take a message up to the second wall," Reed ordered. "Try to find Sir Caddox or whoever is in charge of the mangonels. Tell them to stop."

"My Lord?"

"They are wasting ammunition. The greylings haven't committed yet. Tell them to wait until the enemy attack in force."

The spotty youth saluted again and ran off. Reed looked around for the Da'arran woman, but both she and the stretcher-bearers had disappeared. Shrugging, he followed Praedora and Aldarin back along the battlements to the gatehouse, stopping near a basket of spears and picking one at random. Its polished blade gleamed in the yellow light of the braziers. Decorative, ostentatious, but well-made nonetheless. He reached up with one hand and ripped off the tassel.

"Reed!" Aldarin shouted exuberantly, raising his voice over the sound of thrumming arrows and the shrieks of the enemy. He clapped Reed on the shoulder hard enough to make him wince. "A joyous day. My friend Ka'arka is among us once more."

"I am happy that you have been reunited with your friend," Reed replied, massaging his shoulder, "although you appear to have forgotten the horde of greylings trying to kill us."

"If we die, we die," said Aldarin with a smile. "And I will die in battle surrounded by my friends. Surely one could not wish for a better end."

Dying in my sleep at the ripe old age of eighty-five sounds better to me, Reed thought wryly. He swallowed and changed the subject. "Any movement from the main force of greylings?"

"No, nothing. They still seem to be probing the wall for weaknesses. I do not think they will find any. I studied the stone myself: it's polished granite. Incredibly hard and durable. Well-maintained too. I couldn't see any cracks or fissures. Arelium and the Southern Pit were both badly in need of repairs, perfect for greyling claws. Klief is the exact opposite."

As if to confirm Aldarin's words, a brood mother let out a piercing shriek, and the greyling advance guard broke off the attack, scuttling back out of arrow range. Hundreds of corpses littered the ground before Klief, and not one greyling had gained a foothold on the ramparts.

"What are they doing?" Praedora asked.

"Retreating," Aldarin replied. "There are still a few hours of night left, however. I fear we have not seen the last of them."

Far above, on the second wall, the mangonels had fallen silent. Reed could see the occasional flash of silver as the Knights of Brachyura reloaded the deadly machines.

"Movement," Aldarin said calmly, pulling Reed's gaze

back to the attackers. The entire host was advancing now. A dozen Knights of Zygos were scattered among them. Two brood mothers brought up the rear, their gross bodies carried on wooden litters. At some unspoken signal, the greyling army split in two, forming a duo of curved prongs reminiscent of Aldarin's horned helm.

"They are targeting the left and right walls simultaneously," Reed said. "I would recommend sending the reserves from the gatehouse to reinforce our flanks."

"Agreed," Aldarin said, beckoning at a messenger and relaying the order. "Hopefully, the bowmen have had time to restock their quivers; they are about to have plenty of targets."

Four boulders sailed over the wall and crunched into the attackers. Four out of twelve. The central mangonels would have to be repositioned and recalibrated to fire at a different angle.

"BOWS! AT WILL!" Aldarin bellowed, his words echoing down the defensive line as they were repeated by the unit sergeants. The arrows reaped a deadly harvest. Scores of greylings died with every volley. Yet, they advanced without faltering.

"How close are they?" Praedora said to Aldarin. "I am still feeling the after-effects of saving Ka'arka, but I have enough in me for one more salvo. You tell me when."

Reed frowned. The first priestess was hiding it well, but she was tired. Drained. "Perhaps we should not be too hasty," he said carefully.

"We wait until they gain the ramparts," the big knight replied, watching the greylings with interest. The tip of each prong had reached the base of the wall, and there they stopped, milling around aimlessly. Their proximity to the defences protected them from the mangonels, but they were being massacred by the steel-tipped arrows and sharp rocks of the men of Klief.

Grey-skinned bodies piled up, forming a great heap of bloody flesh. More greylings scrambled up the morbid mound, only to die in turn. It was over eight feet high now and growing steadily. Ten feet. Twelve feet.

Reed felt the familiar feeling of dread squirm in his chest. He knew what the greylings were doing. "ALDARIN!" he shouted. "TELL THE ARCHERS TO STOP! CEASEFIRE!"

The Knight of Brachyura repeated Reed's orders in his strong baritone, and the hail of arrows slowed to a trickle. The two grisly pyramids stood at fifteen feet, over half the height of the first wall. Reed breathed a tentative sigh of relief. "Look!" he said loudly to Aldarin over the shrieks of the injured greylings. "Crafty bastards were trying to use their own dead to reach the ramparts. Nearly managed it, too. We're going to have to find a way to clear the bodies from the base of the wall!"

A brood mother screeched, cutting through the churning sounds of battle. One of the attacking threshers clumped over to a surviving greyling. Picked it up almost tenderly.

And snapped its neck.

"NO!" Reed cried in panic.

The thresher threw the corpse onto the pile, grunting triumphantly as his fellows tore into the surrounding greylings, ripping them to pieces and adding the dismembered remains to the steadily-growing pyramid.

"Archers! The threshers! Aim for the threshers!" Aldarin commanded.

"I can help," Praedora said in a small voice, snapping open her medallion. "Tell me where."

"Prae ..."

"I'll be all right, Aldarin." She shuddered as her right hand burst into flame. "I told you, I need to feel useful. Guide me."

The Knight of Brachyura took position behind her and gently moved her arm.

"Hurry, Aldarin."

"Now!"

A crackling ball of blue fire leapt from her outstretched fingertips. Aldarin had aimed well. The pile of corpses to the far right caught alight, long-tongued tendrils lapping at the hundreds of greyling dead. The heat was so immense that Reed could feel it on his face. The mound of the fallen became a pyre.

"Turn ... me ... round," Praedora stammered, her body shaking. A thin trickle of blood escaped her left nostril.

"No," Aldarin replied, his face creased with worry. "You are spent, Prae. I saw you like this before, in the Great Hall of Kessrin, just before you lost your sight. You've pushed yourself too far."

"Do it ... initiate. I can feel it. I can hear it. They have ... reached the walls." She tried to turn by herself, lost her balance and crumpled against the parapet, unconscious.

"Prae!"

"No time!" Reed yelled, pointing. "She's right, they've reached the eastern battlements. We have to push them back!" The pile of dead was now high enough to allow the greylings to scamper up the last few feet and leap from the apex up onto the battlements, pouncing on the startled men of Klief. A desperate melee had broken out. A golden-armoured guard screamed as he was pulled over the edge by three of the monsters, crashing into the climbing greylings below.

"PIT!" Aldarin cursed. "You!" he ordered a group of nearby guardsmen. "No one gets near her, understood? Anything happens to her, and you'll answer to me!" He gave one last anguished look at Praedora and ran after Reed, drawing his axe as he did so. The greylings had established a foothold and were fixing ropes to the merlons, just as they had in Arelium. Threshers would be joining them soon.

"FOR BRACHYURA!" Aldarin cried, barrelling into the enemy like a charging stallion. The greylings in front of him were scattered. He decapitated two of the creatures with his axe and broke the neck of a third with a steel punch. Reed was at his side, his borrowed spear thrusting in and out like a piston, piercing dark grey flesh.

A greyling sprang from the battlements, trying to land on Aldarin's exposed back. The knight swivelled and tilted his pronged helm, impaling the unfortunate attacker on one of his pincer-shaped horns.

A distant clamour made Reed turn his head. Praedora's flames had been extinguished, and the second pile of bodies was high enough to enable the greylings to attack the western ramparts. The defenders were now fighting on two fronts.

More and more greylings swarmed over the walls. Aldarin's axe was reaping a terrible toll, but he was just one man. The Kliefien town guard were poorly trained and badly equipped. And they had never fought an enemy like this before. They were losing.

Reed screamed in frustration, unable to prevent the first of the threshers from using a rope to gain the ramparts. The town guard were so disorganised, each unit fighting individually without an overall sense of cohesion; a handful of isolated islands of gold being slowly overwhelmed by the grey tide.

Worst of all, Aldarin had been right about the fancy golden armour. It was heavy and cumbersome. The soldiers could not react quickly enough; their spear thrusts were easily avoided by the more agile greylings whose sharp talons had no difficulty penetrating the soft metal.

A booming sound resonated from below the gatehouse. Eight threshers had made a makeshift battering ram from a fallen tree trunk and were pounding it against the doors, flattening the embossed eagle with every earth-shattering impact.

Reed scanned the battlements. There were more greylings than Kliefien. They had to retreat.

"WE HAVE TO PULL BACK!" he shouted at Aldarin, dodging a pair of blood-stained claws and thwacking the butt of his spear into his opponent's face.

"NO!" Aldarin yelled, his blue eyes hard and menacing, his armour sullied with so much black ichor it no longer gleamed.

A thresher was advancing steadily along the ramparts, killing anything in its way. Its enormous two-handed sword cut a trembling guard nearly in half.

Reed grabbed Aldarin's arm. "Listen to me! Look around you! The wall is lost." Aldarin snarled and pulled away, charging at the sword-wielding thresher. He ducked under a horizontal sweep and brought his axe up into the thing's stomach, releasing its intestines.

"ALDARIN!" Reed tried again. "You can't leave Jelaïa! You can't leave her alone!"

At hearing her name, some of the battle lust faded from Aldarin's eyes. He shook his axe blade free of blood and surveyed the carnage with a clear mind. His face fell as he understood.

"RETREAT!" he roared, as loud as he could. "Back to the second wall! Fall back!"

The closest set of stairs was only a few paces away. Reed pulled a dazed guard to his feet and dragged him to safety. Others followed. The Captain of the Old Guard held the top of the steps alone, feet firmly planted on the ichor-spattered stone, his spear lashing out at any greyling that came within range as the beleaguered town guard streamed past him. Aldarin dispatched another thresher and moved to join him.

Several hundred feet away, the gate at the base of the second wall gatehouse swung open, allowing the defenders inside. The western ramparts were completely overrun and without Aldarin and Reed's aid, scant few guardsmen had escaped.

"Go, Reed," Aldarin said, breathing hard. "I can hold them."

"No. We go together or not at all."

"Pit, Reed! GO!"

"I cannot. I … swore to Jelaïa I would stay by your side. No way I'm going to tell her I left you here. She'll burn me alive."

"You are … most persistent," the knight replied with a

ghost of a smile. "Together then." He swept his axe in a wide semi-circle, pushing the greylings back, then turned and ran down the steps, Reed chasing after him. They were among the last to leave the wall, the enemy snapping at their heels.

The second wall's gate began to close with a squeal of protesting hinges. Reed's booted feet flew up the main road, his thighs on fire, his weakened lungs struggling to provide him with air. He tripped over a loose stone and went sprawling. Strong arms pulled him up.

"Stop dawdling," Aldarin said. Arrows hummed past them, drilling into their pursuers. The two men reached the shadow of the wall, hurrying through the heavy doors just before they slammed shut. They were greeted by a scene of chaos. Blood-soaked town guards wandered aimlessly, dazed and exhausted. Knights of Brachyura were using rope pulleys to haul great boulders up to the second wall ramparts where they would be used as ammunition for the mangonels.

There was a clanking of scimitars, and Sir Bansworth appeared at the head of a unit of Kessrin swordsmen.

"Gentlemen," he panted, saluting wearily. "I am here to take you to the infirmary. I must warn you that Kumbha is doing what she can, but the cots are overflowing despite her efforts."

"That won't be necessary," Aldarin replied. "I am fine. My fellow Knights will need all the help they can get now that the first wall has been breached. Reed, it is here that our paths diverge."

Reed massaged his aching chest. "I'll go give my report to Jelaïa, then I'm coming right back, Aldarin, you won't get rid of me that easily."

"SCRIER!" someone called down from the wall. It was Caddox, his face grim. "GET UP HERE NOW!"

Something in his voice sounded off. Aldarin frowned and ran for the nearest set of steps. "What is it?" he asked, reaching the battlements. Caddox didn't answer, only pointed with one gauntleted finger at the first wall, several hundred feet below.

A signal fire burned there, brighter than the others, the conflagration so hot it was almost white.

Or a brilliant sky-blue.

Aldarin let out a terrible moan. "Prae ... No ... What is she doing?"

The first priestess of Brachyura was alone on the roof of the gatehouse, her entire body clothed in flame, her long hair writhing as if it were alive. She was an island of light in an ocean of greylings, the last human to stand on the first wall. She was pure. Untouchable. Every creature — greyling or thresher — that came close to her magnificence was swallowed by the raging inferno.

"The Kliefien guard tried to make her retreat, but she refused," Caddox said softly. "She told them that now is her time."

"Her time?" shouted Aldarin in disbelief. "No. She doesn't get to decide that. I'll stop her." He made to leave. Caddox blocked his path.

"If this is what she wishes, we must respect it, Aldarin," he said sadly.

"Let me pass."

"No."

"LET ME PASS!" Aldarin cried in a choked voice. He

slammed his fist into Caddox's pauldron, but the other knight held fast.

"It is too late, Brother."

The flames surrounding Praedora were becoming brighter, throbbing like a beating heart.

Reed came to stand beside him. "This is her choice, Aldarin. You must let her go."

"No, I cannot. She is like a mother to me, Reed. And not just me. She is like a mother to all of us Knights of Brachyura. Why is she doing this?"

"You know why. She is doing what every mother does. She is trying to protect her children."

"PIT!" screamed Aldarin, ripping his helm from his head, tears mingling with the scars on his face. "She should have told me. I didn't have time to prepare. I didn't even have time to say goodbye."

Reed smiled sadly. "Why don't you do so now?"

The cerulean firestorm was so bright it was almost impossible to look at. Brighter than the stars. Brighter than the moon. The shape of Praedora's body was lost inside the miniature sun. Electricity arced and crackled along its surface. It pulsed faster and faster. Stronger and stronger.

It was beautiful.

Then, with a supersonic detonation that cracked the thick stone of the gatehouse and rattled the stained-glass windows of the cathedral, it exploded.

A tidal wave of blue flames scoured the wall clean, incinerating thousands of greylings in a single second. The two huge piles of corpses were reduced to ash. Yet, the purifying fires of Brachyura were not satiated. They crept towards the enemy lines, devouring, burning, killing, leaving nothing but charred corpses and blackened grassland in their wake.

"Goodbye," whispered Aldarin sorrowfully, his eyes red and raw.

Ten thousand greylings died before the rolling curtain of flame began to dissipate. It had happened so quickly that the attackers had had no time to run. No time to scream.

Far below, on the gatehouse roof, the last tiny spark flickered and died.

Aldarin cried out in grief.

A surge of hot air rolled over the battlements of the second wall, carrying with it the gruesome stench of burnt flesh.

And perhaps, just perhaps, a lingering scent of honeysuckle.

CHAPTER 13

A MATTER OF TRUST

"I have often heard it said that between two people 'love is enough'. I do not think it is. It cannot stand alone for long, it must be supported with trust and understanding or it will start to be washed away, like grains of sand on a beach."

MERAD REED, CAPTAIN OF THE OLD GUARD, 426 AT

JELAÏA FOUND ALDARIN sitting on one of the benches in the empty dining hall, his plate armour scattered around him like fallen petals. She sat down beside him and took his hand. It was strangely cold-and clean, in stark comparison with his damp hair and grime-stained face.

"I should never have agreed to her foolish wish to stand on the first wall," he muttered angrily. "She was a blind old woman. What was I thinking?"

"You seem to be under the impression that she was

asking for your permission," Jelaïa replied with a sad shake of her head. "Knowing Praedora, she was only doing you the courtesy of informing you where she was going to be. I don't believe anyone in the nine Baronies could stop that woman from doing what she wanted, even one of the Twelve themselves."

"Yet, I abandoned her when she needed me the most. I only meant to leave her for a moment. I just ... I let myself be overtaken by that boiling red cloud. When I am lost in the throes of combat, the pain in my head fades away. I can actually hear my own thoughts without the constant throbbing of my skull. I strayed too far ..."

"She knew the risks. We all did. If she hadn't been on that wall, Ka'arka would have died. With her final breath, she single-handedly beat back the greyling assault. Even now, they do not attempt to attack us. She has bought us time to reinforce the second wall, restock the mangonels, and see to the injured."

Aldarin sighed and picked absently at his scar. "You don't seem too upset about it."

"I am. Of course, I am. It's just ... certain things give me comfort. I think she always wanted to end her life on her own terms. I think she missed Sir Manfeld terribly. And I think that what she did here will be remembered by thousands for generations to come. You said she was a blind old woman. Do you really believe that is who the name 'Praedora' will bring to mind? Or will people recall instead the most powerful priestess of Brachyura who ever lived?"

Aldarin thought for a moment, then turned and kissed her cheek. "There is some truth in what you say. I have no idea how you manage it, but you always find a way to chip away at the darkness surrounding my heart and let in a ray of sunlight."

Jelaïa kissed him back. "You're not too bad at that yourself, you know, when you put your mind to it. I came to tell you that Ka'arka has been healed by Kumbha and is ready to give us his report if you feel up to it."

"Naturally," Aldarin said, cracking his neck and getting up. "Just give me a moment to pick up my armour."

"Oh, no time for that," Jelaïa replied with a wave of her hand. "I'm sure someone will be along to tidy it up sooner or later. The others are waiting."

"Where?"

"In the cathedral."

The sun was just rising from behind the rugged hills to the east as they left the keep, crossed the small square, and ascended the stairs to the three-doored portal. The engraved sculptures of the Twelve seemed somehow more sinister to Jelaïa now that she knew the truth about what had happened in the Morlakian Pit. Dawn's shadows left harsh lines on the stone and gave the statues ebony eyes. The eyes of the fallen. The eyes of the dead.

A small group of men and women surrounded the strange circular slab of stone at the far end of the nave. The four members of the Twelve. Reed, Vohanen, Derello, Syrella, Ka'arka, and his travelling companion, the Da'arran woman with dusky skin and hard eyes. There was no sign of Azael.

"Ah, there you are," said Makara in his wheezing voice. "You are the last of us. I sent Baron del Klief to tour our defences. It should be safe enough. We have plenty of time to discuss recent events before he returns." He paused for a moment, his eyes probing Jelaïa's face. "I am sorry for your loss," he said. "Praedora seemed to be a wonderful person. She will be missed."

"If my patron had stepped out of this ... morgue and joined us on the wall, the wonderful person of whom you speak might still be alive," said Aldarin hotly to Brachyura.

The Fourth of the Twelve exhaled sharply. "She might, or then again, my presence might have doomed us all," he said. "We cannot participate in the defence of Klief until we have dealt with the weaver. Who knows what she has done to our minds? You were there in the Great Hall of Talth, Aldarin, you saw how she used her link with the brood mother to bring me to my knees. What is to say she will not do so again? Or worse, what if she can see through our eyes? Read our thoughts? Our situation is precarious enough. Kriari and I will not fight. I have been helping Kumbha in the infirmary, but that is all I dare do."

Jelaïa, seeing that Aldarin was opening his mouth to reply, interceded, steering the conversation in a more neutral direction. "How many Kliefien escaped the first wall?" she asked.

"Less than a third," Syrella said morosely. "And it would have been fewer if not for the efforts of Aldarin and Reed." She shot the Captain of the Old Guard a grateful smile.

"Then, we no longer have enough men to hold the ramparts," Jelaïa said. "We have no other choice but to abandon it."

"That's not the only issue," Makara continued. "Once the greylings are over the first wall, the mangonels will be practically useless. The abandoned buildings offer excellent cover, and even if we recalibrate the siege weapons to the shortest possible firing arc, they still have a minimum range."

"In that case, we should do the opposite," Derello said, hands clasped behind his back. "Set them to their maximum range. We'll hit the greylings from as far away as we can. The first wall might well be unmanned, but it's still an obstacle. We can rain boulders down on them while they attempt to scale it."

The Da'arran woman made a tutting sound. "If I may speak? You have yet to hear what we came here to tell you."

"My Lady," Derello bowed eloquently and motioned for her to continue.

"My thanks. For those who do not know me, my name is Xer'ana del Da'arra, Daughter of the Baron and Knight of Luridae."

Pit! thought Jelaïa. She could see that Aldarin was looking at the woman with newfound respect.

"Yesterday, I walked the golden sands of the Shakalla Desert. Today, I stand before you on the plains of Klief. This Knight of Brachyura and I have discovered how the greylings can move so quickly from Barony to Barony, allowing them to bring such massive armies to bear in so short a time."

She went on to explain all they had seen, from the buried eggs, to the black liquid filling the pools and archways, to the portals enabling passage from one Pit to another.

Makara paled when Xer'ana described the archway and the strange symbols carved into its stone frame. "This is far worse than anything I could have imagined. When we first fought against the weaver three hundred years ago, we destroyed a portal near-identical to the one you describe. I had hoped that in doing so we had trapped her on the other side … However, it appears that she has managed not only to return from wherever the archway leads but also to construct several more. Simply destroying one portal is no longer a viable solution."

"We have to take the fight to her," Vohanen said fiercely, punching the palm of one hand with his fist. "If all those portals lead to the same place — to wherever she came from — we will have to travel through the nearest one and kill her in her own domain."

"Careful," Brachyura warned. "She may be watching and listening."

"Aye. I almost hope she is. That way she'll know how it feels to be the hunted rather than the hunter for a change."

Makara leant on his cane to hobble over to one of the many pews lining the central aisle and sat down heavily. "I think … you may be right, Knight of Kriari. Unfortunately, you are forgetting one essential point: the weaver is immensely strong. It would take an entire army to defeat her. An entire army or …"

"The Twelve," Brachyura finished. "We are the only ones who can stop her and the only ones who cannot be trusted to do so."

"Yes," Makara said. "There is no way of knowing what will happen if you go through that portal. You could save the nine Baronies or precipitate their demise."

"Like the sea serpent that devours its own tail," murmured Derello.

Aldarin coughed uncomfortably. Brachyura turned to him with a frown. "Yes, initiate?"

"Lord, I am hesitant to bring this up, although I feel that I must. As you reminded us earlier, when you last stood before the weaver, she defeated you with a simple song. How do we know that will not happen again?"

"A song?" Makara asked with renewed interest. "You omitted that detail, Brother. How, exactly?"

Brachyura shook his head. "I am not sure. It was as if she had set my blood on fire. Every note wrenched my insides in a different direction. There was pain … pain like I had never known."

"And you heard her voice in your mind?"

"No. Nothing like that. Only the song. The same as everyone else."

"Hmmm." Makara took his lorgnette and wiped the lenses with the corner of his robe. "Then, what you are describing sounds similar to the suggestive induction I use with Azael to keep him … unaware of certain things. A series of subconscious commands placed in the mind, to be activated by using specific gestures or sounds."

"So, we cover our ears," Brachyura replied.

"That won't work unless you can find a way to lose your hearing altogether. The slightest hint of sound will be enough to trigger whatever dormant instructions the weaver has implanted. Nevertheless, I believe I can help. I can use my gift. I will not be able to destroy whatever chokeholds I find there, not without irredeemably damaging your psyche, but I should be able to isolate them so they cannot be activated."

"It will have to do," Brachyura said. "We should get started right away—"

"Wait," Kumbha interrupted. "You no longer lead here, Brother. This is too important a decision for you to make alone. We must do what we have always done since our return: guide, not command. It is the leaders of the nine

Baronies who must decide if they trust us enough to place their fate in our hands."

"Three leaders," Jelaïa corrected. "Three out of nine."

"Four counting Azael," Makara reminded her. "And five if we allow Xer'ana to speak for Da'arra."

She nodded, turning the problem round and round in her mind, imagining every possible outcome. *It's simple really,* she thought. *There is no definitive answer. It all comes down to one thing. Trust. Who did she trust?*

"How much free will do the Twelve really have?" she pondered aloud. "That is the crux of the problem. And we can only make an educated guess based on what has happened since they returned. I saw Brachyura denounce the Pact and join our cause. I saw him fight for us at Kessrin and Talth. He has told me many times that he will do all he can to halt the greyling tide, and I believe him. I cannot comprehend why he would do all these things if he was under the weaver's complete control. I ... believe that the Twelve, or at the very least those standing before us now, are responsible for their own actions, and I vote to let them go through the portal."

Derello was next to speak. "I watched Brachyura nearly kill his sister to protect us," he said. "He chose us over his own family. And his counsel was invaluable during the siege of Talth. Kumbha has worked tirelessly to save Kessrin lives, despite the pain she feels each time she uses her gift. I vote yes."

"I do not." Xer'ana glared at them. "Makara told me what the weaver has done to you. Implanted false memories in your minds. Brought you back to life by some nefarious means. Or maybe she has not even done that. Maybe you are not even the Twelve but something else entirely. Something alien. I have seen no proof of your benevolence and cannot, in good conscience, risk the lives of my people on a hunch. I am sorry."

Syrella cleared her throat. "Morlak votes yes," she said. "Kriari braved great danger to ring the bell that warned my people. In doing so, he spared many Morlakians from the wyrm's wrath. And it was Kriari who led us here to Klief. We would not be here without him. I vote yes."

"Then, the War Council has decided," Jelaïa confirmed. "Three votes to one. We will … we will …" she clutched at her head.

"Jelaïa?" Aldarin said with concern. "Is everything—"

She didn't hear the rest as the vision hit her with the force of a hurricane, driving her to her knees.

Three golden statues, glowing brightly in the sun. Black tar drips onto them from above. The glow fades as more and more of the sticky liquid trickles down until the statues are swallowed by it.

"Twelve. Failure," she heard herself say in a monotone voice. A second vision pushed away the first.

A wolf cub stands over the first statue, protecting it. The tarry substance drips onto its back instead, blackening its white fur.

A vermilion cloak is placed over the second statue, shielding it from harm.

A ram's horn covers the third.

"White wolf. Vermilion cloak. Ram's horn."

With a sob, she opened her eyes. There was blood on the floor in front of her. She had bitten her tongue. Aldarin pulled her up gently. "Jelaïa?"

"I'm fine. Did you hear what I said?"

"We did. The vision is telling you that the Twelve will fail."

"Only if they go alone. Three of us must go with them."

"The vermilion cloak," Reed said slowly. "The Old Guard. I am one of the three." He gave a wry smile. "I mean, of course I am, aren't I? A dangerous, possibly mortal, mission with little chance of success. It had to be me."

"I'll be going with you," Vohanen growled. "The ram's horn. It represents my family heirloom. Shattered by Mithuna."

"Well, I'm slightly more reassured knowing you'll be with me," Reed said. "So, that just leaves the third. The wolf cub. Who is—"

"It's me," Jelaïa said. "The Lady of the White Wolf. It's me."

"I see," Aldarin said in a distant voice. "We had better prepare then, time is of the essence."

"You can't come with us, Aldarin."

"Jelaïa ..."

"The visions. Three protectors, not four. They have guided us well so far. It would be folly to stray from them now."

"But ..."

"I will look after her, my friend," Reed said reassuringly. "Although after having heard tales of how she wields the fires of Brachyura, I imagine it's more likely that she will be the one looking after me."

Aldarin said nothing in reply, but Jelaïa could see the anguish in his eyes.

"I have to do this," she said in a low voice only he could

hear. "Please, Aldarin. I love you. I love you so much, but you have to let me do this. I will be careful. I will use my gift sparingly. Trust me."

He stared back at her, then nodded, once.

"Thank you."

"Three humans and three demi-gods," said Derello brightly. "An unlikely combination. All I can think of is the fact that we are betting the future of the Baronies on a half-baked mystical prophecy."

"It was the visions that led us to Kessrin," Jelaïa chastised him. "And to Da'arra. In fact, it was the visions that led Aldarin to the Southern Pit. They were what set this whole mission in motion. It seems fitting that they will also be what ends it." Her gaze drifted to one of the stained-glass windows depicting a knight in shining armour. "Loré will speak for Arelium while I am gone. And if anything happens to me … he is my first choice to take my place as Baron."

"We will try and make sure you have something to come back to," Aldarin said. "Caddox and I will take charge of the Knights of Brachyura on the second wall. Derello, we will need any archers you can spare. Every greyling we can take down at range is one less that reaches the battlements." He looked at Ka'arka and his healed shoulder. "It is Kumbha we will miss the most. Without her skills, the infirmary is going to be put under a lot of strain."

"Belen and Xandris are both excellent healers," the giantess said. "You should not underestimate them. Some of their techniques are nothing short of astounding."

"And we have plenty of volunteers," Syrella added. "Jeffson and Taleck have been helping in surgery. Citizens of Klief, too. We can handle it."

"We don't have any choice in the matter," Makara added. "Kumbha must go through the portal. I'll try to convince Azael to let us expand the infirmary into the keep."

"Kriari." The bear-like First of the Twelve made a serpentine movement with his hand.

"The wyrm," Brachyura translated. "In focusing on the armies battering at our door, we have forgotten the even greater threat. I have lost track of time. When will it arrive?"

Jelaïa felt the positive momentum drain from the room. "Tomorrow," she said dejectedly. "If the weaver makes good on her promise, it will be here tomorrow."

"Hah!" barked Reed. "So, we have a day to find and stop the weaver or we're wyrm food. Perfect."

"I may be able to help with that too," Makara interjected. "If the weaver communicates with the wyrm in the same way as I speak to the Twelve ... I might be able to slow its progress."

"Do what you can," Reed said. "I saw that thing once; I definitely do *not* want to see it again." He looked round at the others. "I suppose we should set off straight away. How far are we from the Kliefien Pit?"

Makara gave an embarrassed cough.

"Ah, about that," the Tenth of the Twelve said. He looked almost embarrassed. "I'm afraid I might not have been entirely forthcoming about the Pit's location."

Reed rubbed his tired eyes. "Why am I not surprised? Where is it?"

Makara gave an apologetic shrug. "It's here," he said, tapping the floor of the cathedral with the end of his cane.

"You're standing on it."

CHAPTER 14

AGAMIDS

"You have only met the greylings, friend Reed, but there are other things that lurk far beneath the earth."

SIR ALDARIN, KNIGHT OF BRACHYURA, 426 AT

෨

"T HAT DESPICABLE WITCH!" spat Zygos, pacing back and forth across the plush carpet of his tent. "That withered old hag!"

Praxis felt the Seventh of the Twelve's anger like the blade of a sword, each expletive-filled curse a cut to his psyche. It was the first time he had ever seen Zygos angry, and he knew why: something unexpected had happened. Something *illogical*.

"I should be standing before the cathedral of Klief by now, not in this moth-infested tent," the demi-god continued. "Why did that woman sacrifice herself like that? She has only delayed my conquest by a day. What a waste."

And therein lies the problem, Praxis thought. *Zygos has the same weakness as all of the Twelve possess. They do not understand human emotion. They believe it to be a flaw, a vulnerability to be exploited. It is so much more. For every man who loses himself to rage, another finds strength through love and self-sacrifice. Praedora's death has not only given the defenders time. It has given them hope.*

He tried to ignore the droning voice of his captor and concentrated instead on the little finger of his right hand. *Move!* he commanded, pouring all his will into that one thought, trying to remember what it felt like, the bending of the joints, the softness of the flesh, the weight of his arm.

Nothing.

PIT! he screamed into the empty cavern of his mind. *MOVE! THIS IS MY BODY! MY LIFE! YOU BELONG TO ME! MOVE, YOU PIT-SPAWNED PILE OF TRASH! MOVE!*

The finger twitched.

The movement was so slight, so fast, he thought he must have imagined it. He tried again, abandoning all focused thought, allowing the anger and frustration he had worked so hard to ignore for all of his adult life to bubble to the surface. Another, almost imperceptible spasm.

This is how he would break free from an eternity of captivity. Praxis knew his body was lost to him forever. His muscles, his skin, his nerves, his veins. They all belonged to Zygos. There was only one thing left for him to do. If he could regain control of his arm for just a moment, then he could tear the dagger from his belt and plunge it straight into his putrid heart.

"What are you doing?" a curious voice asked. Praxis peered out through the windows of his prison and saw his own face staring back at him. Zygos had ceased his pacing and was standing in front of the polished full-length mirror he had brought with him from the temple.

"Well?" Zygos insisted. "I can hear you squirming around. There is no escape, Praxis. You would do best to relax and enjoy the ride."

Praxis studied his reflection, aghast at the way his body was changing. His skin, filtered through the colourless lenses of Zygos's pitch-black eyes, looked pale and sickly. He was so thin he appeared almost skeletal, his hollow cheeks and sunken eyes giving him a ghoulish quality. The self-inflicted scar bulged, twisted and wormlike.

"Praxis?"

He focused, willing Zygos to hear his thoughts. *I only share your disappointment, Lord.*

"Ah? A minor setback. We still have ample time to take the city and tell the weaver to call off the wyrm. I would rather it not be destroyed. The cathedral alone sounds fascinating. An entire structure dedicated to the worship of the Twelve."

Yes, Lord.

"Perhaps I will ask her to bequeath it to me," Zygos mused. "She promised to let us go free once the last armies of men have fallen. The greylings will have no use for it. And it is only logical for my brothers and sisters to be rewarded for what they have done."

All except Mina and Mithuna. The thought slipped out before he could stop it.

Careful, thundered a voice in his mind. **You are a pet, nothing more. Disrespect my siblings and I will snuff you out like a candle.**

Yes, Lord.

"Excellent," Zygos said out loud with a half-smile that stretched his skin even tighter across his cheekbones. "Then, let us find something to occupy us until nightfall."

"Lord?" Helios stood awkwardly at the entrance of the tent, his head bowed respectfully. He had a heavy-looking canvas bag slung over one shoulder.

He must think his master is talking to himself, Praxis thought with some amusement.

"What is it?" Zygos asked crossly. "You know I do not like to be interrupted."

"It's the eggs, Lord. They are hatching."

Zygos raised an eyebrow. "Really? Already? Excellent news. Show me." He stalked past Helios and stepped out into the morning sun. Several hundred yards away, smoke still rose from the deserted first wall, its ramparts permanently scarred black by the fires of Brachyura and Praedora's sacrifice.

The greylings had dug trenches and pot-holes all along the perimeter, doing what they could to stay out of the sun. Those who could not find a spot underground huddled together under the shade of the Knights of Zygos's tents. Praxis even saw a trio of creatures squatting in the shadow cast by a hulking thresher. It was a strange, paternal image that surprised him.

They passed piles of rotting animal carcasses hunted and

killed by the greylings during their march north. A paltry amount compared to the astronomical size of the horde, but starvation would never be an issue. Once all available food had been consumed, they would turn to cannibalism.

More knights joined them as they left the camp, escorting them into the valley. Snow had not yet come to Klief, but there was a thin layer of frost on the scraggly grass, and the ground underneath was cold and hard.

The eggs covered the valley floor like a forest of mushrooms. Hundreds of creamy-white shells. Some of them were moving. Darker shadows wriggled under the near-translucent surfaces. Helios pointed to one of the eggs close by.

"This one is ready, Lord."

A tapping sound was coming from the egg, slow and rhythmical like a nail being hammered into a piece of wood. Cracks appeared in the fragile shell. A piece the size of a small child detached, revealing a pointed reptilian snout covered in yolk. The snout pushed through the hole it had made for itself, and the egg shattered. Gooey albumen splashed onto the ground, spattering Zygos's boots.

The hatchling resembled nothing Praxis had ever seen before. It had the body of a large lizard, easily six feet long from tip to tail, its mottled skin made up of tiny, overlapping scales. Four stubby legs ended in curved claws. The strangest appendages were two folded flaps of red skin that ran the entire length of its body like fleshy curtains, stopping just before the prehensile tail.

The creature opened its jaw and hissed, its forked tongue darting through a row of needle-sharp teeth.

What is it? thought Praxis.

"The weaver calls them agamids," Zygos said, observing

the newborn as it licked the last of the orange yolk from its body. "Their species made their homes in the deep caverns and tunnels of the nine Baronies. Until the greylings arrived and slaughtered them all. Well, most of them. A few were kept for breeding purposes. The eggs need both sunlight and warmth to hatch so the Da'arran desert was the perfect place to incubate them. Helios! The leash!"

The Knight of Zygos set down his bag with a clinking sound and took out a metal chain that he looped over the thing's neck and pulled tight. The agamid hissed again and tugged at the chain with its claws, but Helios held fast.

"Remember, they must be leashed just after they have hatched," Zygos told him. "While they are still disorientated. Now, hand me the chain and get to work on the others. I am going to test this one right away."

"Yes, Lord."

Zygos turned and started up the closest hill, dragging the agamid behind him. "They must all be tested," he explained to Praxis. "Those too weak to serve will be fed to the strong. As it should be."

He crested the rise. The greyling army was spread out below them like a swarm of flies while beyond was the city of Klief, the sparkling windows of its cathedral mocking them.

"Now, let us see," said Zygos, and with a grunt of effort, he flung the agamid off the top of the hill.

It shrieked in fear as it fell, its back arched and forelimbs spread wide. Then the wind caught the flaps of skin, filling them with air, stretching them out like …

Wings, marvelled Praxis. The agamid pulled smoothly out of its dive, using its rigid tail and forelimbs to steer itself.

"Not wings, but patagia," Zygos replied. "Magnificent,

aren't they? The lines you can see in the membranes are the thing's ribs. They can fold or unfold them at will."

The agamid banked sharply, gliding past them and back down into the valley below.

"Good. This seems to be a suitable launch site if the wind holds. I am not sure they will have enough lift to reach the third wall, but they should have no difficulty in getting as far as the second. Agamids do not fear the sun. We will launch the aerial assault as soon as the colony has hatched. The defenders will not be expecting an attack during the day. And then, when pandemonium reigns and the walls of Klief are wet with blood, I will unleash the full strength of the greyling horde. Klief will fall. And I will not even need that useless traitor to let me in."

How will you control them? Praxis asked, hating himself for engaging with Zygos but unable to restrain his curiosity.

"I do not need to. Agamids inherit the diet of their progenitors. The hatchlings are half-starved and will search out the closest source of food as soon as they take flight."

What were their progenitors fed with?

"Flesh," Zygos said dispassionately. "Raw human flesh."

"What is this madness?" Ka'arka blurted out. "You built the entire city of Klief over the Pit?"

Makara was about to reply when the doors to the cathedral opened and two of his bearers appeared, carrying suits of burnished silver plate. Aldarin's armour and a second suit for Ka'arka to replace the one lost somewhere in the hills near the city. The Da'arran frowned when he saw the helm.

"No helm," he said curtly.

"Are you sure? It would be better—"

"No helm." Ka'arka took the other pieces of armour from the bearer with a nod of thanks.

"Our axes and helms are forged by our own hands," Aldarin explained, retrieving his own plate. "Part of the ritual leading to our knighthood. They are an important part of our identities. Buried with us, when possible. Offering a Knight of Brachyura the helm of a dead comrade is considered ... poor etiquette."

"Aye," added Vohanen, "just like the Knights of Kriari and our shields. Took ages to make mine. Had it with me all my life until I gave it away to ... to my son, Avor ..." he trailed off, his eyes clouding with grief.

"Ah ... apologies. To both of you," Makara replied, waving his bearers away. "I did not know."

"Well, now you do," said Ka'arka, buckling on his greaves. "Just look at what interesting things you could have learnt if you hadn't spent all your time hiding in this monument to lost ideals and lies."

"Enough," Brachyura warned.

Jelaïa was looking at the Fourth of the Twelve strangely. "You knew! You've known ever since we arrived. When you touched the wall." She wheeled on Kriari and Kumbha. "You all knew!"

Brachyura sighed. "I had a memory, yes. A memory of the Kliefien Pit being here. But you have to understand, Baroness. Makara tells us that these bodies are not our own. That our thoughts are not our own. How can I trust my memories? How can I be sure which are true and which have been planted or changed by the weaver? I am sorry, but since learning who I am, or rather who I am not, I will only place my faith in what I have seen with my own eyes, not a faded recollection. Tell us, Brother. Tell us what happened."

Makara shifted uneasily. "After the Battle of the Northern Plains, our first priority was to trap the greylings underground. We spent ten years collapsing tunnels, filling in caves and crevices, doing everything we could to prevent their return. In the end, six enormous craters still remained, all far too large to fill, or at least that is what we thought at the time. Our palliative solution led to the creation of the Old Guard and the construction of Brachyura's walls. The Kliefien Pit was thus protected, just like the others. You have seen what remains of this Pit's defences. Some of you have even walked along it."

"The first wall," Aldarin murmured in disbelief.

"Indeed. The first wall once ringed the Kliefien Pit. As the population of the nine Baronies grew, their knowledge of engineering evolved exponentially. We began to realise that maybe, one day, the Pits *could* be closed. It would take an extraordinary amount of time and raw materials, but it was no longer an impossibility. Alas, this option was never discussed further as, shortly afterwards, our priorities changed."

"Peace," said Jelaïa.

"Yes. We were tiring of the constant warmongering. Our initial policies of eradication and isolation were no longer effective. Not only that, but we were all beginning to feel that our own reserves of strength were failing. We pivoted from extermination to conciliation. The Pits were not to be touched. Instead, we would attempt to make contact with the enemy to discuss a truce."

"The damming of Terris Lake," Vohanen said, glancing at Kriari.

"Kriari dam," the scruffy giant agreed.

"It all seems terribly ironic now," Makara continued. "But the Morlakian Pit was where Mithuna was concentrating her ... diplomatic efforts. We couldn't let it be flooded."

"The weaver tricked you."

"Maybe. Or maybe she really thought we would capitulate. In any case, as you know, I escaped to Klief. The capital city was originally situated further north, in the mountains, close to the gold mines. When it was decimated by an avalanche shortly after my return, I suggested we relocate to the plains and attempt to fill in the Pit."

"Why?"

Makara shrugged. "I think a part of me knew that the greylings might one day try to return to the surface. It was the perfect way of keeping the Barony safe."

"The Barony ... your Barony, you mean," Jelaïa said. "What of Morlak? Of Arelium?"

"It took me *fifty years* to get the Kliefien Pit filled. And that was with a steady supply of stones from the quarries as well as gold from the mines to hire a substantial workforce. Close to another fifty years to rebuild Klief. To erect this cathedral. By then, I was no longer Makara. I had become the High Priest of the newly created church of the Twelve. All who had known me and my siblings had died of old age. Our faces were forgotten. The Pits were silent. I believed our struggles were over. I ... I was tired. So tired. I needed to rest. Or so I told myself. I understand that some may see my complacency as cowardice. I am sorry."

Jelaïa was shaking her head. "What is so frustrating is

that you have such a wealth of knowledge and yet you chose to run away and hide instead of face your responsibilities. Did you not even think to keep a record of all that came before?"

"Or course I did," Makara said, gesturing with a withered hand at the vaulted ceiling of the cathedral. "What do you think all this is?"

"I'm not talking about religion. I'm talking about *history*. You wrote the book of the Twelve, the perfect opportunity to share your knowledge, but you twisted the truth. You were so adamant about not exposing your failure and tarnishing your siblings' memories that you didn't stop to think of the consequences. So many lives lost. You sent hundreds of false prophets out into the world, preaching from a book of lies, then went and hid your head in the sand!"

Makara said nothing. The nave was silent save for Aldarin tightening the straps of his breastplate.

Jelaïa could feel herself becoming agitated. She wrapped one hand around her medallion and tried to calm her frayed nerves. "The lies of the Pact were not your fault," she continued. "But they were made worse by your isolationism. If you had kept in touch with the Knightly Orders. If you had attended the Council of Baronies. If you had opened the borders of Klief ..."

"I know ..." the last surviving member of the Twelve replied in a voice barely louder than a whisper. His gnarled, bony hands trembled on the pommel of his cane. "I know ..."

"This is not a persecution," Brachyura said sternly, his black eyes narrowing dangerously. "Nor a tribunal."

"No," agreed Jelaïa. "It is not. It is a stark reminder of

what awaits us if those who survive all this do not record it. It must not happen again. What happens here now will be remembered."

"And shared," Syrella added. "History is not something to be hoarded like a chest of gold coins. The more people who know of it, the more chance we have that it will not be forgotten."

Reed stood. "The day is not getting any longer. So, you filled in the Pit. That doesn't seem to have stopped the weaver though, does it? She still managed to build her portal. How do we get to it? Don't tell me we have to go back the way Ka'arka came? The whole valley is crawling with greylings now, and I don't think I can outrun all of them."

"You won't have to," Makara said. "I … I left a way in." He gestured to the circular slab of stone. "My own little wall. Press the fourth, tenth, and twelfth signal towers."

Reed did as he was asked, hearing a small click as he touched each tower. There was a clanking sound, and the stone rolled aside, revealing a round hole five feet wide, covered by a set of steel bars. A lock was set in the centre.

Makara reached inside his priest's robes and produced a key. "This is the only copy. It will unlock the gate here and a second gate that you will find when you reach the bottom. There is a length of rope hidden under the altar in the chapel of Makara. We will close the way behind you; the same sequence will need to be repeated on the opposite side for it to open again. Oh, and we won't be able to leave the rope. You'll have to shimmy back up using your back and feet … or find some other way out."

"What about torches?" Reed asked.

"My eyes, like those of my brothers and sisters, no longer need such things," Brachyura said. "We will guide you."

"Right, but — sorry to say this, Lord — what if we find ourselves ... without you?"

Syrella took a reel of thread from a pouch on her belt. "The healer uses this for stitching up wounds, it's well-made and resistant. I have a couple on me. Would that work? There are plenty more in the infirmary."

"Perfect," said Reed.

Makara looked at the entrance to the shaft. "Then, say your goodbyes. It is time."

Xer'ana went to fetch the rope, leaving Reed to unlock the door. Syrella bent down next to him and kissed his cheek before whispering something into his ear, making him laugh. Aldarin and Jelaïa were standing a few feet away, locked in each other's arms. The tall knight was speaking softly to the Baroness and stroking her chestnut hair.

"Brachyura, Kumbha, Kriari. Join me."

Each of the Twelve kneeled before Makara, and he placed his palms flat on their foreheads, muttering something unintelligible as he did so.

"It is done," the Tenth of the Twelve said wearily. "I have blocked her, I think. Before you go, I just want to say ... I am sorry. Sorry for all of this."

Brachyura hesitated, then held out his hand.

"I do not know exactly who or what I am," Brachyura said, his usual stoicism crumbling under the weight of his inner turmoil. "Everything is a puzzle. Whereas before I had answers, I now have only questions. There is one thing I am sure of, however. You *are* my brother. And I am grateful to have seen your face again, if but for a short time."

Makara took Brachyura's outstretched hand in his own, and they grasped wrists.

"You will succeed, Brother," he replied. "I know it. And when you return, we can try to make up for the years of lost time."

"Kriari."

Makara smiled sadly and gave Kriari's wrist a squeeze, followed by Kumbha.

Xer'ana secured the rope to one of the elaborately carved columns lining the nave and threw the other end into the hole. Brachyura descended first, followed by Kumbha, Kriari, Reed, Vohanen, and finally Jelaïa who gave one last fleeting look at Aldarin before vanishing into the darkness.

"May the Twelve guide your path," Aldarin said quietly.

Those who remained stood silently in the glow of the multi-faceted stained-glass windows. After a few moments, there were three strong tugs on the rope. Xer'ana pulled it up out of the shaft while Derello slid the stone slab back into place. It locked itself shut with a resonating clang that echoed up to the vaulted ceiling.

"And now we must wait," Makara said. "I will stay here. It is as good a place as any to try to counter the wyrm. I will send for you all the minute I hear anything."

There was a noise from outside, a high-pitched wail that sounded eerily like a scream.

"What was that?" Ka'arka wondered.

The doors to the cathedral burst open, and Azael del Klief stumbled inside, his golden jacket torn, his hair in disarray.

"They are attacking!" he shouted.

"Attacking? Who are attacking?" Makara said. "Surely not the greylings, the day has not yet run its course!"

"I don't know what they are … Creatures! Creatures from another age!"

"Talk sense, man!" Xer'ana snapped. "Start acting more like a Baron and less like a child."

Azael took one look at her and burst into tears.

"Pit!" she cursed. "We'll have to go and see for ourselves. Knight of Brachyura?"

"Yes?" Aldarin and Ka'arka replied simultaneously.

Xer'ana rolled her eyes. "Fine! Both of you! With me! The battle for the second wall has begun!"

And together they charged out of the cathedral.

Out into smoke, fire, and death.

CHAPTER 15

A Crown of Flowers

"Humanity's technical and scientific evolution seemed to accelerate exponentially after my brothers and sisters disappeared, almost as if we had been stifling their progress. And maybe we had. The greatest inventions are the consequence of a group of talented people attempting to solve one of society's problems. By systematically providing the human tribes with all the answers, I fear we inadvertently stopped them from asking any questions."

MAKARA, TENTH OF THE TWELVE, 131 AT

❧

JEFFSON PLUNGED HIS hands into the basin of water and scrubbed vigorously to remove the dried blood staining his cuticles. He had already forgotten who it had belonged to. The Kliefien town guard with the lacerated neck? The other one with the broken leg? The stretcher-bearer who had been set upon by greylings as he was carrying the wounded from the wall? After a time, the faces all blurred together.

Since Kumbha had been summoned to the cathedral, the infirmary beds were filling faster than Belen, the healer, could empty them. Praedora's sacrifice had certainly bought them some time, but the wounded continued to flow in through the infirmary doors like ants drawn to sugar.

"Jeffson," Belen called from the surgery, his half-moon spectacles perched precariously on the end of his nose. "When was the last time you took a break?"

"I … I'm not sure, my Lord."

"I'm not your Lord. Take five minutes. I can manage on my own."

"But—"

"Healer's orders. You're no use to me dead on your feet. I suggest a quick meander around the gardens if you haven't visited them yet. Best place for a bit of peace and quiet."

Jeffson bowed, smiling inwardly. Belen could barely string two sentences together when talking normally, but the infirmary transformed him from a meek mouse into a proud lion. The master of his domain.

The gardens were a short stroll away, hidden behind the Baron's keep. Jeffson was relieved to see that they had been spared Azael's over-zealous decorative tastes. No golden banners or marble statues, just a series of gravel paths winding in and out of colourful floral compositions.

He closed his eyes, relishing the silence after the frenzied chaos of the infirmary. A pair of robins fluttered past, heading for the taller trees at the back of the garden. He heard a faint cry of laughter. A child's laughter.

No, not again, he thought, searching the empty path.

For years, the guilt of being indirectly responsible for his daughter's death had caused him to hear echoing memories of her laugh. But that had stopped when he had learnt that his family was still alive.

Another high-pitched giggle. He wasn't hallucinating this time. He rounded a bend and almost bumped into Cerra who was watching Daelle and Mila racing up and down a short stretch of gravel. The two girls wore crowns of flowers and held sword-like sticks.

"I am Syrella del Morlak, Lady of the White Rose," Daelle was saying haughtily. "Look upon me and weep!"

"No, *I* am Baroness del Morlak," Mila retorted, waving her stick menacingly. "Do not listen to this imposter! Look upon me and sleep!"

"Pfff, it's look upon me and *weep*, not sleep," Daelle sniggered. "Why would people who see you want to sleep?"

"Obviously, they are overwhelmed by my beauty."

"What? That doesn't even make any sense! How do you even—"

"Girls. Girls," Cerra chided. "Play nicely. Or I'll take you back inside."

Jeffson gave a polite cough. "Good afternoon, ladies. I hope I am not interrupting anything?"

Daelle's face lit up, and she dropped her stick. "Jeffson!" she squealed, running over to him and wrapping her tiny arms around his legs. "Where have you been? I haven't seen you in ages!"

Jeffson shot a sidelong glance at Cerra. "I have been busy. Very busy." After a moment's hesitation, he reached down and patted his daughter's hair.

"This is the man I was telling you about!" Daelle

shouted to Mila. "He saved me and my Mummy from the bad people!"

Mila looked him up and down critically. "Are you sure? He doesn't have much hair left, and he's not even standing up straight. If someone hit him, he would just fall over."

Jeffson smiled despite himself. "Appearances can be deceiving, little girl. Why, your friend Merad Reed is just as scrawny as me, and he has saved Lady Syrella's life on numerous occasions."

"He has more hair, though," Mila replied stubbornly.

"Enough, children, enough," Cerra repeated. "Why don't you go and find some more flowers for your crowns?"

The girls wandered off down the path, hand-in-hand. Jeffson watched his daughter leave with a mixture of happiness and regret.

"I would like to thank you for keeping your distance," Cerra said suddenly. "It has been a ... difficult time for all of us."

"Of course," Jeffson replied, inclining his head. "Ner'alla has been treating you both well, I hope?"

"The Da'arran has been the perfect gentlemen. It's his manservant who's a bit less amiable. I've caught him giving me the odd dirty look. Not that he's around much."

"Oh?" Jeffson asked innocently.

"Yes. Disappears without a trace for hours at a time. No idea what he gets up to."

"Cerra?"

"Yes?"

"You all shared Ner'alla's tent on the trip north. Was that Stick fellow by any chance with you on the very first night we arrived, the night Verona was killed?"

"The priestess? I ... don't remember. I distinctly recall a lot of drinking and lewd behaviour. But I was in my bed long before the others. No ... wait ... I think Ner'alla came back alone. Why? Do you think this Stick person was responsible?"

"Anything is possible. It's the motive I don't understand. He never gave us any indication that he had encountered Verona before. Why murder someone you have just met? And in such a gruesome fashion?"

"It sounds like we're missing something. I'll talk to Ner'alla. If anyone can tell us more about Stick, it's him."

"Thank you."

Daelle and Mila had returned. Jeffson's daughter was carrying a massive piece of wood taller than herself. "Mummy! I found a lance!" she said proudly. "I'm going to be a knight now! I need a trusty steed. Can I have a pony?"

"Not today, dear," Cerra said, not unkindly. "It's about time we headed back. I promised I'd help prepare the vegetables for this evening's stew. We wouldn't want our valiant defenders to starve, would we?"

"I know how to peel carrots," said Mila smugly.

"You do? Well then, you can be my assistant. Come along."

She took the children by the hand and pulled them back towards the Kliefien keep.

"Cerra!" Jeffson called. She stopped and looked back over her shoulder.

"I ... I enjoyed talking with you," he said tentatively. "Perhaps we could do so again soon?"

She hesitated, then smiled briefly. "I think I would like that." Jeffson smiled back, watching as they rounded the bend and disappeared. He sat down on one of the benches lining the garden path.

There is still hope, he thought. *Even when all seems lost. Even when the currents of the river of life drag us apart, there is always a way back. It just takes patience and dedication.*

He sat for a while in the sun, listening to the chirping of the birds and the soft whispering of the wind. A crunch of gravel made him open his eyes. Xandris, the healer's apprentice, was plodding towards him, his triangular goatee bright and yellow in the afternoon light.

"Jeffson," he beamed. "Belen said I would find you here."

"Yes. I am … relaxing."

"As well you should be. I heard you worked for nearly ten hours non-stop in the infirmary. There's only so much a man can take. I remember my first amputation as if it were yesterday. I nicked an artery. Blood everywhere. I passed out, hitting my forehead on the operating table as I fell. Belen had to finish the amputation then patch me up too. I still have the scar."

"Blood doesn't bother me."

"No, I suppose it wouldn't. Hmm. It's quite fortuitous I've run into you, actually. I would like to show you something, something I've been working on. If you have a minute?"

Jeffson shrugged. "It's not like I have anything else planned. The greylings are cowering in their holes, and the last time I saw Sir Reed he was heading to the cathedral. I was not invited."

"Excellent. Follow me, please."

Xandris led Jeffson out of the gardens, past the infirmary,

to a small, nondescript building that may have once been a tavern but, like many of the other houses, was now deserted. Inside waited the unlikely trio of Ner'alla, Bansworth, and Krelbe, clustered around a bowl filled with hundreds of tiny black pellets, each no larger than a grain of sand.

"I've been working on this ever since Kessrin," Xandris said, plumping himself down into a chair and motioning for Jeffson to do the same. "Belen was helping Kumbha in the infirmary, the Baroness and Lord del Conte were leading the troops, and I was just sort of ... tagging along. I felt like I needed to *do* something, you know?" He picked a half-dozen pellets out of the bowl and rolled them around in his hand.

"I'll be the first to admit I'm not the best healer. But I have a great memory. Twenty years of cataloguing every single substance in Belen's dispensary. And I enjoy figuring out how things work. So, I got to thinking ... out of all the herbs and powders we have at our disposal, could we not find some way to weaponise certain compounds?"

He rolled up the sleeve of his right arm, revealing an inch-wide burn that ran from wrist to elbow. "My first experiments were unsuccessful. But on the road to Klief, I finally cracked it."

He held out one of the little black grains. "We use charcoal to draw toxins out of the body and reduce stomach ailments. Sulphur is used for burns or rashes. Both are quite harmless. Add saltpetre, however, traditionally used as a cure for food poisoning, and you have something quite flammable."

He put the grains on the table, grabbed a nearby candle and brought it close. With a whoosh, the powder caught fire, burning with a bright yellow-white flame.

"Impressive," Jeffson admitted. The flames sputtered and died, leaving a charred patch of wood in their wake.

"Thank you."

"If we put the contents of that bowl into some sort of container, the explosive force would likely be enough to topple a thresher."

Xandris grinned, enjoying himself. "Sorry, you've misunderstood. What's in the bowl is just a small sample. As soon as I realised what I'd discovered, I spent my every waking hour making more of the stuff. Since we arrived in Klief, it's become even easier. The dispensary here was overflowing with raw materials."

"And he managed to convince us to help with his harebrained scheme," said Krelbe with a scowl.

"Convince you? I had to give you a crate of Morlakian red!"

"That was just for me to come and listen. I didn't realise I'd be stuck with a pestle and mortar for hours on end."

"How much do you have?" Jeffson asked, ignoring the surly Knight of Kriari. Xandris gestured towards the far wall of the tavern where casks of ale were stacked against the wall.

"A barrelful? You had time to make enough to fill a whole barrel?"

"No," Xandris said with a sly smile. "We've filled all of them."

Jeffson sprang up from his chair. "Are you mad? If a flame gets anywhere near that, you'll blow a hole the size of the cathedral!"

"That's the plan. Not here, of course. Listen, we all saw what Praedora did atop the first wall. The number of enemies she killed. The way she slowed their advance." Xandris licked his lips. "The four of us were thinking ... um ..."

"Well, spit it out!"

"It's just ... the second wall won't hold indefinitely. I'm sorry, but it won't. The greylings are too many. It's not a matter of *if* the wall will fall but *when*."

"Go on."

"What if we placed the barrels at strategic locations along the inner side? At ground level? We could link them together using rope as a fuse. Then, once the last of the defenders are clear, we wait until the greylings reach the ramparts, light the fuses and watch the entire second wall explode. Take out a whole lot of greylings and create a great mountain of rubble that the survivors will have to climb over to get to us."

Jeffson mulled it over. "It's ... it's genius," he said appreciatively. "If timed correctly, it may even give us a slim chance of victory. What do you need from me?"

Xandris glowed with pride. "Another pair of hands to help us get the barrels down to the wall. And perhaps you could put in a good word to Syrella and the others?"

"You haven't told them about this?"

"No. I've tried to talk to Lady Jelaïa about it several times, but I've never quite managed to. And now they're all holed up in the cathedral."

Jeffson glanced outside. "We shouldn't wait. We only have an hour of sunlight left at the most. The greylings will almost certainly attack again at dusk. Let's get started. We can worry about gaining the support of the Barons later."

Xandris nodded. "I've already commandeered a cart. I'll bring it round, and we can begin loading."

Bansworth gave one of the barrels an experimental tug.

"By the Twelve, they're heavy!" he exclaimed. "This one must weigh at least a hundred pounds. How are we going to carry them?"

"Tip 'em onto their side and roll 'em," Krelbe remarked.

Xandris looked horrified. "Are you out of your mind? We have no idea how volatile the powder is!"

Ner'alla hauled himself to his feet. "When I was working at *The Crimson Wing*, we used a technique called the rim roll. You tilt the barrel slightly to the side so it's resting on a part of its metal rim." He demonstrated with the barrel Bansworth was standing next to, moving it easily.

"That should keep the powder stable enough," Xandris agreed. "Unless—" He was cut off by a terrible screeching sound followed by a loud human scream.

"What in the Pit was that?"

They rushed outside. Another cry of panic. On the far side of the courtyard, the doors of the cathedral burst open. Aldarin, Ka'arka, and Xer'ana appeared, weapons drawn.

"It's coming from the second wall," Krelbe shouted. "We're too late, the enemy are already attacking! Xandris, stay with the horse and cart. The rest of you, with me! Let's see what we're up against."

The others followed Krelbe as he ran through the third wall gatehouse, yelling at the couple of Knights of Kriari stationed there to go fetch the rest of the men. The battlements below were under assault by a host of winged creatures, swarming over the Knights of Brachyura and their mangonels like wasps.

Jeffson watched, stunned. Kessrin and Kliefien archers were firing up into the air, but even at this distance, he could see that it was useless. The lizard-like beasts were far too agile. One twirled effortlessly through the storm of arrows and kicked a defender square in the chest with its stubby legs, knocking him off the wall to his death on the cobbles far below.

Sir Caddox was galloping up the road, two knights at his side. He arrived with a hammering of hooves and a cloud of dust.

"They came out of nowhere," he said angrily as he dismounted. "And we have no way to counter them. I've lost nine archers already. Aldarin, we have to get Jelaïa to come back with us. She's the only priestess still alive, and the only one who can drive them off."

"Jelaïa, Reed, and Vohanen are ... unavailable," Aldarin replied evasively. "We'll have to think of something else."

"Well, think fast," Caddox snarled. "Or I'm giving the order to abandon the wall."

Ner'alla had been silent, observing the creatures skim across the battlements. "They don't appear to be flapping their wings," he said, half to himself. "In fact, they aren't flying at all, really, they're ... *gliding.*"

Caddox glared at him. "No. I know what you're going to say but no. Never again. Never in a million years. I would rather break all the bones in both my hands."

"What's he talking about?" asked Aldarin, confused.

"There is a way to fight back," Ner'alla said. "It's extremely dangerous, highly unorthodox, and to be honest, rather stupid. But with the right pilots ... experienced pilots ... it just might work."

He looked up past the gatehouse where the sharp spire of the cathedral was rising into the afternoon sky like a dagger.

"I call them my Crimson Wings."

CHAPTER 16

THROUGH THE PORTAL

"The Twelve were always very evasive when discussing their origins. I'm not quite sure whether it was because they did not want to share their secrets or that they really didn't know where they came from. It did make me think more and more about how they conveniently appeared among us just as humanity was facing its darkest hour. Serendipity? Perhaps. Or something else entirely."

BARONESS JELAÏA DEL ARELIUM, 427 AT

REED LOWERED HIMSELF carefully down the circular shaft, Kriari's untidy mess of hair below him, Vohanen's steel-capped boots brushing against the top of the spear tied to Reed's back.

I can't believe I allowed myself to get roped into this again, he thought moodily as his nose picked up the familiar scent of sulphur. He had always believed that after meeting Aldarin and fleeing Jaelem all those months ago he would never have to smell that dreadful stench again. But events always conspired to send him right back into the depths of the Pit, the one place he was trying so hard to escape from.

He wondered what Vohanen must be feeling. For Reed, returning to the underground darkness reminded him of his friends and comrades of the Old Guard. Vohanen would be thinking of his son, Avor, who had sacrificed himself to save the Morlakian prisoners, including Lady Syrella herself.

"How are you doing?" he called up softly to the grizzled old knight.

"Better than you, laddie," the voice of Vohanen floated back down. "I'm as fresh as a daisy. Spent most of yesterday on the third wall trying to avoid Baron del Klief, sharing the contents of Lord del Conte's flask, and running errands for Lady Jelaïa. Not the most heroic of afternoons, I must confess. Just make sure you don't poke a hole through the soles of my boots with that spear of yours."

"Laddie? I'm nearly as old as you," Reed replied grumpily.

"You're what? Forty-one? Forty-two? A pipsqueak. Ah, to be young again."

"Vohanen, you can't be older than fifty-five!"

"Shame on you, Reed! I don't know how you were brought up in Arelium, but in Morlak it's considered very rude to ask a man his age."

"Uggghhh. I'm beginning to think that whoever or *whatever* is sending these visions to Jelaïa has it in for me. It's the only reasonable explanation as to why I'm always being paired up with you."

"Nonsense. Now, what did Syrella tell you before we left? Something romantic, I hope?"

"She … she told me that when I get back, she's going to shave off my beard."

"I've not heard that innuendo before, but it sounds like an open invitation to me."

"What? No! It's because it scratches—" His feet hit Kriari's head. They had reached the bottom of the shaft.

"Kriari?"

"Sorry," Reed apologised, sliding down the last few feet of rope and standing aside to let the others descend. "It's your initiate's fault. He was distracting me."

"Quiet," Brachyura shushed. "We're in enemy territory now. We speak only when necessary."

Kumbha tugged three times on the rope before swinging the barred gate closed, sealing the shaft behind them.

The darkness was so absolute that Reed might as well have been blind. He closed his eyes and gently massaged his eyelids just like Jeffson had taught him. When he opened them again, he could just make out the colossal form of Brachyura.

"Where are we?"

"In a small cavern," Brachyura replied, "with numerous exits. All appear to have been made recently." He sighed. "My brother was a fool to think filling in the Pit would stop them."

"He was unaware of the portals," Kumbha reminded him. "Collapsing all the tunnels was not necessarily an ineffective strategy … if the greylings had no other way in."

"Which way?" Reed asked impatiently.

"I don't know," Brachyura answered honestly. "I am unsure of which path we should take."

"Kriari," the First of the Twelve uttered confidently, pointing down one of the passageways.

"I agree with our brother," Kumbha said. "I feel it tugging at me. It calls to us all. It's almost as if it's ... calling us home."

"Or leading us to our deaths," muttered Vohanen.

"That's enough of that," Jelaïa said to him sharply. "We voted to trust in the Twelve's guidance. This expedition will never work if we start second-guessing every decision. Reed, do you have the thread?"

"I do, although I can't see much further than the end of my nose."

Brachyura huffed, took the reel and tied one end around one of the many lumps that protruded from the bedrock. He gave it an experimental pull.

"That should hold. Attach it to your belt, Old Guard, so you have both hands free. It's wide enough here to walk two abreast. We will guide you."

The tunnel chosen by the Twelve sloped steadily downwards. Reed was helped along by Brachyura, who was not the most careful or attentive of guides. Kriari was even worse, steering Vohanen into the wall of the tunnel by accident or becoming distracted and failing to prevent him from bumping into Jelaïa.

"We're close," Kumbha said in a hushed tone. "Prepare yourselves."

They stepped into another small cavern. The stone archway was much as Ka'arka had described, covered in indecipherable inscriptions that glowed in the dark.

"They ... are moving," Reed said, fascinated. "Ka'arka did not tell us this. See, look at that one, it rotates like a wheel."

"Do not stare at them for too long," Brachyura cautioned. "We do not know what damage they might cause to the human mind."

The strange runes gave off enough light for Reed to make out the five pools surrounding the archway. The one closest to him bore the carving of a wolf. "Arelium," he said quietly, tracing the deep gouges that made up the wolf's head.

"We will see our Barony again," Jelaïa said, reading his thoughts.

"I ... am not sure that Arelium is where I wish to go when all this is over," Reed replied. "There are so many other places to visit, so many other people to meet."

"Like Syrella, you mean?"

"Pit, is it really that obvious?"

Jelaïa smiled. "It is to me. Just don't do what I did. Don't wait too long before you tell her how you feel."

"We should hurry," Brachyura interrupted. "I will go first." He drew his axe and stood before the portal, the glittering runes reflected in his eyes. He took a step and faltered.

"Courage, Brother," Kumbha said, coming to stand beside him. "We will go through together." The dark-skinned giant took her hand, and the two siblings walked through the portal. Reed watched as the liquid covered their arms, faces, and necks. Then they were gone.

"Kriari!" The shaggy figure leapt fearlessly after them, creating even more ripples in the tarry surface.

Vohanen scowled. "He seemed particularly eager," he

said warily. "I wonder what's waiting on the other side that he's so impatient to reach?"

"There's only one way to find out," Jelaïa said, stretching out her hands. Reed took her left hand in his right. It felt so small and fragile. *She's still so young,* he thought. *Yet, she's already lived through so much. She possesses such strength and self-confidence. Resilient. Like her father.*

The portal loomed over them, the runes swirling.

"Any last words?" Vohanen ventured, clasping Jelaïa's other hand.

"I am glad you are both here with me," Reed said. "My comrades. My friends. Let us finish this. On three. One, two—"

The darkness enveloped them.

⪜

"Wake up, Merad!" He opened his bleary eyes to see the concerned face of his mother. "Something terrible has happened." Behind her, his big frame filling the doorway of the hut, stood Terrin, the stablemaster, a guttering torch in one hand.

Reed threw off his goatskin rug and laced up his leather jerkin.

"Hurry, lad," Terrin growled. "He hasn't got much time left."

It was still dark out but the full moon lit the path that led from Reed's hut through Jaelem's wooden palisade and down to the grove of oaks surrounding the lake. A semicircle of villagers had gathered around one of the largest trees that had seemingly toppled over, its age-old roots poking up into the air like knobbly fingers. Soft torchlight illuminated a crumpled shape half-obscured by the massive trunk.

A bush or a pile of autumn leaves, Reed told himself. His pace slowed. He found he didn't want to go any further. His mother tugged on his arm. "We have to go, child. We have to see."

"I don't want to. I want to go back to bed." He tried to wriggle free from his mother's grasp, but she held him fast, dragging him closer to the fallen tree.

His father lay on his back, his pelvis and lower body crushed by the oak. His eyes were dull and unfocused. An axe lay next to him, just out of reach of his twitching fingers.

"Went out to chop wood all alone in the middle of the night, stupid man," Terrin said to Reed's mother. "He's normally so conscientious, I don't know what came over him."

"It's my fault," Reed's mother replied tearfully. "We argued. I said some things I shouldn't have. He said he needed to get some fresh air …"

"Aye, well. You didn't tell him to go cut down a tree, did you? He made that decision on his own."

Terrin turned to Reed. "Merad, lad. He's asking for you."

A dreadful terror clawed at Reed's throat. "I … can't."

"It wasn't a request. Go to him, or I will carry you there myself."

Reed inched closer. His bare feet trod in something sticky. Blood. His father's blood. Another couple of steps brought him to the dying man's side.

"Merad," his father coughed.

This is not my father, Reed thought. *My father is so strong he can lift me onto his shoulders with one arm. His voice is so*

loud that it scares away the frogs when we are out in his boat.
This wasted, broken thing is only his shadow.

"You will have to look after your mother now, Merad,"
his father continued weakly. "It will be up to you to provide
food and lodging. You fish well, at least. I taught you that
much."

His body was wracked by a jerking spasm. "I am sorry
we could not spend more time together. There are so many
things I wanted to show you. Be true. Be true to yourself.
I hope … I hope you will remember me." His head lolled
sideways, slack-jawed.

Lifeless eyes. Like a dead fish.

Reed opened his mouth and screamed.

∾

"Reed. REED!" A rough hand on his shoulder, shaking him.
He was on his knees, black liquid dripping from his face and
hair.

"I'm all right," he croaked. His stomach heaved, and he
vomited more of the stuff. "What in the Pit just happened?"

Jelaïa was sitting next to him, fresh tears on her cheeks.
"I saw my father die," she said in a small voice. "I saw Praxis
stab him in the stomach and sit on the edge of the bed until
he bled to death. What sort of a person does that? Watches
calmly as another being expires?"

"A person with no compassion. No empathy," Brachyura
said. "A person like Zygos, my brother."

Reed spat in an attempt to remove the oily taste from his
mouth. "I also relived my father's last moments," he said. "I
had almost forgotten them. It happened when I was a young

boy. He was killed by a falling tree. An accident. A stupid accident." He sighed. "What did you see, Vohanen?"

The Knight of Kriari was standing apart from the others, his back turned. "Avor," he said softly. Reed knew not to press him further.

"Wh ... what is this place?" Jelaïa asked hesitantly. Reed wiped the last of the liquid from his eyes. The portal had brought them to a bleak, monochromatic wasteland; a featureless expanse of grey mud and blackened tree stumps stretching out in all directions. Dense clouds the colour of lead hung menacingly overhead, blocking out the sun and casting a pallid sheen across the landscape.

The air was thick and stale. It reminded Reed of when, many years ago, the Old Guard had reopened one of the abandoned signal towers. He had unbarred the door himself and had been the first to enter and breathe the air that had been trapped there. Dry and musty, like the inside of a tomb.

There was an uncomfortable stillness about the place, not just quietness, but the complete absence of sound. No animals, no plant life. Nothing.

"We are no longer in the nine Baronies," Brachyura said darkly. The dim light dulled the brilliance of his plate armour, making it look worn and tarnished. "But I can't shake this odd sense of familiarity, as if I have been here before."

"You're right, I feel it too," Kumbha agreed.

"Kriari."

Behind them the archway thrummed, the runes squirming as if alive.

"How do we even orient ourselves?" Reed wondered out

loud. "There are no landmarks. No variation in the terrain. Everything is flat and grey."

"It pains me to say this, but we will have to split up," Brachyura answered reluctantly.

"Wait," Jelaïa said, squinting at something on the horizon. "Isn't that smoke?"

Reed followed her gaze. About a mile or so away, a patch of cloud looked significantly lighter than the rest. "I'm getting old, my Lady. It could be."

"Where there's smoke, there's fire," Vohanen quoted, peering at the distant smudge.

"Yes, but whose fire? For all we know, it could be an army of greylings."

"Aye, or it could be the weaver. The sooner we slit her throat, the better."

"Well, we won't find any answers by staying here," Jelaïa said, clutching her axe-shaped medallion protectively. "Let's at least start heading in that direction. If it turns out to be something dangerous, we can always turn back."

They squelched off through the mud. Reed's leather boots were soon covered in grey slime. It felt as if the earth was purposefully trying to slow him down; clinging to his feet and forcing him to exert himself for every step he took.

A soft breeze caressed his face, bringing with it the smell of something sweet and sickly.

His thoughts turned to his father. The dream had been so real, the images so much sharper than the hazy memory he had of that terrible night. He could almost see him now, a blurred figure waiting on the path ahead, arms outstretched in greeting. Reed blinked, and the figure became another scraggly tree, its leafless branches mimicking human limbs. Reed sighed and lowered his gaze.

They slogged onwards. No one spoke. All were lost in their own misery. The changeless, never-ending plains were soul-crushing, and the oppressive weight of the low-hanging clouds only added to the burden. Again, Reed was reminded of the suffocating blackness of the Pit, slowly draining the Old Guard of their sanity. The same thing was happening here, the grey of the mud blending with the grey of the clouds to form an ashen void.

What if it's not smoke? What if it's a mirage? Will we be able to find our way back to the portal? Or will we be stuck here, trudging round and round in circles until we die of madness or starvation? Turn back. We have to turn back.

He was about to voice his discontent to the others when something changed on the horizon, its uniformity broken by a flash of colour.

"Pit, you were right, Jelaïa," Vohanen murmured happily. "It's a building. The smoke you saw is coming from its chimney." He uncorked his wine skin and took a congratulatory swig.

Reed felt a flood of relief at hearing this, and his mood improved considerably. "Maybe they've spotted us and are cooking up a feast to celebrate our arrival!"

"Careful," warned Brachyura. "You have already forgotten what I said earlier. We are in enemy territory. We have no idea what manner of beast stalks these lands."

The building turned out to be a stone cottage roughly the size of Reed's old barracks, with a sagging roof and round glass windows. Someone had painstakingly painted the door a dark shade of blue, enough to make it stand out from the hues of grey.

Brachyura readied his axe and motioned for Reed and Vohanen to do the same. A shadow passed in front of the window. A creaking of floorboards. Someone was inside.

"If it is the weaver, we give her no time to prepare herself," the Fourth of the Twelve stated firmly. "We must strike fast and hard."

He rapped on the door with the butt of his axe. "Coming, coming," a female voice grumbled from inside. There was a series of clicks, and the door swung open. The voice belonged to a wizened old woman with a walnut-shaped face and a prominent flat nose. Whatever hair she had once had was nearly gone; a few snowy-white wisps were all that remained on her liver-spotted scalp. She was dressed in a simple woollen tunic that had been patched so many times it was impossible to identify its original colour. Two wrinkled bare feet poked out from under the tunic, and the end of a metal chain was clamped around one ankle.

Brachyura dropped his axe. It hit the mud with a squelch. "I ... I know that face," he stammered. "You are—"

"Shala," Kriari said mournfully. "Sister."

Shala, Sixth of the Twelve, smiled sadly, revealing dirty yellow teeth. "I always knew this day would come. That you would break free from her control."

Kumbha looked puzzled. "What do you mean? What day?"

"The day you would come back here to punish me, Sister." She gazed at them with rheumy eyes. "The day you would finally decide to take my life in retaliation for all I have done."

"You speak in riddles, Sister," Brachyura said with a frown. "In retaliation for what?"

"For bringing you back. For helping her bring you back from the dead."

CHAPTER 17

THE HARDER THEY FALL

"It has been said that the definition of insanity is doing the same thing over and over again and expecting different results. I disagree. If I swing an axe at a tree once, it will stay standing. However, if I continue swinging, eventually it will fall. Sometimes repetition, no matter how strange it may seem, can lead to a different outcome."

JEFFSON, 427 AT

❦

I N THE TIME it took Ner'alla to explain exactly what the gliders were and how they worked, a sizeable number of Knights of Kriari had joined the group. Krelbe sent two of them off to find the man named Stick and escort him to the cathedral with the Crimson Wings. Xandris had also disappeared, mumbling about having something else that 'might help'.

"We only had time to make six, I'm afraid," Ner'alla said as they crossed the square. "I brought what little willow wood and fabric I had left with me from Morlak, and I haven't been able to find much more here. Plenty of rope, though."

"Six. Who should pilot them?" Jeffson asked, already fairly sure of the answer.

"With Vohanen gone and Taleck not yet fully healed, the command of the Knights of Kriari falls to me," Krelbe said reluctantly. "Much as I hate the responsibility, I can't go."

"Ka'arka and I will organise the Knights of Brachyura," said Aldarin with an inappropriate amount of cheerfulness. "So, Sir Caddox has no reason not to be one of the pilots. Unless you have any objection to my orders, Caddox?"

"No ... Scrier," the broad-shouldered knight muttered through a clenched jaw.

"Excellent. Then, you will not be needing your horse." He swung himself up onto Caddox's panting stallion. "I'll do my best to move the men off the ramparts and into the abandoned buildings. They should be safe there. Xer'ana. Ka'arka. Join me as soon as you are able. May the Twelve be with you." He wheeled his horse around and thundered off down the road.

Ner'alla flashed a smile. "A man of action, I see. Jeffson, you have flown before, I take it you will be participating?"

"I suppose so. You're enjoying this, aren't you?"

"Just happy to be of some use at last. My manservant is especially proficient at manoeuvring the gliders. He will be your third. I suggest Sir Krelbe chooses three Knights of

Kriari who have already used the Wings in Morlak to make up your numbers."

"That'll be easy," Krelbe growled. "Only three survived the battle with Mithuna. I'll send for them. What about our ... other plan?"

"The powder? It can still work, but we'll have to wait until those flying beasts are distracted, otherwise they'll tear us to pieces before we can get the barrels in place. Then the fuses need to be set. That's a lot of work; it'll be us versus the setting sun. We'll be cutting it close. Cutting it very close indeed."

"Those who risk nothing, gain nothing," said Jeffson with mock seriousness. "I believe that was the motto of a particularly narcissistic band of hot-headed thieves. What were they called?"

"Those idiots? The Red Sparrows," Ner'alla replied, his eyes twinkling. "Stupid but courageous. Maybe I should take a leaf out of their book, eh, Nissus?"

Jeffson grasped the other man's wrist. "I'll see you when I land ... my friend. We have not always seen eye to eye, but I do wish to thank you. Thank you for what you did for Daelle and Cerra. I think you made the right choice."

"It was my pleasure. I only wish I could have done more." The portly Da'arran bowed and ambled off to find Bansworth.

There was a metallic clank as Caddox pulled on the straps of his steel breastplate. He had been removing his armour as they talked, keeping only his gauntlets and vambraces. After a moment's hesitation, he added his axe to the pile. "Why the cathedral?" he said gruffly, staring at the large building with a hint of trepidation.

"It's the highest point in Klief, Sir Knight," Jeffson explained patiently. "Remember what Stick told you. You're not flying. You're falling. A controlled fall but falling nonetheless."

"I hate this. Having to follow orders from that *scrier*. I cannot fathom why Manfeld made him first master of the temple."

"I'm sure he had his reasons, Sir Knight," Jeffson said as they passed into the shadow of the cathedral spire. "Although if I understand correctly, Sir Aldarin has made known his intention to relinquish his title. Something about having already sworn a previous oath to the Baroness of Arelium."

A spark of ambition flared to life in Caddox's eyes. "Stepping down, eh? Then, we will need a new first master. And with both Manfeld and Praedora dead, my only real competition will be that bumbling scrier Ka'arka. And who will the Knights of Brachyura choose? The man who saved them from the flying lizard-beasts or the man who has spent the last few months in the Shakalla Desert?" He pushed open the heavy doors. "This is good news, Jeffson. Very good news. I can come out of this a hero, as long as I don't kill myself with this infernal contraption of yours."

A strange man, thought Jeffson. *So much anger and resentment. Hiding his feelings of inadequacy behind a layer of bluster and insults. Yet, there is bravery and courage in him also. I saw it in Morlak. What a great man he could become if he stopped comparing himself constantly to Aldarin and found his own path.*

"You have no need to prove your worth to me, in any case, Sir Knight. If you had not stepped out of that alleyway in Morlak, I would be dead. Thank you for that."

Sir Caddox seemed quite taken aback by Jeffson's casual remark and fell silent. They walked up the aisle to the altar where Xandris and three Knights of Kriari were talking with Makara.

"The agamids are fast and agile but not very bright," the Tenth of the Twelve was saying. "Work together and try to use the element of surprise to your advantage."

"Agamids?" Caddox queried.

"Yes, that is what we used to call them. We fought a small number of the creatures during the Battle of the Northern Plains and came close to wiping them out. There were some sightings in the years that followed, but they became increasingly rare before disappearing altogether. I must admit, I thought they had been completely exterminated."

"Where's our launch point?" asked Jeffson.

"There's a balcony near the top of the spire. It's cramped but there should be enough space to deploy the gliders. The bad news is that there is no runway. You will have to launch from the balcony itself and hope that the initial dive will provide sufficient acceleration."

"I see you are familiar with the working principles of gliders, Lord," said Jeffson respectfully.

Makara gave a tired laugh. "I am. One of the many projects that were still in their infancy when my siblings were alive. Mina was working on her ballistae. Guanna on his weapons of war. Brachyura on his walls and fortifications … Who knows what the nine Baronies would look like today if we had all survived another three hundred years?"

Jeffson chose his next words carefully. "Sir Reed told me what happened, Lord. Down in the Pit. How they died. It wasn't your fault."

"Not their deaths, no. But my behaviour in the years that followed ..." Makara looked up at the multi-faceted stained-glass windows. "Have you heard the saying 'If enough people believe in a lie, it becomes the truth'? My siblings and I were venerated like gods. And despite knowing full-well what we really were, I think, somewhere along the way, I became so self-deluded I started acting like one."

"Lord, apologies, but we need to hurry," Xandris cut in urgently. "Daylight is fading fast."

"Of course. It is I who am sorry. Please ignore the idiotic ramblings of this old man. Tell them about your jars."

Xandris smacked his forehead with the palm of his hand. "Yes! I almost forgot!" He pulled out a bag from under one of the pews. Jeffson could see that it was full to bursting with glass containers.

"Something else I have been working on," Xandris said proudly. "It actually dates back to when I was in Kessrin and an assassin nearly killed Jelaïa, but I digress." He fished around in the bag and produced a glass vial. Green smoke swirled around inside.

"It's poisonous, I think," he continued, giving the vial a shake. "Derived from the same substance that the assassin used in the wine. I've only been able to try it out on rodents so far, and I am happy to say none has survived."

"What if the vials break before we can throw them?" Caddox asked warily.

"Um, you'll have to hold your breath? Look, it's not perfect, but it should give you some means of harming the enemy without getting too close. Unless anyone has any better ideas?"

"We'll take them," Jeffson said firmly, filling his pockets with a half-dozen vials. "Where's Stick?"

"He went on ahead with the first two gliders. The remaining four are by the stairs."

The disassembled gliders were each roughly the size of a rucksack with two long poles of spruce protruding from their backs. Jeffson picked one up and began the long, arduous climb up the hundreds of spiralling steps that would take him to the balcony.

Minutes later, he arrived at his destination, his chest heaving with effort. Stick had already finished work on one of the gliders and was close to finishing the second.

How in the Pit did that man climb all those stairs with one leg? Jeffson thought to himself, studying the Morlakian as he pulled the dark red fabric tight over the wooden frame. "Don't just stand there, Nissus," Stick admonished. "Come 'ere an' 'elp me with the 'arness."

Jeffson crouched down beside him, uncoiling the length of rope that would be used to attach the pilot to his craft. "I've already told you, I don't use that name anymore."

"Ah, yes. Why is that? You can't change a man just by changing his name."

"Then, why keep yours a secret?"

"Apples an' oranges," smirked Stick. "I 'aven't changed my name, I just choose not to throw it about willy-nilly. Pull that tighter."

Jeffson gave the rope an angry tug. There was something that infuriated him about the other man, but he couldn't quite put his finger on it. He thought back to what his mother used to tell him. *A good core.* Maybe that was it? He had spent so long around loyal, brave, and fundamentally good people recently that it was becoming harder and harder to tolerate people who were obviously the complete opposite.

Caddox was the next to arrive, panting and puffing. "So. Many. Stairs." He leant against the balcony, the columned parapet the only thing between him and a two-hundred-foot drop.

"Ain't enough space up 'ere for all the gliders," Stick said. "You two take these, and I'll get the next lot ready."

Jeffson risked a glance over the edge, the cold wind making his eyes water. Directly below them stood the infirmary, the keep, and the third wall — the last line of defence between the greylings and the inner city. Red-uniformed Arelians kept watch, armed with bows and spears, reinforced by a scattering of Knights of Kriari. By the gatehouse, Bansworth and Krelbe were loading the last of the black powder onto the cart.

From there, the main road cut straight through the half-abandoned buildings to join the second wall where the attack was still underway. The allied forces were fleeing the ramparts, running for the relative safety of the dwellings and storefronts closest to the wall. The agamids circled lazily overhead, occasionally diving down to plunge their claws into the exposed backs of the retreating soldiers. Jeffson could make out the miniature form of Aldarin, still on the battlements, waving his hands in the air, trying either to keep the defenders moving or to draw the enemy's attention.

"Wind's against us," Stick commented. "Don't forget to use the altitude to your advantage."

Jeffson didn't reply, only walked over to the glider and pulled on the harness. The last time he had used a Crimson Wing it had been a never-ending nightmare. No, that wasn't true. It *had* ended but in a tree instead of in the field he had been aiming for. He had smacked into it with enough force to break his leg. And now he was about to do it all again.

His thoughts turned to Cerra. The thick wall of ice she had built around herself was slowly thawing. Time, patience, and understanding were the keys to bringing her back. Unfortunately, all three were presently in short supply.

The wind filled the dark red wings strapped to his back. He stepped up onto the parapet. Jeffson was not a religious man, but his view of the distant cobbles prompted him to utter a brief prayer to the Twelve.

He jumped.

Or rather, he dived, keeping his body ramrod straight, tilting his head downwards. The cathedral spire flashed past in a blur as he accelerated. Choosing exactly when to pull out of the dive was critical. Too soon and he would lose valuable speed; too late and they would be scraping him off the cobbles.

He caught a glimpse of stained glass and yanked on the harness while simultaneously dropping his legs. The glider levelled out, and he shot over the third wall ramparts, so close to the battlements that he could have reached down and touched them. He felt an updraught to his right and turned slightly to use it, gaining a little lift.

The sun was low on the horizon, a visible reminder of the imminent greyling assault. Jeffson risked a glance behind him and saw that Caddox and a Knight of Kriari had launched, although both were at a lower elevation. They would soon be spotted by the agamids. He, however, was much higher and still had the element of surprise; the creatures were looking everywhere except up.

From orphan, to thief, to killer, to manservant, he thought, reaching prudently into his jerkin pocket where he had secreted a handful of vials. *And now, a killer once again.* He brought out a glass vial, aimed at the head of the nearest agamid, and sent the deadly projectile hurtling towards it with a flick of his wrist.

The vial span past the startled creature's snout and shattered on the wing of another just below it. Acrid green smoke spilled forth, eating through the thin membrane. Dissolving. Destroying.

The wounded reptilian screeched in pain. Its remaining wing was not enough to keep it aloft, and it plummeted earthwards, rebounding off one of the mangonels with a crack of broken bone.

Jeffson was so focused on the thing's plight that he was nearly disembowelled by his original target, its sharp claws raking a line along the leather of his jerkin. Sixty lizard-like heads swivelled in his direction.

He had their full attention.

Four more creatures broke off their assault on the second wall and swerved northwards on an intercept course. One lucky swipe of those claws would tear his Crimson Wing to shreds. He had to keep his distance.

He clipped an updraught, bouncing over his attackers, releasing vials as he soared overhead. He was rewarded with a chorus of hissing shrieks, and three more agamids fell from the sky like stones, their flesh corroded by Xandris's concoction.

The glider was well past the second wall now and approaching the scarred remains of the first. Jeffson shifted his body to the left, wheeling round in a wide one-hundred-and-eighty-degree arc. The wind was at his back. Looking down, he saw something that made his body grow ice-cold.

The greylings were beginning to move.

Pit!

The second wall was deserted. There was nothing standing between the greyling horde and the allied defenders cowering in the shelter of the abandoned buildings. Aldarin, Ka'arka, and the rest of the Knights of Brachyura were going to be butchered.

Their one last hope was the black powder, *if* Krelbe and Bansworth could get the barrels to the wall unmolested. The five other Crimson Wings had joined the fray, lighting up the sky with flashes of green as they hurled vials left and right. More viridescent smoke billowed up from the ramparts below, adding to the confusion. A young bearded Knight of Kriari misjudged his turn and collided with the agamid he had been trying to avoid, sending them both to their deaths.

And then they were five.

Caddox was in trouble, an agamid hard on his tail. The Knight of Brachyura threw a vial behind him, but the creature dodged it easily with a flick of its wings. Jeffson pulled up to slow his descent and dispatched Caddox's pursuer with a well-aimed shot. He whisked past the astonished knight, tapping two fingers to his forehead in an unofficial salute as he flew by.

A laugh escaped his lips, and Jeffson realised that he was enjoying himself for the first time in many years. A blur of movement from down below caught his eye: Krelbe and the cart! They had to keep the agamids busy just a little longer.

The arrival of the dour-faced Knight of Kriari had not gone unnoticed. A trio of enemy fliers banked in perfect formation and homed in on the unprotected barrels. Jeffson scanned the skies. They had lost another Knight of Kriari. Four left. Caddox and the last knight were in the process of landing, they would be no help. Stick was holding his own against a half-dozen agamids, bobbing and weaving like he had been born in the harness. But he was far away. Too far.

There was no one who could reach the creatures in time.

No one except Jeffson.

He pushed his glider into another dive, the wind slicing painfully into his face. A trembling hand dug around in his pocket. Three vials left. Three vials for three agamids.

The sound of thousands upon thousands of clawed feet echoed across the plains. The greylings were minutes from the first wall, chanting and howling, herded into position by scores of threshers. There was no vanguard this time. Zygos had sent the full strength of his army. No tactics. No scheming. Simply an overwhelming grey tide.

Jeffson swooped within range of his trio of targets. His first throw hit an agamid on its tail. It listed sideways like a rudderless boat.

One.

Another vial. Another creature down, the green fumes eating at its face like acid.

Two.

A single agamid remained. Jeffson took a deep breath. An image flashed before his eyes. His daughter playing in the gardens of Klief, her head wreathed in flowers. He smiled, his hand steady. The battlements loomed.

Jeffson tossed the flask.

And missed.

The agamid hissed, its claws outstretched. Krelbe looked up at the sound, his eyes widening in terror.

There was only one thing left to do.

Jeffson grabbed hold of the thing's tail and yanked with all his might. He let go of his harness and wrapped his arms around its squirming body, crushing its wings in his tight embrace. The wooden ribs of his glider snapped. Jeffson and his captive fell from the sky.

The wind roared in his ears.

The hard stone of the ramparts rushed up to meet him.

Then his world became pain, and he blacked out.

CHAPTER 18
THE SHROUD

"Initially, I thought that using the church of the Twelve as a means to keep the memories of my siblings alive was the perfect solution, but I had not taken into consideration the myriad alternative religious cults that gained traction over the same period. For example, the Knights of Kriari and some Morlakians believe that the dead go to rejoin their ancestors, whereas the Da'arrans are devoted to the idea of The Great Lake. I fear now that there are places in the nine Baronies where the priests of the Twelve will be ridiculed."

HIGH PRIEST OF THE TWELVE, 313 AT

᠅

"Y OU HELPED HER?" Reed exclaimed. "How could you have even considered such a thing? She was your mortal enemy. Makara told us what happened. She killed your brothers and sisters!"

Shala replied with a wan smile. "Why don't you come inside? I was just brewing a spot of tea." She turned with some difficulty, stepping over the chain attached to her ankle, and shuffled back into the gloom.

"A trick?" growled Vohanen, shifting his grip on his tower shield.

"I don't think so," Kumbha said. "If it isn't Shala, then it's a perfect imitation. She may have aged, but her mannerisms and gestures are just as I remember them."

"Or what the weaver wants you to remember."

"Oh, stop it," Jelaïa huffed. "Not everything is an ambush waiting to happen. I, for one, am tired, thirsty, and in need of a cup of tea." She strode confidently inside. Reed, with an apologetic shrug at Vohanen, followed.

He wasn't quite sure what he was expecting, but the interior was drearily ... normal. No greylings lying in wait, no dead bodies on the floor or symbols painted on the walls. There was a round table, some chairs, two large cupboards, a bed, a washstand, and a small curtained-off area that was presumably a latrine. The only light came from the fireplace opposite the door. Over the fire hung a clay teapot, steam already pouring from its spout with a petulant whine.

The furniture had an odd look to it. There was no metal to be seen, only wood: handmade but appearing grown rather than put together. Each chair was one unique piece without any visible joints or nails, and the table seemed to sprout out of the floor like a gigantic mushroom, supported by a single leg at its centre. Wrapped around the leg was a long length of iron chain, the same chain as the one attached to Shala's ankle. She was a prisoner, then. A prisoner of her own house.

The old woman hobbled over to the fire and used a glove to lift the top of the teapot, giving the contents a tentative sniff. "I can't promise it will be good," she said. "Weaver brings me comestibles back from the nine Baronies occasionally, as an afterthought really, so I end up with all manner of things. Little girl, would you bring me some mugs, please?"

"My name is Jelaïa del Arelium."

"Oh, an Arelian, are you? Now you say it, you do look a bit like the Baron. Nice man, he was. Very nice. Top shelf of the cupboard, dear."

Brachyura ducked under the lintel and propped his axe up near the door. "This resembles your handiwork," he said to Shala, gesturing at one of the chairs. "Your gift still works here?"

"It does," the old woman replied, carefully using the glove to remove the teapot. "Although it is possible it only works because Weaver allows it."

"What is your gift?" asked Jelaïa curiously, setting four mugs down on the table.

Shala looked at her strangely. "You ask what you should already know, little girl. The initiates of my Order kept detailed records of what the Twelve could do. Have you not read them?"

"I ... no, Lady, none of us has. The location of your temple has been lost, and as for your knights ... I am not sure any still live."

Shala's mouth opened and shut soundlessly. "My Order is ... no more? Since when? How did this happen?"

"Sixty years ago. We call it the Schism," Vohanen said as Jelaïa returned to fetch more mugs. "The Orders were split apart on what we now know to be false pretences."

"Split apart ..." Shala muttered to herself. "She told me no one would get hurt. She *promised* me no one would get hurt." She poured out seven cups of steaming hot brew. It smelt of moss and damp leaves.

Her rheumy eyes found Brachyura's. "Sixty years! Have I really been gone that long?"

"No, my Sister," Brachyura said gently, taking her hand. "It has been much, much longer than that."

It took them a good half-hour to explain, from Makara's escape, to the Schism and the shadow war that followed, to the return of the greylings and the battles of Arelium, Kessrin, Morlak, Talth, and Klief. Shala was weeping by the time they had finished, her tea cold and undrunk.

"Three hundred years," she moaned. "Weaver hid this from me. I can't believe it ... three centuries stuck here. I try to keep track of the time, but it's impossible. There is no sun here. No day-night cycle. No weather. No seasons. When I sleep, I do not know if it is for twelve hours or twelve days. The same overcast skies and endless flat grey earth greet me every time I open my eyes."

Reed thought back to his weeks spent in the damp cell under Morlak keep, so bored and lonely that he had started talking to a rat. What Shala had been through was worse. Infinitely worse. It was a miracle that she was still sane. In fact, come to think of it, maybe she wasn't.

"A prison," he said out loud. "One of considerable size but a prison nonetheless. What do you call this place?"

Shala dried her eyes with the sleeve of her tunic. "Weaver uses the term 'Shroud'," she said, and Reed noticed, not for the first time, that she had dropped the determiner 'the' before weaver.

"The Shroud?"

"Yes. She suspects we are in a sort of limbo, a space on the border between the lands of the living … and whatever comes after we cease to exist. A final barrier before the unknown. A Shroud that covers the faces of the dead."

Reed shivered despite the warmth of the fire. "She suspects? This isn't her home?"

"Now, maybe, but she wasn't born here, she arrived from somewhere else."

"Why did you choose to help her?" asked Brachyura suddenly, his voice low.

"Kriari …" his brother warned.

Shala wrung her hands nervously. "No, no, Kriari. Brachyura has a right to know. You all have a right to know. Little girl, would you help an old woman and pour me some more tea? Thank you. Where shall I start?"

"The portal," Brachyura said, rubbing his bald scalp. "You fell through. Or rather, I pushed you through. Start from there."

Jelaïa emptied out the cold tea and refilled the cup. Shala took a long sip. "Hah! I was stronger then. Much stronger. We fought … I think, at first, we were evenly matched; the wounds she had received at the hands of our brothers and sisters had made her weak. But for every minute spent here, she seemed to grow stronger and I weaker. Once she had recovered enough to suppress my gift, it was over."

"Your gift!" Jelaïa said. "You haven't yet told us what it was."

Shala drained her cup and slammed it down on the table, cracking it into several pieces. She placed one large shard of clay in her hand and concentrated for a moment.

After a few seconds, the shard came to life, wriggling like an earthworm. Reed let out a surprised yelp and stumbled backwards, nearly setting his vermilion cloak on fire.

"It's difficult to explain," the Sixth of the Twelve murmured, her eyes focusing on her palm. The piece of clay became a ball of putty then stretched into an oblong shape. Four tiny legs appeared as the putty was moulded into a miniature horse, complete with tail and mane.

"It's like the earth sings to me," she continued. "Earth, wood, flesh, rock. I can hear them. And I can sing back."

"This house ..." Reed stammered. "This table ..."

"Yes. My gift does have obvious limitations. The song of metal still eludes me. Anything metallic you see here was brought through the portal by Weaver. Also, the larger the target, the harder it becomes, and anything over nine or ten feet long is nigh impossible for me to manipulate. Oh, and I can only transform the shape of an existing object, never create matter that isn't already there." She set down the finished horse and gestured at the cottage walls. "Plenty of trees in this forsaken place, but I still have to cobble the planks together myself."

"The weaver allows you to use your gift," Brachyura said. "What did you have to give her in return?"

"I ... It's not that simple. Once she had beaten me into unconsciousness, she chained me to the largest tree she could find, a tree that has now become this table." She gave her leg a shake, making the chain around her ankle jangle. "There she left me. She was angry. Angry that her plan had failed. She had been utterly convinced that we would agree to her terms. The Twelve were to be allies, wiping out the human race so that the greylings could prosper. She could not comprehend that we would be willing to put their lives above our own."

Kriari snorted contemptuously.

"That's what I tried to tell her," Shala said with a smile. "But she would not listen. Her only priority was rebuilding the portal. Not the one here, which was still standing, but the one in the Morlakian Pit. Without it, not only could she not travel physically to the nine Baronies, but she had no sure means of communicating with the greylings."

"No *sure* means?" Jelaïa asked.

"Yes. From what little I understand, she could still send her thoughts through the portal. It's just that there was no anchor point. No fixed destination. It was like writing a message, putting it in a bottle, and throwing it into the sea in the hope that it would reach its recipient."

"And yet, the portal was rebuilt," Kumbha said.

"Eventually. As I've already explained, it is difficult to track the passage of time here, but it must have taken years. Hundreds of years. Sending instructions haphazardly through the void in the hope that they would be heard. And during that time, I plotted. I schemed. I searched for a way out. Nothing."

Reed swallowed a mouthful of tea. "What about food? How did you survive without any sort of nourishment?"

"Another side-effect of the Shroud. There is no hunger here and no starvation. The body withers but does not die. The mind rots but does not dissolve. I no longer need to eat or drink. The tea is an eccentricity, nothing more."

"And so, the portal was rebuilt," Vohanen rumbled. "And yet ... we are no closer to understanding how the Twelve were reborn."

Shala stroked the miniature horse. "One day, Weaver came to me. I was delirious, talking to ghosts and shadows, pretending I was somewhere else. She asked me if I would like to see my brothers and sisters again."

A tear rolled down her cheek. "I was so lonely, Brachyura. So, so, alone. You cannot imagine what it was like, waking up every morning knowing that the only company I would have all day was my own conscience. Dreading that very moment, the moment my eyes opened and my day began, condemned to the same grey sky, the same solitary, repetitive existence. I ..." she hesitated. "She offered me the one thing I could not refuse ... What would you do if your worst enemy told you there was a way to be with your brothers and sisters again? To touch them? To talk to them?"

"I do not know," answered Brachyura truthfully.

"I resisted for a time, but depression wore me down until, eventually, I capitulated ... no longer a prisoner but an accomplice. And my gift was restored."

"She needed your gift to bring us back."

A look of terrible anguish crossed Shala's face, there and gone again like a flash of lightning in a storm. "Yes. Perhaps it would be better if I show you." She twisted her wrist, and the floor under Reed's feet turned to mud, the wooden planks sluggishly reshaping themselves into a trapdoor five feet wide. Shala rose to her feet, swaying slightly as if drunk. "Down we go. Down into the depths of my greatest shame. My greatest guilt. Old Guard, open the trapdoor if you would?"

It took Reed a moment to realise that she was talking to him. He crouched down. There was no discernible lock, only a small hole in the surface wide enough for five fingers. He thrust his scarred right hand into the aperture and pulled. The trapdoor opened easily.

"Humans, you will need some light," Shala said, pointing at the fire. Vohanen set down his tower shield, chose a stick from the woodpile stacked next to the fireplace and set it alight. The flame reflected off the metal of the short sword that he held in his other hand.

"You will not need that," Shala said.

Vohanen glared at her. "I only take advice from those I trust. And you, Lady, I do not trust in the slightest."

"I understand. Then, I will go first." She shuffled over to the trapdoor and lowered herself down the ladder into the darkness, her chain trailing after her.

"Well, what do we think?" Jelaïa asked.

Reed sighed. "I think the only way we are going to find the answers we seek is by going down into that cellar." He peered into the open trapdoor. No sign of Shala.

So, here I go again, he thought, putting his foot on the first rung. *Descending into obscurity and danger. It would be ironic if I wasn't trembling with fear.*

The cellar was as dark as the Pit. He waited for a few moments until Vohanen joined him, his torch revealing walls and a ceiling of hard earth. Crates lined one side and further back, Shala stood before a row of animal carcasses hanging from meat hooks. She beckoned them over.

"Through here," she said. Behind the row of meat was a plain wooden door. Reed went to push the nearest carcass aside when something caught his eye. A gleam in the torchlight. Frowning, he examined the carcass more closely. There was a ring stuck fast in the crimson flesh, surrounded by flecks of white bone.

"Vohanen, your torch." The pieces of bone reminded him of something. Oval, concave, and about as long as his …
Pit.

"They're fingernails," he whispered, aghast. "Human fingernails." He was looking at a flayed, headless corpse, its arms and legs flattened against the torso to reduce space. He wheeled on Shala, his rage bubbling to the surface.

"You have dead bodies hanging from hooks in your cellar?" he growled. "You witless old crone! Vohanen. Jelaïa. We've wasted enough time here. For all we know, the second wall fell while we were sitting drinking tea!"

"Please," Shala begged. "Five more steps. Through the door. You've come this far."

Reed didn't answer. He ducked under the glistening hunks of flesh and pulled the door open with such force it bounced off the cellar wall. Beyond lay ten stone plinths. Two were empty. On the other eight rested more corpses, their faces shrouded in darkness.

Reed stalked angrily over to the nearest corpse. It was large, larger than a man. Dark-skinned and hairless.

Then everything slotted into place, and Reed didn't need the illumination of Vohanen's torch to see whose body he was standing over.

It was Brachyura, Fourth of the Twelve.

CHAPTER 19

ONE TINY SPARK

"Krelbe is, without a doubt, the worst gambler I have ever seen. A glutton for punishment too, always coming back for more. I got a quick peek at his hand once, nearly pissed myself when I saw the number of trump cards he had. And yet, he still lost! I suppose that explains why he constantly has that dour expression plastered on his face."

VOHANEN, KNIGHT OF KRIARI, 425 AT

᷍

"JEFFSON!" THE VOICE was a lighthouse in an ocean of pain. He struggled towards it, fighting to stay afloat. More sounds filtered through, an inhuman chittering. A scraping of claws.

"Jeffson!" the voice called again sharply. "I can't hold them much longer. They're nearly at the top of the wall. Pull yourself out of whatever drunken stupor you're in and help me!"

He opened one eye. The agamid lay inches from his face, one of the wooden ribs from his Crimson Wing protruding from its skull. More remains of the broken glider were strewn all around him, including a large piece of fabric directly under him that appeared to have partially cushioned his fall.

"Jeffson!" Krelbe had his back to him, the fur mantle of his half-plate stained grey with ash, his tower shield planted on the slick stone of the ramparts. The closest mangonel had caught fire, belching greasy black smoke that mixed with the green fumes of the broken vials.

"I'm awake, Sir Knight," Jeffson tried to shout, but it came out as an incoherent jumble of syllables. Another jolt of pain. His left leg was sending urgent messages to his brain. He looked down to see the shinbone had torn through the soft tissue and was protruding through the skin like a huge tooth.

He had broken his leg. *Again*. Something cracked inside his mind, and he began to laugh at the absurdity of it all. His mirth alerted Krelbe, who glanced over his shoulder with a strange look somewhere between anger and concern. His expression only made Jeffson laugh louder.

"I have bad news, Sir Knight," he gasped in between chuckles. "I can't walk. Not sure I can even stand. You'll have to leave me here. Are the fuses set?"

"Are the ... No, they're not set, you dim-witted Arelian! They're not set because I came up here to save your sorry hide instead of doing my job." A grey, wrinkled head appeared over the top of the battlements, and Krelbe slammed it with the metal boss of his tower shield.

"The latest stupid decision in a whole line of utterly stupid decisions. You and Reed have been nothing but trouble for the Knights of Kriari since we first met."

Two more greylings gained the ramparts, only to be swiftly dispatched by a flurry of thrusts from Krelbe's short sword.

Jeffson took hold of his left leg with both hands and gave an experimental pull. He nearly blacked out again from the pain. "It's no use, Sir Knight. Time for you to go. I thank you for your altruism. If you would kindly leave me with a weapon, I will do what I can to cover your retreat."

"Nonsense, Friend Jeffson," came a familiar booming voice. Aldarin strode onto the battlements, his armour covered in dirt and blood. "Your heroic efforts have saved many lives here today. My men have used the distraction provided by your aerial assault to vacate the buildings and retreat to the third wall. I will not abandon you now. Neither will my fellow knights. Ka'arka! Xer'ana! Protect our rear if you would? Sir Krelbe, if we use your shield as a stretcher, we can carry Jeffson to safety." The Knight of Kriari grunted and dropped his tower shield.

The enemy had arrived in force, pouring over the wall, many of them armed with ropes to aid in the inevitable arrival of the threshers. Ka'arka drew his axe with a ringing of metal and swept the space in front of him clean of greylings with a couple of wide swings.

Aldarin knelt down next to Jeffson. "This is going to hurt," he said unhappily. "I'm going to pick you up and put you on the shield. Ready?"

"No—" Jeffson started to say before Aldarin slipped both arms under the manservant's wounded body and lifted him hurriedly onto the makeshift stretcher.

Jeffson screamed.

Aldarin winced. "Apologies."

A shout from behind them. Ka'arka had been pounced upon by three greylings that were now scrabbling over his back like spiders, searching for a chink in the plate.

"Hold still!" Xer'ana said peevishly. Her glaive blurred, and a trio of severed heads rolled past her feet.

"Get Jeffson away!" Ka'arka yelled. Blood was running freely from a cut above his eyebrow. He shook his head to clear his vision and threw himself back into the fray.

Aldarin pulled the tower shield to the top of the steps, kicking away the bodies of the fallen to make a path. "Krelbe! Help me carry him down!" The Knight of Kriari nodded without turning round, retreating slowly, step by step, never showing his back to the enemy.

Jeffson lay on the shield looking up at the sky. The sun was setting, sending glorious reflections of pink and mauve across his field of view. It was quite beautiful. A shadow flashed past, shattering the perfection. He caught a glimpse of sharp teeth and mottled skin.

"Agamid!" he called to his rescuers, the effort of speech sending new waves of pain coursing through his body. With a screech, the creature dived low, skimming over the battlements in search of prey. Aldarin grabbed hold of Krelbe and yanked him to his knees just before two sets of razor-sharp talons raked the air where he had been standing.

The agamid shrieked in frustration. It changed course with a swish of its prehensile tail, passing over the burning mangonel and using the hot updraught from the fire to gain elevation.

"It's coming back for another pass," Aldarin warned, watching as it turned. "We have to get off the wall! Krelbe! You first. Take the front." Jeffson was hoisted into the air as the two knights began carrying him down the steps, his legs resting fully on the shield, the top of his shoulders pressed uncomfortably against the knight's bloody breastplate.

"Ka'arka! Xer'ana!" Aldarin called. "We're leaving!"

"One minute," the Da'arran woman replied, eyeing the approaching agamid.

"We don't have a minute."

"You are not my superior," she snapped back. "Knight of Bra— Ka'arka, I mean. Down on one knee."

"What?"

"Just do it."

The agamid was diving. Ka'arka cracked the butt of his axe against a greyling skull, reversed his swing, and cut through the hip of another opponent. He dropped to one knee.

The agamid screeched long and loud, reptilian eyes locked on the Knight of Brachyura. Its mouth opened wide.

Xer'ana sprang into action. She ran at Ka'arka and jumped, using his knee as a means of propelling herself even higher into the air, glaive held over her head. The agamid saw the danger coming far too late, the momentum of its dive carrying it straight onto the steel-tipped point. The blade ripped through its jaw and on into its brain.

Xer'ana landed gracefully, the dead body of her foe bouncing twice off the paved ramparts before slithering to a halt.

"What in the Pit ..." marvelled Ka'arka.

"Training and dedication," she answered with the ghost of a smile. "Now, come. The wall is lost." They ran down the steps, catching up with the others as they reached the bottom.

Aldarin and Krelbe were both sweating and red-faced. "Friend Jeffson," Aldarin said, breathing hard. "Have you been overindulging in Morlakian delicacies during your recent stay there? How can someone so slim be so heavy?"

Jeffson only smiled weakly.

"We can all drag him," Ka'arka offered. "It's not far." He started to help Aldarin pull the shield up the slope towards the third wall.

"Wait," Jeffson croaked. "Where's Krelbe?"

The Knight of Kriari hadn't moved. "The black powder," he said grimly, gesturing to the cart stacked high with barrels. "It's not too late. I can still set it off."

Jeffson shook his head. "You told me you didn't have time to set the fuses. There's no way of doing so safely. Leave it."

"I have my flint. A spark will be enough."

"Not if you want to get out alive, it won't."

"I ... I don't."

Jeffson frowned, thinking he must have misheard. "What did you say?"

Krelbe stared at him. "She caused the death of Vohanen's son, do you understand? She ruined the life of my closest friend. After losing Avor, he became a ghost ... it was as if he had died too. Even looking at her caused him pain. It tore me up inside to see him like that. I knew he wanted her gone, but he couldn't do it. Despite his anger and his hate, he couldn't do it. He is a good man. I, however, am not."

Jeffson thought back to the tree and the frozen corpse of Verona with her crimson smile, bright against her pale skin, her blackened tongue staining the fallen leaves.

Greylings were streaming over the abandoned second wall. Aldarin was yelling in his ear. He looked deep into Krelbe's eyes, past the scowling exterior, and saw the terrible guilt eating at his soul. Guilt, anguish, and something else. A yearning for something he so desperately wanted and would always be out of reach. Feelings for another that would never be returned.

"If this is your choice, I will not dissuade you from it," Jeffson whispered, trying to ignore the terrible throbbing in his leg. "And I will tell Vohanen of your sacrifice. He will be proud. You ..." he coughed. "... You were never bad at cards, were you?"

Krelbe's permanent scowl softened slightly, and Jeffson saw him smile for the first and last time. "Do you know how hard it is to lose on purpose over and over again?" he answered quietly "How amazing you have to be to fake being bad? Pit, I wasn't just good, I was the best player in all the nine Baronies!"

Then the Knight of Kriari nodded resolutely and set off for the cart and its barrels of black powder.

Aldarin and Ka'arka started moving again, pulling at the shield. Jeffson could only watch helplessly as Krelbe and the first group of greylings both reached the barrels at virtually the same time. Krelbe disembowelled one, kicked another away with his boot, then dropped his sword, reaching instead into his armour for his flint and steel.

An emboldened greyling, seeing Krelbe was defenceless, darted in and stabbed him in the leg. The knight cried out and faltered but remained upright, scraping the steel along the stick of flint. There was a tiny flicker.

"Come on. Come on," Jeffson murmured.

A greyling jumped onto Krelbe's back, claws slashing across the side of his unprotected neck. Blood gushed from the wound, soaking the knight's fur mantle. He stumbled against one of the barrels, nearly dropping the flint, then regained his footing with a desperate roar.

He raised his flint one last time as a dozen greylings closed in.

One trembling hand brought the steel down.

One last chance.

One tiny spark.

Praxis watched through Zygos's monochromatic vision as the greyling forces swarmed unopposed up the second wall. The Seventh of the Twelve was standing on the blackened remains of the first wall gatehouse. He had told his knights that he wanted to see the exact spot where the priestess of Brachyura had immolated herself.

"Incomprehensible," he muttered, running his hand over the burnt stone. "Inconceivable."

Not far above, an agamid careened erratically through the air like a leaf caught in the wind, a ragged hole in one wing. It disappeared from sight behind the ramparts and moments later, there was the sickening crack of splintered bone.

Praxis could feel his captor's anger. Twice now Zygos had been thwarted by unforeseen circumstances. Illogical circumstances. His worst nightmare. The agamids had been the weaver's trump card, a tactical advantage years in the making. Pushed back by human ingenuity.

The toxic fumes still hung over the second wall battlements. The first greylings to gain the ramparts had tried to push through them and had died screaming as the gas ate away at their throats and lungs. Those that followed were more cautious, giving the glaucous patches a wide berth.

It was Xandris, Praxis thought. *Xandris and his healer friend. It had to be. Those two have been a thorn in my side ever since I botched Listus's murder. And they are the only ones who have the medicinal knowledge to create something so utterly destructive. Well, they are Zygos's problem now.*

Helios was approaching, threading his way through the army of greylings. None of them tried to touch him. Zygos had lost one knight to a thresher in the early days of the alliance, and the weaver had made sure it would never happen again. She had ordered the thresher to be tied to a post and eaten alive. It had taken several hours.

The Knight of Zygos sprang lithely up the steps to the gatehouse roof and performed an elaborate bow.

Lucky I can't move, Praxis thought, *or I would punch him right in the middle of his smug face.*

"Message from the traitor, Lord," Helios said, handing over an arrow with a small piece of parchment wrapped around the shaft.

Zygos unrolled the sheaf of paper, his ebony eyes skimming the page.

Traps on second wall. CAUTION!

"Pull them back," he said hurriedly. "Pull them back now!"

Helios gave him a puzzled look. "Lord?"

"NOW, FOOL! NOW!" Spittle flew from Zygos's mouth, his backhanded slap catching Helios on the jaw and knocking him to the ground.

"H ... how, Lord?" the knight stammered. He was right. They had no direct control. Zygos knew a few words of the greyling tongue, but only the weaver or one of the brood mothers was capable of directing such a large number of creatures. And the surviving brood mothers were still behind the front lines. Zygos, in his hubris, had not thought them needed. This was supposed to be the final assault.

"Return to our camp. Drag one of those slugs here. Do it yourself if you have to. We have to retreat."

Praxis was only half-listening. *That slap*, he thought jubilantly. *That wasn't Zygos. I did that! He doesn't even realise it, but that was me!*

"Y ... yes, Lord. I—" The world went white.

There was a boom louder than thunder. The second wall gatehouse ceased to exist. Chunks of masonry the size of hay bales were flung violently into the air, trailing dust and grit like deadly comets. They rained down on the attacking greylings.

Wounding. Maiming. Killing.

This was not the fires of Brachyura. This was something else.

More falling debris cut a bloody swathe through the enemy ranks, accompanied by the gruesome remains of thousands of mutilated greyling corpses. A hailstorm of broken bodies, severed limbs, and shattered skulls. The smoke cleared, revealing a smouldering crater where the gatehouse had once stood; as if a giant hand had scooped up a circle of earth.

A ripple ran through the greyling horde. The wailing shrieks of the dead and dying filled the air. Another ripple and they were routed, turning away from the shining cathedral of Klief and scampering back to the safety of their camp. Zygos looked on, running a finger up and down his scarred cheek, as they passed underneath the roof where he stood.

"I have *never* been defeated," he said in a tight voice. "Not in a hundred years. I could predict every move the enemy would make, counter every stratagem. But this … this illogical way of conducting warfare … I can no longer anticipate what they will do next."

"What are you saying, Lord?" Helios asked, unable to tear his eyes away from the macabre field of battle. "Have we lost?"

"Hmm? Lost? You disappoint me, initiate. Despite these unforeseen setbacks, our army is still fifty thousand strong. Klief will fall. That is not the issue."

He still wants the town for himself, thought Praxis suddenly. *A multitude of dead greylings and the only thing that bothers him is that the wyrm might destroy Klief before he can lay claim to it.*

Avarice. Anger. Frustration. In the last few days, Zygos had shown more emotion than Praxis believed possible. Not only that, but the Seventh of the Twelve was contradicting the core philosophy of his Order: the credence that feelings are a weakness to be suppressed whenever possible.

Praxis had a theory as to why this was happening. Maybe when Zygos took over his body, he also inherited a small part of Praxis's psyche, a subconscious core of emotions that were now slowly bleeding into his mind, contaminating him. And for someone who had never felt emotion, this unwanted influx of feelings must be immensely hard to control.

One slip-up, he thought, trying to move the hand again and being rewarded with a satisfying twitch. *One mistake and I will end you.*

"The issue is time," Zygos continued, giving no indication that he had picked up on Praxis's ruminations. "The wyrm will soon be here to rob us of our hard-fought victory." His gaze travelled from the remains of the gatehouse up to the cathedral and the wall that surrounded it. The final wall. The last barrier standing between him and his reward.

Zygos sighed. "I can see no other option. My deck of cards grows thin. Send word to the traitor. Tell him it is time for him to open the gate ... and let us into Klief."

CHAPTER 20

WHO WE REALLY ARE

"How did the humans manage to learn so much in so little time? Three hundred years ago, they couldn't even smelt iron or make steel without the Twelve's guidance, and now the Knightly Orders roam the surface clad in suits of plate armour. Their cities are protected by walls five times higher than my tallest children. The seas are patrolled by great ships of wood and metal. They have evolved far beyond what I thought was possible. I must re-evaluate my strategy. Victory is no longer a certainty."

'WEAVER', 298 AT

✌

"WHAT IS THE meaning of this?" Brachyura had entered the underground chamber and was staring down at the body on the plinth, his ebony eyes narrowed to tiny slits. "Why do you have a … facsimile of me under your house, Sister?"

"The rows of skinless corpses," said Jelaïa slowly. "They are your raw materials, aren't they? You have been using your gift to create copies of your siblings."

"Kriari," came the mournful tone. The First of the Twelve had found his likeness on one of the other slabs and was studying it with a mixture of sadness and incomprehension. "Kriari. Brother."

"Answer the Baroness," growled Brachyura, his gaze still locked on the plinth. Jelaïa studied the two figures. This close together, she could see that they were not, in fact, identical. The corpse looked younger; *newer* somehow, unmarred by physical imperfections. Its skin was silky smooth, unwrinkled and waxy like a ripe apple. It had no eyes, but the backs of its eye sockets were covered in the same strange skin as the rest of its body.

When Jelaïa was twelve or thirteen, Nidore had smuggled her out of the keep to go and see one of the travelling puppet shows. The puppeteers had deftly jiggled the strings to make the three-foot-high figures of Listus del Arelium and Loré del Conte dance and sing. That was what the corpse reminded Jelaïa of. An expressionless, emotionless carved puppet … without its strings.

"I was … so lonely," said Shala in a quavering voice. "So very lonely. As I told you, I tried to resist. Tried to block out the images that her words conjured in my head … but the temptation was too great. She chipped away at my resolve; each visit to my prison was another drop into the sea of my misery until I found myself drowning in it."

"I can understand the appeal," said Vohanen from his place by the door. "I too have had a loved one taken from me, and I would do almost anything to see his face again."

"And so, you made these sculptures," Kumbha murmured, purposefully avoiding looking towards the end of the room where her own copy was to be found.

"I did. At Weaver's insistence. I made them from the last memories I had of you. Memories that are now several hundred years old."

"Memories and dead flesh," added Reed disapprovingly. "Brought to you by the weaver, I imagine. Did you not think to ask her who had to die so your brothers and sisters could live?"

"No, I did not. All I know is that once the Morlakian portal was rebuilt, she began to travel to the nine Baronies again. Sparingly. Carefully. Taking great pains not to draw attention to herself. She still needed time to marshal her depleted forces. As her confidence grew, she sent scouting parties above ground and was amazed at what they reported back. The Twelve had been forgotten. Scant few remembered their names. The Knightly Orders still existed, but instead of sharing what knowledge they still had with the Council of Baronies, they kept to themselves, holed up in their temples."

"She told you all of this?" asked Jelaïa curiously. "What did she hope to gain by doing so?"

"Gain? Nothing. Maybe she wanted to gloat … or perhaps she was just lonely too."

"Perhaps, although it's more likely she had some ulterior motive. You have yet to explain why she wanted you to recreate the bodies of the Twelve."

Shala coughed, her breath misting in the cold air of the cellar. "After her initial forays to the surface, Morlak became the centre of her web, her tentacles slowly spreading outwards across the nine Baronies, gathering more and more information. She learnt that the human race was far more numerous than before and that they had not been idle but had developed and expanded the weapons of war designed by the Twelve before their disappearance. Carracks, trebuchets, ballistae, mangonels … A plethora of machines each more deadly than the last."

"Enough to tip the scales in our favour," said Brachyura.

"Yes. Conversely, the greylings had suffered greatly during her absence. Without Weaver's leadership or guidance, thousands had died from starvation and thousands more from vicious infighting as cannibalism ran rampant among the survivors." Shala coughed again. "Might we return to the warmth of the fire? I can feel the chill seeping into my bones."

"No," Brachyura replied impassively. "Finish your tale."

Shala leant heavily on her cane, the chain around her ankle clinking as she shifted position. "As you wish. Where was I?"

"The stalemate," prompted Jelaïa. "The weaver realised she could not win."

"Ah, yes, thank you, dear. I did not see her for a time after that. It could have been months or even years. My solitude gnawed at me. I began hoping that she would return, that she would free me from this unending monotony. Then one day, she did. And told me she had found a solution. A way to even the odds. She would ally the greylings with the Knightly Orders."

Shala smiled, the movement stretching her lips tight and deepening the wrinkles around her eyes. "I laughed, of course. I thought she had gone as mad as me. But she

hadn't. Far from it. I told you this … purgatory we find ourselves in … this 'Shroud' … is on the edge of something else.
Something infinitely greater. The final destination we travel
to after our deaths. All of us. Even the Twelve."

"Folly!" snorted Vohanen. "When I die, I will be reunited with my ancestors in the Great Hall, just like all the
Knights of Kriari who died before me, and all who will
perish after. It has been this way since the dawn of time. The
weaver is playing mind games with you, Lady."

Shala shook her head. "She could *hear* them, Sir Knight.
Whatever gift she has that allows her to communicate with
her progeny stretches beyond the realm of the living. She can
pierce the thin veil that exists between the Shroud and what
lies beyond. She senses the dead. She senses the Twelve."

"If she could sense the Twelve, then why did she need
you?" Reed asked.

"To lure them here. She needed me to be the bait. All
my longing and grief would act as a beacon. A burning fire
in the black of night. And the spirits of my dead brothers
and sisters would be drawn to me, like moths to the flame."

"You helped her tear us from our rest …" said Kumbha
dejectedly, her face mirroring Brachyura's disappointment.
"You agreed to this … defilement of our psyche …"

"I did. As I told you earlier, the tapestry of my mind was
in tatters. My only thought was to see you all again. To speak
with you once more. And were you really resting? What lies
beyond the Shroud? No one knows. Perhaps your existence
there was filled with pain and suffering—"

"I am sure that is what you tell yourself," the Fourth
of the Twelve interrupted. "What you whisper in the dark

when you lie awake at night, unable to sleep. Unacceptable. There is nothing you can say that justifies this enslavement."

Shala said nothing, only started to weep silently.

"We need to hear the end of it," Jelaïa said. "What happened when you managed to entice your siblings here?"

"That was when Weaver intervened. The deceased spirits could only manifest physically for a few minutes before being dragged back beyond the Shroud. The only way to keep them here was to use a combination of these flesh simulacrums and the black liquid from the portals ... to trap them in their own corpses. Then Weaver would use her gift to attempt to repair the disjointed pieces ... to link body and mind."

There was a thunking sound. Kriari was lifting and dropping the lifeless arm of his copy, watching it hit the plinth like a slab of beef.

"You said 'attempt'," Jelaïa continued, as Kumbha gently took her brother's hand and guided him away. "It didn't work at first, did it?"

Shala glanced at Kriari, and fresh tears trickled down her cheeks. "No. We started with the First of the Twelve. A total failure. His mind is in there somewhere, but we could not successfully combine the two ..."

"Monster," whispered Brachyura in horror.

"We tried again," Shala whimpered. "Guanna was better, yet wild and untamed. He had no idea who he was. Mithuna, the Third of the Twelve, only regained part of her identity, a twisted, bitter shadow of who she was in her former life. I think Weaver pushed too hard and part of her psyche ended up entangled with Mithuna's. Then, at last, we had our first success. The Fourth of the Twelve."

Brachyura gave a deep sigh and gazed down at his palms, turning them over and over, examining his fingernails, his knuckles, the veins under the skin. "I cannot believe it," he said. "These are *my* hands. This is *my* voice. I *am* Brachyura! Not some pale imitation. And why the false memories? I remember standing on the shores of that lake. I remember signing the Pact. I remember being encased in stone."

"That is because all of those things *did* happen," the old woman said, wringing her hands. "Weaver's initial idea was total subjugation, but it didn't work. Your psyche was far too strong and systematically rejected it. Her manipulation needed to be more subtle. A concept that your mind could be made to accept with minimum subterfuge. Thus, the idea of the Pact was born. And to strengthen that false reality, she took each of you back to the Morlakian Pit. She made you *sign* the Pact. Well, most of you. A few, like Kumbha, she could not quite convince entirely. Once it was done, I myself used my gift to cover you in stone ..."

"So, the Twelve were revived, indoctrinated, and scattered among the nine Baronies in statues," Jelaïa said. "But there is one thing I still don't understand. For the plan to work, the Knightly Orders would have to be convinced that the Pact was real. Praedora told us of the Schism and the scrolls found in the temple of Zygos."

"Mithuna," Reed said, aghast.

Shala was nodding in agreement "Her mind was so unhinged that she was completely converted to Weaver's cause. And all she needs to take the form of another is spit, hair, and blood, elements Weaver could easily obtain. Mithuna got the statue of Kumbha into the gardens of

Arelium. The statue of Zygos into his temple. And more besides."

"She planted the scrolls," murmured Jelaïa.

"Not just planted them. Mithuna *was* the first priestess of Zygos for several years, until the person she was imitating died. Weaver told me that it was *Mithuna* who showed the scrolls to the other Orders, although she failed to reveal to me what happened afterwards …"

"Then, Mithuna is responsible for the Schism," said Vohanen angrily. "That thrice-accursed whore."

"She is not responsible," retorted Brachyura flatly. "She was used. We were all used. Defiled. We should not be here. We are freaks of nature, neither dead nor alive. Once this war is over, once the weaver is dead and the greylings have been wiped out, I will throw myself off the cliffs of Kessrin and end this farce. As for you, Sister, you have betrayed not only your siblings but the sacred principles of life itself. Because of your weakness, the Barony of Morlak is lost, and Klief is soon to follow. I do not see how you can be allowed to live." He cracked his knuckles. "I will make it quick."

He balled his hands into fists, and a shadow blocked his path. Kriari, First of the Twelve. The giant interposed himself between Brachyura and Shala, his black eyes unreadable.

"Step aside, Brother," Brachyura warned.

Kriari shook his head.

Brachyura lashed out. His swing caught Kriari in the lower jaw and split his lip.

"Step aside."

A second blow. Blood splattered onto one of the nearby plinths. Kriari coughed and spat out a broken tooth. "No."

"Why, Brother? Why protect her?"

Kriari shrugged. "Sister."

Brachyura let out a soft growl and pummelled his brother's stomach.

"Stop it!" Kumbha shouted. "What are you doing? Stop it!"

"She must pay!" Brachyura yelled back. He threw another punch, and Kriari caught it. Brachyura struggled to free himself, but his brother's grip was like iron.

"Let me go," the Fourth of the Twelve said, almost pleading now. "She must pay. She must pay."

"Look at her, Brother," Kumbha said quietly. "I think she already has."

Brachyura stared at Shala. At the old, half-mad woman with rotten teeth and a balding scalp. Hunched over her cane, the skin of her ankle rubbed raw by the chain that held her captive in her own house, living one long, endless day for the last three hundred years, waking up to the same empty sky and desolate surroundings. Unable to die from hunger or thirst. Unable to flee her prison. Death would have been a blessing.

He let the tension drain from his body. Kriari released his grip. "I cannot forgive you, Sister," Brachyura said sternly. "But I cannot kill you either. You must know why we are here. To kill the weaver and end the terrible suffering that plagues the nine Baronies."

He bent down slowly, took hold of Shala's chain, and broke one of the links with a sharp twist.

"You are free. I am not the weaver. I will not force you to help us. I will not try to negotiate or offer you some sort of deal. You decide what you want to do with your life. Choose your own path."

Shala shuffled forwards and put her wasted fingers on Brachyura's chest. "I will help you. Of course, I will help you. You are my brother."

Brachyura looked down and removed her hand. "I am. Although I do not recognise what *you* are anymore. Do you know where the weaver is to be found?"

"Not exactly, but she always arrives from the same direction. I can show you."

"Something is bothering me," Reed said suddenly. Jelaïa almost jumped out of her skin. The guardsman had been silent for so long that she had almost forgotten he was there. He was standing at the very end of the room, just after the last two plinths.

"A terrible thought has crossed my mind," he continued. "And I hope to the Pit I am wrong. Lady, you said you returned the Twelve to life with the help of the weaver. That you moulded new bodies for them from the flesh of the dead. So, tell me, what are *these* bodies doing here if your work is done?"

Shala's brow crinkled. "They are ... replacements. Copies of copies. Weaver wanted to account for all possibilities. If the hibernation process failed or one of the Twelve was killed, their spirits would return once more to the place beyond the Shroud and Weaver could call them back again. She said that" — she swallowed — "she said that, in this way, they would be bound to her forever. Her eternal servants."

Brachyura sniffed and looked away in disgust.

"I had a feeling you were going to say that, Shala. Tell me, why are there only eight corpses? If Makara and yourself are the only members of the Twelve still alive, should there not be ten?"

Jelaïa sensed the familiar feeling of dread uncurl in her stomach, like a wyrm awakening from a long slumber to devour her from the inside. She let out an involuntary moan.

Reed tapped one of the empty plinths. "The weaver had you bring them back, didn't she? The only two of the Twelve who we actually managed to kill?"

Shala gave a hesitant nod then hung her head.

"Where are they now?"

"Mithuna and Mina are with her. They will protect her. And they will obey her. You will not be able to reason with them."

"Pit," cursed Reed with feeling. "Why do I always have to be right?"

Brachyura turned to him, his eyes hard. "This changes nothing. If my sisters try to stop us, we will have no other choice but to cut them down. They will die. As they did before. And this time, we will make sure that they do *not* come back."

CHAPTER 21

THE FIDDLE'S LAMENT

"Brachyura has once again been lauded by his siblings for the construction of another perfect wall. I wanted to scream at them for their naivety. Walls do not protect a castle from being taken by its enemies. It is the soldiers manning those walls who do. And if just one of those soldiers can be swayed to our cause, the castle will fall."

MITHUNA, THIRD OF THE TWELVE, 42 AT

❧

K A'ARKA COULD HEAR the chimes of the cathedral bells through the walls of the tavern. The Baron had ordered them to be rung a hundred times as a eulogy for those who had given their lives defending the second wall. Jeffson was the only Crimson Wing pilot to have returned. Stick, Caddox, and the others were still missing, presumed dead.

Aldarin clumped over and sat down next to him, a tankard of ale in each hand. The wooden chair creaked in protest
at having to support the bulk of a fully-armoured knight.
"I left Jeffson with the healer," he said, pushing one of the
tankards across the table to Ka'arka. "Kumbha has still not
returned to the surface. Belen will have to do what he can."

Ka'arka took a gulp of ale and raised his tankard in
thanks. "He'll pull through. He's a tough one. You can tell
just by looking at him. Caddox was telling me he used to be
some sort of mercenary when he was younger—"

"A mercenary? Jeffson?" interrupted Aldarin.

"Don't judge a book by its cover, my friend. You have a
terrible tendency to underestimate people. They are saying
he killed Mithuna, one of the Twelve. Stuck a dagger through
her eye without even flinching."

"To Krelbe!" came a cry from up near the bar. Taleck,
Ner'alla, and Bansworth stood there, tankards raised. There
was a smattering of applause. One of the last surviving
Knights of Kriari brought out a fiddle and began drawing
his bow slowly across the strings.

Xer'ana joined the two knights at their table, sitting
down carefully as if not used to that particular movement.
"Gentlemen," she said in greeting. She looked at the tankards and pursed her lips. "Drinking, are we? I am not sure
that is wise. The Knight of Kriari has bought us some time,
but the greylings will renew their assault within the hour,
you can be sure of it."

"We are honouring a dead comrade, my Lady," Aldarin
replied seriously over the fiddle's lament. "The Knights of
Kriari believe that when they die, their spirits join those of

their ancestors in the afterlife. It is something to be celebrated, and tradition dictates we should toast his memory."

Xer'ana's face softened. "I see. I did not realise this. I … apologise. The Da'arrans have spent so long among themselves that I sometimes forget that there is a whole world out there with traditions different from our own. Like sitting on chairs to eat, for example. A most uncomfortable practice."

"What do the Knights of Luridae believe?" asked Aldarin curiously.

"We … No, it is nothing."

"I disagree. It is far from nothing," Ka'arka said softly. "Our faith is important. And it is a part of me I have neglected, much to my shame. For too long, my Da'arran heritage has suffered from my commitment to my knighthood. Tell Sir Aldarin of our ideology."

"After death, we give the body back to the desert. The mind … the mind rejoins the Great Lake. An expanse of cool, fresh water. Our thoughts combine, our consciousness is shared with all who came before. A communal eternity of peace and tranquillity."

"That sounds beautiful," Aldarin said.

Ka'arka was silent for a moment then raised his tankard in salute once more. "To Shen'alla. May the Great Lake welcome her into its waters."

Xer'ana looked at him in amazement. "What a touching sentiment. I cannot figure you out, Knight of Brachyura," she said. "You are constantly defying my expectations."

"Yes, it's annoying, isn't it?" agreed Aldarin, his tankard obscuring his face. "He does that to me, too. Makes you wonder why anyone would want to be around him, really."

"Oh, I don't know," Xer'ana replied, extricating herself

from the chair with some difficulty. "I am starting to find his erratic behaviour quite exhilarating. Now, if you would excuse me, I will leave you to your drinks."

Ka'arka watched her go, the fiddle keening in his ears.

"Exhilarating," repeated Aldarin with a smile. Ka'arka punched him on the shoulder, hitting his pauldron with a clang. "You weren't this amusing before, Aldarin," he said in mock frustration. "I think Jelaïa is having a bad influence on you."

Aldarin's face fell on hearing her name, and Ka'arka cursed himself for his mistake. "I am sorry, friend," he said softly. "I did not wish to trouble you. I take it there is still no news?"

"None. I'm sure she is fine. Reed is with her, and there is no man I trust more. And, of course, three of the Twelve. They will bring her back safely."

"I do not doubt it."

Aldarin raised his tankard once more. "They *have* to, Ka'arka. She is everything to me. She has opened my mind to so many things. Changed me for the better. Helped me … enjoy life. When I wake in the morning and see her lying beside me, I still can't believe this is real. Losing her is inconceivable. She—"

He was cut off by a deep rumbling sound. Behind the bar, glass bottles rattled. One fell to the floor and shattered. Ka'arka looked down at his half-finished ale. The surface of the liquid was rippling with miniature waves.

"The greylings?" he asked. "Already?"

Aldarin frowned. "I think not. It's not coming from the wall."

Derello burst into the tavern, his hair hanging wild

about his face. His eyes alighted on the two knights, and he called out to them. "Aldarin, Ka'arka. Mak— The High Priest requires your presence in the cathedral, immediately."

They followed the distraught Baron out of the tavern. A squad of Knights of Brachyura marched past, their horned helms looking strange and warped in the light of the braziers. Golden-armoured soldiers of the Kliefien town guard were unloading cartloads of arrows for those stationed up on the ramparts.

Another tremor of the earth. Candles flickered in the windows of the infirmary. Faint moaning and whimpering could be heard from within. With Kumbha absent, the beds were rapidly filling with the grievously wounded. Syrella and the healer staggered outside, carrying a dead Arelian between them. A row of bodies already lined the infirmary wall, and the Arelian was laid down next to them. The chill night air would keep the corpses as cold as any morgue.

Derello led Ka'arka and Aldarin up the steps of the cathedral. The bells had fallen silent. The interior was empty of people save for Makara and Azael, sitting side by side on the marble floor, their backs against the stone representation of the Pit. The Tenth of the Twelve was speaking to the Baron in soft tones, one scrawny arm around the boy's shoulders. He looked up as they approached.

"Ah, Knights of Brachyura. Thank you for coming." He muttered a few words to Azael, and the Baron's eyes closed immediately, his breathing slowing as he fell asleep. Makara gave him a look of affection then hauled himself up, using the stone behind him for support.

"He is the closest I have had to a son," he said sadly. "I will miss him."

"My Lord?" queried Ka'arka.

"It is the wyrm, Sir Knight. The rumbling. I can sense its approach. I must attempt to stall it. The closer it gets, the more susceptible it will become to my gift. I wanted to say goodbye to the Baron before I began."

"Goodbye, Lord? Why?"

"The wyrm has the mind the size of a house, Sir Knight. It will crush me. The longer I try to restrain it, the greater its weight will become. I will not survive, that is a certainty. The only unknown factor is how much time I can give you."

Aldarin was only half-listening, staring past Makara at the stone plug and the grate beneath. "Do you have any idea where the wyrm will emerge?" he asked in a strained voice.

"I expect it will take the most direct route," Makara replied, rubbing his tired eyes. "It will come up through the Pit."

"Then, Jelaïa, Reed, and the others …"

"If they are still down there when it breaks through, they will die, Sir Knight."

"Pit!" shouted Aldarin, slamming his fist into one of the pews hard enough to crack the wood. "I knew I should never have let her go!"

"Have a little faith."

"Faith? In what? In whom? In the Twelve? Everything I have been told about you and your siblings was a lie. And ever since Brachyura crawled out of that damned Pit, he has made one bad decision after another."

Makara looked at him with his amethyst eyes, and Aldarin heard a voice in his skull. **No, Sir Knight. Not in the Twelve. Faith in your friends. Faith in her.**

"I have one last task to ask of you," he said aloud. "I want you to get Azael out of Klief."

"I leave with Jelaïa or not at all," countered Aldarin immediately, crossing his arms.

"Of course. I am not asking you to leave permanently. I have a cabin hidden in the hills behind the city; there is a huntsman stationed there at all times. He has his instructions. It's less than an hour's walk away, you would be there and back again before dawn."

"Then, why did you not send Azael there earlier?" fumed Ka'arka.

"A Baron fleeing before the battle had even begun?" Makara answered, raising a sceptical eyebrow. "He would have been ridiculed and most certainly forced to abdicate. No, now is the right time."

"And how do we get him out?"

"There is a postern gate at the very back of the gardens behind the keep, between two arrowwoods growing against the eastern wall."

"Arrowwoods?"

"Viburnum. Oval-shaped leaves and pink flowers."

Azael moaned in his sleep. Makara sighed. "You should go before I change my mind."

Aldarin tapped his fingers against the side of one of the pews. "Once again, you have kept important information from us, Lord," he said unhappily. "The War Council should have been informed earlier that there was another way out of the city."

"I think not. We would have lost half the population as soon as it was revealed."

"After all this time, you still consider yourself a ruler

rather than a priest, don't you? If only you had tried to serve the best interests of your people instead of the other way round. Imposing this ridiculous religion and locking them away from the outside world has done more harm than good."

"Will you help me?" Makara repeated.

"Why are you so attached to the child?" asked Ka'arka curiously. "Is he of your bloodline?"

"No. Not at all. Just two lonely people using each other's grief to soothe their own. One looking for a father. Another looking for a son …"

Aldarin nodded and gathered the Baron in his arms. "Very well. We will do this, Makara, but once it is done, I will inform the War Council of the postern gate's existence. Agreed?"

Makara nodded. "Good luck."

Aldarin hesitated. "Thank you for buying Jelaïa some much-needed time. And thank you for your sacrifice. May the Twelve be with you,"

"They are," the eldest of the Twelve replied with a melancholy smile. "And they always have been."

Zygos crouched in the ruins of the second wall gatehouse, running his hand over a piece of split masonry.

"Impressive," he admitted. He stood, surveying the damage wrought by the black powder. "Whatever they used, it was more destructive than the fires of Brachyura. A waste, of course."

"A waste, Lord?" asked Helios, hovering nearby like a

lovesick puppy. Seven other knights accompanied him, clad in close-fitting black leather.

"To use such a powerful substance in such a crude and simple way. Think if they found a way to add it to their arrows? To the ammunition used by the mangonels? If they'd used it correctly and efficiently, they could have slaughtered every greyling that came within range of the second wall. The agamids would have been ripped from the sky."

"Maybe they are just stupid, Lord," smirked Helios.

Zygos frowned. "You are not thinking logically, initiate. As is your wont. The defenders are anything but incompetent, otherwise we would be having this conversation in the cathedral of Klief. No, I believe they simply did not have the time."

The ground trembled, making the shards of stone and dirt bounce up and down like fleas. "The wyrm," Zygos said. "It is nearly here. There is still time. If we can take the city, the weaver will put the leash back on her pet. Has the traitor been contacted?"

"Yes, Lord. He will be ready."

"Excellent. This must be timed perfectly. The greylings will renew their attack soon. I intend for the third gate to be open so that they can completely bypass the last line of defence. The gate consists of a portcullis and a barred door. Two of you will be enough to use the crank, the rest of you will protect them while they work."

And die in the process, thought Praxis. *Zygos knows this, but he doesn't care. Was I also like this before? So blinded by loyalty? It was a suicide mission, more lives thrown away on a whim.*

"It shall be as you command, Lord," said Helios, pulling

his hood up over his head and motioning for his men to do the same.

Zygos nodded in satisfaction. "Then, we move. The night will hide us well. Use the shadows of the buildings. Short bursts from cover to cover. Our destination lies at the far end of the eastern wall."

The Seventh of the Twelve drew his own hood close to his face and set off, slipping easily from one building to the next.

Praxis watched silently from his prison. He had to find a way to stop them. If Zygos won, if there was no one left to challenge him, then Praxis would be trapped in this body forever. The wall drew steadily closer. They were within range of the archers now. If Praxis could make his patron stumble, if he could force him out into the open, he would be peppered with arrows.

MOVE!

He pulsed the command down the length of his arm, willing his hand to pull his body off balance. Nothing happened. Zygos angled right, heading for the more sparsely defended eastern part of the wall.

Pit! thought Praxis, trying again, focusing on his fingertips, remembering how it felt to fold the skin, to bend the joints. Still nothing.

It's not working! Why isn't it working?

Then it hit him. There was no anger. In all his previous attempts, Zygos had been angry, an emotion he had never felt before, a side-effect of melding his spirit with Praxis. It had weakened him, made him more susceptible to manipulation. Praxis could sense none of that now. On the contrary, Zygos seemed entirely composed and serene, fully committed to his plan. Praxis retreated, brooding, to the depths of his cell. There was nothing he could do but wait.

Zygos sprinted across the last few feet of open ground and threw himself against the base of the wall, flattening his body against the stone. Helios arrived a moment later, breathing hard, followed by a fellow knight, then another. The third knight tripped on a loose cobble. His ankle twisted painfully, and he was sent sprawling.

A tasselled spear poked over the battlements. A boyish face peered down at them, its spotty pallid skin as white as the moon shining overhead.

"Wha—" the boy began to exclaim, his eyes widening in shock.

Zygos flicked his wrist, and a throwing dagger shot upwards with the speed of an arrow. It was a superb throw, catching the young guard under his chin and boring through the soft flesh of his mouth up into his brain. He toppled over the parapet and fell without a sound.

Zygos quickly calculated the dead body's trajectory and intercepted it before it could hit the ground. He lowered the corpse carefully into the shadows at the base of the wall.

"Helios," he said, not looking round. "Deal with that."

The initiate swallowed hard, drawing his dagger and turning on the fallen Knight of Zygos who was clutching his sprained ankle and grimacing in pain.

"I am sorry," Helios said and rammed his stiletto through his brother knight's eye.

"Incompetence will not be tolerated," warned Zygos as the second body was manoeuvred into place beside the first. "There is too much at stake." He began slowly moving up the eastern wall, stopping once every so often to rap his hand against the blocks of stone.

A high-pitched shriek echoed through the night from down by the first wall. A brood mother. The greylings were on the offensive.

There was a muffled *thunk* of flesh on wood. Zygos had found the postern gate, cunningly concealed, its planks expertly painted to look like stone. It was extraordinary work, enough to stand up to all but the closest scrutiny.

Zygos knocked three times, paused, then three times more. For an instant, nothing happened. Then, slowly but surely, the postern gate creaked ponderously open. On the other side stood the traitor, his face pale against the dark shadows of his hood.

Zygos grasped the man's wrist, congratulating him. "You have done well."

"Thank you, Lord," replied Lord Taile Bansworth. "Welcome to Klief."

CHAPTER 22

THE MEMORY OF
THOSE WE LOST

*"Many believe that there are five stages of grief. Denial, anger,
bargaining, depression, and finally acceptance. Acceptance does
not mean that we have moved past our loss, only that we have
embraced its inevitability and are learning to live again, all the
while keeping the memories of those we lost close to us."*

BARONESS JELAÏA DEL ARELIUM, 426 AT

᠊ᢙ᠊

T HE WEAVER'S TOWER was easily found. Tall and thin
like the charred tree trunks clustered around its
base, its black sides made it appear as if someone
had torn a hole in the sky itself. Jelaïa trudged stubbornly
towards it, her hand clenching her axe-shaped amulet hard
enough to draw blood.

She studied her companions: Reed, Vohanen, and the

three members of the Twelve. All were silent, lost in their own nebulous thoughts, digesting the information they had just received and preparing themselves for the challenges to come.

They had left Shala behind; she was still far too weak from her prolonged captivity to match their frantic pace. They were to meet her by the portal when they returned. *If* they returned.

Her thoughts drifted to Aldarin and the others. Was the second wall still standing? She had no idea how long they had been in the Shroud. There was no sun, no way of recording the passing of time. How anyone could survive for so long in a place like this was beyond her understanding.

A gust of wind tugged at her hair, and she thought she heard a tinkling of laughter. Echoes of the dead, perhaps. A glimpse into what lay beyond the Shroud. The nearby trees took on strange humanoid shapes. Listus. Praedora. Manfeld. Calling to her. Jelaïa shivered and tried to ignore the chill breeze, focusing instead on Reed as he plodded along in front of her, his spear bobbing up and down on his back.

Brachyura called for a halt a few hundred feet away from the tower. "I have been thinking about how to approach this," he said to them, his black eyes unreadable. "If we trust Shala, then we will face three opponents: Mithuna, Mina, and the weaver herself. Six against three. The odds are in our favour."

"Did you not say that the weaver decimated the Twelve when you last met?" asked Reed, sounding unconvinced. "She alone may be more than a match for us."

"She did," Brachyura replied. "But we were disorganised

and bewildered. That will not happen again. And we have two other significant advantages. The first is that I do not believe Mina and Mithuna will be armed or armoured. When Kumbha and I were resurrected, we were … unattired."

"Kriari," the First of the Twelve agreed with a grin.

"Precisely. The second advantage we have is surprise. They do not know we are coming."

"Unless one of them looks out the window," remarked Vohanen candidly.

"True. Then, let us hope they do not. Mina is, without a doubt, the stronger of my two sisters. I have fought her before. She is easily goaded. I will deal with her. Kriari, Kumbha, you should be able to take down Mithuna if you work together. Once our siblings are out of the way, the six of us can tackle the weaver. Questions?"

"I don't think so," said Reed, his voice pitched slightly higher than normal. "Kill one demi-god, then kill the other, then kill the creature that controls the wyrm, the one who is probably the god of the entire greyling race. Is that all? Pit, I thought this was going to be difficult."

Jelaïa could only smile at the absurdity of the situation. "Well, you did volunteer," she said matter-of-factly.

"What? No, I didn't! You had a vision! I just said that the vermilion cloak sounded like it referred to me, that's all. A simple supposition. There are other members of the Old Guard around somewhere, you know. I rescued some from Morlak Pit myself."

Vohanen pulled his well-worn skin of wine from his belt and drank deeply. "It's not too late, friend Reed," he said, wiping his mouth with his sleeve. "You can turn back. No one will think ill of you for it."

Reed sighed. "Is that a Morlakian red?"

"The finest."

"I'm going to need some of that."

"Are you sure? Last time you drank some wine, you ended up kissing a Baroness."

Reed grabbed the skin from the smirking Knight of Kriari and brought it to his lips.

"Watch out, my Lady," whispered Vohanen conspiratorially to Jelaïa, who laughed.

"It is time," came the leaden baritone of Brachyura. He had drawn his axe. Jelaïa felt her good humour drain away, replaced by an all-too-familiar feeling of mounting trepidation. Reed returned the skin to Vohanen with a nod of thanks and brought out his spear.

"Courage," Brachyura said solemnly. "You will need to find your courage. I have faced uncountable greylings on the Northern Plains. I have fought to the death beneath the Morlakian Pit. I have traded blows with the Last of the Twelve. Yet, this will be my greatest trial. And it will be yours. Have courage in yourselves. Trust yourselves. Believe in yourselves."

"And may the Twelve be with us," added Jelaïa softly, thinking again of Aldarin.

"We go," Brachyura said curtly. "Try to keep up."

He turned and charged towards the tower, his sabatons kicking up great clods of grey mud as he accelerated. Kriari raced after him with a loping, animalistic gait, his long hair streaming in the wind.

Pit, what am I doing? thought Jelaïa, setting off at a sprint. Ahead, there was the explosive sound of a door caving in, thunderously loud in the quiet of the Shroud. She passed through the broken remains of whatever had been protecting the entrance to the tower and skidded to a halt, almost bumping into Brachyura. She peered around his impressive girth to see what had arrested his spirited charge.

They were in a spacious, circular chamber. It had no visible ceiling, the black stone walls rising steeply until they were lost to the darkness above. At the far end of the chamber, on a throne moulded from the rock itself, sat the weaver, her taloned hands tapping on the arm rests, a thin smile on her face. She did not seem surprised to see them.

On either side, like well-trained bodyguards, Mina and Mithuna stood silently. Both wore rough woollen tunics and dull, vacant looks.

In the centre of the chamber was what had made Brachyura pull up short. Dangling in mid-air from a score of chains bolted into the walls hung an enormous heart, crimson-red and slick with fluid. It must have been close to eight feet in length, its single ventricle and dual atriums covered in tiny throbbing veins. As Jelaïa watched, the heart pulsed weakly, the cavities deflating and inflating as it filled with blood.

"What is this ... folly?" murmured Brachyura.

There was movement on the opposite side of the room. The weaver stretched, stood, and cocked her head. "Greetings to you all." Jelaïa was once more struck by the strange intonations in her voice. She spoke in a series of syllables chained haphazardly together, stressing parts of the sentence seemingly at random. "I was wondering how long it would take you to get here. Shala betrayed me much faster than I had anticipated. How unfortunate. She will have to be disciplined."

Mithuna let out a bark of laughter. The weaver shot her an angry look. "Do not be uncouth, Mithuna. We are not here to gloat. We are here to compromise."

Kumbha pointed at the slowly-beating heart with a trembling hand. "Explain this. It is not human; I can see that much. What have you done?"

"The fulcrum? Ah, I thought you would have figured that out by now. Once more, I appear to have overestimated you. It is very frustrating. Your creators supposedly endowed you with superior intelligence and reflexes, yet you still bumble around like children."

Jelaïa tore her eyes away from the suspended heart, forcing her tired mind to try and understand what the weaver was saying. "Your creators?"

"Later," growled Brachyura. "This is a reptilian heart, is it not? This is how you control the wyrm."

The weaver clapped her hands together in delight. "Yes! Excellent! Not quite so bumbling after all! I tried to manipulate its mind directly at first but soon realised that it was far, far beyond my abilities. The size of the thing … fathomless. I almost lost myself in the depths of its thoughts. I was an ant drowning in an ocean. Most unpleasant. So, I studied it. They are fascinating creatures. Little to no verbal communication, but there is an intrinsic familial link, a passive transmission of thought between shared blood."

"Shared blood?" repeated Reed, his eyebrows drawn into a frown. "Like between father and son?"

The weaver nodded emphatically. "Father and son, or mother and daughter. I stole one of the creature's eggs, hatched it myself, and cut out the newborn infant's heart. It makes a perfect conduit. The fact that the wyrm could feel her child's pain as I was ending its life only strengthens my hold."

"How could you do this?" asked Kumbha softly, horror plain on her face. "You have desecrated the most sacred of bonds, that between mother and child. You are subjecting her to unspeakable torture; using her own child's heart as a leash. No wonder she weeps tears of fire." She glanced at her brother. "Brachyura, we must put a stop to this."

"Agreed. Weaver, or whatever your name is. This is your final chance. Do not send the wyrm to Klief. Destroy this ... monstrosity that binds her to your will. Order your forces to pull back. We can still find common ground, I am sure of it."

The weaver made a clicking noise with her tongue. "I see no reason to do so. Besides, I have already given the order. The wyrm is on its — *her* — way, homing in on your despicable human scent. Do you know she is half-blind? Compensates with her extraordinary sense of smell. It's quite fascinating. I wouldn't have needed to send her at all if your brother, Zygos, had done his job properly, but he has turned out to be another disappointment. The biggest greyling army ever assembled in three hundred years, and he has squandered it."

Klief still stands! thought Jelaïa.

"Then, you die," uttered Brachyura simply, hefting his axe. Mithuna and Mina made to step forwards, but the weaver raised a clawed hand, stopping them in their tracks.

"So strong, so brave, so self-assured. The opposite of Makara. How far he has fallen. Once maybe the greatest of you all, now a scared old man who is frightened of his own shadow. I can feel his mark on you. On all three of you. His *gift*. He hopes it will protect you."

The weaver smiled. A terrifying sight, her thin, bloodless lips pulled tightly across her face revealing two rows of crooked razor-sharp teeth.

"So strong, so brave ... so stupid."

Something surged to the forefront of Jelaïa's mind. A recent memory. Brachyura's surprise at learning Shala's gift worked in a place like this. "It does," Shala had replied. "Although it is possible that it only works because Weaver allows it."

Oh no.

The weaver, still smiling, began to hum.

Brachyura let out a cry of agony and fell to one knee, his black eyes bulging in their sockets. Kumbha screamed as her left eye burst, covering her beautiful golden hair with black tar.

"Kri ..." began Kriari, before coughing painfully, dark ichor dribbling from his mouth. He managed one more step before collapsing.

"What's happening?" shouted Reed in horror, as the three members of the Twelve writhed on the floor before him.

"Makara's gift! It doesn't work here!" Jelaïa replied in panic. "They are no longer protected!"

"The perfect way to keep us tame, is it not, little man?" said Mithuna. She was studying Reed with her obsidian gaze, and he wilted under her scrutiny. "I ... know you, do I not? Your face is familiar to me, although I cannot quite place it. Have we met before?"

"Have we met ..." Reed looked past Mithuna to where the weaver was swaying back and forth, her eyes closed, humming softly. "Do you not see what you are doing to them?" he called to her. "Your constant meddling is causing permanent damage. They are losing what little identity they have left. Stop this! Free them!" He took a step towards her, and Mithuna quickly interposed.

"Run away, little man," she cautioned. "This is not your fight."

Reed replied with a spear thrust to her ribs. The tip opened a thin line in Mithuna's tunic but failed to penetrate the tough skin beneath. Her answering punch knocked him to the ground.

"Silly little man," she said with a sigh and raised her foot to crush his skull. Vohanen leapt desperately to Reed's rescue, his tower shield held high. There was a squeal of metal as Mithuna's bare foot flattened the central boss, but the shield held.

"A thrust to the ribs won't work," barked Vohanen, pulling Reed back out of range. "Their skin is tougher than a thresher's. Aim for the weak spots: back of the knee, armpit, groin, back of the neck. Got it?" Reed nodded and readjusted his cloak, his left cheek already swelling from Mithuna's punch.

There was another scream as Brachyura tried to come to their aid. He struggled to rise, tar-like tears streaming from his empty eye sockets, then collapsed again.

"My Lady!" Vohanen called over to Jelaïa. "A little help?"

"That would not be wise," said Mina menacingly from somewhere over to Jelaïa's left. "I have no quarrel with you, whoever you may be. But intervene and I will gut you like a fish."

Jelaïa smiled sweetly at her. "I suppose that's meant to scare me, is it? You don't recognise me, do you? No idea who we are. What we have been through. I have faced far worse than you, Last of the Twelve. We met once, very briefly, before the walls of Kessrin. Just before you killed my aunt's closest friend."

She raised her axe medallion and began to slowly unscrew the top. Mina scowled. "An effigy of Brachyura. You are one of his whores? You wield the fires?"

"I do. And the one who taught me to use them burned the flesh from your bones. She is gone now, but she was a good teacher. I do not see why it will not work a second time." Jelaïa brought the vial of Aldarin's blood to her lips and downed its contents in a single gulp. She steeled herself, waiting for the flood of angry memories and raw power to come coursing through her veins. Mina was staring at her, something akin to fear playing across her face.

Come, thought Jelaïa. *Let us finish this.*

Nothing happened.

She began to panic. Closing her eyes, she willed the feeling to return and those terrible memories to scythe into her brain.

Silence. Jelaïa moaned. It was not just the Twelve, the weaver was suppressing her gift too.

She was defenceless.

"Trouble, little one?" asked Mina mockingly, regaining her composure. "That is a pity."

"Stay ... stay back," warned Jelaïa. The empty amulet fell from her shaking fingers. Glancing to her right, she saw Reed and Vohanen still locked in combat with Mithuna. The Third of the Twelve had managed to grab hold of Vohanen's jaw and was squeezing it slowly, deftly avoiding Reed's clumsy attacks.

Mina approached calmly. Jelaïa looked into her obsidian eyes and despaired. *We will never know what the Twelve were really like*, she thought, battling waves of fear. *All we have are these pale imitations. Twisted copies of fallen gods.*

An enormous hand closed around her neck, and she was lifted bodily into the air. She beat at Mina's forearm with her fists, but it was useless. Jelaïa felt the hand tighten ever so slightly, almost tenderly. Just enough to cut off her supply of air.

She coughed. Her lungs screamed at her for oxygen, but she had nothing left to give. Through a haze of black spots, she could see Mina looking at her curiously. "I know you," the Last of the Twelve was saying to herself. "Why is this memory hidden from me?"

Jelaïa opened her mouth to reply but no longer had the strength to talk. *Aldarin!* she thought suddenly, the very name causing a surge of sadness. *Aldarin, I'm so sorry. Forgive me.*

There was a distant whinnying of horses. Of course, she had almost forgotten! Her father had promised he would take her riding today! She had been looking forward to it for weeks. The perfect escape from her boring parchments and stuffy bedroom. They would ride down across the valley, through the villages and farmsteads of Arelium, and up into the hills beyond. Turning, she could see him now, coming to meet her, resplendent in his golden armour, a glint of mischief in his steel-flecked eyes.

Darkness further clouded her vision, and soon all she could see was the shining brilliance of her father's plate. He smiled, and her heart almost burst with her love for him.

"Father," she said. "Have you come to take me away? Is it time for us to go riding together?"

He raised one gauntleted hand and tucked a stray lock of her chestnut hair back behind her ear. "That is up to you, Jeli. Are you ready?"

"I don't know. I—"

A pair of mismatched shoes. The smell of wildflowers. Aldarin.

"No ... No, I don't think I am."

Her father's eyes twinkled, and he nodded.

There was a muffled cry of pain, and her father vanished. She felt herself falling. She hit the ground hard and tasted blood in her mouth. Sight and sound rushed to meet her. She took a great lungful of air and blinked to clear her blurred vision. There was something lying close by, long and flesh-coloured. A finger. Mina's finger.

Jelaïa took another deep breath and tried to focus. The Last of the Twelve was crouched a few feet away, her jaw twisted into an ugly snarl as she clutched her ruined right hand with her left, attempting to staunch the flow of blood that bubbled and spurted from her severed middle finger. The demi-god was shouting wildly at her aggressor. The man who now stood between her and Jelaïa. The man whose blade had mutilated her hand.

"WHO ARE YOU? TELL ME! TELL ME WHO YOU ARE! TELL ME YOUR NAME!"

The man lashed out. His bastard sword sang as it bit into Mina's flesh, forcing her back. Fresh blood mingled with the glittering rubies set into the wolf's head hilt.

"My name," the man said, flicking the blade, "is Listus."

He looked back over his shoulder at Jelaïa and grinned his feral grin. "Listus del Arelium."

CHAPTER 23

THE OBSIDIAN
EYES OF KLIEF

"Balance (noun): a situation in which all the different parts are equal in strength or importance.

In the balance (idiom): in an uncertain, undecided, and often critical condition."

UNKNOWN

✣

*B*ANSWORTH? THOUGHT PRAXIS as the Knights of Zygos stepped through the postern gate into the town of Klief. *Bansworth is the traitor? I didn't think that blubbering fool of a noble could tie his own shoelaces without help, let alone betray an entire Barony.*

The disgraced Kessrin vassal pulled the postern gate shut. "You should encounter only minimal resistance between here and the gatehouse," he said nervously. "The men on duty will be distracted by the imminent greyling attack, and the reserves are holed up in one of the taverns honouring the dead."

"Just as I predicted," Zygos retorted with a quick nod. "Helios. Take your men and make your way to the wall. Slowly and stealthily. Keep to the shadows. Try to conceal yourselves for as long as possible. I will join you shortly."

Helios inclined his head and drew his stiletto. The blade had been coated in mud to dull its gleam in the moonlight. Pulling his hood close, he faded into the darkness of the gardens, slinking away between the bushes and benches.

The traitor found himself alone with Zygos, who studied him with his jet-black eyes. "There was, however, something I could *not* predict. The destruction of the second gate."

"Ah … yes, Lord. An invention of Xandris, the healer's apprentice. He calls it black powder. I did all I could to stall them, working as slowly as possible without arousing suspicion. Thanks to my efforts, there was not enough time to distribute the barrels all along the wall, only under the gatehouse itself. The damage to your forces could have been significantly higher."

"Perhaps. And yet, your warning came too late."

Bansworth began to sweat. "I did what I could, Lord," he squeaked. "I followed your orders. You told me not to do anything that would compromise my infiltration."

"Yes, I did, didn't I? Do you remember when my initiates found you, Bansworth, in that pigsty of an inn in Haeden? You had passed out drunk in your own vomit. Despicable behaviour. You would be dead from alcohol poisoning by now if we hadn't dragged you out of the gutter."

Bansworth shuffled his feet, his cheeks flushed with shame. "Yes, Lord."

"I told you I would help you, and I did. I simply needed to allow you to 'save' a handful of villagers, and you could return to Kessrin a hero. I even let you take Haeden back without putting up much of a fight — another glorious feather in your cap."

"I am most grateful, Lord."

"As well you should be. I believe the scales are nearly balanced. I owe you one more thing if I recall. What did you ask of me in return for your treachery?"

Bansworth raised his head, tears welling in his eyes. "To be free of the guilt," he whispered. "To no longer feel the shame of cowardice. To have the strength to never run away again."

"Correct," Zygos replied. His hand shot out, fingers flat, and crushed the soft cartilage of Bansworth's windpipe like an eggshell. The Kessrin opened his mouth to scream but could only manage a hoarse wheeze.

"Balance in all things," said Zygos dispassionately as Bansworth sank to his knees, suffocating slowly. "I did envisage several other ways to fulfil my side of the bargain, but statistically I believe this is the only surefire way you will never experience guilt or cowardice again."

Bansworth could only gargle an answer, his face an ugly shade of purple. Zygos pushed the dying man with the toe of his boot, rolling him into the dense foliage of a nearby arrowwood and out of sight.

This man is a monster, thought Praxis, still reeling from what he had seen. *Those who say the Seventh of the Twelve is*

governed by logic and reason have failed to understand that it is
just an excuse to disguise the rampant sadism that lies beneath.

"Enjoying the view, Praxis?" murmured Zygos, as if
he had guessed what Praxis was thinking. "Do you understand how lucky you are, now? If I had not needed a new
body, your corpse would be rotting in that dank cave next to
Aldos's. Food for the worms. Instead, you will be part of the
greatest victory over the nine Baronies since the greylings first
crawled out from the bowels of the earth."

There was the scrunch of metal on gravel. Two figures
were approaching, garbed in near-identical suits of armour.
The taller one was carrying a sleeping child in his arms, his
ocean-blue eyes searching for something.

Aldarin! cursed Praxis, the very name conjuring up a host
of conflicting emotions. First among them was hatred. The
arrogant Knight of Brachyura was the reason why the siege of
Arelium had failed. His incessant meddling had saved Jelaïa's
life — twice. Once on the banks of the River Stahl and again
in the Great Hall of Kessrin. He was the splinter in Praxis's
finger, the thorn in his side, the itch in the middle of his back,
always out of reach. An annoyance.

But he was also one of the only people who could stop
Zygos. *Pit!*

"Gentlemen," the Seventh of the Twelve said in his monotone voice. "If the information I have received is correct, it is
Sir Aldarin and Sir Ka'arka who stand before me? Bansworth
described you well. You appear to be in the wrong place at the
wrong time." He studied the sleeping child. "Baron del Klief,
I take it? Attempting to flee the city? I suppose it's only logical
that the rats would try to leave the sinking ship."

Aldarin said nothing. His companion, a knight of

Da'arran origin who Zygos had identified as Ka'arka, drew his axe.

"I have no quarrel with the Baron," Zygos continued. "However, the weaver has bequeathed Klief to me, and I cannot allow any of the del Klief bloodline to jeopardise that."

No! Praxis tried to call out, sensing what his captor was about to do. It was too late. There was a flash of steel followed by a soft whimper as the throwing dagger flashed across the space between them and thunked into Azael's skull. The tiny body spasmed then went limp. The Baron would never wake. The line of del Klief was no more.

Ka'arka cried out in grief and anger as he charged at Zygos like a raging bull.

My patron is doing just what I did to Hirkuin, Praxis thought. *Antagonising. Goading. Using the enemy's fragile emotions against them.*

Zygos did not try to stop the Da'arran's charge, only stepped aside at the last minute and gave the surprised knight a shove that sent him careening into one of the arrowwoods. The demi-god whirled back around to face Aldarin, who had dropped the dead Baron and was advancing menacingly, his breastplate wet with the child's blood, storm clouds gathering in the depths of his blue eyes.

Zygos baited him with an infuriating half-smile. Aldarin replied with a flurry of strikes. His opponent stepped back out of range, then dived forwards before Aldarin had time to react, using his momentum to tackle the big knight to the ground. The two men grappled like wrestlers, each trying to gain the upper hand.

They were not evenly matched. The Seventh of the Twelve may not have had the colossal strength of Brachyura or Mina — especially since inhabiting Praxis's body — but he was still a demi-god. He rolled sideways, pulling Aldarin with him. Once he had his back on the gravel and the helpless knight on top of him, he stuck a booted foot into Aldarin's stomach and catapulted him into the air. The Knight of Brachyura crashed into a nearby marble bench, splitting it in two.

I should be elated, Praxis thought, watching Aldarin stagger unsteadily to his feet and hawk a mouthful of blood. *Zygos is beating that sanctimonious idiot to a pulp. So, why am I so nervous?*

"Ka'arka," Aldarin shouted to his brother-in-arms, who was extracting himself from the arrowwood. "Zygos will not have come here alone. You must sound the alarm. The defences of the city have been compromised."

Ka'arka eyed Zygos warily. "Are you sure, Brother? He is stronger than he looks. The two of us working together would certainly not be superfluous."

"I can handle it."

"If you say so."

"Now, wait a minute," Zygos said with a frown. "Who's to say I will let you go anywhere? I don't think—" Aldarin's gauntleted fist hit him hard in the stomach, expulsing the air from his lungs. Zygos bent over double and was rewarded with a knee to the face. There was the crack of breaking teeth.

"RUN!" Aldarin shouted at Ka'arka, moving in to attack Zygos again. But the Seventh of the Twelve was ready this time. A low, sweeping kick hooked around Aldarin's ankle. He hit the ground hard.

Zygos stood over him, and Praxis could feel that his captor was beginning to get angry. "Flies," he said irritably,

spitting out a loose tooth. "You are nothing but flies, testing my patience with your constant buzzing." Aldarin tried
to rise, but Zygos stamped on his breastplate, pushing him
back down. "Stay in the mud where you belong, Knight of
Brachyura."

Aldarin groaned, rolled onto his stomach and began to
crawl towards the fallen body of Azael. Zygos watched him
with amusement. "Flies were the wrong analogy," he said.
"Worms seem more appropriate." He pulled his stiletto from
his belt and walked unhurriedly after Aldarin.

"Perhaps once Klief is mine, I will head to Kessrin next.
Then on from there to the temple of Brachyura. That eye-
sore has been left standing far too long. And given that your
Order took my temple from me, it seems only logical that I
destroy yours. Balance. Balance in all things."

The temple, Praxis thought. *That's it! Before he took over
my body. Before he knew real emotions. The only time he lost his
composure was when speaking of the defilement of the temple of
Zygos.*

"Let me look you in the eye, Sir Knight," Zygos was
saying, pushing Aldarin onto his back. "Ah, that's better. I
can see such hatred there, ebbing and flowing like the tides
of the Sea of Sorrow. Know that it is reciprocal."

Praxis felt it. It was time to decide. Another crossroads,
two radically different paths diverging. The satisfaction of
Aldarin's death followed by an aeon locked inside his own
body, controlled by an entity that was obviously insane …
or one last roll of the dice. One last trick. One last chance.

He chuckled to himself. Who was he kidding? He had
spent years trying to convince himself that he was something
he was not: a Knight of Zygos. And what were the three

most important pillars that all initiates must strive to abide by? Balance, Order, and Logic. It was not Balance that had pushed him to become Regent of Arelium. It was not Logic that had made him side with Derello instead of Mina. And it was not Order that had led him to defy Aldos and, ultimately, Zygos himself. He was no longer an initiate. He was simply ... Praxis. Praxis the gambler. Praxis the risk-taker. Praxis the victor.

He plunged deep into the depths of his own memories. He could barely remember his mother's face, but what she had told him of her flight from the temple was engraved onto his very soul. He tore her words from the confines of his mind and let them bubble up to the surface where Zygos would find them.

"They attacked without warning," his mother had said. "Our role in the Schism made us the perfect scapegoats. We were the Order that had revealed the Pact, and it was deemed that we should be the first to suffer. We could not see their faces, only the twisted horns of their helmets. They were the stuff of nightmares. We were unarmed, but that did not stop them. They flowed unimpeded through the temple like a plague of locusts, leaving none alive."

What are you doing? echoed the voice of Zygos in his head, loud enough to cause him pain. **Why show me this?**

So that you know, Praxis replied. *So that you understand.* He forced more of his mother's story up into the light.

"Your father and I would have surely died if not for a stroke of luck. We had been training together, fully-armoured and with real blades. There were several secret ways out of the temple, paths known only to the temple masters like your father. We abandoned our brothers and sisters. We abandoned our Order. We escaped."

Traitors, seethed Zygos. Praxis could feel the Seventh of the Twelve's anger crackling and popping like flames on kindling. He concentrated, and for the briefest of moments, he made his little finger twitch. Nearly there. Just one more memory.

"Our escape route took us across one of the galleries spanning the Conclave Hall," Praxis's mother had told him. "We could see what they were doing down below. They had tied ropes around the statue of our patron and were trying to pull it from its pedestal."

What?

"Their leader had removed his helmet. He was laughing. Laughing as they tore out the heart of our temple. I had to stop myself from crying out as they finally managed to rip the statue free. I could only watch helplessly as it fell, both arms shattering like glass, its noble face cracking. And still, they laughed. Laughed and praised the name of Brachyura."

"BRACHYURA!" Zygos cried aloud, and the burning fire of his anger erupted like a volcano. He wheeled on Aldarin, mad with rage, his stiletto raised high, poised to strike the killing blow.

Aldarin lowered his eyes in resignation as the blade began to fall.

NO! ordered Praxis. He poured all his mental strength into the command. His body's right arm slowed, then stopped, as if encountering an invisible wall. It spasmed, fighting to break free, but Praxis held it fast.

Aldarin looked up at Zygos in astonishment, his gaze

travelling between the trembling arm and the look of hatred on his opponent's face.

Come on! Praxis thought. *Think! For once in your stupid, arrogant, good-for-nothing life, actually try to think!*

"Praxis?" asked Aldarin quietly.

Yes, you idiot! Praxis raged, knowing full well that the knight couldn't hear him. *Do something!*

I do not understand why you continue to defy me. The voice hit Praxis like a punch to the face. **You gain nothing by doing so. All you have bought yourself is an eternity of torture. You will never know rest. I will scrub your mind raw every morning. I will tear off little strips of your sanity, leaving you with just enough to beg for mercy. But there will be none. And all for what? A few seconds of freedom? A few seconds of control?**

The agony was nearly too much for Praxis. He could feel his grip slipping. The intense pain was making him lose his focus. Then he saw a glint of metal on the edge of Zygos's vision and knew it was over.

Sometimes, Lord, a few seconds of freedom is all that I need.

Aldarin hefted the throwing dagger that he had pulled from Azael's skull, exhaled slowly, and let it fly. It was a clumsy throw, lacking speed and grace. But at such a short distance, there was no need for either. The needle-like tip entered Zygos's obsidian eye, smashed through the hard bone of the socket behind and lodged itself deep in his brain.

Praxis jubilated as he felt the invasive spirit of Zygos fade screaming into the dark, draining from his body like pus from a wound.

I made the right choice, he thought, relieved. *Better to die free than live as a slave.* Something tugged at his mind. It wanted to lead him ... somewhere. Somewhere else.

Somewhere better? Praxis asked.

That depends, the thing replied. *You will be ... judged.*

Ah, the eternal philosophical question, thought Praxis dreamily. *Does a handful of good deeds make up for a hundred bad ones? Would helping save Klief be enough to balance the scales? For there must be balance ... Balance in all things.*

There was only one way to find out.

Praxis sighed contentedly and let his guide take him away.

Away from Aldarin.

Away from Klief.

Away from the living.

Towards the light.

CHAPTER 24

NEVER TRULY GONE

"I am no Lady. I am the weaver, the stitcher, the seamster. I am the one who guides. The one who shapes. The one who leads. I am the mother, the father, the god, and the general. I am nothing, and I am everything."

'WEAVER', 123 AT

I MUST BE GOING *mad*, thought Reed as Listus del Arelium flickered into existence. *This place has finally drained me of the last dregs of my sanity.*

Then Mithuna's head whipped round, as fast as an adder, and he realised that the long-dead Baron was no hallucination. The Third of the Twelve released her hold on Vohanen. The knight fell to the ground, coughing and spluttering. Reed could see bruises already starting to form on his cheeks and around his plaited beard. A few moments longer and he would have choked to death.

"Memories," wheezed Vohanen, his voice cracking. He rubbed at his sore throat.

"What do you mean?" asked Reed, helping him up.

"What Jeffson told me was true. As long as the memory of those we loved and lost still remains, then they are never truly gone. They are here, Reed! Remember what Shala told us? They can be drawn to us! Let us call them to our aid!"

Reed opened his mouth to reply, but Mithuna beat him to it. "What are you prattling on about, little man?" she said testily, her ebony eyes still on the Baron.

"Avor," Vohanen replied simply.

A look of confusion crossed her features. "I've … heard that name before."

"Avor," the knight repeated. He was smiling.

"Stop that."

"AVOR!" he cried hoarsely, his face red with effort.

"I said, stop that," Mithuna repeated. She backhanded him across the mouth, splitting his lip. Vohanen laughed back at her, his teeth and beard stained with blood.

A whistling wind swept through the room, cutting through the weaver's humming. The chains holding the wyrm heart jangled and shook. The wind was not silent; it carried with it a song, sung in a strong, energetic tenor. Something about a girl at a fair. Reed knew that song. And he knew that voice.

The embossed ram's head set in the centre of the tower shield cracked Mithuna on the knee cap with enough strength to dent the metal. She sprang back with a yelp of pain and surprise.

"Father," tutted Avor reproachfully. "You look terrible. And is that a skin of wine I see at your belt? Honestly, you're supposed to be setting an example to your children, not the other way around!"

Vohanen, tears streaming down his face, enveloped his son in a bear hug. "Avor, Lad! You have returned to me!"

"Only for an instant, Father," Avor said, trying unsuccessfully to free himself. "Your presence in the Shroud is visible to those beyond, but my corporeal form is held together through sheer force of will. We need to use this time wisely." He jerked his head in Mithuna's direction. The Third of the Twelve was studying them from a safe distance.

"Shieldwall?" proposed Vohanen, wiping his eyes and bending to retrieve his tower shield.

"Naturally," Avor replied, locking his own shield with that of his father's.

"You've only had it for a few minutes, and it's already damaged," grumbled Vohanen, taking in the crushed ram's head. "It took me ages to carve that."

Avor sighed. "This shape is a memory, Father, pulled from your mind. Your shield is sitting safe and sound in a flooded tunnel somewhere deep in the bowels of the Morlakian Pit. You are quite welcome to it, if you can hold your breath for long enough."

"Always contradicting me, aren't you? Why I—"

"The weaver, Father. The humming must stop."

"Right, yes."

"I cannot let you do that," Mithuna said. Reed saw with surprise that the Third of the Twelve was trembling. Could these near-invincible demi-gods actually know fear?

"Careful," he said to the two Knights of Kriari. "Do

not underestimate her. Remember the Great Hall of Morlak, Vohanen. She was a formidable foe."

"Aye."

Father and son advanced. There was a cry from the other side of the room as Listus del Arelium scored another bloody hit on Mina, deftly dodging a rapid counterattack. The Baron moved with an inhuman fluidity as if his golden plate weighed nothing at all.

And why should it? thought Reed. *Why should a figure constructed from light, air, and memories be constrained by physical limitations?*

Mithuna cursed at hearing her sister's shout of pain and barrelled forwards, crashing into the shieldwall. Miraculously, both shields held. Vohanen slashed wildly at her exposed left flank. The giantess whirled and caught the short sword between her thumb and index finger.

"You will have to do better than that," she snarled.

"Agreed," said Avor and stabbed her in the stomach. He leant hard into the blow, pushing his blade in up to the hilt. Mithuna screamed. The young knight ignored her, yanking his sword free and twisting it as he did so, widening the wound. Steaming hot coils of intestine spilled from the gaping rent in her flesh, hanging down far enough to cover her bare feet.

Mithuna opened her mouth to say something, only for bile and black blood to vomit forth, spattering against the knights' raised shields. She grasped feebly at her entrails, clutching at the slippery ropes, trying hopelessly to force them back inside her body. Then her eyelids flickered, and she fell over backwards.

"NO!" Mina cried, turning her head as her sister's body

hit the floor. It was the only distraction Listus needed. His first cut, slicing across the back of her knees, made her kneel while the return swipe took her head from her shoulders in a geyser of blood. The Last of the Twelve joined her siblings on the hard earth, her feet twitching. Brachyura, Kriari, and Kumbha lay close by, no longer moving, dark liquid still seeping from half-closed orifices.

"It's … over," said Reed, not wanting to believe it, his addled mind still playing catch-up with his eyes. *Two of the Twelve. They defeated two of the Twelve in minutes. How is that even possible?*

"Not quite," Avor replied. His voice sounded tinny, as if coming from the other side of a locked door or from another room. He raised his sword to point at the weaver, but the movement was sluggish as if made under water.

"Are you all right, Lad?" Vohanen asked, his brow creased with concern.

Avor nodded, his face blurring as he did so. "This echo is falling apart. We must strike now while she is still weak."

"Are the other members of the Twelve even still alive?" Reed wondered, looking at the motionless bodies.

"I think so. I can feel their … spirits. The weaver's song is severing the link that ties the mind to the body. If we do not act soon, it will become permanent."

"Then, we do so together," said Jelaïa. She was leaning heavily on her father's arm, her face pale and drawn, but Reed was relieved to see that she seemed otherwise unharmed.

"Together," he agreed, tightening his grip on his spear.

They approached, three warriors and two shimmering evocations, surrounding the hunched form of the weaver.

She stopped humming and slowly opened her almond-shaped eyes.

"You have found the power of this place," she uttered wearily. "I hoped you would not. Shala could make the Twelve appear in this way but only for the briefest of moments. The bond between them is strong, but it is not love. Love is what keeps our memories alive. There is nothing more to say. Do what you must."

"For the Old Guard," answered Reed solemnly, thrusting his spear into the weaver's chest. A black, pitch-like substance spurted from the puncture wound.

"For Morlak." Vohanen's short sword pierced the creature's side just above her hips.

"For Arelium," whispered Jelaïa, stabbing into the thing's back with her dagger. More viscous darkness welled forth.

The weaver shuddered. The strips of fabric she wore were now drenched in black liquid. Her yellow eyes found Reed's. "You have not won," she said softly in her discordant speech. "A god can never be beaten. And to my children, I … will … always … be … a god." There was a flare of light deep within those eyes, so bright that Reed had to tear his gaze away. When he looked back, the weaver was dead.

Jelaïa let out a sob and threw herself into her father's arms, heedless of the blood that covered his armour.

"I am … so proud of you, Jeli. My daughter. My Lady of the White Wolf." The Baron's voice was distant and muffled, his face becoming more and more distorted. It reminded Reed of catching sight of his reflection in a glazed window. The shape was there but smudged, the imperfections in the glass making it a blemished copy.

"Must you go, Father? Must you leave me again?"

"You do not need me any longer, Jeli. You have become more than I ever hoped you would. Do not squander this new life that you have won through so much sweat and blood. Stay true to your friends and loved ones. Spend all the time you can with them. Listen to them. Heed their advice. They will make you stronger still."

His voice was barely audible now. He released Jelaïa, and Reed could see *through* him, the slowly beating heart of the fulcrum mixing with the gold plate of his armour.

"I only wish I could see my wife again," Listus said wistfully, trying and failing to catch a loose strand of Jelaïa's hair. "Without her by my side, a part of me is still missing. Tell her …"

He could no longer be heard. His translucent, blurred face moved, but no sound emerged from his fading lips. A flurry of wind tugged at his body, unravelling it like fog, leaving a shimmering golden mist until even that dissolved into nothing.

"A good man," said Reed respectfully.

"A good father," Jelaïa replied with a forlorn smile. She was no longer crying. "I will miss him dreadfully. It's strange. I am not overwhelmed with sadness. I think … I have already mourned his passing. There is no more room left in my heart for grief."

"It is the living that need us now," Reed agreed. "Aldarin, Syrella, Jeffson, and the others. They are counting on us to stop the wyrm."

"Sage words," Avor added, his image jittering like the flames of the fire. He turned to Vohanen. "Does that mean you will stop moping about, Father?"

The old Knight of Kriari looked indignant. "Pit, Lad, subtlety is really not one of your strong suits, is it?"

"You're hurting my brothers and hurting my mother," Avor continued stubbornly. "Strong emotions bleed through the Shroud, I can feel her pain. Her incomprehension. By hurting her, you are hurting me."

"It was my fault you died," Vohanen said in a soft voice. "It should have been me."

"By the Twelve, Father, it sounds like you have repeated such idiocies so often you are starting to believe them. I chose to do what I did, not you. If you had stayed behind in that tunnel, we would not be ..." his voice faded for a moment, then returned "... talking right now. Mithuna would be ruling Morlak. You would not be here to stop the weaver. The past cannot be changed. Look to the future. To your family."

Vohanen went to put his hand on his son's shoulder but passed through it as if it were empty air.

"Swear you will take care of Evie and my brothers," Avor pleaded through gritted teeth, each word an effort. "Swear it."

"You have my word, Lad," Vohanen replied solemnly. "You have my oath."

"That is ... good. And Father?"

"Yes, Avor?"

"I will be waiting. When it is time ... We will see each other again."

The two stood looking into each other's eyes. Father and son. So different, yet so alike. Then Reed blinked, and Avor was gone. Vohanen stood immobile for a moment, lost in his own thoughts, before untying the wineskin from his belt and throwing it against the far wall with enough force to split the leather. He saw Reed looking at him and glared. "Lost the taste for it," he grunted with a sniff.

"Kriari!" The First of the Twelve was on his feet, both hands clutching his skull. "Weaver hurt Kriari!"

"Not anymore," Reed replied, jerking a finger towards the rapidly-cooling corpse. "You are still alive, then, Kriari? I am glad. We have been through much, you and I."

"Kriari," the giant agreed sagely, wiping the sticky black muck from his face.

Brachyura stirred. "Although alive is not quite the right word, friend Reed," he muttered, sitting up with a wince and spitting out a mouthful of liquid. "We are creatures of flesh and shadow, powered by this muddy filth and an old woman's memories." Kriari grabbed his brother's arm to help him up, slapped him amicably on the shoulder and went to help Kumbha.

"There is more to you than that," Jelaïa said. "You chose to break the Pact, to go against the weaver's falsehoods. As did Kumbha. You have the will to forge your own path. Do not forget it."

"Speaking of paths," Reed added. "How about we finish what we came here to do?"

Brachyura turned to the enormous, pulsating heart that dominated the room, untouched by the recent skirmish. Grasping his colossal double-headed axe firmly with both hands, he lifted it above his head and brought it scything down. The blade bit deep into the fleshy organ. The Fourth of the Twelve ripped his axe free in a shower of blood and torn flesh. Despite a gaping hole in one of its ventricles, the heart continued to pump feebly.

Brachyura yelled something incomprehensible and swung his weapon again and again. Crimson liquid sluiced down his arms and pooled around his sabatons. Finally, inexorably, the heart split in two with a sickening tearing sound, each half still suspended by its own set of chains. Blood gushed across the floor as the two ventricles were emptied of their contents, lapping at the dead bodies of the Twelve and staining the leather of Reed's boots.

No more fulcrum and no more weaver, Reed exulted. *For once, the odds are in our favour.*

Wait.

The weaver.

He looked around frantically. *Where was her body?*

"Wh … where is she?" he stammered out loud, drawing Jelaïa's attention. She searched the room, her face growing pale.

"We stabbed her," she said hurriedly. "We all did. God or no god, she can't have survived that."

Something skittered in the darkness high above. The tap-tapping of talons on stone followed by an inhuman peal of laughter. A voice echoed out of the black.

"Foolish children! I keep telling you, but you never listen. This is the Shroud. I cannot be killed here. This is *my* domain. I am a part of this place, and this place is a part of me."

The weaver appeared suddenly, scuttling down the wall like a spider, her back arched at an impossible angle, her mouth wide open, spittle dripping from her pointed teeth.

"STOP HER!" cried Reed, throwing his spear like a javelin. The weaver tensed then sprang from her perch, sailing over their heads to land on the opposite wall.

"YOUR KNIFE!" Brachyura shouted at Jelaïa. She stared at him in befuddlement. What could her tiny knife do against a god?

"HURRY!" urged the dark-skinned titan. Some sixth sense made him leap backwards. The weaver slammed into the ground where he had been standing, splashing into the blood that still covered the chamber. Vohanen charged at her rear, his short sword drawn. The weaver kicked out with a clawed foot, and the Knight of Kriari went flying, rebounding off the floor and rolling to a stop a few feet away.

"NOW!" Brachyura implored. Jelaïa threw him the knife just as the weaver pounced. She screamed as a long nail stabbed straight through her right shoulder and pinned her to the ragged remains of the fulcrum. She could feel the mangled flesh pressing into her back, rubbing against her dress.

Reed, weaponless, punched the weaver hard in the face. She laughed again and batted him away, knocking him into the pool of the heart's blood.

"Let me go!" Jelaïa moaned, tugging ineffectively at the length of bone holding her prisoner.

"I think not," the weaver replied, her lips stretched into a terrible rictus, somewhere between joy and madness. "You dared attack a god. Such a heinous crime deserves an appropriate punishment. I will flay the flesh from your body and rip those beautiful eyes from your face. But first, let us make sure we are not interrupted."

And closing her eyes, she began to hum.

CHAPTER 25

Speaking in Tongues

"People often underestimate Ka'arka. He is so different in character from the stoic Aldarin, always laughing and joking. If there's mischief to be found, you can be sure he'll be in the thick of it. In fact, he's probably the one that started it. But underneath that carefree exterior lies a solid core of prowess, bravery, and loyalty."

Praedora, First Priestess of Brachyura, 419 AT

⤳

K A'ARKA SPED ALONG the paths of the secluded garden. Another tremor nearly knocked him off his feet. He stumbled into a rose bush, the sharp thorns raking his face.

Pit! That sounded closer than last time, he thought, passing through the garden gates and out into the courtyard. He was greeted by scenes of pandemonium. The third wall was under heavy assault; the greylings appeared to have gained footholds in two separate locations and were attempting to lower ropes for the threshers.

The ramparts themselves were a maelstrom of whirling colours: the red of Arelium fought side by side with the blue of Kessrin and the sparkling gold of Klief. Tall Knights of Brachyura in burnished silver congregated where the fighting was the thickest, their skill and determination instrumental in halting the enemy advance. Derello was among the defenders, employing a particularly grandiose style of swordsmanship that made it look like he was dancing.

One of the few remaining agamids soared overhead and was quickly peppered with arrows from archers stationed on the balcony atop the cathedral's spire. The dying reptile plummeted, splattering onto the cobbles below like a piece of rotten fruit.

The cries of conflict mixed with the angry screeching of the greylings and the screams of the wounded. Ka'arka scanned the field of battle, forcing his tired brain to think. Where was the weakest link? What would be the best way to hasten the defenders' demise? His eyes alighted on the gatehouse, and he saw a flash of metal in the shadows. Muttering a curse, he began to run towards it, yelling at the top of his lungs as he did so. "The gate! We are betrayed! They are trying to open the gate!"

His shouts were swallowed by the ambient cacophony. Drawing closer, he spied the shaved head of Orkam on the western parapet, leading a contingent of spearmen. "ORKAM!" he bellowed as loudly as he could. "THE GATE!"

The guard captain's head swivelled round. His face was

covered in sweat. A greyling claw had taken off the top of his left ear, narrowly missing his eye in the process. He tapped the backs of the rear rank of the spearwall and made for the nearest stairs.

Ka'arka skirted around an empty cart and tripped over the body of a golden-clad Kliefien. The guardsman's throat had been cut. Two of his companions lay close by, breastplates riddled with dagger holes.

They were taken completely by surprise, thought Ka'arka. *And their golden armour did nothing to protect them.*

The gatehouse loomed ahead. Ka'arka saw figures locked in combat around the crank at the base of the portcullis. Two town guard against a half-dozen of the enemy wielding long knives and wearing black leather. He was still over fifty feet away. Too far to save them.

One soon fell to a jab to the neck, blood spraying from a punctured artery. The last survivor gave a terrible cry of despair and rushed forwards, his spear held out before him like a lance. He impaled one of the Knights of Zygos on the tasselled tip before being overwhelmed. There was a creak as the crank began to move.

Ka'arka drew his axe and kissed the word 'Brachyura' inscribed into the hilt. *Give me strength, Lord*, he prayed silently. And then he was among them.

His first victim never saw him coming, Ka'arka's axe cleaving through his back before he could turn. The knight pulled his gore-spattered blade free. One down.

Two Knights of Zygos were turning the crank as fast as they could, and thanks to their efforts, the portcullis was already half-raised. Three others stood between Ka'arka and his goal, blocking off all angles of attack. He feinted left, but it was clumsy and his opponent read his intentions easily, deflecting the follow-up swing and countering with a low thrust that screeched along his armoured thigh.

Careful, he thought. *These are Knights of the Twelve I am fighting not simple greylings. I must not treat them as such.*

His eyes flickered to the portcullis. There was only a foot-and-a-half of metal still visible. His opponents made no move to attack, and why would they? Time was on their side, all they had to do was keep him from reaching the crank, and they would soon be joined by thirty thousand greylings.

Pit! He needed to think. A well-thought-out plan that would—

A lithe female shape shouldered him aside and slammed into the three Knights of Zygos, her tongue-like glaive twirling so fast it appeared to be alive. Something dark and wet landed at Ka'arka's feet, and it took him a moment to realise that it was a severed arm.

"Move yourself, Knight of Brachyura!" came the shout from within the whirlwind of bodies. He shook his head in disbelief and rushed to her aid, ducking under a wild cut from a stiletto and taking off his attacker's right leg with a two-handed axe stroke. Leaping over the falling body, he used his momentum to tackle another knight to the ground. The man fought hard, but there was no escaping two hundred and fifty pounds of armoured Da'arran. Ka'arka knocked him senseless with the butt of his axe.

"KA'ARKA!" yelled Orkam. "THE GATE!"

The portcullis had been raised. The final obstacle to the greyling horde was a set of barred double doors. Two Knights of Zygos were in the process of manoeuvring the thick beam of oak out of its supports.

Ka'arka growled a string of expletives and hauled himself to his feet. His axe felt slippery in his gauntleted fist. His calf muscles ached from his frenzied run from the keep's gardens. He gauged the distance to the door. There was no way that he would get there before they managed to free the bar. Xer'ana was still trading blows with a Knight of Zygos. It was up to him.

He widened his stance, planting his feet firmly on the blood-stained cobbles, and held his axe at arm's length with both hands, one thumb pressed against the back of the handle to keep it straight.

"Distance," he muttered to himself. "Distance and rotation."

He inhaled, brought his axe up behind his head, then swung his arms forwards in one fluid motion, releasing his grip on the haft just as the blade passed in front of his face. The weapon flew towards its intended target, rotating once … twice … before bisecting the skull of a Knight of Zygos like a ripe melon, showering his companion with shards of bone and brain matter.

"So perish all enemies of the Twelve!" shouted Ka'arka ecstatically. *Wait until Aldarin hears about that throw!* he thought. *I doubt even Brachyura himself could have done better.*

"It was … quite proficient," agreed Xer'ana from behind his right shoulder, wiping the blade of her glaive on her tunic. Orkam and a score of Arelian town guard followed after her.

Ka'arka inclined his head and called out to the lone enemy survivor. "Knight of Zygos! It is over! Lower your weapons and come with us peacefully. Do not throw your life away in needless fanaticism."

The man cackled, the whites of his eyes clear and sharp against the blood and brain that plastered his once-pale face. "Fanaticism?" he said mockingly. "So much hypocrisy. I have never known such joy since being reunited with our long-lost patron. He understands me like no other. You confuse fanaticism with adulation."

"Keep him talking," whispered Xer'ana, inching forwards step by tentative step.

"Adulation?" Ka'arka scoffed. "You are being tricked. The Pact is a lie. The man you follow is not Zygos, or at least not the Zygos who walked these lands three hundred years ago. Think about it! Would someone who based his whole life around logic abandon humanity to the greylings?"

The Knight of Zygos was shaking his head. "Is that how you hope to sway me? I do not care about what happened in another life. I do not care if this man is Zygos or not. Whoever he is, he has brought our Order back from the brink of destruction. He has given me purpose. And most of all, he has helped me be proud of the name Helios."

Xer'ana took another step. The ground rumbled.

"You talk of greylings," Helios continued. "Yet, you know so little of the creatures. Do you realise that they have learnt the rudiments of our language? And that the ones you call threshers are well-versed in their own tongue? A tongue that we humans never thought to learn?"

Ka'arka glanced at Xer'ana. She was nearly within striking range. A few seconds more.

"Zygos assimilated what he could. He believed in capitalising on all possible advantages. It is a difficult language, but he did teach us one word." His eyes glittered triumphantly, and Ka'arka knew he had made a terrible mistake. "The word 'Now'."

Xer'ana sprang. Helios opened his mouth and screamed a coarse, guttural sound, cutting through the clamour of the defenders up on the ramparts. He continued to scream until Xer'ana's glaive nailed him to the wooden door.

Ka'arka felt a flutter of trepidation as Helios's death cry was repeated back to him from the other side of the wall. It started with a single echo, then a dozen, then a hundred as the threshers lying in wait took up the call.

"GET BACK!" he shouted in panic to Xer'ana. There was a whip-like crack. The oaken bar split, its broken halves falling uselessly out of their supports. The Baroness's daughter whirled round and Ka'arka saw a flicker of fear in her proud eyes. Then the doors slammed open with the force of a hurricane, splattering Helios's remains against the stone wall and hurling Xer'ana into the air. She landed badly, her left arm twisting under her, and slithered to a halt.

Pit! raged Ka'arka, as a mass of threshers boiled through the opening, pushing and shoving each other to be the first inside. He reached over his back for his axe, and his hand closed on empty air. His weapon was gone, buried in the skull of a Knight of Zygos.

Someone tapped him on the arm, and he turned to find Orkam glowering up at him. "You would do best to join us in the spearwall, Knight," he growled, jerking a dirty thumb at the flimsy-looking ranks of guardsmen lined up behind him. "It didn't do much to save us last time, but it's better to die together than alone. And we've learnt a lot since Arelium. Just make sure you follow my lead. Got that, Da'arran?"

Ka'arka quickly took up position in the second rank, the threshers now only a few yards away. He had lost sight of Xer'ana, her prone form swallowed by clouds of dust. Someone passed him a spear.

"Wait!" cautioned Orkam. "On my mark."

The enemy had worked themselves into a frenzy, several of them frothing at the mouth or hitting their naked torsos with the flats of their primitive blades. They picked up the pace. Ka'arka had never been on the receiving end of a cavalry charge, but he knew it must resemble something like this: a pounding, rolling wall of sound ... impossible to avoid.

"Wait ..." repeated Orkam.

Ka'arka could feel the sweat dripping down his braided black hair and neck. The men around him shifted and muttered, but none broke ranks, a testament to their tenacity and courage. *I am a Knight of Brachyura*, he thought, standing a little straighter. *I will show no fear.*

The threshers were so close that he could smell their stench. See their puckered scars and dirty yellow eyes.

I will show no fear.

"BREAK!" bellowed Orkam suddenly, and the spearwall scattered like leaves in the wind. The confused threshers lumbered clumsily through the gaps left by the guardsmen, most of them too surprised to retaliate. Ka'arka saw one of the beasts lash out almost instinctively at one of the men as it passed, breaking his nose.

"COUNTER!" barked the gruff captain, and the Arelians turned ... perfectly positioned to attack the threshers' unprotected rears. Spear-tips that were mostly useless against the thick, leathery hides had no difficulty piercing the thinner skin behind the knee or groin. Orkam aimed lower, cutting through one of the creature's hamstrings. Ka'arka, standing almost a foot taller, punched his own spear through a grey-skinned neck.

"SPEARWALL!" The men reformed, breathing hard. Six enormous corpses lay scattered on the cobbles.

"Six threshers felled by twenty men!" cried Ka'arka in awe. "I've never seen such a feat. Captain Orkam, what you have done here is nothing short of heroic."

"Aye, a pity no one will live to tell anyone about it," Orkam replied dourly, pointing with the tip of his spear to the flood of greylings and threshers pouring through the ruined doors of the gatehouse.

"Aldarin told me you were not the most optimistic of men, Orkam," Ka'arka said, hefting his spear. "But I think on this one occasion, you may be right."

The ground rumbled again. Ka'arka could feel the vibrations ripple along his tired bones.

"Pit-spawned wyrm is nearly here," he said. "I suppose all that remains is to see which of our enemies kills us first."

"That's no wyrm," countered Orkam in a strange tone of voice. He sounded almost … happy. Ka'arka looked at him with concern. The gruff captain appeared to be smiling, a rather unsettling expression, as if he were trying it for the first time. "You didn't think I'd come down here without sending for reinforcements first, did you? I may be brave, but I'm not suicidal."

The rhythmic thundering grew louder, and Ka'arka could now tell that it wasn't the same sound as he had heard in the gardens. It pounded against his senses like a beating heart, a banging gong … or a host of galloping hooves.

"Horses," he murmured just as Loré del Conte rounded the side of the cathedral of Klief at the head of fifty vassals on barded war steeds, his lance held high, the red and white banner of Arelium fluttering from its tip. The handsome noble had his visor up and was grinning like a man half his age.

"FALL BACK!" yelled Orkam, and his spearmen dispersed just as the heavy cavalry hit the first of the threshers. They ploughed onwards without stopping and crunched with impressive force into the enemy closer to the gate. There the charge dissolved into a chaotic melee as lances were dropped in favour of axes and swords. Ka'arka caught a glimpse of Loré, still smiling manically, before he was carried away by the tide of battle.

"They won't hold long," Orkam remarked, pulling one of his men out of the path of a riderless horse. "Cavalry is most effective when charging. Once they've lost all momentum, they'll get bogged down by the greylings, just like they did in Arelium."

"We need to find some way to block the gate, then," said Ka'arka.

"Aye. What do you suggest? When I was on the walls of Kessrin, I remember Brachyura using a cart to—"

"Of course! That's genius! I passed an empty cart on my way here. There are enough of us to manoeuvre it into place in front of the doors. Come on!"

The cart had not moved from where Ka'arka had first seen it, the unlucky members of the Kliefien town guard strewn pitifully around its wheels.

"Six of us should be enough to push it," said Orkam pensively, scratching at his bald scalp. "The rest of you move those corpses out of the way — respectfully — then get your backsides up top and poke at anything that comes within range." The unpleasant sound of a horse whinnying in pain was carried to them over the wind. "And let's hurry it up. Move, guardsmen. MOVE! Da'arran! As you made the excellent choice to throw your weapon away, you can have the honour of pushing the cart with us."

"Why doesn't anyone call me by my name?" grumbled Ka'arka, moving round to the back of the cart and starting to push. "It's always Da'arran this or Knight of Brachyura that. It's not like it's difficult to pronounce."

"I know your name," Orkam said mildly, adding his considerable strength to the rear end of the cart. "It's the sound a chicken makes when you wring its neck. Ka'aaaarka!"

"When we are finished here," Ka'arka replied in an equally mild tone, "I will take you to the mustering field before the walls of Arelium and teach you a little respect."

Orkam let slip a bark of laughter. "Sounds like a date, Knight of Brachyura. I look forward to it."

The cart was nearing the gate. They were forced to turn abruptly to avoid the carcass of a large warhorse, its entrails steaming in the cold night air. Greylings and Arelians were everywhere; cutting, biting, stabbing, clawing. Ka'arka saw three of the vile creatures jump onto a horse's back and pull a struggling noble from the saddle. The stallion reared, throwing the greylings free, and crushing their small bodies with its steel-shod hooves.

Loré was still mounted, his exquisitely-crafted longsword rising and falling like a lumberjack's axe, each stroke killing or maiming those who dared challenge him. Before him lay a dead thresher, its eye pierced by the tip of Loré's lance, the colours of Arelium covering its face.

"MAKE WAY!" bawled Orkam. A greyling leapt high over Ka'arka's head, only to be expertly skewered by one of Orkam's spearmen.

"CLOSE THE GATES!" came Loré's reply, and his nobles surged forwards with renewed vigour. For a few miraculous seconds, the third gate was cleared of the enemy, and Orkam wasted no time in pushing the cart into place. Ka'arka heaved a sigh of relief and rolled his shoulders, cracking his bones.

Loré del Conte rode to meet them in a flurry of dust. He beamed at them. "Good thinking, brave men of Arelium! A cart! Excellent!" He laughed. "By the Twelve, it feels good to be killing greylings again! We'll mop up the remnants here and find some more rubble or wood to reinforce the entrance. You have earned yourselves an ale or two at the tavern! Well done! Well done indeed!"

He wheeled his agitated warhorse around and charged back into the fray, yelling an old Arelian battle cry.

"He seems ... excited," said Ka'arka wearily. His tired eyes roamed the space before the gatehouse, but there was still no sign of Xer'ana.

"He has suffered much," agreed Orkam, leaning wearily against the cart. "Imagine thinking you would never ride a horse into battle again, never hold a sword, never lead a cavalry charge. All these things were essential to Lord del Conte's life. He lost them, then regained them. I can under-stand his happiness."

"And I can understand why Baron del Arelium made you captain of the town guard, Orkam," said Ka'arka, clapping the man on the shoulder. "You are brave, authoritative, and resourceful. Arelium is lucky to have you."

"Thank you, Da'arr— Ka'arka," the bald captain replied, looking almost embarrassed. "You are not too bad yourself. There are worse people I would wish by my side in a fight. Oh, and here comes Aldarin."

Ka'arka followed his gaze and saw his friend limping towards them, his face and breastplate covered in dark ichor.

"Where were you?" Ka'arka asked, grasping Aldarin's wrist. "Your presence here would have been most beneficial."

"I ... apologise," Aldarin replied. He looked exhausted. "I was delayed. Zygos is no more."

"You killed one of the Twelve?"

"No. Praxis killed him. I only helped."

"Praxis? What? Never mind. Where is the Baron? Where is Azael?"

Aldarin sighed deeply. "We must return to Makara."

His gaze wandered to the cathedral, its stone walls untouched, rising stern and resolute over the third wall.

"I must tell him that the Baron of Klief is dead."

CHAPTER 26

THE OAKS OF JAELEM

"Nothing can stop the unpredictability of life. We cannot know how our actions will shape the world around us, just as we cannot know how the actions of others will affect us. So, instead of trying to plan every future step along the path we walk, maybe we should stop for a moment and cherish the present. For it is only by first understanding who we really are that we can begin to discern where we are going."

PRAEDORA, FIRST PRIESTESS OF BRACHYURA, 425 AT

❧

THE WEAVER'S HUMMING resonated around the enclosed chamber, the echoes bouncing off the walls again and again until it sounded as if the chant had been taken up by an entire choir. Reed struggled to focus. His chest was on fire; his old wounds from the siege of Arelium were making it hard for him to breathe. He tried to ignore the pain and the heart blood that dripped from his vermilion cloak, inhaling a great lungful of air and searching for his thrown spear.

Jelaïa writhed under the creature's talons, a dark red circle spreading rapidly from her injured shoulder across the fabric of her dress. The weaver gloated and, still humming, raised a clawed hand.

"The eyes," she said. "We will start with the eyes."

Brachyura's axe sliced through the soft flesh of the weaver's neck and ripped her head from her shoulders. The Fourth of the Twelve took another step and crushed the disembodied skull with the butt of his axe. He was holding Jelaïa's dagger in his free hand — it looked about the size of a toothpick clenched in his massive fist. Blood was running from both his ears, two red streaks on either side of his neck.

"I was not sure it would work," he said, much louder than necessary. Reed winced.

"The humming," Brachyura continued, tapping at his ear with the dagger. "Makara told us that we could only block it out if we lost our hearing altogether. He appears to have been correct. Kriari, you next." He threw the weapon at his brother's feet, then grabbed the still-twitching corpse of the weaver and tugged it off Jelaïa.

"Wait, what are you doing?" asked Reed, catching Kriari's arm as he lifted the dagger to his ear.

"Kriari."

"The weaver is dead!" Reed gestured towards her headless body. "She's not going to recover from that. The wyrm has not yet arrived in Klief; we can make it back to the cathedral if we hurry!"

"You don't understand," said Kumbha sadly. "The weaver

is not invincible, but she *is* immortal. We must stay here and make sure that she never troubles the nine Baronies again."

"Nonsense! All we have to do is destroy the portals, right? Then, she would be trapped here."

"You're not thinking straight," Kumbha replied patiently. "We tried that before, remember? We buried the portal under the Morlakian Pit. It didn't work, only slowed her down."

A huge hand landed on Reed's shoulder, and he looked up into the ink-black eyes of Brachyura. "We must stay here, Lord Reed," he said loudly. "It is the only way to be sure she will not return. Not while we still draw breath. Besides, we do not belong in your world. We do not belong ... anywhere."

"Not belong," echoed Kriari softly.

"We are not the Twelve. We were only created in their image. We are neither alive nor dead. Our place is neither among the living nor beyond the Shroud. It is here, in this ... purgatory. In this wasteland, this *in-between*. Where we were born."

The weaver's corpse jerked.

Reed felt a terrible sadness for these three demi-gods. Lied to, manipulated, their minds torn from a well-deserved rest to serve their sworn enemy. An enemy they would now spend the rest of their lives fighting. They deserved better.

"Do not be troubled," said golden-haired Kumbha, sensing his thoughts. "There are worse fates. At least we will have each other. And maybe ... maybe we will be able to convince the weaver that violence is not the answer. Whatever she is, she appears to have real empathy for the greylings. They will suffer without her guidance. Peace may eventually become more enticing to her than war. Now go, gather your friends, and leave here with all haste. The weaver will soon awaken, and we must be ready for her when she does." She paused. "When you see Sir Loré again, would you please tell him … would you tell him I thank him for lending me his jacket when I awoke, cold and frightened, in the gardens of Arelium? It was a simple thing. A selfless act of kindness that reminded me of the good that can be found in humanity."

"I will, Lady," said Reed in a forlorn voice. "And know that you will be missed. All of you."

Jelaïa and Vohanen approached. The Knight of Kriari was sporting an enormous bruise the size of an apple on his forehead, but it didn't appear to have affected his capacity to whine and grumble.

"We could be having a celebratory drink right now," he was saying, "if my son hadn't made me throw away that perfectly good skin of Morlakian red. Dunno what I was thinking. Caught up in the moment, I suppose. I'll know better next time, that's for sure."

The weaver's corpse jerked again. An ovoid protuberance was forming where her head had once been, like the bulb of a winter crocus.

Reed held out his arm for Jelaïa to lean on, and they started their long trip back to the portal, hunched together like an old married couple.

"Reed!" Brachyura called out. He was standing between Kumbha and Kriari at the entrance of the chamber, his armour gleaming, his axe held high in one final salute. A smile tugged at the corners of his mouth. Kriari stood to his right, his tangled mane tossed by the wind, blood trickling from his pierced ears, his burnt face at peace. Kumbha looked radiant, her long golden hair cleaned of black tar, glowing softly like the rising sun.

Three demi-gods. Three members of the Twelve. Three siblings. The last bulwark between the weaver and the lands of men.

"May the Twelve be with you," Brachyura said serenely, his obsidian eyes sparkling.

Reed raised his own hand in return. "They are, Lord. They are. And this time, I swear we will not forget your sacrifice."

There was a screech from the darkness behind them, and the Twelve turned away, fading from sight to confront the weaver once more.

❧

Shala was waiting for them by the portal, her wrinkled face lined with worry.

"Where are the others?" she asked, searching their faces.

"They have chosen to stay," said Jelaïa simply. She had not spoken much on the return journey from the tower, the wound in her shoulder still leaking blood.

Shala nodded as if she had been expecting this. "Then, it is as I thought. The weaver cannot be defeated." She sighed. "I would have liked to see the Redenfell Mountains one last time, to walk along the banks of the River Stahl, to hear the larks singing in Kaevel Forest ... but I was deluding myself."

"No," Reed said. "You can still come with us. It is not too late."

"And abandon my brothers and sister here? Could you do something like that? I may be old, but my gift may yet be of some use. Once you are through the portal, I will destroy it. Then I will unmake those flesh-covered abominations in my cellar. And once there is no trace left of Weaver ... *the weaver's* handiwork, I will travel to her chambers and lend my strength to that of my siblings. Who knows? Maybe my gift will work long enough for me to craft something that can contain her and buy us some respite."

Vohanen grunted and bowed stiffly. "Then, we wish you luck, Lady. Reed, Jelaïa, let us hurry. We need to reach Klief before the wyrm does."

Reed was assailed by the same sweet, sickly scent he had smelt earlier. He recognised what it was now. Tree sap.

"You two go," he said in a strained voice. "I'll follow on in a minute."

"Reed ..."

"It will be all right. I need to do this."

"Very well. Don't take too long."

Vohanen took hold of Jelaïa and helped her through the portal. Reed watched as the inky liquid enveloped their arms, legs, and faces until they disappeared entirely. He turned, scanning his surroundings until his eyes alighted on a familiar figure standing under the charred remains of a small tree.

The man was rugged and broad-shouldered, dressed in a simple tunic and boots. He had a fishing rod slung over one shoulder.

"Father," murmured Reed, his heart thumping in his chest.

"Hello, Son," his father replied kindly, ruffling Reed's hair with a calloused hand. "I told you I would see you again. How have you been?"

"How have I been ... I have failed you, Father," Reed said tearfully. He could feel himself starting to cry but found that he didn't care. "I am sorry. I tried to follow your guidance. To stand firm. To bring people together. But so many have died. Ferris. Avor. Nidore. Praedora. I failed. I failed to protect the Old Guard who I rescued. I failed to stop the wyrm from destroying Morlak. And now, Klief will fall. I promised before Mother's grave to try to change, to be better, to do something — anything — that would make a difference ... what a disappointment I must be."

Reed's father furrowed his brow. "Was it you who toppled the tree that killed me? Was it you who sent the fever that ended your mother's life? Stop trying to carry the responsibilities of the world on your shoulders, Son, the weight will crush you. When I look at you now, I see the man who stood fearlessly against a horde of greylings before the keep of Arelium, the man who ventured deep into the Morlakian Pit, and the man who walked beside the Twelve themselves to end the greatest threat the nine Baronies have ever known." He laid a firm hand on Reed's shoulder. "There was a saying my own father used to repeat to me when I was a lad. He said that real heroes are those who don't even realise who they are or what they have done. That is who you are, Merad. That is who I see. A hero."

Reed smiled through his tears. "Thank you, Father. I miss you. Give my love to Mother."

"I will. We have a place ready for you by the fire when your time comes." Reed's father hesitated. "I came here because I wanted to ... tell you something. To warn you." His face shimmered, and he grunted with effort. "Time is no longer linear beyond the Shroud. We see glimpses of the past, the present, and sometimes the future." He faded out of focus, then returned. "Destroying the fulcrum is not enough. When you return to Klief, you will be tested. You must stand firm."

"Father? I don't understand!"

"Stand firm, Merad. And be true. Be true to yourself. That is all I can say. Stand firm, and be true. I love you, Son." Then he was gone.

"Father!" Reed cried in anguish. There was no answer but the wind.

⁓

Ka'arka and Aldarin walked slowly up the steps to the cathedral. A horn sounded somewhere atop the third wall battlements, signalling that the greylings had been cleared from the ramparts. Below, Orkam and his fearless Arelians were piling chunks of masonry and any other heavy objects they could find onto the back of the cart now blocking the gate. Loré's cavalry stalked among the dead and dying, offering comfort to allies ... and a merciful end to any of the enemy that still drew breath.

Just like boiling water left to cool, the frenzied, bubbling roar of battle had dimmed to a quietly simmering aftermath; rippling pockets of sound emanating from hushed conversations and mournful lamentations.

"We are holding, Aldarin," Ka'arka said to his friend. "I can scarcely believe it, but we are holding. They cannot break through the third wall. We are ... winning."

Aldarin stopped abruptly and looked at his fellow knight as if he had told a bad joke. "Winning? There is no winning here. We are surviving, that is all. If Jelaïa and her companions fail, it will not matter how many times we push the greylings back. The wyrm will devour all."

His gaze left Ka'arka and travelled up to the entrance of the cathedral and the carved statues of the Twelve glowering down at him.

"Nothing can be built on a foundation made of secrets and lies," Aldarin continued. "If our so-called protectors had been more open with their knowledge. If Makara had chosen courage over cowardice ... maybe the person I care about the most would not be risking her life."

Ka'arka tried a reassuring smile. "I'm sure Jelaïa is fine."

"Makara had better hope she is. Now, onwards. We have an unpleasant task ahead of us."

Two Kliefien town guard stood to attention at the top of the steps, their spears crossed before the doors of the cathedral, barring passage.

"The High Priest is not to be disturbed," one of the guardsmen said sharply with a disapproving glare. "Even by Knights of Brachyura."

Ka'arka saw Aldarin's eyebrows twitch dangerously and slipped swiftly in front of his friend. "Your duty is commendable, soldier," he said in what he hoped was a respectful tone. "Alas, we have an urgent message for his holiness that must be delivered in person."

The guardsman licked his lips nervously. "That may well be, but his *holiness* was quite specific in his instructions. No one is to enter."

"Of course. Although he obviously did not foresee the possibility of there being a message of such importance."

The Kliefien's resolve was melting like a lump of sugar. "Nevertheless—"

"And my fellow knight and I both concur that the message *must* be delivered, by any means necessary. No matter the obstacles that might ... present themselves. Wouldn't you agree, Aldarin?"

The big knight grunted menacingly. He had still not cleaned his face of ichor and stank of sweat and blood.

"Ah ..." the guardsman stammered. "Well, if you are prepared to take full responsibility for disturbing his holiness, then—"

"We are. Thank you," interrupted Ka'arka, breezing past the other man. "Come on, Aldarin. Oh, and close the doors behind us, guardsman. No one else is to enter. Understood?"

"Yes, Sir!" replied the Kliefien, saluting mechanically.

They entered the cathedral and were greeted with a terrible sight. Moonlight streamed through the stained-glass windows, illuminating the prostrate form of Makara in the throes of a violent convulsion, urine staining his robes. It reminded Ka'arka of something he had seen before, a villager of Ak'Shah who had the misfortune to be afflicted with what the Da'arrans called 'the Jester's Kiss'.

"He has lost control!" he shouted to Aldarin as he rushed to help. "We must hold him down or he may injure himself."

Makara was frothing at the mouth, only the whites of his eyes visible in the hollows of his haggard face. Ka'arka tore a strip of fabric from the Tenth of the Twelve's robes and forced it into his mouth.

"Grab his legs!" he ordered, pinning down Makara's arms. The old demi-god was surprisingly strong, and it took all of Ka'arka's considerable vigour to hold him down. After a couple of minutes, the spasms slowed. Then, with a shudder, Makara opened his eyes.

"It is so empty," he murmured, traces of spittle still dripping from his chin. "So vast. A mind the size of a thousand cities." A solitary tear ran down one cheek. "And so much anger. So much pain. So much loss. Surrounding me constantly. Battering at my defences. She is enraged."

"She?" asked Ka'arka softly.

Makara gazed past him at something only he could see. "Yes, the wyrm is a *mother*. A mother who has had her child taken from her. Is there any greater form of grief?" Another tear, red this time, followed by another, then another. The Tenth of the Twelve was weeping blood.

"I tried," he said. "I tried to talk to her. To reason with her. I do not know if she listened. In fact, I do not know if she could hear me at all." Makara flicked his head left and right, his face a crimson mask. "Where is Azael? Where is my boy? Is he safe?"

Aldarin glanced at Ka'arka, who shook his head. "We took the Baron to the postern gate as you asked, Lord," he said carefully.

"Ah, good. That is good. I cannot hold her any longer, you see? The wyrm is coming ... she is coming ..." He gave one last, terrible shudder then lay still. So perished Makara, Tenth of the Twelve. Aldarin leant forwards respectfully and closed the old man's eyes. "May he find peace."

Ka'arka stood, his armour creaking. It would take him hours to remove the encrusted filth and lubricate all the joints. If he was still alive to do so, of course.

"What now?" he asked. "With Makara and Azael gone, who decides the fate of Klief?"

"I don't know," Aldarin admitted. He winced. "My Pit-spawned head is throbbing so hard I can barely hear myself think. I suppose—" he was cut off by a series of clicks from beneath the stone altar. There was a muffled curse, then more clicks before the whole structure slid aside to reveal the exhausted face of Vohanen. The Knight of Kriari looked like he was sitting; his back against one of the walls of the shaft and his legs pressed to the opposite side. Jelaïa, blurry-eyed and dishevelled, lay on his knees.

"Don't just stand there gawking," Vohanen growled, his voice strained with effort. "Help us get out of here!"

"Where's the key?" asked Aldarin hastily, frowning at the wound in Jelaïa's shoulder.

"Here." She removed it from her neck and passed it through the bars to Aldarin, who unlocked the grate as fast as he could and pulled her into his arms, visibly relieved. "Jelaïa," he murmured, holding her close. "Thank the Twelve! Promise me you will never do anything like that ever again. You had me worried sick."

"I promise," she replied weakly, relaxing against his chest. "Aldarin?"

"Yes?"

"I think I am going to pass out now." She closed her eyes, and Aldarin felt the tension leave her muscles. He picked her up gently.

"Do I get a hug too?" Vohanen was being assisted out of the shaft by Ka'arka.

"She needs to go to the infirmary," Aldarin said. He paused. "Where are the Twelve? Where is Sir Reed?"

Vohanen's good humour vanished. "The Twelve will not be coming back. Reed's still down there. Something he had to do. He'll need help getting out. Jelaïa only made it two-thirds up the shaft, and I nearly sent us both tumbling to our deaths several times ascending the last twenty feet or so. If you trust me to take the Baroness to the infirmary, I would ask you to wait here a few minutes longer."

Aldarin looked down at Jelaïa's unconscious face. "Of course," he said reluctantly. "I am sure that is what she would want me to do."

"Were you successful?" Ka'arka asked, unable to contain the question any longer. "The weaver? The wyrm?"

Vohanen pulled at his beard as he tried to frame his thoughts. "I ... we did not kill her. I am not sure she *can* be killed. We contained her, imprisoned her in the land beyond the portal. And we destroyed the object helping her to control the wyrm."

"That does not answer my question." As if to prove his point, the ground trembled once more. Steam wafted up from the open shaft. One of the statues lining the nave teetered precariously on its pedestal. "If the weaver is defeated, then why does the wyrm still come? Why has it not retreated to the deep?"

Vohanen's brow creased in confusion. "I don't know," he said wearily. "But we have done all we can. There is no more time. If we have failed, then Klief is lost. And us with it."

CHAPTER 27

REED'S DECISION

"There is a very thin line between stubborn determination and reckless stupidity."

ALDARIN, KNIGHT OF BRACHYURA, 427 AT

❧

REED COULD NO longer smell the sweet sap of Jaelem's venerable oaks. It was over. He blinked to clear his eyes and walked back to the portal where Shala was waiting patiently.

"Goodbye, Sir Reed," she said, her gaze studying him from glistening irises set deep within an ocean of wrinkles. "Let us hope that your kind does not squander the time we are buying you."

"I give you my oath that we will not," Reed replied seriously. "Farewell, Lady." He took a deep breath and stepped through the portal, shuddering as the liquid flowed over his skin.

There were no sudden visions this time, no revelations, just an endless blackness as dark as the Pit itself. In an instant, he was through. The heat on the other side almost made him collapse. It was like being imprisoned in an oven, the stone walls of the small chamber trapping and absorbing the hot air. Reed began to sweat profusely. The portal's runes were no longer glowing. He groped around blindly for the line of thread, his questing hands eventually finding it and holding on fast.

He inched forwards, one arm held out before him like a blind beggar, the stench of sulphur snaking up into his nostrils.

Where were Jelaïa and Vohanen? Had they managed to escape?

The thread led him down a tunnel, then up another. Reed began to wonder if he was even going the right way. Did it really take them this long on the way down? There was a deep rumbling sound, and the tunnel shook. Bits of loose dirt and stone fell from the ceiling, one shard sharp enough to cut a line in Reed's face. He coughed. The smell of sulphur was becoming worse, as was the heat. Something was drawing closer.

The wyrm.

The thread petered out, and he almost cried with relief when he looked up and saw a halo of light high above. His way out and an end to this whole ordeal. Now, he just had to get to it. He eased into the shaft and placed his feet on opposite wall surfaces, then did the same with his palms. The stone felt warm under his fingers.

Up we go! he thought giddily. The hot air and fumes were starting to make him feel lightheaded. He shifted one foot up while pushing against the walls with his other three limbs. Once that foot was firmly in place, he did the same with the other. He was now three feet off the ground.

Easy!

He tried again, focusing on moving his feet first and using his arms for balance. He was about a third of the way up the shaft when his calves began to ache. Steam was rising from the cavern floor, obscuring his vision. His salt-and-pepper hair was matted with sweat from the heat and exertion, drops of the salty liquid dribbling down into his eyes. He could feel his soggy vermilion cloak squelching against his back.

"Just a little further," he murmured to himself, raising his left foot. It was then that his palms slipped. He yelled out in surprise and lost his balance, slithering back down the shaft. He flailed about desperately with his hands and pushed them against the walls: enough to slow his descent but not stop it. He jabbed out with his free foot and jerked abruptly to a halt. There was a loud pop and a sudden flair of intense pain in his lower leg. He had torn his calf muscle.

He moaned as the pain began to spread, from his ankle to his knee. The bottom of the shaft was roughly twenty feet below him. He would not survive the fall. Reed gritted his teeth and tried to move his injured leg. A spike of agony almost made him black out. Screaming in frustration, he hung there, supported by his palms and remaining leg, his salvation so close and yet so far.

He screamed again, louder, venting his anger and helplessness at the world. He would not fail now. He had helped bring the weaver to her knees. He would not be thwarted by a torn muscle.

Something obscured the circle of light at the top of the shaft. A pronged helm.

"Friend Reed!" Aldarin's deep voice boomed. "We were starting to worry! You must rejoin us with all haste! The wyrm approaches! Allow me to assist you!" He let go of what he was holding, and a length of rope spiralled down, uncoiling as it fell, narrowly avoiding Reed's upturned face.

"With all haste ... damn you, Aldarin," Reed muttered.

He gripped tightly onto the rope with both hands and allowed himself to be pulled slowly towards the light. There was a roar from somewhere in the caverns below, and the pace quickened. Reed tried to concentrate on the top of the shaft and forget the constant pain in his leg. It felt like he had been stabbed. With a final heave, he was pulled over the lip of the hole and onto the marble floor of the cathedral.

Reed lay there for an instant, shaking like a fish out of water, frayed nerves and tiredness making his limbs quiver. Aldarin and Ka'arka dropped their end of the rope. The Da'arran staggered over to one of the pews and sat down gratefully.

Reed turned his head and found himself staring into the bloody face of Makara, Tenth of the Twelve. He recoiled in shock, scrabbling backwards until he hit the stone altar topped with the model of the Old Guard sentry towers.

"He used his gift to slow the wyrm's advance," explained Aldarin dejectedly. "I believe that if it had not been for him, then the creature would already be here ... and you would be either dead or trapped underground."

"Jelaïa?" Reed croaked, his throat raw from the sulphurous fumes.

A flicker of worry crossed Aldarin's features. "Vohanen took her to the infirmary. She has lost a fair amount of blood. You don't look much better, to be honest. I suggest you join her. What in the Pit did you see down there?"

"Ghosts," Reed whispered. "Ghosts and broken promises."

Aldarin looked at him strangely. "Enigmatic, indeed. You need rest, Reed. But first, you need to tell me what I must report to the surviving members of the War Council."

He locked eyes with Reed, his piercing gaze peeling back the layers of the tired guardsman's thoughts, as stern and as penetrating as it had been when they had first met on the ancient walls of the Arelian Pit all those months ago.

"In my opinion, we have two options. We can continue to fight, or we can flee. If we choose the first option, our forces stay on the wall, denying the greylings any foothold on the ramparts. If we choose the second, we retreat. Makara revealed to us the existence of a postern gate. We could slowly — very slowly — evacuate the non-combatants followed by the soldiers, but our casualties would be horrendous. There are wounded in the infirmary who cannot be moved. And we would have to leave a token force on the walls or we would be overrun. Men who would be left to die."

Reed massaged his temples. He had never felt so tired or so empty, as if his entire body had been drained of all its strength and energy. How could he even contemplate such a consequential decision when he could barely string three coherent words together?

"You cannot ask this of me, Aldarin," he said, hating how much it sounded like a whine.

"I was not chosen to go, Reed. Jelaïa's vision happened for a reason. They always do. Trust in yourself. What must we do? Retreat or stand firm?"

Reed's head shot up. "What did you say?"

"Retreat or stand firm?"

Reed laughed. The answer was obvious.

Thank you, Father.

"We stand firm," he said to Aldarin. "Those who are not needed in the defence of the wall can use the postern gate if they so wish, but the third wall must hold. Advise the War Council to keep fighting."

"You are sure of this?"

"I am," replied Reed without hesitation.

Aldarin studied him for a moment longer, then nodded in agreement. "I too agree that this is currently the best course of action. Very well, that is what I will tell them. Ka'arka? I think Reed will have need of your assistance. May the Twelve be with you both." He turned and walked briskly towards the narthex.

Ka'arka ambled over and offered Reed his forearm. "If his Lordship would be so kind as to accompany me to the infirmary? I hear the nurses there are breathtaking. Especially the one with the multi-coloured eyes."

Syrella! thought Reed, and the idea of seeing her again gave him a slight surge of energy.

"My thanks, Sir Knight," he replied warmly. "I—"

There was a loud crack as a marble pillar, five feet away, split nearly in half down the middle. A chunk of rubble smashed onto one of the pews, reducing it to a pile of broken wood. The tiled floor buckled, scores of hairline fractures appearing and widening rapidly into fissures as the ground began to thrum.

"Time to move," said Ka'arka, raising his voice over the mounting sounds of splitting stone and rumbling earth. Another pillar toppled over, hitting the one behind it, which did the same to the one behind that, and all three collapsed like a line of falling dominos.

Reed let himself be pulled along, his injured leg sending lightning bolts of pain up his side each time it touched the ground. A curtain of steam vented from a fissure to his left, close enough for him to feel the intense heat on his face.

A stained-glass window exploded, raining deadly red and blue shards. Ka'arka cursed and pulled Reed sharply towards him, raising his arms over both their heads in an attempt to shield them with his armoured form. Glass rattled off his pauldrons and vambraces like hailstones.

"Nearly there!" he shouted. Reed risked a glance over his shoulder. The shaft he had used to descend into the Kliefien Pit was now a gaping hole over ten feet wide and growing larger by the second, vomiting sulphurous smoke and consuming all around it like an insatiable monster. The iron grating had already been lost to the depths, and now the void preyed on Makara. The inanimate corpse of the Tenth of the Twelve slithered unceremoniously along what was left of the marble floor and plunged over the edge, disappearing from sight.

It's happening again, thought Reed, fighting against the familiar feeling of rising panic. *Just like Morlak.*

Ka'arka kicked open the entrance doors and dragged Reed outside just as the vaulted ceiling began to collapse.

Numerous allied troops still lined the third wall. Either the War Council had agreed to follow Reed's advice, or they had not yet made their decision. On the far side of the courtyard, silhouetted against the open door of the infirmary, Syrella stood waiting for him, a nurse's apron tied over her fine dress, her long hair stuffed under a net. To Reed, she had never looked more beautiful.

Ka'arka helped Reed down the steps and began half-carrying him across the courtyard. Behind them, the cathedral roof caved in on itself, the last few columns unable to support the weight of the vaulted ceiling. Only the spire remained, standing tall and proud against the night sky until it too toppled over into the ever-widening chasm.

Reed watched it fall with mixed emotions. The cathedral had been the epitome of everything Makara had tried to achieve with his new reimagining of Klief: grandeur, beauty, opulence, architecture ... but it had also been the perfect representation of all that was wrong with his misguided vision of society: mistrust, secrets, isolationism, religious zeal ... these were not the values needed to govern a Barony.

The line between guidance and control is so thin, Reed thought as great clouds of steam and dust billowed up from the hole where the cathedral had once been. *How many times over the Twelve's long lifespans were good intentions unravelled into something far more sinister? Mithuna's desire for peace. Makara's choice to deify his brothers and sisters. Choices that led us here. To this moment.*

"Reed," warned Ka'arka. "We are too close, it—"

He was cut off by an ear-splitting roar as the wyrm blasted out of the chasm like an erupting volcano, a monstrous vision of smoke and fire. It rose into the night sky, higher than the third wall, higher than the fallen spire of the cathedral, an impossibly huge behemoth of destruction.

Reed craned his neck back as far as it would go to gaze at the creature. Strangely, he felt no fear, only stupefied incomprehension at what he was seeing. Its serpentine head was large enough to block out the moon.

She, he corrected himself. *Not it. She.*

The wyrm looked much the same as when she had first appeared to Reed in Morlak, her diamond-shaped skull and writhing body covered in thousands of gleaming red scales, each one the size of a shield. Golden orbs of flames boiled in the depths of her lidless eye sockets, illuminating the two spiralling horns rising from her forehead and the row of triangular spikes along her snout.

The wyrm opened her maw and let out a deafening bellow, full of anger and grief. Reed clapped his hands over his ears as the sonic vibrations rattled his bones. All along the third wall, men shrieked in fear, throwing down their weapons and running for the relative safety of the keep.

"Reed!" Ka'arka shouted again, gesturing at the soldiers fleeing the ramparts. "They have the right idea. We cannot stop it! We can only run!"

Sluggish magma bubbled up from the mouth of the chasm, spilling into the courtyard and melting the cobbles. More and more of the defenders abandoned their posts until soon the battlements were completely deserted.

"Why isn't she moving?" Reed asked Ka'arka. "What is she waiting for?"

"I don't know, and I don't care, Reed. I'm not staying to find out."

Reed scratched his beard.

Stand firm.

"I'm going up to the ramparts," he said calmly. The light from the slowly expanding river of magma was reflected by the wyrm's ruby scales, giving everything a reddish hue.

Ka'arka nodded as if half-expecting this. "I thought you would. Aldarin told me you were stubborn. Maybe I should stay—"

"No. Go tell the others to begin the evacuation."

"Very well. Then, this is where our paths divide. Good luck, Merad."

Reed was no longer listening, limping painfully to the closest set of stairs. He began to mount them one by one, each step feeling as high as a mountain and twice as treacherous. He glanced back. The wyrm was motionless. Only her slitted nostrils opened and closed rhythmically, sniffing the air.

She looks confused, Reed thought, arduously pulling himself up another step. *As if she were awakening from a long sleep. Or a bad dream. How long did the weaver have her hooks in the poor creature's mind?*

He stopped abruptly as he realised that he had reached the top of the third wall, the stone beneath his feet slick with the blood of the dead. Before him stretched the decimated city of Klief; the second gatehouse a crumpled mess of rubble, the first a charred skeletal husk. Greylings and threshers were everywhere, huddled together in their thousands along the main highway, packed tightly among the alleyways and backstreets, wandering in and out of the abandoned shops and homes.

This will be the fate of every town and city of the nine Baronies if we do not stop them here.

And yet, something was not quite right. The third wall was defenceless. Why were they not attacking? Where was the screeching, the cajoling, the wild cacophony that had assaulted his senses ever since his first encounter with the greylings above the Arelian Pit? He leant over one of the merlons and looked more closely at those nearest to him. Much like the wyrm, they seemed lethargic, dazed even, slack-jawed and dull-eyed.

Reed felt himself start to smile. This must be an unanticipated consequence of the weaver's death. Or, if not her death, the destruction of the portal and her only means of direct communication from the Shroud.

At last. Something is actually going my way.

Then, as he watched, one of the greylings shook its head groggily, raised its dirty talons and shrieked. Reed's smile vanished. There was an answering shriek from further away, then another.

They are waking up, he thought in fear. *They are returning to their senses.*

And I am all alone.

CHAPTER 28

BE TRUE TO YOURSELF

"Every experience impacts us. Positive and negative. We cannot change that. What we can change, however, is how they impact us. We can let a bad experience fester, slowly poisoning us, making us grow resentful and bitter. Or we can accept it. Learn from it. Grow stronger from it. Sometimes, through failure, we can find success. And sometimes, through loss, we can find love."

BARONESS JELAÏA DEL ARELIUM, 427 AT

REED GRIPPED THE stone of the parapet tightly to stop his hands from trembling, fighting to control the waves of nausea that he could feel seething in his stomach. Before him, the greylings continued to stir, isolated groups of stragglers congregating around the larger, menacing threshers. It would not be long before they would turn their attention to the wall and realise that it was no longer defended.

Behind him, the wyrm had still not moved, her gigantic head swaying leisurely back and forth, probing with her long snout. Searching for something. Magma simmered and bubbled where the cathedral had once stood, the steam it created slowly covering the courtyard. Already, the door to the infirmary was shrouded from sight. Reed hoped that Syrella was no longer standing there. That she had been among the first to depart through the postern gate.

He scratched at his beard again. Pit, the thing itched. Syrella was right. He should shave it off. He nearly laughed at the absurdity of it. Trapped between a wyrm and an army of greylings. Wondering about his beard. What was he *doing*?

I'm trusting the words of my father, he thought, trying to revive his fading confidence. *Stand firm. And be true to yourself.*

There was a guttural roar from down below. He was running out of time.

A crackle of pain raced up his leg from his torn muscle, made worse by the clenching of his anxious stomach. *I am here, Father. Standing firm. What must I do now? Help me!*

Be true to yourself. Pit, he hated riddles. But his father knew that. He had hated them too. There was no hidden meaning. He just had to be himself. Remember who he was. But … who was he?

An orphan, his parents taken from him too soon, lost to the unpredictability of life? A coward, disillusioned by his years guarding the Pit but lacking the courage to do anything else? A captain, training farmers and merchants to fight, only for them to be torn to pieces in front of his eyes?

A prisoner? A friend? A leader? A failure?

Another authoritative bellow followed by the pattering of claws. The greylings were moving, advancing on the wall. Reed began to despair. What was he missing? Hot steam swirled around him, pulling at the hem of his vermilion cloak.

The cloak he had been wearing when the greylings had first crept over the edge of the Arelian Pit. And again, on the walls of Arelium. Again, when braving the dark tunnels of the Morlakian Pit. Lost during his imprisonment, then returned to him by Vohanen. Keeping him warm on the road north to Klief. And, finally, it had travelled with him into the Shroud.

He had changed and grown, yet the cloak had always been his anchor, clinging to him like a second skin. A part of him, not just the cloak itself, but what it represented. What he always would be, no matter what came after. The last of the Arelian Old Guard. The watcher, the protector, the guardian of the wall. The light against the darkness, the burning sun against the cold of night, the mighty shield against the unknown.

Be true to yourself.

He smiled now, as he understood what the wyrm was searching for. What faint scent she had picked up. He undid the wolf's head clasp and tore the cloak free. It was so saturated with the fulcrum's blood that it was still slightly damp, despite the surrounding heat.

"HERE!" he screamed, waving his cloak over his head like a madman in the hope that the movement would attract the wyrm's attention. "THIS IS WHAT YOU ARE LOOKING FOR!"

It wasn't working. The creature's massive head was way too far above him, half-hidden by the steam. A snickering sound made him turn. The sound of nails on stone. Two greylings were pulling themselves over the ramparts, bulbous yellow eyes fixed on Reed. More would soon follow. He was out of time.

So close. So, so close. "Well, at least I tried," he murmured helplessly. He looked around for a weapon, but there was nothing within reach. His leg was on fire. He could barely walk, let alone run. He sighed and dropped his cloak. The nearest monster snarled and pounced at him, claws and mouth stretched wide. Reed lifted his hands in a feeble attempt to ward off the blow.

A bolt of pure cerulean flame streaked past his face and punched the greyling out of the air, sending it flying over the battlements with a surprised shriek.

"You are a most difficult person to have as a friend," came the reproachful voice of Aldarin from the top of the stairs. He was carrying Jelaïa in his arms, her skin crackling, her eyes filled with liquid fire. She raised her arm, and the second greyling burst into flame. Aldarin came closer. "When Ka'arka charged into the infirmary, babbling about what you were doing, I wanted to leave you to rot, but Jelaïa convinced me that we should come and assist you."

The Baroness smiled. "You're a terrible liar, Aldarin. Now, put me down, I can stand on my own two feet for a few minutes." A layer of bandages was wrapped tightly around her shoulder, her axe-shaped medallion glittering on her chest.

Reed stared at them both in shock, unable to speak. He attempted to pull his rattled mind together, shaking his head in disbelief. "What ... What are you doing here? Are you mad? Did you fail to see the astronomically-sized lizard? The huge pool of magma? Why are you risking your lives for me? I didn't ask you for any of this!"

Aldarin looked at him quizzically. "Of course, you didn't, Merad. You didn't have to. And you never will. That is what friendship is." He glanced over the ramparts. "Although whatever you're planning, please proceed with haste. There are more of the enemy attempting to climb the wall as we speak."

"It's the cloak," Reed explained. "It's still drenched in the blood of the fulcrum, the heart of the wyrm's child that we found in the Shroud. We destroyed it, and in doing so, I think we succeeded in breaking the weaver's hold on the wyrm, but severing the link appears to have sent her into some sort of fugue state. The weaver said the wyrm relied heavily on her excellent sense of smell. Maybe the memory of her child's blood will set her free."

"Foolhardy, illogical, and with little chance of success," said Aldarin good-naturedly. "Just as I've come to expect from you, Sir Reed. What do you need us to do?"

"I was looking for a way to get the wyrm's atten—" A bright blue ball of flame rocketed into the air like a comet, burning through the clouds of steam, eclipsing the moon with its blinding light.

"That should suffice," said Jelaïa in a satisfied voice, lowering her hand. The wyrm blinked, her aureate globes dimmed for an instant by a thin, transparent membrane. She turned ponderously towards them, her forked tongue darting in and out as she drew closer.

Reed bent to pick up his cloak, the movement sending

fresh pain jolting up his leg. He winced as he held the damp bundle up over his head one last time. The diamond-shaped head filled his vision. Even at this distance, he could feel the wyrm's breathing pulling at his hair. He faintly heard more greylings gaining the wall and Aldarin rushing to meet them, but none of that mattered now. He stared into the wyrm's burning eyes, hypnotised by the inner fire that spiralled and rippled like golden whirlpools.

What must I look like to her? he thought. *An insignificant blur. Does she even see me at all?*

The forked tongue emerged slowly and descended upon him. One flick of that fleshy appendage would be enough to crush him.

Stand firm. Stand firm.

The pronged tip brushed against his vermilion cloak, then the tongue retreated, returning the olfactory information it had gathered to the wyrm's mouth. Her eyes dimmed once more then burst back into flame, brighter than before as if infused with a new light. Molten fire spilled over the edge of her sockets and trickled down the side of her face. She was weeping once again.

Remember, Reed willed. *Remember what they did to you. To your child.*

The wyrm raised her maw to the stars and cried out in grief. Reed would never forget that sound, a miserable amalgamation of sorrow, remorse, and heartache. Then her head snapped down. Her serpentine body rippled. Her cheeks expanded. And her vengeance began.

A torrent of flame roared over Reed's head, aimed at the greylings massing at the base of the wall. The creatures didn't even have time to scream. Their bodies and everything else in the immediate vicinity were reduced to molten slag in a matter of seconds.

The wyrm advanced at last, revealing more of her immense body as she slithered forth from the pool of magma, her red-hot scales melting the cobbles of the courtyard. The thick stone and iron of the third gatehouse barely slowed her down. Ka'arka's cart was flattened under a thousand pounds of flesh, the portcullis liquified in a single breath. Then she was through, running amok among the greyling army, crushing hundreds with her body, obliterating hundreds more with every snap of her jaw.

"Fetch the others," murmured Reed in awe to Aldarin. "They should see this. They deserve to see this." As his adrenaline faded, the pain in his leg became too much, and he hobbled painfully to sit down on one of the crenels before he collapsed.

Derello was the first to arrive, his arm in a sling. He grasped wrists silently with Reed and went to stand on the very edge of the battlements. Loré came next, his expression grave. Orkam and Ka'arka followed while Xandris, Syrella, and Belen came shortly after. Jeffson was carried up the stairs by Cerra and Ner'alla. Vohanen was last, unarmoured, rubbing his eyes as if emerging from a deep sleep.

Barons and knights. Scientists and healers. Thieves and watchmen. Merchants and nobles. All stood silently witnessing the destruction of the greatest threat the nine Baronies had ever known. The greylings were wailing in panic; even without the weaver's guiding hand, they recognised defeat. They scurried from building to building or attempted to flee across open ground back towards the relative safety of the southern hills, out beyond the first wall. But there was no

escaping the wyrm's wrath. Her entire body had now sur-
faced, and she used her long tail like a whip to block off
all avenues of retreat, herding her hated enemy back into
her killing zone. Firestorms blazed. Each deadly cascade of
flames scorched the earth.

The slaughter continued. More soldiers joined the initial
group. Arelians. Kessrin. Kliefien. Knights of Brachyura and
Kriari. All were drawn to the tremendous spectacle unfolding
before their eyes. Once more, the wind carried the stench of
burnt flesh to the survivors on the wall. They could hear the
shrieks and screams of uncountable thousands, punctuated
by the wyrm's deep roars.

"For Hirkuin," said Derello, breaking the silence.

"For Praedora," said Jelaïa and Aldarin almost
simultaneously.

"For Listus."

"For Nidore."

"For Hode."

"For Manfeld."

"For Ferris."

"For Fernshaw."

"For Shen'alla."

"For Krelbe."

"For Yusifel."

"For Avor."

"For the Twelve," finished Reed softly.

"Witness this," came a voice. Jelaïa was standing on one
of the crenels, her hand resting lightly on Aldarin's armoured
shoulder. "Witness what is happening here. Do not look
away. The wyrm aids us due to the valiant efforts of the
Twelve. Brachyura, Makara, Shala, Kumbha, and Kriari.

Makara gave his life to protect us, and even now as I speak, the others are still fighting to keep us safe. Remember their names. Remember their sacrifice. Remember this day. Then share what you know. If you can write, record it. If you can draw, commemorate it. If you can weave a tale, tell it. If you can sing a song, sing it. Shout it to the very boundaries of the nine Baronies. Let us never forget this moment. The moment of our victory!"

"VICTORY!" shouted Aldarin, his face filled with love and admiration.

"VICTORY!" yelled Reed. He felt a sudden warmth in his hand and turned to see Syrella had interlaced her fingers with his, a joyous smile on her lips.

"VICTORY!" whooped Vohanen, punching the air.

And the cry soon echoed like thunder along the third wall as the wyrm crashed through the charred remains of the Eagle Gate and took her vengeance on the last remaining greylings with fire and fury. With a final roar, she turned to the southeast, snaking into the low hills close to where Ka'arka and the Knights of Luridae had escaped the Kliefien Pit.

"It seems strange to hear people cheering the beast that destroyed my city," said Syrella to Reed. "I know she was only a thrall, but I still dream of seeing my subjects trampled underfoot by the fleeing crowds, or Morlak keep — my home — melting like a wax candle. It is … hard."

Reed gave her hand a squeeze. "It is. And now, at last, it's all over."

"Over?" she repeated sadly, bowing her head. "Oh, Merad, it hasn't even begun. Morlak is defenceless. Its capital in ruins. Kessrin has no fleet. Arelium has no food. The forests of Talth are burned to the ground. The Old Guard depleted. Klief a mountain of rubble. How can we ever hope to come back from this?"

Reed gently placed his hand under her chin and raised her tear-streaked face to meet his. "One day at a time," he murmured. He smiled and bent to kiss her tenderly.

"One day at a time."

CHAPTER 29

SPRING

"It is not what we have in our life, but who we have in our life that matters."

❧

"W HOEVER INVENTED THIS Pit-spawned uniform should be flogged," fumed Aldarin, trying for the third time to button up the high-collared shirt of his dress uniform.

"It's called an Atilla jacket," said Jelaïa from the other side of the bedroom, purposefully avoiding his gaze. "I hear they are all the rage in the northern Baronies."

"Rage is certainly the term that applies." He gave the jacket an angry tug, and a piece of braided frogging came loose, dangling from his torso as if to mock him.

"Now look what you've done!" Jelaïa admonished,

coming closer to assess the damage. "We'll have to ask Mava to repair it or, at the very least, reattach it. Pit, Aldarin, we are late enough as it is."

"You are the Baroness of Arelium, my Lady," Aldarin replied seriously. "The most important person in the room. You are never late. It is the others who are early."

She smiled. "Nice try. But I won't be the most important today, will I?"

"No. I suppose not. Although to be fair, if you spent less time engrossed in your writing, we wouldn't be the last ones to arrive everywhere."

"The book's not going to write itself, is it? Now, take your jacket off. I'll go and see if I can find Mava." She practically tore it from his shoulders and hurried away, leaving Aldarin alone with his thoughts.

He felt a stab of pain ripple over his skull and mechanically reached up to trace the thin scar on his scalp. He was getting better at anticipating the surges, but they still bothered him. He sighed. It was a small price to pay for what he had achieved. What they had all achieved.

He gazed out of the window. Jelaïa had refused to move into her father's old rooms, preferring to keep the chambers she had lived in since a young child. The view down into the valley of Arelium was magnificent.

The new barbican was almost finished; Arelium's own carpenters were adding the finishing touches to the interior. It was pristine, the shining blocks of stone in sharp contrast to the ageing curtain wall that surrounded the city. Aldarin made a mental note to ask Orkam to have the old wall surveyed for damage and erosion.

Beyond the city and its bustling docks, reinvigorated

by Derello and Jelaïa's profitable trade deals, the fields of Arelium were being reborn. Sir Manfeld had been right; despite the heavy damage to the topsoil, fertile earth had still survived underneath, enough to be tilled and sown. Aldarin could see a handful of green islands in a sea of brown. It was not much, but it was a start. And even better, it gave the people hope. He had accompanied Jelaïa many times on tours of the farmsteads, and whenever he spied those little green shoots pushing up valiantly through the hard ground, it made him smile. If the plants and crops could manage to find new life, so too could the nine Baronies.

His eyes wandered closer to home, alighting on the construction site just below him in the inner courtyard. A new stone edifice, built with materials from the quarries of Morlak. A tower. Men were already hard at work, using pulleys, ropes, and scaffolding to reach the higher levels. A host of stonemasons, glaziers, and knights. The roof was not yet completed, but a flag already flew proudly from the parapet. A silver axe on a field of blue. The Order of Brachyura. A barracks. Ready to house and train a score of initiates who would be his to command. Protectors of the Realm.

The core of the Baron's defences, he thought, remembering his conversation with Jelaïa in the temple smithy. *His honour guard and the final rampart against the enemy.*

He smiled as he recognised the ebony form of Ka'arka, stripped to the waist, shouting amiably at one of his fellow knights as they manoeuvred a large slab of granite into position. Aldarin knew his friend would not be staying long. He had been talking about leaving for days now, and Aldarin thought he knew why. There were vague reports of unrest brought north by traders and travellers. Disturbing news from Da'arra. An ailing Baron. Dwindling water. Ka'arka felt the need to help his people. Or, more specifically, to help one person.

The door banged open, and Jelaïa practically ran into the room with his ceremonial jacket. She stood there panting, her chest heaving, her cheeks red with exertion. Aldarin gazed at her in admiration. She was attired in the colours of Arelium: a crimson dress trimmed with white fur and diamond earrings. The silver axe-shaped medallion hung from her bare neck while her chestnut hair was styled in a conical coif held in place by a forest of hairpins.

"Stop gawking, Aldarin!"

"I wasn't—"

"Put your Atilla back on, and try not to break it this time. Suck your chest in or something."

"Suck? A Knight of Brachyura does not hide his physical stature, my Lady. Besides, I do not see why I cannot wear my armour."

She gave an exasperated sigh. "The worst thing is that you really don't, do you? I'll let you in on a little secret."

"I'm all ears," Aldarin replied, carefully threading his arms through the sleeves of the jacket.

"You use your armour as an excuse to shut people out. No, let me finish," she said as Aldarin opened his mouth to reply. "Think about the moments over the last seven months that brought us closer together. Our time spent on the boat travelling to Kessrin. The smithy under the temple of Brachyura. The forest of Talth. When you cannot hide inside your silver casing, you are vulnerable, like a crab without its shell."

"You mock me."

"Quite the contrary. I did not fall in love with Aldarin, the Knight of Brachyura. I fell in love with the man who sang me to sleep when I was tired and afraid. Who comforted me when my father died. Showing emotion is not a weakness, it is a strength. It takes great confidence and self-esteem to allow others to see you as you really are."

Aldarin relaxed slightly. "Pit! I sometimes forget just how astute you are, Baroness. You are right. I will ... suck my chest in. But it had better be worth it."

"Oh," replied Jelaïa with a mysterious smile. "I think it will."

It was fitting that the ceremony be held in the gardens of Arelium, a place still lauded as a symbol of resistance, hope, and healing. It had not changed much since Aldarin had last walked its gravel paths with Merad Reed, revealing to his friend what he knew of the Twelve. Knowledge that, in hindsight, had proved to be partially wrong. The Twelve. The Pact. Lies upon lies upon lies.

Jelaïa guided him to the central fountain where the marble statue of Kumbha had once been located. A replacement sculpture had recently been unveiled to unanimous acclaim: Listus del Arelium stared down at them proudly, his infamous bastard sword held high, a feral grin eternally etched on his marble face. Cold, clear water bubbled up from the upturned palm of his free hand, cascading into the pool below.

A small group of people was gathered around the marble benches in front of the fountain. Merad Reed and Syrella del

Morlak stood apart from the others. Aldarin's friend looked
particularly uncomfortable in his ostentatious clothes: a
starched collar, burgundy brocaded jacket, and tight leather
trousers. He was scratching furiously at a spot on his neck
where the collar was rubbing against the flesh. Over his
noble clothes — and looking rather out of place — Reed
had thrown on his well-worn vermilion cloak, held together
by his traditional wolf's head clasp.

Another shell, perhaps, thought Aldarin, ruminating on
what Jelaïa had told him earlier. *We all have our talismans,
it seems.*

Standing opposite Reed, Syrella looked radiant. Her
dress was pure white, decorated with hundreds of ivory
roses, from the bodice down to the end of the long train.
More flowers had been fixed to her braided black hair. Daelle
and Mila held up the end of the train. They were wearing
matching yellow frocks and regarding the proceedings with
a mixture of wonder and excitement.

Jelaïa let go of Aldarin's hand. "Now, stay here and try
not to be too much of a nuisance," she said teasingly.

"I'll make sure of that," said Jelaïa's mother, detaching
herself from a huddle of ladies-in-waiting. "I've had plenty
of practice." Listus's widow had made great progress since
Jelaïa had returned to Arelium, emerging skinny and weak
from her self-imposed isolation with a new fire kindling in
her eyes.

"I needed an excuse to escape from those women," she
confided to Aldarin. "They talk of nothing but clothes and
men all day, it bores me to death half the time."

"I can imagine," he replied, his gaze roaming over the
groups of guests. "Perhaps we can find you someone more

stimulating. Ah, I have the perfect fit." He offered his arm. "If I may escort you, my Lady?"

He led the Baroness to a trio of figures gesticulating animatedly. Lady Arkile and Xandris were engaged in lively banter about the River Stahl tolls. Unfortunately, Derello seemed to have been sandwiched between the two and was attempting to make the best of the situation.

"Ever since Lady Jelaïa named you steward, you have become much more disagreeable, Xandris," Lady Arkile was saying to the rotund little man, one eyebrow arched as only she knew how.

"I know, I know, it's wonderful isn't it," steward Xandris replied jubilantly. "It's as if our title offers us some sort of diplomatic immunity. We can say what we want to whom we want without the risk of repercussion. And there are *so* many things we can do together if we just put our minds to it."

Help, mimed Derello soundlessly. Aldarin suppressed a smile.

"Steward Xandris. Steward Arkile. I believe the Baroness would be most interested in what you are discussing. May I entrust her to your capable hands?"

"Of course!" Xandris beamed.

"My thanks. I will leave you—"

Derello coughed loudly.

"Baron del Kessrin and I will leave you to it, then," amended Aldarin with a respectful nod.

"By the Twelve," Derello muttered, straightening his feathered hat. "I was drowning in there. As if the daily meetings aren't enough."

"They have passion. It is a good thing."

"Hmm. You say that, but you weren't at any of the meetings. How is the Baroness's book coming along?"

"Slowly. She seems so tired at the moment."

"Sorry to hear that. Has she decided on a title yet?"

"No. I have offered several excellent ones, but she has categorically refused all of them. Ah, look, Jeffson is here! I did not have time to greet him yesterday."

Reed's old manservant was sitting next to Cerra on one of the benches, holding her hand and speaking to her in his soft, monotone voice. They looked up as Aldarin and Derello approached.

"Apologies for not meeting you at the gate," Aldarin said, holding out his forearm so they could grasp wrists. "I was out surveying our western borders and did not return before nightfall."

"It is good to see you," Jeffson replied, his eyes twinkling. "What do you think of Sir Reed's attire? I dressed him myself. We had a … long conversation about the cloak. It lasted most of the journey from Lostthorn to Arelium, in fact. He ended up getting his way, just like he did with his beard. Syrella never did manage to make him shave it off. I fear he is becoming more and more stubborn in his old age. I feel sorry for the poor soul who has taken my place."

"And the tavern?"

"Oh, Ner'alla and Cerra run it mostly. I just help. Keep the cellar well-stocked, that sort of thing."

"What did you end up calling it?"

Jeffson paused for a moment. "*The Second Chance,*" he said slowly in a tight voice.

"A good name."

"It is," Cerra agreed, giving Jeffson's hand a squeeze. "We are hoping it will stand for many a year."

"Ladies and Gentlemen," called Jelaïa from the base of the fountain. "If I could have your attention? We are gathered here today to witness the joining of Baroness Syrella del Morlak and Sir Merad Reed, Captain of the Old Guard. Let the ringbearer approach."

"Oh, that's me!" Mila squealed excitedly, dropping the train and digging around in the pockets of her dress. She produced the two rings and handed them to the smiling couple.

"These rings are more than just baubles," Jelaïa continued seriously. "They are symbols of who you are, crafted by your own hands. Please gift them to one another and relate to all present what they represent."

Syrella took Reed's hand and slipped a yellow-brown band onto his finger. "Merad. With this ring, I ask you to be mine. I returned to the shores of the Morlakian Pit. It is so peaceful there now, surrounded by towering pines that survived the flooding of the valley. From their resin, I forged this ring, and with this ring, I ask, will you be mine?"

"I will," Reed replied in a choked voice. He held out his own creation. "Syrella. With this ring, I ask you to be mine. I travelled to Jaelem, the place where I was born. From a branch of a great oak, I forged this ring, and with this ring, I ask, will you be mine?"

"I will," answered Syrella happily.

"Merad Reed. Syrella del Morlak. Your vows ring true. You have chosen to accept one another. To support one another. And to love one another. Does anyone here today refute these claims?"

Total silence.

"Then, as Baroness of Arelium, it is my great pleasure to declare you man and wife. Let all here celebrate the Baron and Baroness of Morlak!"

"HEAR! HEAR!" roared Vohanen, rising to his feet amid thunderous applause. Reed, his face beetroot-red, bowed awkwardly and raised his hands.

"Thank you. It warms my heart to see you all once more. It has been too long. In fact, Syrella still thinks the only reason I agreed to get married was so that I would have an excuse to be with you again!"

His words were greeted with laughter and more applause.

"She is not entirely wrong. You are the greatest companions a man could wish for. You have seen me at my best and, unfortunately, at my worst, yet your friendship has never faltered. If not for all of you — *all of you* — I would not be here today. I would be dead on the ramparts of the Arelian Pit, or on the streets of Arelium, or in the depths of the Morlakian Pit ... and the list goes on and on." He paused, overcome with emotion. "I am the last of the Arelian Old Guard, but I do not stand alone. *You* are my watchers, my protectors, my guardians, and my shield ... and for that, I am eternally grateful. Now, enough with the boring speeches, I know for a fact that the two wild boar Loré brought back from the hunt yesterday are slowly roasting at the spit as we speak, and they are not going to eat themselves. Let us feast!"

After some enthusiastic cheering, the guests began to disperse, heading for the keep and the banquet prepared for them in the Great Hall. Aldarin, his mouth already watering, waited patiently for Jelaïa, but she didn't move to join him, staying instead by the fountain in the shadow of her father's statue. Soon, they were alone.

"Are you not hungry, dear?" he asked, walking over to her. She was crying. "What's the matter?"

"Oh, it's nothing. Memories of my father. He would have loved to have been here today. To see what we have managed to accomplish. Friendships from hardships."

"Remember what he told you in the Shroud. He is watching. And he is proud."

"Yes … I know. But it's not the same."

"It is not," agreed Aldarin.

"I … have something I wish to tell you," Jelaïa said hesitantly. "I have been trying to find the right time, but what with the construction of the barracks and the running of the Barony we have not seen a great deal of each other. I …" she withdrew a hairpin and pricked her finger. A bead of bright red blood welled up from the tiny hole.

"May I?" she asked, holding up the pin. Aldarin nodded and felt her puncture his skin and press her bloody finger against his.

Aldarin steeled himself as unwanted memories flooded his vision. He felt the pang of loss as an image of his dying mother flashed before his eyes. Anger at the violent upbringing his father had subjected him to. Shame and frustration as he was bullied and beaten again and again by the initiates of the temple of Brachyura.

My past is my past, he repeated to himself as his scar began to throb. *I am not defined by my past. It is a part of me, but it will never control me.*

Praedora, her honeysuckle scent filling his senses. Meeting Ka'arka. Growing strong enough to fight back and protect others who could not protect themselves. Meeting Reed. Meeting Jelaïa.

Jelaïa.

And just like that, the circle was joined. He crossed over into her mind and was immediately confounded by the extent of her feelings for him. It suffused every fibre of his being, and he cried out from the joy of it. Her love raced along his veins, easing his pain, soothing his thoughts. The dull ache of his old wound was snuffed out by an emotion far, far stronger.

He laughed, caught up in the majesty, when something gave him pause. A shining star in the core of her thoughts, twinkling playfully. He chased willingly after it, following it deeper into the swirling intermingling of their shared emotions. It stopped suddenly, somewhere dark, comforting, and silent.

No, not silent. There was a distant sound, so quiet it was almost indistinguishable from the roaring tide of love and affection. But it did not need to be loud for Aldarin to know what it was, and what it meant.

The sound of new beginnings.

The sound of renewed hope.

The sound of a slowly beating heart.

The beating heart … of Arelium.

End of the War of the Twelve

AFTERWORD

THE SECRETS OF THE TWELVE

❧

WHEN I WAS younger, there was a Japanese anime I was captivated by. It was called *Saint Seiya: Knights of the Zodiac*, and it followed the eponymous character as he battled his way through various representations of the constellations, including — you guessed it — the twelve signs of the zodiac. The story was fairly flimsy but allowed for spectacular duels between our plucky hero and the golden-armoured personifications of Cancer, Sagittarius, and many others, peppered with more twists and heel-turns than a full season of wrestling.

Years later, when researching another story I wanted to tell, about the unreliability of history, I came across the zodiac again, this time in an essay on how astrology has evolved over the centuries, and consequently how the celestial system developed in Babylonia some 2,500 years ago has not only changed but splintered, shaping astrology in other parts of the world. That was how I first learnt of Vedic astrology.

Vedic astrology, also referred to as Jyotisha (meaning light) or simply Hindu astrology, comes from the word Vedas, India's ancient system of knowledge. It is much older than western astrology, possibly dating back as far as 5000 BC, and uses the sideral zodiac, which puts the planet's position against a backdrop of stars, rather than the tropical zodiac, which is based on the seasons and Earth's relationship to the Sun.

Despite these differences, Vedic astrology has twelve Rāśi, or zodiacal signs, the first of them being Mesa (Aries). The First of the Twelve. And so, the pieces clicked together in my head and I knew I had my Twelve Knightly Orders. Well ... almost. Below is some further insight into how I merged both western and eastern descriptions to create the characters you have read about in the last four novels. I also tried to subtly integrate aspects of the signs into the traits and traditions of the corresponding Knightly Orders, little Easter eggs that may have given you a few hints without breaking immersion.

❧

KRIARI, FIRST OF THE TWELVE – THE RAM

Ram in Greek is zygouri or ... kriari, and I liked the hard-sounding 'k' from the second translation. The Order of Kriari wear fur pelts (not sheep pelts, of course, that would have been too on the nose), and Vohanen carries a ram's horn, which he uses to raise Kriari from his fugue state. Rams are flock animals and strongly gregarious, which is why the Order of Kriari is based on a philosophy of broth-erhood, unity, and mutual protection; ideas that naturally spawned the creation of the shieldwall.

❧

GUANNA, SECOND OF THE TWELVE – THE BULL

From the Sumero-Babylonian name Gu.an.na, meaning Divine Bull of Heaven. Unfortunately, we do not see a great deal of the Knights of Guanna or their patron, but I wanted to try and convey some of the sheer power of these large, muscular bovines and the fear they could inspire. And so, they became the siege-breakers, using their strength to pummel the enemy into submission.

∽

MITHUNA, THIRD OF THE TWELVE – THE TWINS

From the Sanskrit name Mithuna. One of the most interesting signs, its mythology encompasses everything from the stars Pollux and Castor to the less well-known Babylonian god of plague and pestilence, Nergal. A charming, if somewhat unpredictable, deity, his tales often involve him using a combination of guile and violence to achieve his goals. Nergal was a good starting point for the Order of Mithuna, to which I added the gift of metamorphosis, drawing from the myths about the duplicity and interchangeability of identical twins.

∽

BRACHYURA, FOURTH OF THE TWELVE – THE TOWER

Without a doubt the hardest of the Twelve to develop, as he is not only the first we encounter but also the patron to Aldarin, one of the main characters. The Latin word Cancer was out of the question, and the Sanskrit Karka sounded too similar to Makara. In the end, I went with Brachyura, the infraorder for decapod crustaceans, from the Greek brachys (short) and oura (tail).

The Order of Brachyura carries the most references to

the original zodiac sign. The knights are encased in a hard shell of plate armour (in fact, Jelaïa tells Aldarin to come out of his shell at one point), the horns on Aldarin's helm are shaped like a crab's pincers, and even their double-bladed axes look slightly pincer-like.

They are, like crabs, usually defensive but can be aggressive towards one another when fighting over females or hiding holes (as is the case with the power struggle between Caddox and Aldarin). In a final etymological nod, I named one of the knights Ka'arka, going back to the original Sanskrit.

∽

SIMHA, FIFTH OF THE TWELVE – THE LION

The exact transliteration of the original Sanskrit term Simha. Again, we do not see much of Simha in the novels but hopefully, our glimpse of him is enough to give an idea of his alpha-male-like character. Good-natured and brave, but impatient and reckless.

∽

SHALA, SIXTH OF THE TWELVE – WHEAT

Shala was an ancient Mesopotamian goddess of grain, sometimes represented as the sixth sign of the zodiac through the Sumero-Babylonian Ab.sin (meaning furrow). Additionally, in Greek and Roman mythology, Virgo is closely associated with wheat, Demeter, the goddess of the harvest, and her daughter, Persephone.

The themes of harvest and growth morphed into the

idea of her being able to 'sing to the earth' and shape it to her will, leading to her eventual terrible alliance with the weaver. From Persephone came her connection to the Underworld, or rather the place on the border of the Underworld, and her many unfortunate dealings with the dead.

ZYGOS, SEVENTH OF THE TWELVE – SCALES

From the Greek word Zygos. Obviously, the scales lead naturally to themes of balance and order. The seventh astrological sign also has ties to the goddess Themis, the personification of law. Other connotations include rationality and detachment. I was especially interested in the latter and wanted to explore how emotionless logic can have disastrous consequences when used incorrectly.

LURIDAE, EIGHTH OF THE TWELVE – THE DAGGER

As with Brachyura, I didn't want it to be immediately obvious that the Eighth of the Twelve was the sign of the Scorpion. The Iuridae is a family of scorpions in the order of Scorpiones, which I changed slightly to Luridae. The scorpion's stinger became the glaive used by the Knights of Luridae, a dagger-like single blade on the edge of a long pole.

I also wanted to incorporate their geographical distribution into the story. Scorpions are primarily xerocoles, hence the Knights of Luridae live in the hot Da'arran desert.

DHANUSA, NINTH OF THE TWELVE – THE SHORT BOW

From the Sanskrit name Dhanusa. Sagittarius is interesting, often represented as a bow-wielding centaur, although certain illustrations show him as a human archer. In both cases, the bow and arrow are always present. This sign is linked to prophecies (the flight of the arrow being compared to the passage of time), something that was never explored in the War of the Twelve.

∽

MAKARA, TENTH OF THE TWELVE – THE BOOK

Another literal transcription of the Sanskrit name Makara. The horned goat, or sea goat. Also, the crocodile in Hindu astrology. The sea goat aspect appears to come from the Sumerian god of wisdom and waters, Enki, which gave me the idea of using the Book as the sign of his Order and making Makara himself one of the more erudite members of the Twelve. Unfortunately, after the deaths of his siblings, he becomes fervently devoted to preserving their memory, at the cost of sharing his knowledge.

Indians still celebrate the sign of Makara with the Makara Sankranti festival (also known as Maghe Sankranti), held every January to mark the transition from one period to the next. During Makara Sankranti, believers bathe in holy rivers in the hope of being absolved of their past sins.

∽

KUMBHA, ELEVENTH OF THE TWELVE – THE AMPHORA

From the Sanskrit name Kumbha, the water bearer. Traditionally, the water carrier is a young man or boy, but I ended up swapping genders to counterbalance the two antagonistic female members of the Twelve, Mithuna and Mina. There is no real documented link between Aquarius and medicine, although water carriers — who collected drinkable water from a natural source and transported it all the way to people's homes — must have been seen by some as healers. In fact, as centralised water supply systems became more prevalent, water carriers diversified their profession and became unofficial community nurses, helping the elderly and the sick.

MINA, LAST OF THE TWELVE – THE TWO FISHES

From the Sanskrit name Mina. Despite its similarity to Mithuna, I opted to keep Mina. Pisces is the twelfth and final astrological sign. From my rough outline, I knew that the second book in the series would take place at least partly at sea, so Mina was the obvious choice. An element that has been lost from more recent representations of Pisces is the cord or string joining the two fish together, by either the mouth or the tail. The fish are often portrayed swimming away from each other, in opposite directions, leading to a certain unpredictable duality, which I tried to convey in both Mina and her Knights.

A Brief Timeline of Events

The calendar used throughout the nine Baronies is intrinsically linked to the Twelve, with the year of their first appearance among the scattered tribes termed 'The Arrival of the Twelve' (AT). The events described here take place in the year 426 AT.

❧

-58 AT	A series of natural disasters, later known as the Calamity, wreaks havoc on the land and its inhabitants
00 AT	The first appearance of the Twelve among the human tribes
13 AT	An innumerable host of greylings is defeated in the Battle of the Northern Plains
14 AT	The Twelve separate, dispersing to aid the

	surviving tribes and eliminate the remaining greylings
33 AT	The Old Guard is established, sworn to defend the Pits
35 AT	The Council of Baronies is created by the Twelve, who gradually concede rulership of the nine provinces to the tribal leaders
41 AT	The first founding of the great temples of the Twelve and their Orders
122 AT	The battle of Hellin Pass
123 AT	The building of the wooden dam at Terris Lake
123 AT	The Twelve depart into exile after signing a Pact with the leader of the greylings, a creature known as the weaver. The Pact states they will return in three hundred years to aid in the greylings' conquest of the nine Baronies. If they refuse, the weaver will set loose a creature known as the wyrm
313 AT	The naval battle of Torc
365 AT	Birth of Listus del Arelium
366 AT	Documents detailing the Pact are discovered by the Order of Zygos, leading to a Schism that divides the Knights of the Twelve into two factions, those who believe the Pact to be real, and those who refuse to acknowledge it
368 AT	The First Temple of Zygos is destroyed, and the statue of its patron torn down. The survivors flee and eventually settle in Nightvale.
370 AT	Birth of Loré del Conte
386 AT	Birth of Merad Reed
394 AT	Birth of Aldarin

404 AT   Merad Reed joins the Old Guard

404 AT   Birth of Nidore del Conte

405 AT   Birth of Jelaïa del Arelium

407 AT   The Scrying. Aldarin is accepted as an initiate at the temple of Brachyura

411 AT   Syrella del Morlak becomes Baroness

416 AT   Praxis begins his tenure as steward to Baron Listus

418 AT   Auguste Fernshaw is elected Mayor of Jaelem

421 AT   Derello del Kessrin becomes Baron after the death of his parents, lost at sea, now known to have been killed by Mina, Last of the Twelve

426 AT   Greylings appear in great numbers at the Southern Pit and attack the town of Arelium. Listus del Arelium is killed. The greylings are finally routed by the Knights of Brachyura

Autumn   Mina, Last of the Twelve, is found on Kingfisher Isle. Kessrin is attacked by a group of kraken. Mina is defeated by the combined efforts of Brachyura, Manfeld, and the priestess Praedora, who loses her sight

Mithuna, Third of the Twelve, imprisons Merad Reed in the cells under Morlak keep

Kumbha awakens

427 AT   Jeffson, Syrella, and the Knights of Kriari infiltrate Morlak keep, saving Reed and Kriari, First of the Twelve. Nidore and Mithuna are killed. Morlak is destroyed by the wyrm

Allied forces retake the town of Talth

Praxis is consumed by Zygos, Seventh of the Twelve

AUTHOR INTERVIEW

❧

Where did the idea of the War of the Twelve come from?

I've always been fascinated by the unreliability of history. In a lot of medieval-inspired fantasy I read growing up, *everyone* (from the lowliest peasant toiling in the fields to the richest noble) seems to know *everything* about these hundred-year-old legends. How is history recorded in these stories? Word-of-mouth? A collection of dusty scrolls? How can that be irrefutable? Add to that widespread illiteracy and isolationism (voluntary or not), and you can imagine how difficult it must be to find reliable information ...

This is what first sparked the idea for the series; a scattering of breadcrumbs throughout the first novel that things are not quite as they seem. As one character remarks to another

"History is a malleable thing, changed in an instant with a stroke of the pen."

My basic outline hasn't really changed from this original idea. A few things have been shifted very slightly, but the premise remains the same.

How did you get into writing?

I'm a UK ex-pat living in France; I moved here with my parents and siblings in 1995. I took up writing as a hobby a few years ago after I started to realise that the quality of my written English was slipping. I still speak regularly to my close family in English, read exclusively in English, and watch a lot of UK TV, but actual writing was something I was doing less and less of.

What started as a short story to practise my writing skills then expanded into a longer tale and from there careened headlong into the War of the Twelve series (which started as three books and is now four).

Originally, when I started writing, I thought I would never publish at all. Firstly, as I assumed publication would be horrendously expensive, and secondly, because I didn't believe the quality of the writing would be quite up to scratch. Both of these things, I am happy to say, turned out to be false!

Who were your favourite authors growing up, and who would you recommend now?

Wow, that's a tough one, as there are so many great authors out there, past and present. It's incredibly clichéd, but the first fantasy book I read was *The Hobbit*, drawn to John Howe's brilliant depiction of the dragon on the cover. I was lucky enough to go to a school that had a massive library with two rows of fantasy books. After finishing that, I tried and failed to get through the Lord of the Rings (those first one hundred pages are tough for a ten-year-old) and pivoted instead to some of the great classic high fantasy tales of the late eighties/early nineties: Eddings's *Malloreon*, Weis & Hickman's *Dragonlance Chronicles*, David Gemmell (probably my favourite fantasy author and certainly the one who has been the most influential on my work), Terry Pratchett, Tad Williams …

As for current authors, the closest anyone has got to Gemmell is John Gwynne, an amazing gritty, historical fantasy writer. *The Faith and the Fallen* is a fantasy twist on Anglo-Saxon society, followed by *The Shadow of the Gods*, based on Norse mythology.

How did you settle on your writing style?

That was incredibly tricky. I knew I wanted to write a fast-paced tale that pulled the reader from one action-packed scene to the next. It turned out to be surprisingly difficult to do. The prose needs to be simple, but effective. Descriptive, but not so overly-lyrical that it breaks the flow. World-building and character development are paramount to an engaging story, but they need to be integrated seamlessly into the narrative or they will break immersion instead of reinforcing it. And finally, I gave myself an unofficial limit of 100,000 words maximum (first draft) to try and keep things nice and tight. The first novel had a few missteps in that regard, but I feel like I'm slowly improving with each subsequent book in the series.

What's the best thing about living in France?

The wine. Definitely the wine. Although, the magnificent mountain ranges and beaches we have here are nice, too.

What's next? Is this really the last we'll see of Aldarin, Jelaïa, Reed and the nine Baronies?

Hah! Wouldn't you like to know? This is absolutely the end of the first series of books. I had this idea of a quartet and by some amazing miracle, I managed to pull this off while staying sane. It's turned out to be a nice little self-contained story (and by little, I mean all four books combined have about the same word count as one Brandon Sanderson book!).

One thing I can tell you is that I love writing. I've come to love it as much as I love reading. There are many more stories to be told.

Where's the best place for people to go to find out what you are doing next?

I'm very bad at social media in general (probably because I'm over forty), something not helped by the fact that I'm in a different time zone from a large part of my reader base.

The best thing to do is to sign up for my monthly newsletter via my website at http://warofthetwelve.com. Not only will you be the first to know about my current and future projects, but you'll get a free digital short story, *Praedora*, set shortly before the events of the first novel.

Printed in Great Britain
by Amazon